RHAPSODY IN BLOOD

The Miranda Chronicles: Book II

RHAPSODY IN BLOOD

SUSAN OLD

Zairesue Books
Arlington, Washington
2020

Layout by Roland Trenary
Cover art by Lily Droeven

Inhabitants of Miranda's World

Tarot Card names are used by the rulers of the night to identify stations and communities.
The Magus aka Desmon Dontinae, the first vampire. Born in Mesopotamia.
Lena was the 2nd most powerful vampire destroyed by the Magus for an attempted coup.
The Emperor aka Baron Tristan Mordecai, 2nd most powerful vampire. Born in what is currently Lithuania.
The Empress aka Baroness Miranda Ortega Mordecai, First half-vampire, biological daughter of Sir Omar Sedaghi.
Miranda and Tristan's offspring: Tomas, Desmon, Marie and Jacques.

The Vampire world is organized into and ruled by Houses who are loyal to the Magus.
Sir and Lady denote the ruling class Haute Caste vampires with HH blood.
Angel, House of Plows, Common Caste
Lady Anastasia Romanov aka The High Priestess, significant other of Sir Omar
Antoinella, Common Caste, aide to Sir Borgia, House of Pentacles
Sir Bartholomew aka The Hierophant prefers to be called Bart
Sir Cesare Borgia, Head of The House of Pentacles, London, England
Sir Franco, Knight to Sir Jorge, House of Arrows
Sir Jorge, Head of The House of Arrows, Caracas, Venezuela
Lady Kabedi, Knight to Lady Kananga, House of Wands
Lady Kananga, Head of The House of Wands, Kinshasa, Democratic Republic of the Congo
Lady (Princess) Khunbish of Mongolia, House of Cups
Sir (Dr.) Kyoto, Head of The House of Cups, Tokyo, Japan
Lady (Dr.) Lily, Knight to Sir Kyoto, House of Cups
Sir Omar Sedaghi Head of The House of Swords, Doha, Qatar
Lady Pauline, House of Plows
Sir Ruben, brother and Knight to Lady Sarah, House of Plows
Lady Sarah, Head of The House of Plows, Toronto, Canada
Scheherazade, Common Caste, The House of Pentacles a very ambitious vampiress
Sir Steve, House of Plows

Mortals:
Al Lolly's significant other, F.O.V.
Batu, bodyguard from Mongolia, assigned to protect Miranda and the offspring
Benedetto, mad monk vampire hunter
Camo, a biker friend of Sir Ruben bodyguard to the Mordecai family
Connie Ortega, Miranda's mother, Rossville, IL
Danuta, Miranda's housekeeper in Rossville, IL
Grigoryi, a reformed vampire hunter who owes a debt to Miranda
James friend of Miranda, F.O.V
Lolly longtime friend of Miranda, F.O.V.
Pete Ortega, Miranda's father
Teri, a martial arts expert bodyguard to the Mordechai family
Turlock, mad monk vampire hunters

Glossary

Burnoose - a long, loose hooded cloak worn by Arabs.

Caftan - A robe or tunic worn in a number of cultures around the world. Worn by many Middle Eastern ethnic groups, the caftan is ancient Mesopotamian (modern-day Iraq) in origin. It may be made of wool, cashmere, silk, or cotton, and may be worn with a sash. In some cultures, the caftan has served as a symbol of royalty.

Common Caste – Vampires with blood other than HH. Have lesser rights and power in vampire society. In Rare Blood vampiress Lena organized some of the Common Caste to attempt a coup against the Magus.

F.O.V. – Friends of Vampires. A term coined by James as a way of referring to mortal friends who are aware of the existence of and protected by the vampire society.

Haute Caste – Elite ruling caste of vampire society. Only those with HH blood can be Haute Caste

HH Blood - Called Bombay Blood, or the rarest of blood, because it was first found in some people of Bombay in 1952. Only 0.0004% (about 4 per million) of the human population, though in some places such as Mumbai (formerly Bombay) locals can have occurrences in as much as 0.01% (1 in 10,000) of inhabitants. Haute Caste vampires all have HH blood.

Hierophant - A priest in ancient Greece, who interprets sacred mysteries or esoteric principles. His task is to pass down his spiritual wisdom and maintain the balance between the conscious and subconscious minds and the unlocking of mysteries, which only he can teach.

Keffiyeh - A traditional Arab headdress worn in the Middle East

Knight – An aide-de-camp to the Head of a vampire House, highly trusted and performs important and confidential tasks. A Knight may be a personal representative to the Head of a House at important vampire society functions.

Malachite - Malachite has been used as a gemstone and sculptural material for thousands of years. Colors range from pastel green, to a bright green, to an extremely dark green that is almost black. It is typically found in caves. When cut, the surfaces often exhibit banding and eyes that are similar to agate.

Shorts – Term used in the vampire society for mortals or short-lived.

*"Is it too much to ask
for just one night
without vampire drama?"*
– Baroness Miranda Ortega

The Komodo Dragon

It would have been a perfect evening on the coast above Paradise Cove near Malibu, if not for the sound of crunching bones. The mysterious head of the vampire world, the Magus, turned his gaze on me and said. "She is lovely in a prehistoric way, and I named her Dorcus."

"Calling a Komodo dragon lovely is a stretch, though Dorcus works." I watched her chew up and swallow the remains of a recently deceased turkey through the glass wall of her enclosure. The undead tend to have unusual pets. My husband, the Baron Tristan Mordecai, has a cat, to be exact a black panther.

The Magus, as always, was elegantly dressed, had chiseled features and black hair. He gestured with a jeweled hand. "Her kind should have become extinct, but they found a way to survive. Not unlike our kind." We stood watching a few more minutes. "Shall we go inside?" He turned and led me back to the house.

"You mean your kind. I walk in sunlight and could die if Dorcus got loose and decided that I would make a better meal than turkey."

His mansion surrounded with beautiful ferns, blooming flowers, and a small rose garden scented the air. He entered a security code on the keypad next to the door. There were security cameras hidden discretely around the property. He was big on security and privacy. He held the door open for me, and we walked down a long, elegantly decorated hallway to the library. There were rare, antique objects d'art and original paintings that museums would love to have.

"To be or not to be a vampire, that is the question," the Magus spoke with a knowing smile that lacked warmth. He was handsome in a goth rock star kind of way. Scary sexy. Uncharacteristically, I paused before I just blurted out a response.

It felt like he was staring at prey, but my blood would not be spilled tonight; I was important to him. As the first-ever progeny of vampire and mortal, I was part of some grand scheme he had for the undead world. He wanted me to transform, but I was putting off my decision. His slightly British accent made everything he said sound special and slightly menacing. The Magus' dark eyes did not just look at you; they penetrated. I pushed my dark brown wavy hair back from my face and sat in an antique velvet chair that cost as much as a new car. There was a lot of pressure on me to become one of the undead. The library of his mansion was a lovely place to have an unholy conversation. Most of the furnishings looked like they came from Versailles. The walls lined with dark walnut bookcases were filled with leather-bound tomes, many of which were first editions. Blinds and heavy drapes covered the windows. On one wall, a large fireplace created a false sense of warmth. It had a carved malachite mantel. On top of the mantel was a large ornate gold clock that the Magus probably had owned since the French Revolution. In front of the fireplace was an antique dark blue velvet sofa, to each side were matching gold velvet chairs. Side tables held exotic-looking vases filled with long peacock feathers.

The Magus patiently waited as if he had all the time in the world, which I suppose he did. "Not very original," I finally responded to his earlier comment.

"It was when William said it."

"Shakespeare? C'mon." I leaned back in the chair across from him and sipped coffee from a porcelain cup that had been waiting for me when we entered the library. I may have looked young and innocent, but I had survived vampire attacks, was privy to closely held secrets of the vampire society and was better protected than the nuclear launch codes. I wore a Chicago Bears t-shirt and blue jeans. I had terrible taste in fashion, though I loved my T-shirt collection and my lime green Converse high-tops.

Vamps would dress for an audience with him, but I was still a passive-aggressive mortal. The Magus had recently told me that my biological father was Sir Omar, an ancient vampire, not the man that had lovingly raised me.

He looked a little disgruntled by my doubt. "The Bard modified it for his larger, ignorant audience." The Magus snapped his fingers, and an ornate candle on the table lit up. I ignored the parlor trick.

"Did he become..."

"No, Will was in love at the time, but he managed to base some of his characters on us. I should have paid closer attention when he said Lady Mac Beth was inspired by Lena."

I tried not to think about the ambitious vampiress that had tried to harm my children and me before the Magus destroyed her. "She is one of the reasons I might not join your exclusive club. Transforming might make me like her."

"You are no more like her than a rose is like poison ivy."

Being flattered by the Magus was scarier than his threats. He was the supreme chess master. He had literally ripped out the heart of a vampire who had threatened one of my triplets a few weeks earlier. I had decided to leave the insanity of the vampire world in L.A. and try to give my children a more normal life back in the small town where I had grown up. The Magus and my husband were not happy with my decision but were not going to stand in my way.

I was not quite sure why he was so fond of me and the offspring, except that we were the only part vampire, part mortals in existence.

"Who else has turned you down?" I asked.

"Not many. Genghis Khan, Cleopatra, Mozart, Marie Curie, Jimi Hendrix, and some ancient acquaintances you have never heard of."

"Wow! I will be in remarkable company if I decline. I'm curious, what makes a mortal worthy of becoming a vampire?"

"Intelligence, a personal code, talent, aspirations about to be cut short, and passion."

"I don't fulfill all of the criteria, especially aspirations, cut short, or do I?"

He smiled, "You don't have to meet all those criteria if we find you have an exceptional ability to contribute to our society."

I was pretty sure he meant the royal we. I guessed my breeding ability topped his list of my gifts, but I did not say that. "Do you really want someone who can't get through 24 hours without saying fuck and has difficulty with authority? Honestly, I'm not well-mannered enough to be a nocturnal killer."

Contrary to popular belief, a bite by the undead does not

make one a vampire. You have to desire to become one and be approved of by the Haute Caste, which rules the vampire world before the necessary bloody initiation ceremony can occur.

He ignored my comment and fixed his gaze on me. "Tell me, how do you view us?" The Magus was trying a different tact.

"All the undead?" I knew they did not like that nickname.

"Immortals, but yes…"

I hesitated to respond. I had already severely tested his insolence tolerance, "You heal quickly, you're prone to extreme sunburn, you're powerful, control significant wealth, are extremely intelligent and bloodthirsty." I left out freak.

"I expected brutally frank honesty," he looked disappointed. You are getting much better at hiding your thoughts. I was born disabled but have been able to turn my unique traits into a highly prized state of being and shared it with others so we could create a unique hidden society."

"Since I've got some Haute Caste DNA, I'll go with your version. Still, your gifts keep you from living fully. You take your amazing health for granted, and you can never enjoy the beauty of nature in sunlight."

"Boring mortal options. You would find the thrill of experiencing the world as a ruler of the night more than compensates for battling a painful disease or a day at a public park."

I put down my cup. "How many years do I have before I must decide?"

He appeared concerned, "We have difficulty understanding why you would prefer to waste away. You are a mystery within a mystery. You will continue to age until you transform. Time is your tyrant, not ours."

"You never worry about wasting time?"

"Time has little meaning for us. One year, or a hundred years from now, we will be the same. We have all the time in the world. I have witnessed empires rise and fall. Patience can be a powerful tool."

His words opened my eyes to the meaning of their eternity. I mulled his words over out loud. "You reset every night, your existence, and the vampires you surround yourself with only change on a superficial level. You go from era to era unscathed. You trade carriages for cars."

He gave me a rare smile, "Try chariots. You could be free of the ravages of time."

"Time is concerning you more than you want to admit, the children and I have caused you to think about our limited lifespans, and you're uncomfortable with that."

"Perhaps." he mused. "I'd like you to try something. Look at the candle and focus your mind on extinguishing it. Just see it slowly going out."

"Sure, I'll play." I looked at the flickering flame and imagined it flickering out. The light grew weaker, and then it went out in a small puff of smoke. I looked back up at him. "You did that, not me."

"Try it out when I'm not around. Your powers grow as you mature."

"Does not knowing what the kids and I will become make you uneasy?"

"Living forever can become a bit tedious, but your existence has had fascinating ramifications." He leaned forward, and I could smell his spice-laden cologne. His mysterious gaze and handsome features lost their harshness for a moment.

"Glad you find us entertaining." I sat back, taking a deep breath to clear my head. Normally people would only be allowed to accept the invitation to become undead until they are in their late 20's. I wished I was not an exception. It would make my existence easier. The Magus stood and stared down at me, his thick straight hair framing his haughty features. My audience with his highness was over, but I wanted to know more about this powerful vampire who had orchestrated my conception and that of my children; any knowledge of the Magus could be useful. I pressed my luck since I was about to leave.

"I've never seen you be flirtatious, but there must be someone with whom you are intimate. I've heard rumors but never seen you with anyone. Tristan sees nothing wrong with being unfaithful." My husband was the Casanova of the vampire world. "You all act like sex is a meaningless sport."

"You are a most remarkable creature." He was surprised by my rude question. He stood in front of the malachite fireplace watching me, considering how to answer. The flames of hell seemed to burn behind him. "You have been fated to be with the Baron since you were born. Tristan is very open about his affairs, which is no concern of mine. We regard sex as an activity we enjoy, not something upon which to base a relationship. Because you've brought a generation of mortals with our DNA into the world, your sexual activity is consequential. Whoever I have an intimate moment with is my private affair."

"You're all afraid of love."

He merely shook his head, "Such sang-froid, and you're still mortal. The notion of love consumed Shakespeare. He's dead."

I considered mentioning that the Magus was undead but refrained. "If I decide to become nocturnal, you and Tristan will be the first to know. Since you can read my thoughts at times, you know that I haven't decided. Mostly I think it would be sick and crazy to transform, but some nights I want to avoid death, so I can always watch over my children. In the meantime, at least one of their parents will be able to go to their soccer games."

Chapter 1

Rossville, IL, Several Months Later

I still remember that conversation clearly. It took place just before I left Los Angeles with my triplets against the wishes of my husband, the amazing, seductive, and powerful vampire Baron Tristan Mordecai. I came to Los Angeles as a young starry-eyed optimist from the cornfields of Rossville to make my fame and fortune as a writer. I was unaware that my ancestor Jacques de Molay had made a pact with a vampire, just as King Phillippe of France and the clergy were about to destroy de Molay's Knights Templar. In exchange for the Templar vast treasures, given to the vampire ruling caste, the de Molay's were discretely protected by the undead for generations. The vampires also took pleasure in the downfall of royals and clergy who betrayed the Templars. Loyalty is very important to the undead. It is and always has been one of the reasons they have survived and prospered for centuries.

Vampires rarely lie and see themselves as elite honorable beings. They also take pride in, shall we say, removing from society, people they regard as offensive. Despite their twisted code of serial killer ethics, the nocturnal mafia quietly looked after the last remaining de Molay descendants. They had watched over my parents and then me in our little rural Illinois town. As I grew up, I wanted nothing more than to escape to L.A. and become a famous writer. Baron Tristan Mordechai, second to the Magus, published my first book, then proceeded to seduce and marry me.

The factor which caused the entire vampire world to come out of the coffin and focus on me was my rare blood type. The distinction between Haute Caste and Common Caste vampires is their blood identity. If someone with HH blood becomes a vampire, they automatically join the ruling caste. When my mother, a de Molay descendant, married a mortal man with HH blood, the leaders of the vampire world became obsessed with the idea that an offspring of the de Molay line born with

HH blood would be a signal to expand their population with specially bred human beings. Who better to become a vampire?

When it turned out that my father was infertile, the Magus' grand plan had to change. Instead of my children being the first part-vampire human beings, it was decided to have my mom impregnated by one. The Magus arranged for a vampire with similar appearance to my father to spend the night with my mother. She wanted a child more than anything. My mom just "happened" to meet a charming and handsome guy at a bar in the hotel she was staying at when she was in Chicago for a women's club annual meeting. She rarely drank but, she had wine that night. She was pretty pissed-off at my dad for having an affair with a waitress that worked at their café back home, also orchestrated by the Magus. The handsome stranger charmed her into having more wine and, as they say, one thing led to another, and here I am. After years of unsuccessfully trying to get pregnant my parents said I was, "A miracle!" Maybe it is closer to say I was an undead experiment.

The Magus and my biological father, Sir Omar Sedaghi, head of the House of Swords, kept my half-vampire nature a secret until I was an adult and could handle the revelation. Since I have yet to make my final decision on transformation, my undead nature remains unseen, though, at times, I sense powers that alarm me. At times, I have the ability to pick up others' thoughts. It can be disturbing, but it helped me save my newborn daughter's life when a rogue vampire abducted her.

The Haute Caste Vampires are addressed as Sir and Lady, but, not surprisingly, I tend to ignore that protocol. Vampires are attractive, seductive, rich, and brilliant with the bodies of athletes. Apparently, when you let them take the big bite, followed by a transfusion of vampire blood, it enhances all your best qualities. And some less desirable personality traits as well. Tristan invaded my life under the pretense of wanting to publish my books. I had no idea what he truly was. I tried to not fall for the bloodsucking arrogant chick-magnet who professed his literally undying passion for me, but my response to him was undeniable. I was twenty-three and a virgin from the cornfields of Illinois. The triplets were born eleven months after we met. Though the Magus and my husband were excited by the chaos and challenges the kids and I represented, not all the undead were thrilled. Their jealousy and the ensuing dangers caused me to get the hell out of a city that should have been called Los Vampiros. Even "polite" vampire society was not the best environment in which to raise kids.

My husband had a large colonial-style house built for the kids and me on farmland near the small town in the Midwest where I had grown up. Our first night back in Illinois, Tristan called about midnight.

"All is well?"

"Yeah, the babies handled the flight fine, slept most of the way. My parents are really happy we're here. This house is amazing! I haven't seen the grounds yet 'cause it was dark when we got here, but I know the river runs through the far end of the property. I'll check it out tomorrow. We were greeted by a bearded guy, Bart, wearing a beanie, tunic, and sandals. He just brought out the horses, smiled, and then returned to the barn. I could pick up his Haute Caste scent. I have to say he did seem a little different." As time went by, I had started to develop a nose for vampires.

"I miss all of you, but I'm glad you arrived safely. Try to be respectful of Sir Bart. He is a Hierophant, a sort of monk. He has sworn to protect you and our offspring." I knew that "the Hierophant" was one of the Tarot cards. Each Haute Caste had a card depicting their station. The Haute Caste invented Tarot as a secret means of communication and identification.

"I'll probably have to protect him from the kids! Are you sure he's like you? He doesn't seem to care about his appearance."

"He is unique. Like you, he doesn't seek the company of many of our kind. Some feel uncomfortable around him. He is a spiritual being who chose to stay in this materialistic world. Hopefully, in time he will share his story with you. The Magus personally asked if he would watch over you."

"Wow! The Magus asked, not demanded? He should be interesting. Please thank the Magus' housekeeper for recommending her sister. Danuta had dinner waiting when we arrived and helped us get settled in. She was good with the babies."

"She is well paid to help with the household. I'm sure she will take good care of all of you. Someone else will arrive soon to help with daytime security and the horses. He is a friend of Sir Ruben."

"Sir Ruben, the wild child, do you really want a friend of his around the kids?" He was the punk rock brother of Lady Sarah, the Head of the House of Plows. They were the nearest vampire house with headquarters in Toronto.

"This friend is very loyal to Sir Ruben. I would not have approved if I had any doubts about his ability to protect you and respect confidentiality. You may speak freely around him. I still don't understand how you could be content to return to that uncivilized wasteland."

Tristan had a point. I had gotten a little spoiled living in L.A. Now, I had to drive to the next county to find a Starbucks, but it was worth it to keep my babies safe. We settled into a nightly routine quickly. He would call about midnight, early evening for him, and our conversation would focus on the offspring and the day to day happenings at our rural home. Neither of us wanted to discuss our relationship issues on the phone. Invariably he would share news about the nocturnal folk. His main concern was that there were still rumblings about the Common Caste undead wanting to have the same privileges as the Haute Caste. I was relieved to be away from vampire central in Los Angeles.

A day later, a biker on a Harley Shovelhead chopper loudly announced his arrival. The bike had green trim, which matched his camouflage attire and black leather vest with motorcycle club patches. He had curly red hair in a Mohawk and a tattoo of a black widow on his neck. The babies were taking a nap. I rushed out on the porch. Danuta was already there, obviously not happy, her fists on her hips, glaring at the biker, "Turn that thing off!" she ordered.

He shut off the engine. "Are you the Baroness?" he asked, looking at Danuta. She always had her hair up and wore a nice sweater with jeans tucked into her Uggs. I was barefoot and wearing sweats.

"Yes, what do you want?" I demanded. He looked confused and Danuta had her phone ready to call the cops.

"I'm Camo, Ruben's friend. I owe him a favor, so I'll be your protection as long as you might need me."

"What kind of bike does Ruben ride?" I asked.

Camo shook his head, "A fucking Triumph."

I nodded to Danuta, "It's okay. Tristan sent him." I turned to our new recruit, "Sorry for not being more welcoming. The babies just fell asleep, and we're being careful. Come in and make yourself at home. Danuta will show you to a guest room." He smiled and got off his bike. "Just one more thing, you're not an Outlaw here. No disrespect, but the vest has to be put away while you're protecting us. We don't want the attention of the police.

"Yes, Ma'am," he replied, but I could tell he did not like it. He must have really owed Ruben.

The first few weeks were chaotic. The babies were getting used to new people and a new schedule. I had to establish boundaries with my parents. They wanted me to hang out at the Café all the time with the grandkids. That was not happening. So far, I brought them in once. That day my dad added a triple burger to the menu. The place had never been so packed. It's a small town, and of course, everyone wanted to see the wayward daughter coming home with her offspring. When the kids got older, I'd allow them to help out at the café like I did as a kid, but in the meantime, I just wanted to keep them out of the public eye.

Danuta and Camo settled into a working relationship. He seemed to accept her staff seniority, until one evening when Danuta was making chili. Camo took a spoonful from the pot and declared, "This is fuckin' terrible! What spices did you use? You're a great cook, but Polish chili doesn't fly." I watched them from my cubbyhole office nearby.

Danuta was pissed, "Get out of my kitchen!" She glared at him with her fists on her hips as if deciding if she was going to try to physically throw him out of the kitchen. It was kind of comical considering her petite 5'3" frame.

Camo was 6'2" with broad shoulders. He smiled but did not leave. Instead, he quietly went about making up his own pot of chili. First, he took off a few skull rings and leather bracelets. Then he finely diced onions, peppers, and garlic and added them to browned beef. He spooned in a ton of chili powder and a little extra cumin. Three different kinds of beans, diced tomatoes, and a little cilantro were the final ingredients. It smelled amazing. Danuta glared at him. He handed her a spoonful to try.

Because she was an honest soul, she stated, "Is good." After that, whenever she did not feel like cooking, she would ask Camo to make chili.

It was nice to see people I had grown up with, but I kept my interactions superficial except for two old friends. Katy and Josh, who had been my Scholastic Bowl teammates. Going to competitions with them were some of my fondest high school memories. The year our team made it to the state finals, the football team and basketball team sucked. Only our coaches and family members acknowledged our success. If the football team ever won a game, they would ride around the town on the fire truck with the siren blaring. My friends and I had no bitterness or jealousy about that! My friends found a way to be happy in a culture that was uncomfortable with intelligence, especially bright females. Katie was petite with long brown hair and an impish smile. Josh was a big, heavy guy with curly blond hair. After high school, they became a couple while training to be EMTs. They loved Marvel superheroes, gaming, and they had read my first book. People congratulated me on being published, but few had read it. Katy went on about how "hot" the ghosts were. Josh called my book "Ghost Porn." Josh and Katy were the only "Rossvillagers" who regularly visited, what in our small town was considered a mansion.

They loved helping with the horses during the day.

People in town were pleasant and charitable. I knew that if I got a flat tire, someone would stop to help me. If there was a death, the whole town would grieve with you. I had tried to fit in, but being raised Catholic in a Protestant town did not help. We would drive to the next town, Hoopeston, to attend services and Mass. I returned because I knew it would be a safe place for my children. People looked out for each other here. It was a town of who begot who. Often people called me "Pete and Connie's girl." People liked to be able to place you in the social order. The triplets would always be from California, and their father would be considered a foreigner, really foreign. Just moving back to Rossville was not enough to be accepted into the clan again, but something was going to help bring us into the fold.

For his first visit, the Baron Tristan Mordecai, second in command to the Magus, arrived in a sleek black Lamborghini Aventador. It looked like a racing car that was barely legal for the street. He had driven down from Chicago. It belonged in Monte Carlo, or a James Bond movie, not parked by the barn. He could easily play a Nordic villain with his long blond hair and haughty bearing. When he climbed out of the car, he carried his own suitcase.

"Roughing it?" I asked, nodding at his suitcase as I greeted him on the steps.

He dropped his bag and held me tightly. His kisses made me melt into his arms. The strength of his embrace, the scent of his skin, were overwhelming. I was ready to head for the bedroom. C'mon, it had been three weeks. He released me gently, and as if reading my mind, he said, "First, I must see the triplets."

Camo came around the corner of the house, nodded his silent male greeting, and picked up the suitcase. He followed us into the house where Danuta politely said, "Good evening Baron." Tristan went directly to the nursery without my having to show him the way. After all he had designed the house.

Tomas was fussing, but his siblings were asleep. My husband picked up his firstborn as though handling a delicate piece of china and smiled approvingly. "Tomas, have you set a good example for your brother and sister?" Our son's dark eyes focused on Tristan's face with a look of delight. There was a connection between him and the triplets I could not explain. Early on, they let me know that getting their dad's attention and approval was very important. Desmon and Marie started waking up, so I took Tomas and allowed Tristan to work his charm on them. Soon they were making happy sounds and smiling at him. The housekeeper entered just as a foul smell emanated from one of the baby royals. "What have you been feeding them?" He asked, shocked by the ghastly odor. Like I said, no vamp had ever sired a child.

"My milk and formula," I replied, "You get used to it."

I always remember that moment as the first time the kids stunned Tristan, the Emperor of the undead, and it was just the start.

We left the babies with Danuta and went to my husband's bedroom. The top covers of the huge canopied bed had been turned down. His clothes were already unpacked and hanging in the closet. Now the room had his scent. I wished I could bottle it to spray on my sheets when he would be gone. I sat on the bed as he looked around at the expensive Asian rosewood furnishings.

"This will do," he stated then turned to me, "Why are you still dressed?"

"My parents are coming over." His expression turned to equal portions of dread and disappointment. "Just kidding!" I laughed. "You should have seen your face!"

My sense of humor did not particularly amuse him. He leaped on me, pushing me down into the feather bed topper. His mouth smothered mine with kisses. He stopped and pulled slightly away, staring at me. "You're pregnant," he uttered.

"What?" I gasped for air, "We haven't had sex yet!"

He sat up with a Cheshire grin, "You should see your face, except I'm not joking. I can smell your hormonal change. You are with child again, or perhaps children."

"But I didn't think it could happen while I was nursing…"

"You can be tested. I'll call Dr. Kyoto, but I'm sure. I could not be more delighted." While I lay there in shock, he slid a hand down my zipper then deftly pulled off my jeans.

"Unbelievable. What the fuck!"

"Yes, that was the cause."

"I don't know if my orifice can take it again!"

He started laughing. It was so out of character to see the somber Baron Mordecai to be in stitches that I started laughing too.

"Orifice? I can think of much more pleasing descriptive terms for that part of your anatomy. Honey pot or velvet cave…"

I hit him in the head with a king-size pillow, messing up his hair. "This is war!" he decreed. He grabbed the nearest pillow, and the battle was on. Soon most of the bedding was on the floor, and he had me pinned down on the bed. He allowed me to flip him over, amused by my audacity. We had lost most of our clothing in the scuffle.

There was a knock on the door. Danuta announced, "Baron, Baroness, your parents are downstairs."

"Thanks! We'll be down in a minute," I called out. Tristan glared at me as I scrambled off the bed. "I told them you would be here tomorrow. Did you think that driving that car thru town would go unnoticed?"

I ran out the door pulling on my clothes. I stopped in my room to brush my hair. My dad would care if he thought he had disturbed us, but not my mom. She wanted to see that, 'precious man,' I had married.

Once properly attired, we greeted my parents in the kitchen, where Danuta had just served them coffee and cookies. In the Midwest, folks like to come in back doors and hang out in kitchens, even if you live in a mansion.

Mom jumped up and hugged Tristan catching him off-guard. "It's about time!"

It was hard not to chuckle as he politely extricated himself. He wasn't a hugger. He quickly turned and shook my dad's hand. "Thank you for overseeing the construction of the house. The accommodations are quite acceptable for my family."

"Acceptable?" my mom responded, "This place is the talk of the town. Randie said you wouldn't be in until tomorrow." My mother liked to always be on top of things.

"I changed my plans," Tristan replied curtly, not used to explaining himself.

"That's a nice set of wheels," Dad said, trying to change the subject.

"Stan, why don't you take my father for a spin." He stiffened and glared at me for a second, then looked over at my dad and smiled, "I would be delighted."

When I first told my parents we were getting married, I had told them that Stan was short for Tristan. He still hates being called by a nickname, but I still enjoy it when they call him Stan.

We walked to the front door, and Mom and I watched as dad climbed into the Lamborghini like a kid getting in a wild ride at Disneyland. My husband had a slight smile as he hit the gas, and they headed for the road. I felt a little sorry for my mom who seemed clueless about who and what my husband truly was. It seemed there was a nagging uneasiness she could not put her finger on. As far as I knew, she had no idea about the Templar-vampire connection to our family, or who my biological father was. The undead had filled me in on my pedigree.

"He looks well. I bet he really missed you and the kids." My mom locked up her doubts. "I hope he doesn't mind the humidity."

I breathed a sigh of relief. Mom talked about the weather when she was seeking safe turf. "He'll be fine. The first thing he wanted to do was hold the babies." We went back in the kitchen, and I poured myself and Mom coffee. Danuta had put a plate of fresh-baked cookies on the table. We sat quietly for a minute having our late-night snack. "Do you like the cookies?" I asked.

"Yes. I'll have to get the recipe from Danuta. How long will he stay?"

"A week, then he's off to run his financial empire. We agreed on spending a week together once a month. He wants us back in L.A., but I'm raising the kids here. Though the kids may hate me when they're teenagers."

My mom looked at me with new respect, "Good for you."

We talked about their café. Over the years, it had become a local hang-out. Old farmers could be found there early in the morning gossiping over breakfast. She asked for a new photo of the babies to hang over the register. We heard the rumble of the Italian engine as they parked. They sounded like a couple of excited teenagers as they came back into the house.

"That's a sweet ride, thanks for letting me drive it. Made me feel like an Indy 500 driver. Randie, you be careful," my dad stated emphatically.

"I'll stick with my Jeep."

"I bought it for you," my husband looked a little hurt, "I thought you might need a second car."

"You couldn't just buy a minivan?"

My parents chuckled. Tristan did not see the humor.

"C'mon Connie, we should let Stan unpack," My dad and mom were the only people allowed to call his highness Stan.

"OK," Mom acquiesced, "Call me tomorrow."

My husband liked Dad. It was rare for him to be fond of a mortal. Or 'Short' for short-lived as the vamp world usually called us. My mom's lack of boundaries irritated him, but he was always polite.

As soon as they drove away, Tristan started to walk up the stairs.

"Wait a minute, let's go to Danville. I want to get a pregnancy test kit."

"You don't believe me?"

I gave him the, 'Are you serious?' look, and he just shook his head as we walked to the front door. I told Danuta we were going into town.

"Remind me why I missed you," he said as I got buckled in.

He tore out of the driveway. I said, "Slow down. Look out for deer."

A pair of golden eyes flickered across from our main gate, as we pulled onto Route One. It was probably one of the many coyotes that live in the area.

"Would you prefer to have your mother drive you?"

We rode in silence until we got to Danville. It was the biggest city in the county, with a population of about 30,000. Other than a couple of gas stations, Walgreens was one of the few stores that was open late.

As we pulled up, a rough-looking guy walked out of the store carrying a twelve-pack of beer, followed by a frail-looking young woman who smiled at my husband displaying badly decayed meth-head teeth. The guy's jaw practically hit the sidewalk as he stopped short and stared at the car.

"Do you need assistance?" Tristan asked me.

"Um, no, thanks. You should probably guard the car."

He wasn't too happy, but he stationed himself by the entrance to the store where he could see me through the window and keep an eye on his new toy.

Luckily, I did not know anyone in the store. I was not in the mood to be social or start rumors. If it were true, I would need a minute to take in what another pregnancy meant before telling my parents. Thankfully I was able to find what I was looking for without any help and took the test kit to the register and quickly paid.

As I headed to the door, an older man walked out ahead of me with a bag containing a bottle of whiskey. As we were driving away, I saw him lean against the building and take a drink from the bottle "hidden" in the sack. There are a lot of interesting people out after dark.

"It seems there may be enough sordid behavior in this town to satisfy my thirst," my husband muttered under his breath as he glanced at some wannabe gangbangers walking down the street talking loudly. A restored muscle car with expensive rims and dark windows pulled up to them. The passenger window rolled down, there was a quick exchange, and the vehicle sped off. "I'll have to remember that car."

"Do the kids and me a favor, don't be the vampire vigilante of Vermilion County." I glanced at Tristan who looked a tad disappointed. "If you need a fresh meal, try Champaign. It's a university town with a lot more money for drugs and vice. The dealers drive nicer cars. Please!" I thought adding please was a nice touch.

He perked up a little, "Very well."

I know that seemed like a really weird and jaded conversation, but I had been worrying about my husband's appetite. He could get by on bagged blood, but it was not his first choice.

"Thanks. I don't want any connection to develop between your visits and unsolvable murders, even if you think you're helping society." As the second most powerful vampire in existence, he could eliminate a "criminal problem" if he was in the mood without getting permission from the Magus.

"I'm always very careful when I remove scum from society."

I decided I should leave it at that. As we headed down the street, I noticed a Danville cop following us as we left town. I pointed it out to Tristan.

"You know he could never catch me," Tristan said with a little smile. He was too eager to try out his theory.

"Yeah, but he's got your license plate." A minute later, the siren and flashing lights went on. I put my hand on his arm, "Pull over. Please!" He pulled up to the curb and parked.

A chubby, young, brown-haired officer approached the car. Tristan was pissed as he rolled down the window, and the officer looked inside.

Luck was with us, I recognized him. "Hi, Bob," I called out.

He shined the light on my face, temporarily blinding me, "Randie! I heard you moved back home. It has been a long time. His eyes roamed over the car. "Nice! What is this thing?"

"Lamborghini," Tristan answered in an irritated tone.

"You don't say. I need to see your license and insurance."

As Tristan handed Bob his license and insurance card, I introduced them. "This is my husband, Tristan, Tristan, this is Bob." I hoped to keep things friendly.

"All the way from California," Bob examined the license then handed it back. "Well, Mr. Mordecai, you were a few miles over the speed limit. You're new here, so I figure you didn't know better. Guess I'll let you off with a warning."

"Thanks Bob," I responded quickly.

My husband said nothing until we started to drive away, then he muttered, "Cossacks." After we had driven a couple of miles out of town into the cornfields, he asked, "Who is Bob?"

"My exercise partner," I replied with an evil grin.

He slammed on the breaks and came to a dead stop. Luckily, no one else was on the road. Anger had been smoldering in him since I had left with the babies. His glare made me want to hide under my seat. I realized I might have gone a bit too far. "I was just joking. We went to high school together. First time I've seen him in years."

"If you want me to be sexually exclusive, then come home. You decided to move away from me, remember? Three miles over the speed limit! Inbred idiot! This is where you choose to raise our children?" He put his foot on the gas, almost giving me whiplash. He was going 100 mph! I just prayed the County Sheriff wasn't on this road tonight and thought it best to stay quiet.

When we got home, I bolted from the car clutching the test kit, ran upstairs, and locked myself in an upstairs bathroom. I held the test and just sat there in a fog for a couple of minutes. I sighed, "I've got to know."

The test gave instant results. I sat on the edge of the tub and cried. He was right, "Damn it!" I loved my children but was not expecting a fourth. I started to fill the tub, and I needed some alone time. Then it struck me that I was not alone. I put my hand on my tummy and whispered, "Forgive me, I will always love and cherish you. Welcome to our crazy family."

The massaging jets of water, the pale aqua walls of the bathroom, and lemon verbena scented water were very soothing. Tonight, we would call the Magus and my biological father, Omar. Tomorrow, I would tell my parents and my friends. I knew the town would love the news that their wandering daughter had returned home to have a child. This child would not be an outsider, regardless of rare royal blood, though at times they might wish that he or she was. I started thinking of names.

Chapter 2

The Announcement

I found Tristan in the barn talking with Bart. It was the first time I had heard him say more than a few words besides, "Please don't call me Sir." To my surprise, Tristan was helping him groom the horses.

"Ah, my lady, I hear that congratulations are in order." I could detect a slight, upper class, British accent.

"Thanks," I responded.

Tristan looked at me with concern. He could tell I had been crying.

Bart tried to save the awkward moment, "We were discussing the possibility of getting another royal steed for the boy."

I stared at him. "All I know is that I'm pregnant."

"A son, Baroness, one son." Despite his work clothes, he pulled off the manners of a gentleman.

Resentment shone in my face. My husband dropped the horse brush and came over to my side. I glared at Bart, "How could you know that?"

My husband interceded, "He is a renowned clairvoyant; he had a vision last week. His premonitions are always right." Tristan tried to put his arm about my shoulders, but I moved away.

Bart continued to brush the horse. I wanted to shove his little beanie up his ass. "Why didn't you tell me?"

"I thought it would be better to wait for your husband. Apparently, I was right. Please don't touch my beanie." He stated with a straight face.

"You read my mind!"

"Not intentionally, Baroness, usually it is rather pleasant."

"Bart tends to prefer the company of animals, due to his clairvoyant ability," my husband told me.

"It's why the undead avoid you."

Bart gave me a knowing smile, "I sense the same ability in you, but you fight it."

I had only used it when Marie had been kidnapped in L.A. That was enough. "I really don't want to know what other people think."

Bart looked at me with compassion. "Such talent can be a burden, but I will be honored to help you develop and control your ability if you wish."

"Yeah, don't hold your breath." I turned to go back to the house.

"Jacques Omar is a fitting name," Bart called after me.

"Fuck-off!" I kept going.

I heard my husband say, "Jacques Omar Ortega Mordecai, perfect!"

As I neared the house, I wondered how much distance was needed to keep Bart out of my thoughts. He was probably spying for the Magus and my husband. Maybe I could develop a way to shield my thoughts from him. Though I had to admit it would be good to have someone around who could read my children's thoughts. I was not sure I wanted that ability. At times I could already read my husband's. Another pregnancy would add to his stud-muffin legacy. I was sure he couldn't wait to tell the rest of the infertile vampire world he had impregnated me again.

As I was about to walk up the steps, I realized I had not warned Bart about the coyote I'd seen on the way to town. I turned towards the barn and visualized the golden eyes in the darkness. Then I went into the house.

Bart stopped grooming the horses, turned in the direction of the house then looked at Tristan, "You are a fortunate husband."

"Didn't you just witness her temper tantrum?" Tristan responded with a curious expression.

"In the midst of her anger, she stopped to warn me of danger. She saw the beast's eyes."

"I was afraid she would notice that animal." Tristan looked at Bart appreciating the companionship of another vampire in the cornfields.

"Do you and the Magus wish me to make contact with it?"

Tristan put his hand on Bart's shoulder, "Thank you. We can start leaving it peace offerings. I've ordered a side of beef to be delivered tomorrow. If you'll excuse me, I must see to my wife."

"Of course," he smiled. "Good luck!"

Tristan found me in the kitchen drinking coffee and finishing off the cookies. I looked up at his handsome concerned countenance, and I was still in love.

"Don't worry. It's Congolese decaf." I took a big swig.

He opened the fridge and took out a round of Camembert cheese, "You need protein."

I cut a large triangle and savored the creamy wonderfulness. He was right. I would need to improve my diet. I had to add meat to my diet during my last pregnancy. "All righty," I said, trying to sound chipper,

"Jacques Omar it is. C'mon, we have some calls to make."

He was relieved I had calmed down after taking my anger out on Bart. "Sir Omar and Lady Anastasia are visiting the Magus."

We sat on the couch across from the fireplace, where the fire was burning low. I looked up at the Mordecai coat of arms on the mantle. Another royal off-spring from a Lithuanian undead bastard was going to be raised in the cornfields. I sighed, and my husband glanced at me. "It's just all a bit overwhelming."

"I'll always look after you and the children."

"That's what I'm afraid of," I replied with a grin.

He did not laugh. My husband dialed the head of the vampire world and put him on speakerphone. The Magus, whose legal name was Desmon Dontinae, was in his headquarters near Malibu. He had been a sickly child in Mesopotamia whose mother realized he needed raw, bloody meat to survive. Every vampire traces back to him. Lady Anastasia is a member of the Haute Caste, and a truly royal member of undead society. My father, Sir Omar, and Lady Anastasia are an interesting couple, very polite and very deadly if you cross them. Luckily, they are also devoted to protecting the kids and me. The triplets and I have HH blood making us the darlings of Haute Caste society.

"Hello, dear Magus, I have news. The Baroness is expecting again. Bart has seen one child, a boy. We will name him Jacques Omar Ortega Mordecai."

My husband and the Magus congratulated each other like they had won a football game. Then my biological father spoke, "I am honored that you will name him after me. Do you wish another stallion for the boy?"

"Omar, thanks, but I don't think we'll need another horse just yet. I'm about four weeks along, and you'll have lots of time to prepare for his arrival."

Anastasia was the only one to inquire about me, "Miranda, this is so much, so soon! How are you?"

"I'm okay, and I'll be ready by the time his highness arrives."

"Let us know of anything we can do to help. I'm sure Dr. Kyoto and Dr. Lily will visit this week," she said. I was glad to have the doctor who was also the Head of the House of Cups and his Knight attend to me. They had cared for me during my previous pregnancy.

The Magus urged, "You must consider moving back here."

"Thanks, but it's less stressful in the cornfields, though I'll consider staying at your place in Chicago as the due date approaches."

"I'll have Dr. Kyoto set up a medical office in my home there," the Magus replied, apparently deciding against trying to order me around.

"Do you need more staff?"

Tristan responded, "The household seems to be running well at the moment."

"I like Danuta. She is kind and thinks of everything we might need," I added.

"And Sir Bart?"

"The clairvoyant monk? I think he misses you," I replied and heard muffled laughter.

Tristan added, "I'm relieved he is looking out for my family."

"Very well, Miranda. I hope you will come to appreciate his talents. Goodnight," the Magus was ending the call.

"Goodnight, Magus, Dad, Anastasia. I'll see you all soon in Chicago."

Soon phone calls from the Haute Caste started. First came Jorge, the head of the House of Arrows, and his Knight Franco from south of the border.

Jorge joked, "Miranda, you don't have to be such a good Catholic."

Franco added, "In your case, I think the Pope would agree, though I'm delighted."

From north of the border, "Can't you find something else to do? I know it's boring in Rossville, but try reading a book," Ruben the Knight of the House of Plows quipped. "Lady Sarah went out for a bite. I can't wait to share the news when she gets back."

I did not dare ask if he meant that literally. "Thanks for sending Camo. He is surprisingly good with the horses."

Ruben chuckled, "He grew up on a farm before he joined the Outlaws. I knew he'd fit right in."

Tristan got a text message from Kyoto that he and Lily would arrive in two nights. Mbuyi Kananga, head of the House of Wands, called from Kinshasa. She was a bit grumpy, "Sir Omar dared to wake me with your news. Congratulations. I shall visit when the birth is imminent. Baron do whatever your wife wants! Now I shall go back to sleep."

We heard from every great vampire House, but the House of Pentacles. Sir Borgia had given order that he was not to be disturbed, and his staff were afraid to invoke his ire. He seemed closely aligned with the Magus, but I never quite trusted him. I did not mention my uneasiness to my husband. Tristan was experiencing the pure, innocent contentment that had eluded him until he had become a father. He gently placed his hand upon my still flat belly. I had never seen him so vulnerable. The children and I were his Achilles' heel.

"I'll take Lady Kananga's admonition seriously." He could have added Scout's honor.

"Good! I want a back rub."

In a barren room, of a religious order in the Vatican, Brother Adrian Turlock stared at photos of the Baroness Miranda Ortega Mordecai on his computer set on a rustic desk. A brown hooded cloak hung on his old, thin body. Pale, wrinkled hands clicked the keyboard to reveal more photos. He stared at images of the mansion outside of Rossville, focusing on the security fence and cameras. Then photos of Connie and Pete as they opened their café in town. For years he had hired private investigators to keep him apprised of the Baron's movements, and now his family as well. The monk was focused on Mordecai because he had learned about his "blasphemous" agreement with the head of the Knights Templar centuries ago.

"Satan's spawn!" he slammed his fists on the desk, causing everything on his desk to jump. His hood fell back, exposing his ghostly features. Turlock's face looked like beige silk pulled over a skeleton. His eyes were pale blue and milky, giving the false impression he might be blind. He had several brown age spots on his bald head. Turlock knew his frail health was a threat to his plans to take down the vampire world. Believing the end justified the means, he had bought a small amount of blood from a Common Caste vampiress many years ago. It had been an elixir of longevity, but its ability to sustain his life was failing. He paid an unconscionable price but justified it to himself as the cost of fighting evil. He had even considered becoming one of the undead to use their own powers to destroy them. Turlock had been unable to find a single vampire who would transform him. Not even the vampiress, Simone, who had sold him some of her blood. The young monk who assisted him claimed that the Magus had destroyed the vampiress for betraying him.

There was a tap on the door. "Come in," the monk called out. "Ah, Benedetto, what news do you have for me?"

A tall, gaunt priest entered carrying a tray with soup and bread and placed the tray on a bedside table with a large crucifix above it. "Brother Turlock, I did as you asked. I contacted my old friend Grigoryi, but he has left the priesthood. He wants nothing more to do with our holy work. He is a simple baker now and wishes to remain as such."

Turlock considered this information for a moment, then asked, "Does he have a family?"

"No, his mother passed away last year, bless her soul. He lives alone."

"That is unfortunate. Very well, I shall rely heavily on you. Now all the glory will go to you, Brother Benedetto."

The young monk cringed a little, knowing that Turlock's plan might put him in the presence of the Baron again. He had barely survived an encounter once due to the intervention of the Baroness, who had begged for Grigoryi and Benedetto be spared. That was when Grigoryi vowed never to hunt vampires again. Unfortunately, Turlock had taken that information and used it to convince Benedetto that he was a spiritual warrior that the undead could not kill. He had carefully fed grandiose delusions of a special reward in heaven for Benedetto. It was very appealing to the religious zealot until he recalled the vampire battle on the beach in Southern California. For a moment, the sanity of fearing for his life returned.

"Pardon me, Brother Turlock, but is there no one else who could aid our cause?"

"Father Giuseppe is only able to arrange financial support through the Office of Exorcism," he lowered his voice, "There is another, whose name I dare not mention. That ally must remain a secret for now. I fear we are being watched."

His remarks caused Benedetto to look anxiously about the monk's sparsely furnished room. For a moment, he considered Grigoryi's offer to let him work at the bakery. The ancient monk seemed to sense his sudden misgivings.

"Come, my fellow holy warrior. Let us pray for success and salvation." Turlock put his hand on Benedetto's shoulder pushing him to his knees. He then stood over him and began chanting, "Sanctus Victoria!" The young priest repeated his words. It was obvious Benedetto would remain compliant.

In Los Angeles, at the Narcissus club, Pauline, the newest member of the Haute Caste, was deep in conversation with some of the Common Caste. The generic-looking building was situated in a mixed industrial area. It housed the only vampire club in Southern California. Other than vampires, very few had ever set foot in the opulently decorated club. Though the undead reflections did not appear in mirrors, nor could their images be captured on standard photo or video equipment, they had discovered they could see their reflections in pools of clear still water. Each table had a small reflecting "pool" where the undead could admire themselves to cater to the "enhanced" egos of the undead,

"C'mon," Angel said, "You've met the Baroness. You must have some idea of what she'll do." His real name was Alfredo but being one of the few vampires native to L.A., he chose to use that nickname.

Pauline pushed aside her long blonde hair, "I don't think anyone knows what she is capable of or what she will do. No one controls her, not even the Magus, that's for sure. She took the royal kids away from our community. I was there when the late Lady Lena unleashed her wrath," everyone fell silent, "She was a formidable vampiress, but I never feared her like I do the supposedly mortal Baroness."

"You are wise to respect her," a male voice came from the shadow of an alcove.

"Sir Steve, I didn't know you had arrived," Pauline was visibly startled "I meant no disrespect by talking about the Baroness." She added in an attempt to recover her composure.

The dozen vampires gathered around Pauline nodded nervously to the other member of the Haute Caste. Their reaction amused Steve. He had turned his small stature and quickness to his advantage in hand to hand combat. No one in the room could best him.

"It's all right, Lady Pauline." The diminutive assassin stepped forward. "You all wonder if she will transform. The children have bought her time. I imagine it will be several years before she decides." Someone placed a chair for him beside Pauline.

"I don't understand how she could take those children away from their father," the beautiful Italian remarked, "The Baroness is selfish." She gazed at her reflection in the pool on the table next to her and pulled on her long dark curls.

There were gasps in the crowd. Antoinella's sexual relationship with the Baron had made her bold. Steve and Pauline stared at her coldly. They were both of the House of Plows and suspected that she was a spy for the House of Pentacles.

Pauline responded, "You wonder how the Baroness could be away from the Baron, I know it's a struggle for you."

There were a few muffled laughs as most looked anywhere but directly at Antoinella. Antoinella was about to fire back, but Steve cut her off, "You really shouldn't add to your display of ignorance. Everything the Baroness has done has been allowed by the Magus."

Antoinella acted like his words were not worth a response and began adjusting the spaghetti straps of her little black dress. Suddenly a tiny dagger skimmed her shoulder, cutting one of the straps and leaving a bit of blood on her very pale skin and stuck in the wall behind her.

"You, arrogant prick! Wait till I tell the Baron!" She all but stamped her feet.

"That part of my anatomy has every right to be arrogant," Steve responded with a self-satisfied grin. Someone retrieved and returned his dagger. "Besides, what do you think he'll do if he hears that you were critical of his wife?"

The discomfort in the room was palpable, but no one left. The dozen witnesses would be the darlings of the undead gossip scene for weeks.

"Years ago," Pauline began, "I watched a female polar bear successfully fight off a male twice her size to protect her cubs. It was not the outcome I had expected. Like you," she continued eyes locked on Antoinella, "I have no maternal instincts. The Baroness, on the other hand, took out Johann, a trained assassin, when she was still pregnant with the triplets. Now, she has cubs."

Antoinella tried to look dignified while holding her dress up on one side. "I'd love to hear more about your incredibly boring nature adventures, but I have a Salon appointment." With a toss of her head and clearly pouting, she left the club, ignoring the snickers that followed her.

Pauline turned to Angel, "Did you get it all?"

"Every delicious word." With a grin, he handed a tiny voice recorder to Steve. "It's a good thing her intellect does not match her ambition."

"Conversation with her must be painful for the Baron," Pauline stated.

Steve smiled, "She's brighter than you think. I would not underestimate her or trust her. I'll give this to the Baron when he returns. I imagine their next conversation will be quite short."

Chapter 3

The Arrival

My months of pregnancy with Jacques Omar were some of the happiest of my life. My parents loved having their grandchildren close by and would visit a few times a week.

When the offspring were napping, I found time to write. I finished my vampire book final edits and sent it off to be published. The vampire feedback was that I did a much better job of describing them than Bram Stoker. I had discovered that Bram had invoked the extreme ire of the entire vampire world and had suffered the consequences. Being intimately involved in their world made it easier for me to be kinder.

Tristan had taken Lady Kananga's admonition seriously and asked rather than demanded to stay more than a week at a time. I decided to reinforce good behavior and agreed to let him stay for two weeks. I had heard through the grapevine that Antoinella had gone back to London, which pleased me to no end. The children and my pregnancy distracted us from our relationship conflicts. He stopped pressuring me about transforming.

When Tristan arrived, he always brought presents, exquisite jewelry I would have no reason to wear in Rossville, Belgian chocolate, decaf coffee beans from the Congo, stuffed animals for the babies, and passion that filled our bed. For the last two months of my pregnancy, he was content to just hold me. We sat up nights and talked about how our lives had become entwined. He wanted me to know more about our children's bizarre heritage. He told me about using the map my ancestor, Jacques de Molay, had given him to find the Templar treasure. He said the Magus had taken pleasure in making sure the Haute Caste arranged the downfall of those who had betrayed the Templars, especially the clergy.

I was very plump, though not like I was with the triplets, so this time, I did not need bed rest. Tristan made arrangements, with the help of Dr. Kyoto, to have staff from the Rush Medical Center on call. The Magus' home in Chicago had been equipped with a small delivery room with a supply of HH blood if needed. My parents planned to take me and the triplets up to his mansion before my due date to be on the safe side. Camo adjusted to our household quickly. Belonging to an organization outside of proper society, seemed to help him fit in. At first, when Tristan was here, Camo would take off for a wild weekend with his club in Peoria, but he always came back sober. He never forgot to remove his vest before he got to the house.

Vampires think they can control all the variables in any situation with proper planning. It was how they survived through the centuries. Unfortunately, they had not spent much time in downstate Illinois in winter and had had no experience with pregnancies. Most vampires, and the Haute Caste, in particular, do not do rural well. Among other things, it is much harder to blend in and go unnoticed in small, close-knit communities.

Two weeks before my due date, we were planning to leave for the Magus' mansion, where Tristan would meet us, but heavy snow started falling. It was the beginning of an arctic blast coming down from Canada. By evening the snow was piling up in drifts, and the wind was howling. It was hard to see the road. I decided to finish packing. When I bent over to take a sweater out of the bottom drawer of the dresser, a shooting pain caused me to steady myself. It passed, then I noticed my legs were wet! I yelled for Danuta. I had been experiencing mild labor pains on and off for a few days, but nothing like I had felt with the triplets. I had no idea how imminent Jacques' arrival would be.

Danuta and Camo came running and got me to my bed. Camo, wide-eyed, said, "Baroness, I'm calling for an ambulance."

"No, hand me my phone," I called Josh and Katy. When you have friends on the ambulance service, you can sidestep 911. I didn't know who was on call, but I wanted to make sure Josh and Katy would be the ones responding.

"Josh, it's Miranda, I'm home, and my water broke!"

"Is someone with you?"

"Yes."

"OK, we'll get there as soon as possible. Don't try and go to the hospital yourself in this storm."

Bart suddenly appeared in the doorway covered in snow. "How are you doing?"

"I'm about to give birth in the middle of a blizzard, how do you think I'm doing?" I took a breath as another wave of pain assaulted me. It passed, took a breath, and said, "Sorry. Did you get a premonition?"

"Yes." He threw off his coat and hat, and to my surprise, began giving instructions to Danuta like he was a doctor talking to a nurse.

When Josh and Katy got to the ambulance garage, they called for assistance. That day my opinion of nosey neighbors changed forever. All the police scanners in town picked up the message that help was needed clearing the road to get to a woman in labor. My parents heard it too. In such a small town, the address gave away who was about to have a baby. Despite the freezing temps, howling winds, and heavy snow, a small army of tractors and trucks with plow blades appeared in the road to clear the way. Ralph, the Fire Chief, picked up my parents. His truck had the biggest snowplow. I later heard Mom had yelled expletives to encourage him to go faster. Four feet of blowing snow made it almost impossible to see the road. The ambulance followed behind the trucks. The telephone poles were their only guide to follow the road in the blinding snow. Ralph's truck went off into a ditch. My parents climbed up the embankment and got into the back of the ambulance. It took thirty grueling minutes to cover the five miles to the house. Before the ambulance arrived, Ben, the Chief of Police, got to the house on his snowmobile. He had never delivered a baby and looked a little queasy. Danuta asked him to go downstairs and guide the ambulance staff when they arrived. She told Camo to look after the babies.

The phone rang, Danuta answered then handed the phone to me, it was Tristan, "I'm on my way to the airport, how are you?"

"I'm in labor. What do you think?"

"Can't you slow it down?"

I threw the phone across the room, "Idiot!"

Another wave of pain ripped through me. I was mad and sad because Tristan was not here, even though I knew it was not his fault. Then I got tearful thinking about how Ralph and Ben spent their lives looking after this town. I knew they would have braved the storm on foot, if necessary, to help a pregnant woman. I was a tearful mess.

Bart went into the bathroom washed his hands, then came back in the room carrying a black medical bag. He placed surgical implements, syringes, ampules, and gloves on a clean sheet. He glanced at me, "Don't worry, it has all been sterilized."

"You're a doctor?"

"Surgeon. My medical mentor was one of the founders of Johns-Hopkins."

Before I could respond, a contraction ripped through me, "Damn it!" My hands clenched the sheets until my knuckles went white.

He returned to my bedside, took my vitals, and asked Danuta to time my contractions.

"I should have known you were a surgeon That explains your social skills."

For a moment, his serious countenance turned to surprise, "Do you really want to insult me now?"

"Are you kidding? If I insulted God now, I'd be forgiven."

"Point taken."

Another painful spasm gripped me. "Ow! Fuck a duck!"

"How many minutes?' he asked Danuta.

"About three minutes between, they last about a minute."

"It won't be long. You're in transition. Help me get her into position so I can check her cervix."

In my wildest dreams, I had not imagined this scenario. The same hands that had given painstaking care to the horse's hooves were handling my most private parts. I did not care that a centuries-old barn dwelling vampire was delivering my baby as long as he knew what he was doing.

"Push, then breathe…"

"I don't have a choice, damn!"

Katy and Josh came running into the room, shedding coats. She asked, "How are you doing?" Josh gave Bart a questioning glance.

"I'm…" I paused and gritted my teeth as another contraction hit me, "Son of a bitch that hurts!"

"We'll take over now," Josh started to move Sir Bart out of the way.

"No! He's a surgeon," I said to avoid any issues.

"For real?" Josh was surprised. Bart merely nodded.

Katy set up a blood pressure monitor. "Vitals are normal for a woman in labor."

"Fuck!" I yelled.

I looked up to see my parents standing in the doorway. Mom was tearful and started to approach, but Sir Bart said to her, "Could you two please see to the children, your daughter will be fine."

To everyone's relief, my parents went down the hall without protest. The Fire Chief and Chief of Police stationed themselves at the door but turned their backs to afford a little privacy. At that moment, I would not have cared if the birth was being televised.

Bart instructed Josh, "Keep her legs in position."

Katy put a cool cloth on my forehead, "You're doing fine, Randie."

"Here it comes again!" I felt the pain more intensely than with the triplets. I would have killed for an epidural.

"I can see the head!" Josh called out.

"Try not to push." Sir Bart turned to Josh, and calmly gave him directions, "You must help me move the cord. It's around the neck."

"Oh my god! Something's wrong!" I started to panic.

Katy spoke softly, "They have to reposition the baby It will be fine. Try not to push."

"I can't help it! It's coming…"

"He's turning blue," Josh said quietly, glancing at Katy.

I felt a slight pain as Bart made an incision, which allowed room to pull the cord away from the infant's neck.

"Push now!" Sir Bart instructed. "Support the baby as he comes out," he commanded Josh as he held the cord clear of the infant.

"It's a boy!" Josh held up a bloody, screaming, darling baby boy. Jacques Omar let the world know he had arrived. Katy rushed over to take the baby. She wrapped him in a soft blanket, suctioned his nose and mouth, then lay him on my tummy while Bart clamped and cut the cord.

"Thank God you were here!" Josh said to Bart with admiration. The ancient vampire merely smiled.

With tears in my eyes, I looked around at everyone in the room, "Jacques and I are very grateful to you all, especially Bart." My youngest son lay quiet in my arms, nuzzling my chest.

He had very fine, tiny little curls. I kissed his forehead and fell back against the pillows, exhausted.

Bart picked up a surgical needle and thread. "I'm sorry, Baroness, but I must stitch you up. I'll make this quick as possible." He looked at Katy, "Would you assist?"

"Nothing like having a baby to give you the pain tolerance of a defensive lineman, and the modesty of a stripper."

When they finished, Danuta handed me the phone. It was Tristan again, "Miranda, are you OK, and the baby is he…"

"We're fine. Bart was great, and the whole town came out in this storm," I was tearing up.

"I should have been there. I'll be there as soon as possible with Dr. Kyoto."

"I'm tired and sore, but very happy. Our son is lying across my chest. He is darling." My voice started to crack, "Here's Bart."

"Baron, we were unable to get to the hospital, but the ambulance staff got here in time. Your lovely wife and son are doing well. Jacques is about eight lbs., and twenty inches, quite large for not quite being full-term."

"I cannot thank you enough. I will be forever in your debt."

My parents entered and could not say enough about how handsome Jacques was. My father held him in his arms with his back to me while they cleaned me up and changed the bedding. He looked like he had just won the Stanley Cup. "Wait until you meet your brothers and sister."

Mom helped me into a clean nightgown, "Honey, you need to rest, we'll take care of everything. Little Jacques is just perfect."

I settled into my bed and felt the adrenaline rush wearing off. "He's a Rossville kid," I smiled as I drifted off. The big storm and Jacque's birth would be the talked of the town for years.

Dad gently gave me Jacques, "I'm adding a new French burger to the menu with Brie cheese to honor my newest grandson."

Chapter 4

What's Love Got to Do with It?

Due to the storm, my husband and Dr. Kyoto didn't arrive until the next night. They flew into Indianapolis by private jet since the small airport in Danville was still closed. They arrived in a rented Range Rover about midnight. I heard commotion in the house and hurried footsteps in the hall. Tristan rushed to the bed and gently folded me in his cool arms. His scent, his tender kiss, and the look of relief on his face almost brought me to tears.

"I should have been here," he said in a rare apology.

"It was your son's fault. He chose to make his dramatic entrance during the storm." I responded as Dr. Kyoto entered with Jacques. "Our newest troublemaker."

Dr. Kyoto smiled. "He appears quite healthy, though I'll do some bloodwork."

My husband very carefully took charge of his youngest offspring, "He is handsome. Look at his hair," he gently kissed his fuzzy head.

"Baroness, I must attend to you now."

"Of course," the housekeeper responded and nudged my husband to step out.

"I shall be with the children," Tristan retreated with Jacques.

Dr. Kyoto opened his bag and took out a stethoscope, blood pressure cuff, thermometer, syringes, and some small glass vials. The writing on the vials was in Japanese. He made little eye contact while drawing the blood. He checked my stitches, cleansed the area, and applied ointment, which lessened the discomfort. Kyoto's exam was very thorough. It seemed like he took a lot of blood, but I guess that was normal. I asked, "Is everything okay?"

"Yes, Yes. Sir Bart did a wonderful job. I couldn't have done it better myself. The stitches will dissolve in several days. Take showers, not baths. I suggest you not engage in strenuous activity for six weeks."

"Tell Tristan. He might listen to you."

The next night Dr. Kyoto flew back to Los Angeles. He made a phone call to an ancient vampire before he visited the head of the vampire world. "All is well. I will contact you when I have completed my tests," without waiting for a reply, he hung up.

It was fifty-three degrees which for Angelenos was a cold day. After the frozen prairie of the heartland, it felt quite comfortable to Dr. Kyoto. He was shown to the Magus' master suite. A small fire was burning in the fireplace. Two large red velvet chairs from Versailles, stood on the thick Persian rug, facing the fading fire. The Magus sitting in one of the velvet chairs gave Dr. Kyoto a small nod, Dr. Kyoto nodded more deeply. The Magus wore a black silk smoking jacket over a dark gray silk shirt and matching gray pants. He felt a bit too casual for a meeting with the Magus as he still wore a cashmere sweater and jeans from the flight.

"Please sit down," he gestured to the other chair. "How are the Baroness and the baby?"

"The Baroness and the baby are recovering nicely."

"And the bloodwork?" he leaned towards the physician.

"My limited testing so far showed HH, like his siblings. He carries the same mutation, and I hypothesize that he will be comfortable in the day-light world. When they mature, who knows how their vampire natures will be expressed."

The Magus looked delighted. "Excellent news!"

Dr. Kyoto stared into the fire. "I know their DNA is 75% Haute Caste and only 25% mortal, but do not ignore the importance of environment or maternal influence. They will seem more like their mother."

"I am well acquainted with the Baroness," he replied with a confident smile. "I allowed her to return to that unambitious little town to give her a sense of control and security while raising the offspring, but our influence continues."

"May I speak freely?" Sir Kyoto asked humbly.

"Of course, old friend. I have always valued your insights."

"When the lioness and her cubs come to understand the grand experiment that you are conducting with their lives, I doubt they will be pleased or grateful."

The Magus smiled, "Did I ever tell you that I once worked as a lion tamer in a circus in Italy?"

Dr. Kyoto shook his head, "You must teach the Baron."

The Magus looked back at the smoldering fire, "He is in love. I can teach him nothing." Then he regarded Dr. Kyoto, "Have you ever been so enamored of another that it clouded your ability to see the world as it is?"

Although they had discussed sexual affairs, Kyoto was surprised by the Magus' personal inquiry. They had never talked about feelings for someone. The Haute Caste regarded love as a weakness. "Love? Not since I left tears on my kimono sleeves as a youth. I don't believe the Baron is in love. His relationship with the Baroness was so well planned. The Baron's attachment to her serves a purpose."

"The Taj Mahal was carefully planned, and has meaning, yet the only reason it stands is because of love." The Magus walked over to the fireplace and stood facing his old friend. "Though the vampire world is excited about the offspring, like you, they do not accept the most amazing aspect of the Baron and Baroness. Because of her, a member of the Haute Caste has demonstrated feeling something besides loyalty, arrogance, or lust."

Dr. Kyoto smiled faintly, "Do you believe that the rest of us, so set in our ways, might also have such an experience? I have no desire for such misfortune. I am content to feel and act only on my lust. I do not wish to suffer from love blindness."

The Magus leaned towards him, "I understand. In many ways, the Baroness has opened a vampire's version of Pandora's box. I must disagree with you. Infatuation is blind, but not love. It sees all and still feels unrelenting desire. Have you not noticed how Lady Anastasia and Sir Omar interact?"

"I have noticed their growing fondness, but I assumed it was related to sharing in the violent end of Lady Lena. You know how a good assassination can stir a rhapsody in the blood, and that was epic," Dr. Kyoto responded, hoping it was not more than that.

With a wistful expression, the Magus added, "Change is inevitable, even after a thousand years, even for our kind. We must be aware of change and use it to our advantage."

Dr. Kyoto fired back, "If I had wanted change, I would have stayed mortal."

"There is the curmudgeon I've always admired. All I can say is that I have seen the future, and it is glorious." The Magus said with a small smile.

"You believe in Lady Cassandra's visions. All I know is that I witnessed the Baron changing a diaper, it was quite disturbing to see Baron Tristan Mordechai reduced to such a disgusting menial task."

The Magus replied, "I do not think the Baron views it that way. Maybe we can have a painting of that."

They both started laughing. The butler unused to the sound of laughter, came to check on the Magus and was quickly dismissed.

Tristan stayed for ten nights. I had lots of help between my parents, Bart, Josh, Katy, Danuta and even Camo. We turned the living room into a large playpen for the triplets. I would often find Tristan sitting alone with Jacques when the other offspring had overwhelmed his control-freak tendencies. The triplets crawled over each other in attempts to get to the toy of the moment. Marie quickly developed an ability to hold her own with her brothers. Amazon made a small fortune off us on diapers alone. I relished the normal chaos of babies. When Tristan finally left, I think he was looking forward to going back to his fairly predictable vampire nightlife. The second most powerful vampire in the world was worn out by the kids.

I waited until Tristan went back to L.A. to ask Bart more about his story. I felt close enough to him now that he might open up to me. I found him behind the barn watching the horses. He looked like a Sherpa with his mud boots and colorful beanie.

"Hi Bart, do you have a few minutes to talk?"

"That depends. He replied with a small smile, "What do you want to talk about?"

"You."

Just then, one of the horses came up to me and started nibbling on my jacket. I rubbed his nose. The other horses came over, and I found myself overwhelmed by their affection. Bart reached into his pocket and handed me a few peppermints. "No thanks," I said.

He smiled and replied, "They're not for you. The horses love peppermints!" I was a little skeptical, but I gave one to each of the horses. They loved the treat.

"That's enough treats for now!" Bart said, and led the huge beasts back to the barn. I helped him get them into their stalls.

"So, can we talk? Jacques just fell asleep. Danuta and Camo are watching the triplets."

"Yes. Come into my home. Please remove your shoes."

His apartment was spotless and had a faint smell of pine. I never realized he was a clean freak! Two red glass Victorian lamps lighted the room. I sat on a low velvet tufted couch and admired his Persian rug.

He disappeared for a few minutes then brought out a teapot decorated with red roses and two matching cups. He had changed out of his work clothes and wore a long caftan. His hair hung loose past his shoulders. It was the first time I realized how handsome he was. "Tea?"

Normally I would have asked for coffee, but I did not want to offend his hospitality. "Yes, thanks."

"You may ask one question about my personal life." He sat cross-legged on the carpet a few feet from me. He looked like a wise yogi about to dispense the truth of the universe.

I sipped the tea while carefully choosing my question. "Why and how did you transform?"

He smiled, "That is two questions, but I shall answer both."

"In detail, please."

"I was studying to become a history professor in London, four hundred years after the death of de Molay. Having once considered becoming a man of the cloth, I had an interest in religion, which led me to research the Knights Templar. I was struck by the greed and cowardly attacks by those in power, which ended their order. Your ancestor Jacques de Molay was truly noble. The orchestrated demise of all those involved in the Friday the 13th massacre of the Templars also fascinated me. I went to France, and after a year of investigating clues, I encountered a vampire for the first time, Guillaume de Molay. At first, I was appalled, contact with such a being went against all my religious training. He asked if I wanted to know the truth about vampires or continue to believe folk tales. Though I knew he could have easily killed me somehow, I did not feel threatened by him. Though I feared for my soul, my scholarly brain won out. Guillaume said he could introduce me to the vampire who had actually met de Molay."

He took a sip of tea. I said nothing, not wanting to stop the flow of precious information.

"Your husband only bothered to meet me because Guillaume had detected my, what we now call, HH blood. I had no idea I was so unique, there were no sophisticated medical tests at that time, but the vampires could tell. My first encounter with the Baron was thrilling and terrifying. He still has the most commanding presence. After three meetings, he was able to help me understand my destiny. As you well know, once you accept that vampires exist, life can never be the same. I was given this rare insight into the nocturnal world for a reason. It became clear that I should transform to help with the Haute Caste's efforts to rid the world of injustice."

"Was the title Hierophant given to you by the Magus?"

"That, Baroness Mordecai is another story. That is all I will tell you for now."

"Thank you." I finished my cup of tea and left. A gentleman, scholar, surgeon, and crusader. Maybe he'd be able to handle my kids.

Chapter 5

Just Another Day in the Cornfields

After a few weeks in Bel Air, Tristan returned to Rossville and his paternal role with gusto. He read several books on parenting and tried to be on top of their developmental changes and needs. Like all things he took great pride in, he attacked the task like a quest or mission. It was good he spent most of his time away on business as his head would start to explode when some behavioral model he had read and studied about failed to achieve his goal in the real world. He was sure he could get them to all go to bed and to sleep at the same time. He set up a schedule that involved almost every activity of the day set up on spreadsheets, which I found hilarious. He thought he could synchronize a baby and three toddlers like swimmers. Just when he would think he had them all asleep, one would wake up and start fussing, which would get the others going. Danuta and I were used to the chaos, but not the Baron. He always looked exhausted, both physically and mentally, by the time he went back to Bel Air. It takes a lot to wear out a vampire, but we managed.

The Magus made sure the vampire world left us alone for the most part. Tristan visited on a regular basis without incident besides the rare story about a drug dealer or a child abuser in the university town found dead due to blood loss from a savage wound. I learned to emotionally distance myself from my husband's "calling." Camo and Danuta were good with the children. Danuta encouraged the soft side of the tough biker. She even helped him find little camo t-shirts for the children. To my amusement, the shirts horrified my husband.

My parents managed to accept my husband's weird lifestyle and our long-distance relationship with little comment. Mom just said, "Maybe you should visit the Lithuanian Museum in Chicago, learn more about his culture."

I replied, "I think I know enough about Lithuanians. I'm good."

"I found some Lithuanian cookie recipes online do you think Stan would like them?"

I coughed, then replied, "I don't think so, he's very strict about his diet. Thanks anyway."

The children were brilliant, quick, goal-oriented (which is a mom's way of saying extremely manipulative), somewhat wicked when bored, and loving. Every day was a chess match between two kings and a queen, with swiftly changing alliances. Desmond, Marie, and Tomas treated Jacques, who was almost a year younger, like a knight they could send on fool's errands. He learned to question their authority quickly.

Tomas had black, wavy hair and dark brown eyes like his grandfather. He was orderly and neat, to the point of being a bit obsessive-compulsive. So naturally, Desmon and Marie spent a lot of time moving and hiding his toys. Even when he ate, Tomas arranged the food on his plate like countries with distinct borders. If he looked away, a pea would somehow appear in his mashed potatoes. He learned to be hypervigilant about guarding his stuff.

Desmon had light brown hair that curled in ringlets and brown eyes. He had a way of setting things in motion without seeming to have been involved. He was the most goal-oriented, which reminded me of his namesake. One day Jacques had been playing in the garden with Desmon, suddenly burst into my office with a baby snake he had found. Luckily it was not poisonous. Des knew I was afraid of snakes. He learned that the trail would lead back to him no matter how well he covered his tracks. At least I like to tell myself that.

Marie had straight black hair and blue eyes and could charm the devil himself. She had an amazing way with adults and animals. Her brothers seemed immune to her wonderfulness, which frustrated her to no end. Nothing her father or I said made much of a dent, but if one of the boys were critical of her, they took their lives in their hands. At dinner one night, Tomas was getting under her skin. I stepped away for a moment, and when I came back, I found Tomas' dinner plate empty and the contents in the blender. Sometimes Desmon would run down the stairs with his toys flying past his head. She learned how to protect herself and her self-esteem, especially with males.

Jacques had curly brown hair and green eyes. He was the most coddled by me. As the youngest, he was the most picked on by his siblings. At an early age, he decided to be a great Baron, just like his dad. While the others were playing hockey and soccer, he asked for fencing lessons. He would spend hours reading books about royalty. In kindergarten, when kids at school painted dogs or snowmen, he painted a royal crest. Although wary of his siblings, he learned to not worry about what the masses said or did. Of all the kids, he seemed most likely to be won over by his dad's nocturnal clan.

When they asked me about why we were different from other families, I just said it was because their dad was Lithuanian. I had two rules, never call anyone stupid and never use royal titles in town. When Tristan visited, the kids loved calling each other Baron and Baroness in a snarky tone of voice to annoy me.

Our marital issues fueled a dramatic relationship. The sex was almost as intense as the resentments we both felt. Tristan seemed to go out of his way to set me off about my decision to raise the kids in the cornfields. I knew he continued to have extramarital relationships. If I said anything, he would simply tell me to return with him, and he would give up all his distractions. He loved me on his terms. I knew a time would come when I would either transform or leave him or maybe both, but not while the offspring were so young.

The children were more aware of our conflicts than I thought. One evening when Tristan was about to arrive, I had my hair up in a braid because it was muggy and hot. My husband always told me he likes me to wear my hair down. I overheard Tomas, who was about seven, ask, "Is Mom mad?"

Marie responded, "Why?"

Desmon answered, "She's got her fancy hair. Dad doesn't like it."

Marie added, "Poor Dad!"

To which Jacques responded with, "Dad is rich!"

My youngest always seemed to be on a different wavelength.

It was difficult to raise them in a small town where fitting in was prized almost above all else. Their strength, speed, and agility were obvious to me, and I had to ask them to hold back at times. I worried about them getting attention for standing out in sports. I also worried about what they might do if someone tried to bully them.

They were extremely intelligent and easily bored in school. It was hard for them to accept that they had to restrain themselves even when they knew more about a subject than the teacher. One day in science class, Tomas used all his self-control not to respond when the teacher said that the reason the center of the earth is extremely hot is explained in the Bible. Such is life in a small rural town.

The horses turned out to be a blessing. Bart taught them about taking care of the horses which they loved. When Tristan visited, they would practice hockey. We kept a low profile, and the kids would socialize on a superficial level at school. They participated in plays and band but didn't bring kids home. My parents' café became a place to hang out with other kids after school without having to deal with questions about why their dad was only seen at night, who was that weird guy Bart, how rich they were, etc.

The shadow of the vampire world never left us. We became a tourist stop for the undead. Sometimes I would detect the scent of vampires at night when I ran into town on some errand. They would be passing through on their way to Chicago, St. Louis, or Indianapolis. They were hoping for a sighting of the royals. Several times a year, a limo or other expensive vehicle would drive slowly down our road at night but never pull into the drive. I gave only a few of the Haute Caste I knew well permission to visit. We would visit the Magus' home north of Chicago once a year, and some vampires would meet us there. Even those allowed to visit Rossville disliked the lack of amenities and meager population in our county. It was fine by me as Rossville did not need any more vampires.

The largest gathering to "inspect" the offspring happened when they were four and five years old. My husband and the Magus insisted that it was time to introduce our offspring to the greater vampire community. It was a birthday party in July, even though their births had occurred in winter. Vampires are not fond of the cold. I had no idea at the time how the new acquaintances would foretell the coming crisis in the vampire world and our lives. It was a birthday party for my kids, no big deal. Right?

Chapter 6

The Mongolian Hordes Invade

I loaded the kids into the Jeep with Danuta's help. She was looking forward to a little vacation in Chicago with her relatives. I did not tell my parents about the party for the kids. They thought I was just meeting Tristan there. My biological father would be attending the party. I did not want to take the chance that my mom would recognize him. I did not think she would want to face the truth of how I came into this world.

We arrived at the mansion in Highland Park about five in the evening. It was eerily quiet in the great house. The butler showed us to a den that had games and toys ready for the children. A housekeeper brought in a tray with sandwiches, cookies, and milk. The Magus' staff enjoyed having the children around. It was a bit of normalcy. Our luggage was taken to the second floor, where two bedrooms had been set aside for the kids next to the suite where my husband was asleep. My friends, Lolly, Al, and James, were at a nearby hotel and would be arriving at eight that evening.

Lolly and I became close friends while surviving UCLA together. She is a successful model now, and her fiancé, Al, is a nerdy psychiatrist. James, a dentist friend of Al's, and I had started dating when Tristan first invaded my life. After our second, and last date in L.A., he was abducted by a vampiress as part of a larger plan to seize power. All three had dangerous encounters with rogue undead, but my friends trusted my immortal family, the "good" vampires.

Sometimes I needed a mortal reality check. They were my children's godparents. I wanted to be sure they would have more mortals in their lives. They had come up with the name F.O.V., Friends of Vampires, which stuck. Tristan did not appreciate the humor.

The kids were playing in the den as I looked out the French doors at Lake Michigan. My reverie was broken when I heard Jacques complain. The triplets started playing some game that excluded him. His eyes filled with tears. I asked the housekeeper and butler to watch over the triplets. I took Jacques' hand and asked, "Do you want to explore the garden?"

"Like Chris Robin and Pooh?"

"Yes. C'mon, we'll have a little adventure."

We went out to the garden with a perfectly mowed lawn that went to the water's edge. I stood looking at the clouds in the west, starting to turn pastel shades of pink and orange as the sun began to set. At my back was the dark blue enormous expanse of Lake Michigan. I still thought of it like an ocean since you couldn't see to the other side. We walked to the border of lilies, violets, and small shrubs that sat on the cliff above the water.

"Mom. Look, boats!" A couple of sailboats were making their way back to the harbor at Wilmette.

"Yes, Jacques, it's a big lake, so there are lots of big boats."

"And big fish?"

"Yes, I suppose there are."

He began to take off his jacket, "I want to swim with the big fish!"

"No, hon, you can't swim here. We'll go swimming in the pond, back home."

"Please! I want to swim!" He started to take his pants off.

"Jacques Omar Ortega Mordecai! No!" I pulled his pants back up. I looked back to the west to see that the sun had sunk below the horizon. "Besides, it is too dark for swimming now. Let's see if Dad is awake. I'll race you to the house."

The distraction worked. "OK, but I say go." He looked at me with a mischievous grin, and then he took off running. "Go!"

As I followed behind, I noticed a man with sunglasses in an upstairs window watching us. The windows of the house were tinted, but I could still make out his silhouette. He was fair, with shoulder-length hair, and medium stature. I felt him shield his thoughts from me as he pulled the drapes closed. I got a glimmer of delight when he looked at my son, but nothing more. I knew we were going to meet some interesting vampires tonight. I did not want them to be too interested in my kids.

Just before we got to the door, I scooped Jacques up in my arms.

"Cheater!" he protested.

"I had to grab you, or you would have won."

"I'll tell Dad!"

Tristan was waiting for us at the door. He took Jacques from me and placed him on the ground. "I declare Jacques Omar Ortega Mordecai, the winner!" Then he grabbed me and gave me a kiss that testified to how much he missed me.

"Let Mom go!" Jacques yelled.

He looked down at his son, "It's perfectly proper, we are married."

Jacques thought for a moment then replied in a serious tone, "I marry Auntie Stasia."

I laughed, but my husband responded in an equally serious tone, "Worthy choice, but Lady Anastasia is not available."

Jacques looked confused.

I replied, "She loves Omar."

"OK. Look what I found!" He pulled a tiny frog out of his jacket pocket. It landed on the floor and went jumping down the hall with Jacques running after it, "Froggy!"

I turned to Tristan, "She will be heartbroken."

"He got over his first love rather quickly. Good man!"

We rounded up the children and marched them upstairs to dress for their party. Tristan was already wearing a dark navy silk shirt and matching dress slacks with blue suede shoes. I started humming my dad's favorite Elvis song as we walked upstairs. I got no reaction from his highness. Apparently not a fan of the King.

He and a housekeeper took the children into their rooms to change, allowing me a little alone time to get ready. I walked into our suite and wanted to take a nap. There was a king-size four-poster bed. The dark purple comforter had been turned down, revealing pale lavender sheets. I resisted the urge and forced myself to primp. There were two paintings of lovely Renaissance ladies on the wall. I knew it would be hard to live up to their examples.

I put on a satin teal dress with a plunging neckline front and back, curled my hair in long ringlets then pinned them back. I put on three-inch black strappy sandals and looked in the full-length mirror the Magus had his staff put up, obviously just for me. I was wearing a gold and diamond bracelet Lady Kananga had given me. The small blade hidden in the bracelet had protected me in the past. Although I knew I should be safe here, wearing it gave me added comfort.

Though it seemed like I was ready for the party, I grabbed one more piece of jewelry. A very large ruby pendant that Tristan had given me when we were first married. Lena, who was trying to seize power, was enraged that it had not gone to her. Ultimately, she and her rouge undead cohorts were defeated, but there were still rumblings of Common Caste unrest. I wasn't comfortable wearing it in Rossville, so this was one of the rare occasions I was able to wear it.

Tristan marched our kids into the room for final inspection. Marie ran up to me with tears in her eyes.

"What happened?"

"Daddy brushed my hair," she whimpered.

"I might have pulled too hard," he responded and looked down at the floor. I tried very hard not to laugh.

The boys wore variations of dark pants and striped shirts. Marie wore a pale blue dress with an ivory lace collar and matching lace leggings.

"You all look amazing," I wondered how long it would last. "OK, so here are the rules. When someone gives you a present, you say, 'Thank You.' Stick together. No yelling or fighting. If someone is unhappy, just come and tell us. Got it?"

They all nodded. Then Marie said, "Unhappy!"

I replied, "Your hair looks fine. It will feel better soon."

We went downstairs and entered what had once been a small ballroom. A beautiful crystal chandelier lit up the elegantly furnished room. Tristan whispered, "Do you think she'll forgive me?"

I looked at my husband's worried countenance, "In a few months."

Lolly, Al, and James arrived and greeted us warmly. James made a point of saying hello to my husband before he talked to me.

"How are you? The kids are getting big," he gave me a quick kiss on the cheek.

"I'm still mortal and partially sane, so far so good," I smiled.

He chuckled, "Yeah, me too. I brought my dentist bag so I can give the offspring a quick check-up tomorrow."

"That would be great, thanks. I appreciate that." Because the kids were three-quarters vampire, I was concerned that they might be developing little fangs like their dad. I did not want them to have our local dentist find anything unusual. It was a little difficult to manage routine medical checkups, but the Magus arranged for them to be checked by a doctor in his employ.

Lolly looked great in a tiny black dress with geometric beading in shades of red. She hugged me warmly, "How are you, honey, I really missed you?" Al wore a black suit and shirt with a red tie that I knew Lolly had picked out.

"I'm good. I love your braids!"

"Just came back from filming a commercial in Jamaica."

"I thought Al looked sunburned." He was generally a whiter shade of pale from sitting in his psychiatric practice all day.

"Yeah, the fool thought he would get a tan, I did try to warn him to use sunscreen. I've got to say hello to the kids." She began hugging and teasing them. They all loved their Godmother Lolly. She even got Jacques giggling when she tickled him. I noticed Marie touch her hair and point at her dad. Lolly gave her an appropriate sympathetic look.

Al hugged me, "Hi Randie, everything ok?" He could not help but have personal and professional concern for my situation. He had survived a vampire attack, so I knew it was more than curiosity.

"Same strange life, but yeah, Tristan, and the kids and I are doing fine everything considered. I think raising them in Rossville, away from the craziness of the nocturnal world, was a good decision."

Al and I glanced around the room at the stylishly dressed, attractive and flirtatious vampires who appeared to be in their twenties or early thirties, surrounded by the opulent furnishings. I saw about a dozen vampires that I knew. Some that I did not recognize were staring at the children like they were rare creatures on display at a zoo.

"Stop it!" Tomas cried out and suddenly pushed Des down. It was about to get ugly when my husband stepped in between them and instantly stopped the fight.

I laughed, "We do have enough normal kid drama."

A hush fell on the room as the Magus entered. He was tall with a slight figure dressed in a black suit and a black silk shirt with thin lapels and a thin metallic purple tie. He gracefully walked across the room to us, where a butler suddenly appeared with a stuffed gray velvet chair and placed it near us. Everyone in the room, except for the kids nodded, even the F.O.V. showed him respect. He brushed his straight black hair back from his face and smiled at me before sitting. "Good evening Baroness." Now everyone knew how they should respond to the Baroness Mordecai.

The offspring yelled, "Magus!" almost in unison and ran over to him. He stiffly patted their heads and looked at them approvingly. My husband and I moved them over beside his highness' chair as the Haute Caste started to come by to exchange greetings and compliment him before acknowledging their delight in seeing the children. My gut told me about half of what I heard was sincere. I was relieved when Lady Sarah and her brother Sir Ruben came over. They had looked after my safety since I was born, and I completely trusted them. The ravishing, well-endowed redhead wore a black leather dress and a diamond collar. "Miranda, you look chic and gorgeous, your husband must convince you and the offspring to leave the cornfields more often."

"He has tried, but the world is not ready for my munchkin mercenaries."

Ruben, who typically dressed more casually, usually in a rock n' roll T-shirt and jeans, pulled on his unruly red curls and straightened his tuxedo. "Good to see you! You and the kids do look great!" Then in almost a whisper, "I hate this straight-jacket."

Des cried out, "Uncle Ruben!" and pulled on his pant leg. The other kids gathered around him. He knelt on the floor to his sister's dismay and started playing with the kids.

When my father, Sir Omar, and Lady Anastasia arrived, it caused quite a stir. Her exquisite ivory lace gown had a high neckline, which was covered by strands of pearls, and gold chains encrusted with jewels. Anastasia's hair, in delicate ringlets about her lovely face was dyed platinum blonde to remind her of Russian winters. My father wore his Arab finery with pride. He wore a white flowing burnoose with a gold embroidered belt at his waist. On his belt was a gold, jewel-encrusted sword that hung at his side. His keffiyeh, held in place with a black cord around his head, emphasized his dark eyes and high cheekbones. They were a captivating couple.

They bent down to greet the children, and lavish praise on them. The children thought of him as an indulgent uncle. However, the vampire world knew they were Sir Omar's grandchildren. Tristan pointed out to me that Jacques was holding Lady Anastasia's hand. "Maybe he hasn't quite gotten over his first love."

"Let us give the children their presents," the Magus decreed. It was strange and a little creepy when he fussed over them, like a Goth Santa Claus. Just saying!

It was supposed to be orderly, with one present at a time being taken off a loaded tea cart and given out to a child. The process took too long for the siblings. Not surprisingly, despite Tristan and the Magus' attempts to keep things orderly, it soon dissolved into chaos. The triplets could already read their names and managed to pass them out themselves. Paper was flying along with screams of delight. They loved the wooden swords, sailboats, Legos, toy soldiers, drums, books, and electronic games. Anastasia gave them each a porcelain doll wearing royal robes and crowns.

When all the presents were opened and the decibel level restored to a manageable level, it was time for birthday cake. One of the housekeepers wheeled in a cart with a huge cake with candles. It seemed a bit much to me as the undead wouldn't be partaking in cake, but the Magus liked to do everything with flair. The candles were blown out, and I started to hand out the cake and ice cream. Jacques was missing! I called his name, but there was no response.

"Search the house and grounds for the child!" The Magus commanded. The well-dressed undead ran out of the room, hoping to garner favor by finding Jacques.

I told the F.O.V. to watch the triplets, then looked at Tristan, "The lake!" we both went running through the halls to the back door.

I heard someone yell, "There he is!"

"Jacques!" I called as we ran towards a man who was leading our son back from the water's edge. Jacques was holding his sailboat. It was not well-lit, so it was hard to make out who had saved him. Breathless, I fell on my knees on the wet grass and grabbed my youngest. "Thank you! Jacques, you scared me, never do that again!"

"He said sharks, mom, and crocodiles, this lake bad! I just wanted to sail my boat." His eyes were as big as saucers.

I looked up to see the man who had been watching us from the window earlier. "I think he has been properly dissuaded from swimming in Lake Michigan," he smiled.

"You saved him, we are in your debt," Tristan stated and bowed his head slightly.

Keeping hold of Jacque's hand, I stood and kissed the hero on the cheek, "We are grateful." He smelled great. I looked into his eyes; they were polychromatic. He was as handsome as Tristan with brown wavy hair to his shoulders.

"That kiss was all the reward I desire." He smiled at me, and I melted a little.

As we walked back in the house, I said, "We've never met, I don't know your name."

"You already know my name. You just have not made my acquaintance. I'm Alexander." He had a slight Middle Eastern accent like the Magus.

I took a good look at him in the light. He had one hazel and one green eye, he was medium height and muscular. He smelled of bergamot with a hint of citrus. Like a pinball machine lighting up, I responded, "The Great?"

He bowed slightly. "Some have called me that, but just call me Alex."

After meeting Anastasia Romanov, I had become a little hard to impress, but Alexander the Great? "What the fuck," I muttered.

"I hope you never call me that, though at some point I may deserve it," he replied with a smile and patted Jacque's head before he slipped away in the crowd.

Marie looked at her little brother, "Jacques is in trouble."

Tomas added, "Big trouble."

Des looked at me, "Can I have his boat?"

"No!" Jacques started crying and held on tightly to his toy.

"Stop it! No one is in trouble. Be glad your brother is safe." I just looked at them and shook my head. How the human race had not destroyed itself years ago was beyond me. The kids got quiet and focused on their dessert. I left their grandfather and Lady Anastasia in charge and went to the other side of the room, where the Magus was talking with Tristan.

"It was surprising and fortuitous that Alexander was so attentive to the child," the Magus mused.

"Now I owe him my gratitude," my husband responded.

"So, it would seem," the Magus nodded.

Just at that moment, the House of Arrows arrived. I had known Jorge and Franco since they had taken night classes in order to protect and watch over me when I was at UCLA.

"What did we miss?" Franco asked.

I smiled, "Just Alexander the Great saving Jacque's life."

Jorge looked towards the children "Jacques is okay?"

"Yeah, he's too young to care about more than his toys and birthday cake right now. He didn't even realize how dangerous it is along the cliff."

"I'm glad he is okay," Jorge responded. "You look amazing tonight for a change. That must be annoying to the fine ladies here tonight."

"Thanks, I think."

Just then, Antoinella stood very close to Tristan and started to whisper in his ear. He seemed to be amused by what she had to say.

Franco added, "They aren't all ladies. Excuse us. We must present to the Magus."

I looked around the room and saw that Kyoto and Lily had arrived. Kananga motioned to me to join her. She was sitting like a queen on a throne next to a large bay window. She wore a caftan, made of glistening golden fabric with tiny pieces of malachite embroidered into exotic flower designs about her deep-V neckline. She wore gold bangles, rings, and earrings. About her neck was a lion's head with diamond eyes. She wore a head wrap that matched her caftan, with many long, fine braids pulled off to the side. She looked at me with amber eyes that showed concern.

"Sit down, my dear. It's been a stressful evening."

"Thanks," I pulled up a chair, "Is there something I should know?"

"Too much," she replied and looked around the room. Her eyes rested on Borgia, speaking with Kyoto. "Please take my advice and go back to your farm tonight. Take the children away from these jackals."

"It's not that I disagree, but is there some specific threat I should know about?" I was starting to worry.

Just then, the Magus interrupted us. "Good evening Lady Kananga, you look stunning as always. Miranda, please join us for a final toast to your offspring."

I whispered to Kananga, "If not tonight, we'll leave tomorrow. Thanks for having my back."

I made a point of moving in between Antoinella and Tristan. She elbowed me. I stepped on her foot and said, "I'm so sorry." I imagined that three-inch heels could really sting. Borgia grabbed Antoinella's arm and pulled her away from me. I did not see her after that. Alex, my new friend, moved next to me as small crystal glasses of blood were being handed out to the crowd.

"Your children are delightful. Jacques just told me he was sorry he made you cry. The maternal bond with them is very strong. I was that way with my mother," he looked at me, trying to gauge my response to him.

I looked at him squarely, "They are very close to their father too."

"Of course, as they should be. I have looked forward to meeting you and your children for some time. You are lovely. The Baron is very lucky." His voice was soft and inviting. His gaze was seductive and warm. Damn vampires! I should have had positive feelings towards his greatness, but my gut said something was not right. He was trying too hard. Like he was trying to win me over as part of some agenda. The polite way he presented himself and his true conqueror nature did not jive. I really wished someone else had saved Jacques.

"Yeah, uh, thanks again, please excuse me." I turned towards Tristan, and Alexander walked away.

I whispered to Tristan, "I want to take the kids home tonight."

"I assure you the children will be carefully watched the rest of your visit. Surely you want to spend time with Lolly, Al, and James tomorrow."

He was right about my friends. They had come all this way to see us. I watched them exploring the mountain of gifts with the children. "All right, we'll stay tonight, but I'm not sure about tomorrow night. Not everyone here adores our children. They're just faking it for the Magus and you."

"What did Lady Kananga say to you?"

"To get out of town."

Borgia and Antoinella had withdrawn to a corner of the ballroom to talk more privately. Borgia looked nervous, "I can't be seen in Alexander's company, and I fear he will just dismiss you."

Antoinella whispered back, "I'm hard to dismiss. I could offer cooperation for our shared goals."

"No, Alex does not share well. Offer him allegiance and support." Borgia looked at her with a coldness that shook her confidence.

Antoinella had to seize the chance to impress Borgia and Alexander, "I will not fail you. A taste of Haute Caste blood would be appreciated as a reward."

Borgia responded with irritation, "Only when you have truly earned such a reward. Stay clear of the Baron and Baroness. I want no more scenes."

She knew better than to push him further, "As you wish." She disappeared in the crowd.

The Magus was about to lead the toast when three tall Asian men wearing dark clothing and long colorful vests entered. They were broad-shouldered, with long straight hair tied back. Two had mustaches, one clean-shaven. Each had a knife visible on their belts. The room became quiet as they stepped aside for a tiny woman about four and a half feet tall. Her hair was styled with jeweled combs, and she wore a red silk tunic and matching pants embroidered with black dragons. My offspring stared at her speechless.

"Princess Khunbish, welcome, you finally honor us with your presence!" Remarkably, the Magus extended his arms in greeting. It was not lost on the crowd who bowed their heads.

My husband whispered, "The Mongols have arrived. This is an important show of acceptance and respect for our family."

Everyone cleared the way as we came forward. I whispered to the children, "Bow to the Princess." To my surprise, they did, though Des seemed to trip Tomas in the process. He started to take a swing at his brother but caught the Princess' gaze and stopped himself.

"You're beautiful," Marie uttered, saving the night.

Her highness smiled, "They look strong. Are they riding yet?"

"Not quite yet. Sir Bart has them on the horses and leads them around," I bowed slightly.

"Ah, Sir Bart. Excellent!"

The Princess directed her attention towards other Haute Caste who were waiting to greet her, including Kananga, my father, Anastasia, and Alexander.

Jorge walked over to my side. "She's a descendant of the great Khan. The Magus saved her after a riding accident that paralyzed her. She rarely leaves Asia."

"Are there many Mongol vampires?"

"Very few, she is extremely cautious about passing on the gift. Her guards hope that one day, she will honor them. Her men, like many of us, don't understand why you have not chosen immortality," Jorge looked concerned.

"Children thrive in sunlight. I think that's a good enough reason."

I saw Sir Steve make his way to the front of the line. He was about a half-foot taller than she was. His eyes were aglow as he gazed upon the beautiful small woman before him. He bowed deeply, and she extended her hand. Steve straightened up and gently lifted her hand so that he could lightly kiss her fingertips. Murmurs went through the crowd. The temperature in the room seemed to increase. The Magus broke the tension by introducing Borgia.

"Steve had never met her?" I asked Jorge.

"No. The last time she visited was many years before he had transformed. She is one of the ancient Haute Caste. It is only her curiosity about you and your children that made her less reclusive."

"Will she let Steve get to know her?" I was trying to be tactful.

Jorge smiled, "Thoroughly."

While the F.O.V. entertained the kids, I scanned the room to catch more of the palace intrigue. I felt a twinge when I saw Sarah flirting with James. I liked her as well as any vampiress, but I did not want my friend seduced by the undead. I noticed Jorge was moving to where Franco and Alexander appeared to be sharing an amusing story. There was a heated exchange, and Franco walked off abruptly while Jorge turned his back on Alexander.

A beautiful dark-haired woman in a glistening purple sari approached my husband. He was enjoying her attention a little too much. I considered intervening when I felt someone's eyes upon me. Borgia smiled from across the room and raised his glass of blood. All the lust, jealousy, ambition, and suspicion in the room overwhelmed my senses. I walked over to my husband and said, "It's time to get the offspring to bed."

"Of course. But first, may I introduce you to Scheherazade."

. "Sorry, you'll have to save your story for another night and someone else." I meant to be rude. She looked surprised as I pulled Tristan away.

"That was inexcusable," he whispered. "She is an old friend."

"Yeah, well, I don't have sex with all my 'old' friends."

"That is literally ancient history," he responded. I laughed, which seemed to offend him.

Luckily the kids ran over to us before we caused a scene. We allowed them to take two presents each back to their rooms. Marie picked a princess doll and a sword, Des had an electric game and a drum. I took the drum away as their room was next to ours and told him to pick something else. Tomas had a couple of books about dinosaurs. Jacques clutched a prince doll and his sailboat.

My mortal friends said their goodnights and promised to come by the next day about noon to visit before flying home. I was glad they would not spend too much time with my nocturnal family.

We separated the kids into two rooms. Their doors would be locked to prevent any monkey business, and a butler would make hourly checks on them. Still, I checked out their rooms when we settled them in. I looked out the window in Marie's room and noticed a couple at the far end of the garden. Tristan came over to see what had caught my attention.

I whispered, "I think it's Ruben and Lily."

"Interesting. It's been a great party."

"For back-stabbing crazy fuckers!"

He ignored my comment, and we returned to the party long enough to thank the Magus and say goodnight to a few of the undead. I assured Kananga that we would leave for home by tomorrow evening. Tristan made a point to not leave me alone with her.

I asked Jorge, "Is everything okay?"

"Franco is just restless. It will pass," he replied. "Goodnight, dear friend."

My father and Anastasia kissed my cheeks and expressed regret that they would have to fly back to London that night. The House of Pentacles was still in need of surveillance due to the Common Caste members who had tried to harm the children and me several years ago.

I hugged my father and jokingly said, "Okay, Sultan, but next time you have to stay longer."

He smiled, "It has been a couple of centuries since I have been addressed in that fashion."

The Tsarina looked at him, and flatly stated, "I'm not going to start calling you that."

I would miss the vampires I trusted. Despite my fears, it was a relief to be around family and friends that didn't require us to pretend to be normal.

Later that night, Antoinella found Alexander alone on the balcony, looking towards the dark lake. "Good evening Sir Alexander," she stopped about a foot away. "This gathering is honored by your presence."

"And you are...?" he regarded the Common Caste vampiress who had the nerve to approach him as an annoyance.

She stepped a little closer, "Antoinella, a trusted aide to Sir Borgia. He wished me to convey a message to you."

He turned back to the lake, "He should speak to me personally."

Normally that would make any Common Caste vampire bow and back away, but not Antoinella. "It is a delicate matter."

He turned back towards her, intrigued by her nerve, "Out with it."

She took a breath, "Sir Alexander, the House of Pentacles wishes to be of service to you, if you should desire support for your undertakings."

His eyes took in the beautiful vampiress. "You were sent to deliver this message, so the others will assume you are being seductive, not political. I will consider Sir Borgia's offer. Now let us put on a convincing show."

Sir Alexander pulled Antoinella into his arms and kissed her passionately. Several people saw them from their vantage points in the ballroom. When they broke apart, she stated, "I am flattered."

"Don't be, I was thinking of another. Leave me."

Chapter 7

Snake in the Grass

When Tristan and I headed back to our rooms, we found two tall, handsome, Mongol warriors posted in the hall. I looked at my husband, who did not seem surprised.

"The Princess loaned them to us to assure the offspring's safety. I think Sir Steve is personally seeing to her royal highness' security."

The few hours left of the night were tender. After the door closed, he started to undress me slowly. His lips danced down my neck to my shoulders. When I tried to lean over to take off my heels, he picked me up and sat me on the side of the bed. He got on his knees and tenderly rubbed my feet as he pulled off my sandals. Tender lovemaking was a side of Tristan that always blew me away. "You once said you'd have to be a masochist to be with me," he remarked, "those shoes prove it's true."

I started to fire back, but his hands glided up my legs, causing our interaction to go to nonverbal mode. We quickly shed all our garments and soon my lingerie was scattered on the floor. Tristan looked at me like I was the only star in the sky on a dark night. He gently pushed me over on the bed and lay on top of me, carefully adjusting his muscular form to allow me to breathe. His primal, earthy scent was comforting and elicited expectation. Everything about him made me crave his passion. Then he rolled over and smiled.

I lay there for a moment, surprised, "Seriously! You get me hot and bothered, then stop?"

He laughed softly. "Come here." I straddled him and leaned over to kiss an earlobe. He cupped my breasts, and I moaned softly as I felt his response. I flipped over on my back and said, "Goodnight."

His hands pulled me against him. Every inch of my body responded to every inch of his, and I shuddered with delight when he entered me. My nails sunk into his back as I clutched him. I cried out, hoping the kids did not hear us. His lips caressed my nipples causing exquisite pleasure. The gentle manipulation of my clitoris elicited small eruptions that rocked me. Our bodies collided in delight until we climaxed and cradled in a sweet embrace. He never did return to the party that night.

About noon, I woke and untangled myself from Tristan's arms. He mumbled my name. He was lucky he did not say Antoinella or Scheherazade. The deep sleep of the undead was not easily interrupted. A shower washed away the cosmetic traces of elegance from the party. I quietly dressed in jeans and a denim shirt and pulled my hair into a ponytail. I did not resemble the Baroness of the night before.

I wandered past the Mongol warriors who nodded and tried not to stare. I looked in on the kids, still fast asleep. The kitchen had the wonderful aroma of fresh-brewed coffee. To the horror of the head butler, I poured myself a cup. I took a seat at the table and watched the cook prepare brunch. "Any doughnuts?"

"No Baroness, but we have croissants," she handed me a platter piled high with fresh, delicate croissants.

I heard yelling at the back door.

"What is it?"

The cook smiled, "I think one of the animals got loose."

Puzzled, I went to the back yard, where workers were setting up a small exotic petting zoo with llamas, sloths, an armadillo, a young zebra, a pair of pangolins and a few others. It was amazing!

The head butler followed me and said, "The Magus wanted to provide a little entertainment for the children."

"And for me."

I was wandering around the temporary animal pens when the llamas started jumping up and down and crying out. I thought I had disturbed them, then out of the corner of my eye, I detected movement near my feet and heard a strange sound.

"Snake!" I screamed. It lunged at me and bit my ankle right through my pant leg.

A Mongol bodyguard appeared out of nowhere and cut off the rattlesnake's head with one slash of his sword. My ankle felt like it was on fire. Without a word, the clean-shaven Mongol picked me up, carried me back in the house, and sat me in a chair.

The butler hovered and said, "I'm calling an ambulance!"

"Aren't you going to do something, a tourniquet, suck out the venom?"

The Mongol put one of his hands at the base of my neck, and I passed out.

At that moment, the F.O.V. arrived. The butler quickly explained what had happened. The Mongol had used a pressure point to slow down my heartbeat.

"My God!" Lolly cried out and rushed to my side, and Al began checking my vitals.

James pulled open his go bag with dental supplies and said, "I've got some antivenom." Everyone looked surprised, "I have it for my dog, we live pretty far from a veterinary hospital, and she had a run-in with a rattlesnake a couple years ago. Luckily, I always keep some in my bag."

I started to wake up. I was a little lightheaded, weak, and nauseated, "I'm going to throw…" Too late, my coffee and croissants ended up on James.

He tried to ignore it and drew up a shot of the antivenom, "This will help until we get you to the hospital." I didn't even feel the shot.

All that had just happened came back to me. "I'll be fine, protect the kids!"

The ambulance arrived, and I wondered if we had caused enough noise to raise the undead. As I was loaded on the gurney, the children came running out, saw me, and started crying. I tried to talk but just threw up again. James and Lolly stayed with them. Since Al was a doctor, they allowed him to ride with me. The Mongol who killed the snake followed in the Magus' Maserati.

At the mansion, the other Mongols and the butler were busy interrogating the petting zoo employees. They were scared out of their minds by the sword-wielding strong men. They assured everyone their zoo never had snakes. One of the temporary employees was missing, a tall, skinny man with an Italian accent who had been helping unloading their truck. He was last seen near the llama enclosure. There was no sign of him now, and none of the regular crew knew anything about him.

The children were taken inside to the ballroom where they still had a pile of toys from the party, and Lolly and James did their best to comfort them. The housekeepers came in and closed the heavy black-out curtains on all the windows, completely blocking out any hint of sunlight and turned on the chandelier. The Baron entered in a silk robe talking on the phone to Al. The children ran to him, crying. He finished the call and got on his knees and embraced them tightly.

"Your mom will be okay. She got hurt, so she is on her way to the hospital. She will be fine. Your mom needs to stay there right now so the doctor can take care of her." He wanted to hunt for the man who was responsible, but all he could do was hug his children. He wanted to go to the hospital, but he had to wait for sunset.

Marie looked up at him, "We want mom!"

"Not now, she needs to rest."

"Mom has an owie?" Jacques asked.

"Yes, a big owie, but she will be okay."

Tomas looked like he was about to cry. "I want to go home!"

Des added, "With mom!"

The Baron looked at his children, "I never thought I would say this, but I want to go to Rossville too."

Lolly smiled through tears, "It's not that bad."

One of the housekeepers brought in a tray with breakfast for the children. Despite their concern, they managed to put away a large number of croissants, scrambled eggs, bacon, and orange juice.

At the hospital, I was put on IVs and told I was extremely lucky to have had treatment started so quickly. The doctor explained that keeping me calm was the best response, that tourniquets and bleeding the wound would only have made things worse. They were waiting for more antivenom to be delivered. They gave me medicine to control the nausea and vomiting, and I became very sleepy. Al stayed by my side and told my husband he would notify him if blood would be needed, but it seemed unlikely. I was in and out of it the rest of the day, but I noticed the clean-shaven Mongol who had killed the snake standing guard in the corner of my room. The medication finally wore off, and I woke up feeling hungry. Al stepped out to talk with a nurse.

I looked at my silent guardian, "Thank you for what you did." He didn't respond, so I asked, "Do you speak English?"

The Mongol stepped forward and looked at me intently with soft brown eyes, then he spoke with a British accent, "I have a mechanical engineering degree from Stanford, so I guess I do."

"I'm Miranda, what's your name?"

"Batu, Baroness, the Princess has given me the privilege of guarding you."

"Batu, loosen up, call me Miranda. I'm not big on all this royal formality crap." I detected a slight smile as he retreated to his corner of the room. He smelled faintly of a spice shop and was nice to look at. Just saying! I wondered how long he would be guarding me. I was grateful he and Al were with me. I knew my husband must be going out of his mind waiting for nightfall. Despite their power, riches, and intelligence, they could not best the sun.

Chapter 8

Vengeance Will Be Mine!

The Magus and the Baron were in foul moods as they arrived at the medical center. Al had kept them apprised of my status, which the medical staff said had improved rapidly. Tristan said to the Magus, "I will hunt him down! He will pay...slowly and painfully!"

"That zoo had been checked carefully!" the Magus stated as they walked down the hospital corridor.

Tristan replied, "I'm sure it was one of the maniac monks. I never thought they would come after our children,"

With a grim expression, the Magus replied, "We will punish them, all of them! This, I promise you. It may take time, but we will eliminate the threat."

Heads turned as the two handsome, well-dressed men, walked down the corridors to my room. Once they entered, a couple of female nurses followed them in to 'check' on me.

My husband nodded to Batu, then leaned down and kissed my forehead. "Miranda, my love, I'm so sorry."

"The kids?"

"They're fine. Lolly, James, Lady Kananga, and assorted notables and staff are taking care of their every whim, and we have significantly increased security."

The Magus went over to Batu and whispered something to him.

"We've changed our flights. The F.O.V. will be around for a couple more days," Al reassured me, "though I think you're out of the woods. Your doctor said he is amazed by how little tissue damage is evident at the site of the bite and is amazed at how rapidly you are recovering, and you are ready to be released."

So, vamp DNA recovers quickly from snake bites, I should have known. I wondered if the assailant thought he could kill one of us, or just wanted to scare the crap out of us.

I was just grateful it had not happened to one

The Magus said, "My dear, we will increase t.

as well. The Princess has agreed to assign Batu to y.

sary. Also, Lady Pauline sent another bodyguard to you.

"Time to get you back to the Magus' house," Tristan s.

Chapter 9

A Priest, a Saint and a Monk

Father Rinaldi, who had christened the children, was alone in the Cathedral, in an old section of Los Angeles. He wore dark pants and a matching jacket with a white high-collared shirt. He knelt in front of the altar and prayed that he was about to act righteously. A sound in the back of the church caused him to turn around. The priest watched the petite woman in the hooded denim jacket gracefully come closer, with each of her steps, his anxiety increased. She stopped a few feet away. She pulled back her hood, and long brown hair fell about her shoulders, she wore no makeup, and her jewelry consisted only of a small gold Fleur-de-lis necklace. She exuded a youthful innocence.

"Mon père," she said quietly.

He stared at her speechless for a moment, his eyes went wide in shock as he realized who she was, then bowed his head. "I am not worthy of being in your presence. The Baron said to expect you."

"Father Rinaldi, you have shown yourself to be open-minded when it comes to my kind." She replied with a slight French accent.

"Saints?" he replied with a small smile.

"You are charming, but in my mortal life, I was a simple soldier. I meant to your willingness to be of service to the vampire world."

"I learned long ago not to sit in judgment. I am here to attend to the needs of all, even a saint if I may be allowed."

She responded, "I have not always been greeted with such reverence."

"I thank God, you were spared the fire!"

"What is the old saying? He works in mysterious ways. The Baron paid the executioner to create a lot of smoke but little fire, which hid my escape from the funeral pyre. The clergy did not let anyone know that they could not find my bones. We desire your assistance."

"Yes, yes, please come into my office where we can talk privately." He showed her to a room behind the altar. A small candle cast a flickering light on an image of the Virgin Mary. He gestured for her to be seated on a small couch while he sat in a wooden chair. "The children you baptized for the Baroness are in danger, and we believe you might help keep them safe."

"Whatever I can do!"

"There is a mad priest, Adrian Turlock, who has been funded by someone in the Vatican to go after vampires. He orchestrated an attempt on the life of the Baroness."

"I'm so sorry!"

She sensed that he was truly saddened and outraged by the news. "We understand that you are highly connected in Rome and that only a vow of poverty keeps you at this humble church."

He was surprised by her comment. "My kinship to the Holy Father is a well-kept secret. I would never want to use his relationship for personal gain!"

"But to protect a mother and her children from a sadistic madman who claims to be divinely inspired, could you not use your connections to help us uncover who might sponsor such a monster?" She held her delicate hand up, slowly moving it closer to the flickering candle. "Perhaps you could think of it as a way for the church to make amends."

He started to reach for her hand before she was burned...again, "Please! I do get your point. How can I refuse you?" he sighed, and she lowered her hand. "Perhaps I should call you General Joan."

"I would prefer Jeanne. Let us work together to right a wrong."

A young priest hurried down the hallways at the Vatican to an office in a corner basement of the massive building that was considered exorcism headquarters. He was not comfortable with having to deal with the old priest. Father Antonio squared his shoulders then knocked on the door.

"Enter!" Father Guido called out, then coughed. Father Antonio, the messenger from the Cardinal, came into his office and could not help but think of Scrooge when he looked upon him. Father Guido eyed the young priest with suspicion, "What brings you here?"

"I bring an order and an admonition from His Holiness."

"I trust it is support for my campaign against the evils in our society." he gestured to a chair. Father Antonio declined to sit.

He looked at the old priest with sadness; undoubtedly, he believed what he was doing was right. "The Cardinal has heard disturbing news that one of your staff was involved in an incident resulting in an attack on an innocent woman with young children. This cannot happen again."

His eyes widened as he looked up at the young priest, color showed in his withered cheeks, "No one associated with the undead is innocent."

"Your involvement in this matter has come to our attention and will not be tolerated." Father Antonio's voice was clear and loud, "You will no longer be serving in your current capacity. You will be transferred to the Archives immediately. All funding for your work has been stopped."

"But the vampires, they are among us! We must stop them! They have corrupted you and the Cardinal!" He pulled himself up and leaned on his desk. "This is Satan's work!"

"Trying to kill a young mother, that is Satan's work. You are lucky to have not lost your position completely or your pension. It is only by the Cardinal's mercy that you are allowed to stay in this holy place. I must admonish you to go quietly and be grateful." Father Antonio looked like he had tasted something bitter. "May the Lord forgive you," Father Antonio turned and left abruptly. He had recorded the entire conversation. The Cardinal would have no misgivings about his decision.

Chapter 10

Ice Cream! We Want Ice Cream!

My room at the Magus' mansion had an amazing view of the lake and exquisite Asian furnishings, including a large jade dragon for protection. As I looked around the room to make sure we had everything before we left, I thought, I could get used to this.

I was using a crutch to keep weight off the sore ankle. Danuta had returned that afternoon to Rossville to get a downstairs bedroom ready for me and assure my parents I was fine. By the third night of being hovered over by some of the Haute Caste, the F.O.V., and Magus' staff, I was ready to go home.

The sun had set, time for the undead to rise and shine. Ruben and Sarah came by to say goodbye. "Wow! You know how to stir things up. I have never seen Lady Kananga so pissed."

"Yeah, she had warned me to take the kids and leave. I thought we would be okay waiting until the next afternoon."

Sarah said, "She rarely gives advice, and when she does, it is always worth heeding."

I wanted to change the subject. "James said you might visit his ranch."

She squirmed a tiny bit, "I thought it would be a good idea to look in on him…uh…to check his security. We like to protect the F.O.V. since there are so few insightful mortals."

"Protect?" Ruben chuckled.

She gave her a brother a look that should have at least bruised him badly, "We must be going, take care, Baroness."

"See you later, Tiny Tim," Ruben quipped as I hobbled away on my crutch.

I wondered how they could be related for the hundredth time.

James, Lolly, and Al stopped by on their way to the airport. Al and Lolly were planning on flying commercial, but Sir Borgia offered them a ride on his private jet as he was going to L.A.

I pulled Lolly aside, "Be careful of Borgia, I'm just not sure he is one of the good ones."

"C'mon, he is not going to attack us," Lolly protested.

"It's not that. I get this uneasy feeling around him."

"Al finds him fascinating. He feels honored that Sir Borgia invited us. Antoinella will be going too. Personally, I don't get Tristan ever being with her."

"Just don't let your guard down with Borgia. I swear he is up to something." I turned to James, "My friend, should I worry about you and Lady Sarah?"

He gave me his signature country grin, "Baroness, don't you know I'm used to dealing with difficult women?"

I laughed, "Yes, you are. Maybe I should be worried about Sarah." I would miss my old friends.

The drive home was a bit of normalcy, except that it was a limousine with a Mongolian bodyguard. It was how we rolled.

The kids argued the first half-hour until my husband asserted himself. "Your mother does not feel well, so stop this noise. I expect better from you." Then I heard something snap, and Jacques started crying because Tomas had broken his sailboat mast.

Tomas tried to look innocent, looked at his brother, and said, "You're a cry baby!"

Jacques sobbed, "You're a butt face!"

Des started laughing, which Tomas took personally. "Shut up, Des!"

Noticing a billboard for Dairy Queen near Kankakee, Marie said, "I'm hungry. I want ice cream."

I told Tristan, "Okay, take the next exit to the Dairy Queen. Hot fudge sundaes for everyone." The promise of ice cream brought silence. Blissful silence.

That was when I discovered Batu's weakness. He loved ice cream. He got a banana split with three different flavors. When Des asked for a taste, he looked at him with a grave expression, "No. Eat your own. Remember, never share your ice cream."

I had a hard time not laughing out loud, and even Tristan appeared amused. The kids looked at Batu differently after that. They realized they could not easily manipulate him.

Chapter 11

The Elixir of Life

At a shady hotel in the outskirts of Indianapolis, Turlock paced. Benedetto and Turlock were both extremely nervous. Finally, there was a knock. Turlock signaled to Benedetto to open the door. A tall Chinese vampire came into the room without a word and regarded the two mortals with curiosity.

"I am Chang." He looked about to be sure they were alone. "We are pleased with your services. You have embarrassed the Magus. You handled the attack at his mansion well." He took an envelope out of his suit pocket and laid it on a bedside table. "Twenty thousand dollars." Then Chang pulled a small vial from another pocket and placed it beside the envelope. "You are being honored with this gift. There will be more when you accomplish your next mission."

Turlock grabbed it and proceeded to suck every drop of blood from the vial, leaving nothing for Benedetto. The younger monk merely looked down at the floor. Turlock felt the rush from vampire blood and inhaled deeply, "More, I need more to sustain me."

"Nothing more until your services are required again. Now you must go into hiding. You cannot return to Rome." He handed Benedetto a slip of paper. "Here is an address for a hotel in Memphis. It may be some time until you shall be called upon again. You have been given enough blood to sustain you until that time. Prepare yourselves. Your next assignment will be much more demanding.

Benedetto inquired, "Is the Baroness alive?"

"Yes. All went according to plan. She was only injured."

Benedetto looked relieved.

Turlock responded, "Tell them we will be ready, but more blood would make me stronger, better able to be of service."

Chang responded, "You will do our bidding. Leave tonight." Then he left the hotel room. Out in the parking lot, he sent a text message,

It is done. I shall watch to be sure they leave
for Memphis before returning

Chapter 12

Enter Lady Penelope

After a couple of days, my ankle was feeling better, and soon I was able to give up the crutch. Batu settled into our strange household. He was very helpful with the horses, and Sir Bart welcomed his expertise. He and Camo had a friendly rivalry. They liked to wrestle behind the barn. Camo complained when no weapons were allowed. That was my rule. I appreciated having another mortal around that I did not have to lie to. I got up early on our third day back, got a mug of coffee and headed for the back porch for my moment of Zen on the prairie. As I stepped out on the porch, I was startled to see a wild man, riding a horse at full speed, hanging off the side holding a bow and arrow. I realized it was Batu. His long hair was whipped back by the momentum. I saw an arrow hit the center of a fence post. Then in seconds, another arrow hit the next post. He continued and embedded five more arrows in the fence posts. Then he jumped off the steed and bounded across the field, doing summersaults while he collected the arrows.

"Wow," I uttered. He noticed me and quickly vanished into the barn with the horse. Batu rarely spoke to me, but he spent hours talking with Sir Bart.

I went back in the kitchen and saw Mom watching Batu with the horses from the back window, "How can you trust someone you can't have a decent conversation with. Are you sure he speaks English? I don't think I have ever heard him say more than good morning. Why can't you just hire some regular person, like the Johnson's nephew. He just got laid off at the cannery."

"Batu graduated from Stanford. He speaks perfect English, but he comes from a different culture. I don't want to deal with the gossip that might come from hiring a townie."

My dad agreed, "This Batu guy, he helped save Randie. That makes him okay in my book, even if he's not Mr. Friendly."

That evening my parents were giving Tristan a ride to the Danville airport where the Magus' jet was waiting for him. They had taken the afternoon off from the Café and had a nice time playing with the children. The sun was setting, and they were exhausted and ready to go.

I pulled my husband aside before he left. I tried to question Tristan about who had been responsible for the attack. He mentioned something about zealous monks. "The perpetrators are on the run and will be dealt with," he assured me, "Someone is coming to stay with you."

"Who? Maybe I won't want them here."

"An old friend." He had been impatient and somewhat surly since the attack, and I was ready for him to leave. The kids came out of the game room to see their dad off.

"Bye, Dad," Jacques said sniffling.

"See ya," Tomas said and hugged his leg.

"Don't go!" Marie stated, looking up at him with tears in her eyes. He bent down and hugged them, just as Des came running down the stairs, and almost knocked them over.

"Dad!!"

Tristan stood and said, "My darling children, I'll be back in a few weeks. Be good for your mom."

I even detected Tristan's eyes were watering. When he kissed me goodbye, he blinked as though fighting it.

After Tristan and my parents left, we settled down to dinner and a movie before getting the kids ready for bed.

For the first time in a week, I had an evening to myself after the kids were tucked in. I felt like writing, and the snake incident had given me lots of ideas. I curled up on the couch in the living room with my laptop and a big mug of hot chocolate. I breathed a sigh of relief. I would need to research snakes in the great northwest to use my misfortune in the sequel. I had just Googled rattlesnakes when Batu ran into the room.

"Stay here until I tell you it's safe."

"What are you talking about...?"

Headlights could be seen coming up the long drive. A shiny black Tesla stopped in front of the steps. Through the window, I could see a young handsome blonde man got out on the driver's side then walked around to open the passenger door. Sir Bart approached the car, looked inside at the passenger, and smiled. He looked over toward the house and waved to Batu, signaling that all was well.

Batu turned to me and said, "Haute Caste," and went outside.

So much for my quiet moment. Jorge got out of the car and came into the house, looking upset. He was not his normal, impeccably groomed self. His thick brown hair mussed, and his shirt was a tad wrinkled. Something was very wrong.

"Jorge!" I went over and hugged him "What are you doing here? I hope you're not worried about me; I'm healing up fine. What is going on?"

"I want to kill Franco."

"Wow, I didn't expect that!"

"He is with Alexander."

"I'm so sorry." I touched his hand. I hated seeing my old friend so hurt. "I know how you feel."

"It's not the same. You get upset about meaningless sex. I expect that to happen. I'm talking about Franco choosing another over me."

"Yeah, that's really different from my situation." He looked at me, obviously not happy with my sarcasm. I quickly added, "In any case, it sucks."

"I'm going to get some coffee." I knew the hot chocolate would not cut it tonight. "You want something? There's O positive in the fridge."

He followed me into the kitchen and sat down at the kitchen counter, "No, thanks. I grabbed someone at the airport." A faint smile came to his lips. I just shook my head. He responded, "He had a small bomb in his backpack."

"You took out a terrorist?"

He watched me sip my coffee, "Sad, and the world will never know of my good deeds."

"Good job, citizen! Now tell me why you're here. You could have called me to bitch about Franco."

"I came here because it's the last place he'd look for me. He can lose some sleep over my whereabouts for a change. Why do I even care?"

"So, what are you going to do?"

"Make Alex and Franco suffer." He called to the chauffeur who was waiting in the hall, "Carlos, please invite Lady Penelope to join us."

Carlos entered carrying a chubby black pug with a jeweled pink collar. He gently put her down, and she ran to Sir Jorge, who lifted her into his lap. "Lady Penelope meet the Baroness, Baroness Lady Penelope."

"Charming!" I had to laugh. "I didn't know you had a dog."

"She's not really a dog. She's a Pug. And she isn't mine. She is the treasured companion of Alexander. I left a note saying Lady Penelope was a fair exchange for Franco."

"I have her prescription diet food and treats in the car. If she eats regular dog food, she gets a rash." He picked her up and kissed the pug's head. "I can just hear Alexander yelling at his staff and making Franco miserable."

I looked at the little pushed-in face. Her big, buggy black eyes stared back at me, looking rather clueless but happy. I took her in my arms, "Well, Lady Penelope, welcome to Rossville." I rubbed her head, "You know the children will never give her back."

Jorge smiled, "I'm counting on that."

"You are horrible! Dognaper!" I chuckled. "When should I expect Alex and Franco?"

"I usually spend the summer visiting night clubs in Copenhagen, Amsterdam, and Brussels, so I suspect they will look there first. I purposely told my butler in Caracas that I was going to visit Lady Kananga, to go on night safaris. The Magus has promised to tell anyone who inquires I had mentioned Singapore."

"Would you do me one other favor, would you allow Lady Penelope to sleep with you? She has been keeping me awake since I invited her to run away two nights ago. Apparently, the pug is a day person."

"You really owe me big time for this one," I sighed and patted her head. "Well, Penelope, I'm sure this place is not as grand as what you're used to, but..."

"Mi casa es su casa!" Jorge smiled.

Chapter 13

Meanwhile Back at the Ranch

In Montana, James was expecting company. He had a large log cabin in the middle of fifty acres of grassland with a few wooded areas and a small creek. James liked his remote existence. The nearest neighbor was five miles away. A Triumph motorcycle arrived at 10 p.m., followed by a silver RV worthy of a rock star. He looked at his old Dalmatian and mumbled, "Gracie, the bloodmobile is here."

The rider took off her helmet, and beautiful auburn curls spilled over onto her leather jacket. The faint scent of jasmine filled the air.

James stepped off the front porch and ambled over to the motorcycle, followed by Gracie. "Howdy, Sarah!"

She took off her jacket and leaned over to pet Gracie. The leather bustier she wore displayed her cleavage and small waistline. It was hard for James not to stare.

The driver of the RV climbed out. He wore a tight tailored white shirt and jeans with brown curly hair "Good evening, monsieur James."

"Hi!" James responded, trying to guess if the driver was mortal.

Sir Ruben stumbled out of the side door of the RV and stretched as though he was just waking up. He looked like he had been sleeping in his rumpled Ramone's T-shirt and jeans for a couple of days. His unruly red hair needed to be combed. Hard to believe this was the same member of the Haute Caste he had seen in a tux at the kid's party. He looked around, "Wow! Almost as inhospitable as Rossville." He walked over to James and extended his hand, "Why do you and Miranda choose such primitive surroundings?"

It was the first time a vampire had made such a normal, friendly gesture to James. He gingerly reached out and shook Sir Ruben's hand, "Welcome."

Sir Ruben chuckled, "Don't worry, you're on the No Bite List."

"There's a list?"

"Yeah, since Miranda was born. It's a short list."

Ruben gestured towards the driver, "That's Claude, he's like you but wants to be like me. You can speak freely around him."

James was relieved to have a sort of normal person around while the Lockporte siblings were visiting. Lady Sarah walked over to their host, "James, show us the beast. Claude prepared dinner."

James was a little taken aback by her abruptness, replied, "This way, around the back." He stopped to put Gracie in the house and grab a large flashlight and a rifle. They followed him to a wooded area behind his cabin.

"I've been leaving beef out to try and stay on its good side. So far, it keeps a distance."

Lady Sarah corrected him, "Sir Bart says she is female. Any aggressive behavior?"

"Not yet. I can't figure out if it's, I mean if she's afraid or…"

Ruben added, "Keeping watch."

"Yeah, that crossed my mind." He shined the light near the base of the trees. Golden eyes glimmered for a moment then disappeared into the darkness. "She spends a few months here, but the rest of the time she seems to roam near Rossville, I still can't believe she can travel that distance."

"The vaccine is working." Sir Ruben stated.

"I was not happy when Gracie and I were inoculated with some of that monster Lena's blood, but I guess I should be grateful."

Lady Sarah spoke softly, putting her hand on James' arm, "Lena was a despicable creature, but when she shared her blood with the wolfpack, she unknowingly created an ally for us. This one is the sole survivor. Wolves are pack animals, but this one is a loner. Her scent makes her foreign to other wolves, and it makes her seek us. Having been inoculated with a vaccine created from Lena's blood, you, the Baroness, and the Offspring are bonded to the wolf."

They walked quietly back to the cabin. Without an invitation, the Lockportes just strolled into his home. He was surprised to find Claude setting his rustic table with fine linens, silver, china, and crystal. The Lockportes were raised in the elegant Victorian era. Lady Sarah always wore lace with her black leather. Ruben liked the rebel look. It was clear to James why the sister had become the Head of the House of Plows. Claude poured blood from a decanter into two goblets. There were small bites of raw sirloin on two of the dinner plates. Lady Sarah nodded her approval as Claude pulled a chair out for her. Then he turned to James, "How do you like your steak?"

"Well done."

"Of course, you would," Claude responded under his breath with a touch of disgust.

Lady Sarah looked around the sparsely furnished home, "You should hire a decorator."

"I inherited the homestead from my aunt and haven't had the heart to change much. Besides, Gracie likes it this way."

A few minutes later, Claude placed a large sizzling sirloin on James' plate. It was seasoned to perfection but slightly pink. "I could not allow myself to totally ruin your steak." He then placed a barely seared steak on his plate. When Claude cut into his meat, blood oozed onto the plate. Lady Sarah pointedly looked at James' empty goblet. Claude poured some Perrier into the goblet. Then he poured some red wine into his glass.

"A toast," Sir Ruben said, "To unlikely friends!"

"That's for sure!" James smiled, and they all raised their goblets.

Despite his casual façade, Ruben's table manners were impeccable. The Lockportes had been raised in the upper-class world of Toronto when private schools included etiquette lessons. Lady Sarah sipped from her goblet then dabbed her reddened lips with a linen napkin. She watched James ravage his steak with a slight smile. She and Ruben tasted the small pieces of raw meat like they were savoring a delicacy. Claude tried to mirror their manners. By the time they finished, he had only eaten half his steak. He started to stand so he could clear away the plates, but James put his hand on his shoulder, "Dude, I've got this. The cook gets to eat in my house." Claude looked at Lady Sarah, who nodded her approval.

Sir Ruben helped James clean-up, which meant he stood by the sink and watched. "You just stood up to my sister, and she allowed it."

"I just let a man finish his steak," James responded though he appreciated the compliment.

James handed Sir Ruben a dish towel.

Sir Ruben looked at it, then placed the unused towel on the counter and walked away.

"Claude start a fire," Lady Sarah demanded. Obediently Claude went to the fireplace, laid the wood, started the fire then retired to the RV.

The siblings took a seat on either end of the old leather couch. James pulled up his rocking chair. To James's surprise, Gracie curled up next to Lady Sarah. The vampiress gently patted the old dog's head. He wished Sarah would be that attentive to him.

"Gracie doesn't like her. It was Gracie's growling that first alerted me to her."

"That vaccine might make us safe from the beast, but it won't protect her from Gracie," James joked, but no one laughed. "Does Miranda know about the wolf yet?" James asked. "She thinks it's just a big coyote. But she'll figure it out soon." Sir Ruben replied. "I'll excuse myself and make some calls." He went outside and sat on the front porch.

"Am I that boring?" James asked.

"No. He's having an affair. Trust me. You don't want to know more. Tell me how you want to handle your visitor."

James thought for a minute. "I don't want to kill it. I mean as long, as it doesn't harm or threaten anyone." He got up and put another log on the fire.

"You feel pity for the creature?" She stared at James' handsome face with a new interest.

"I guess. I mean, it did not choose to be part vampire. It's a victim of Lena's."

Her tone became soft, "A victim of vampires."

James shifted uncomfortably. He stood up and walked over to the fireplace staring into the flames. "Yes, a victim, just like I was when I was abducted." Then he turned to Lady Sarah, "Honestly, I'm attracted and repulsed by all of you. I'm glad you are here, but when you go, I know I'll feel some relief. When I stopped drinking, I used to go to A.A. meetings and bare my soul and get support. Now I don't have much to say. If I told the truth, they would all think I had lost my mind. I tried dating, but they would invariably ask about L.A., and I would just change the subject. Women hate that. They probably thought I was hiding something, which I was. So, other than going to my office in town, I stay to myself out here." He had been holding his resentment inside for a long time. He hoped he had not offended Lady Sarah, but it felt good to say it out loud. He turned back to the fire.

"Self-pity is beneath your station," she stated calmly. "You don't seem to be repulsed." Lady Sarah rose and stood behind him. She placed her hands on his shoulders and lightly massaged them. The pleasure from her touch was like a healing balm. He turned and faced her, started to speak, but she placed a finger up to his lips. "James, you may see this twist of fate as good fortune or calamity. Though I would advise just enjoy it." She leaned forward and kissed him. His pulse raced, he pulled her into his embrace in the firelight and kissed her deeply with a passion that he had held in check for years. Her natural, earthy scent combined with her perfume ignited his senses. He felt the soft pressure of her breasts against his chest.

Lady Sarah gently pulled away, "We'll talk more tomorrow night."

"I'm sorry, I didn't mean…"

"I did." Then she walked out.

James stared after her. His eyes never left her until the front door closed. He could not believe he had just kissed a vampiress, and it felt natural. He was affected by the heady undead pheromones. As the contact high began to wear off, he wondered what the hell had just happened. Was he being seduced so he would transform? Was it just a kiss due to somewhat normal attraction? He looked out the window and noticed Sir Ruben sitting on the steps and went out on the porch as Ruben threw his phone on the ground. James looked over at the phone back to Ruben then pulled an old wooden chair up beside him. They both just stared out into the darkness. "What is wrong with women?" Ruben seemed to ask the universe.

"It's what's right about them that bothers me."

Ruben looked over at his phone, still laying on the dirt. "She's impossible and selfish!"

James responded, "She won't let you call the shots?"

He turned towards James and spoke to him as an equal, "Precisely. She thinks I'll wait on her for another kiss."

"I don't know, after tonight I think it might be worth it."

Sir Ruben looked surprised, "My sister? You're joking!"

James nodded and grinned, "I didn't expect her to kiss a regular Joe either, I'm not complaining, but I'm a bit nervous."

"Baroness Mordecai and Lady Lockporte! Don Juan would be envious." He saw James in a new light. "Respect, bro!"

James looked squarely at Sir Ruben, "You know Miranda just kissed my cheek and hugged me."

"We all know that. It's why you're still alive." Sir Ruben scrutinized James, "It's rare for my sister to talk with a short, let alone flirt with one."

"Yeah, not much to say when you're hungry," James quipped. "Sarah mentioned my station, what did she mean?"

"F.O.V., I think. Just be glad she likes you; she can make anyone's existence hell when she's pissed."

"I kind of figured that." James stood and headed to the door, paused, and turned back to Ruben, "Goodnight, Sir Ruben. And good luck with Lady Lily."

"How did you know?"

"I was at the party. It wasn't that hard to figure out, and I'm guessing everyone knows."

"I'm so screwed," Sir Ruben sighed.

In her bedroom in the R.V., Lady Sarah sat back against baby blue satin pillows and called the Magus.

"All is well, dear Magus."

"He took the bait?" The Magus walked out on his patio and gazed at the Pacific in the moonlight.

"And a little more. I sense deep, unexpressed passion."

The Magus was intrigued by Lady Sarah's enthusiasm. "You wish to proceed?"

"Yes. He is much more interesting than I had expected. I like his appetite."

"Good. I thought you might be bored with this assignment."

She responded honestly; it would never do to lie to the Magus. "I was not looking forward to this visit to a western version of Rossville, but this short has potential. He is questioning where he fits in. The poor man said he was repulsed by us and attracted to us."

"The stoic loner opened up to you. Very well, we shall see where his hunger takes him. The beast is not a threat?"

"It seems to be seeking contact, but survival instincts get in the way, it is still keeping its distance. I will try to get closer tomorrow."

"To the wolf or James?"

"Both."

"Excellent. Tristan will be glad to hear of your progress and plans. I have a bit of news. Jorge has run off with Lady Penelope to punish Alexander and Franco."

"Jorge! I never imagined that he would stoop to kidnapping a pug, that's fantastic!" she chuckled. "Alexander must be going out of his mind. I can't help but feel sorry for Franco. Where did he take Penelope?"

"He mentioned something about enjoying Singapore this time of year."

Chapter 14

The Big Bad Wolf

I didn't sleep well the first night with Lady Penelope. She burrowed under the covers for about half an hour, then snored loudly. During the night, she got up, wandered around the bed, waking me up before settling in again. About five in the morning she whined to go outside. I wandered out in my robe with a flashlight and watched while she looked for the perfect place to relieve herself.

Bart walked over from the barn with an amused expression. The pug ran over to him and jumped up on his legs. He picked her up and patted her little round head. "Are you the new Helen of Troy?" Lady Penelope snorted.

"Do you think Alexander will be that obsessed with getting his little dog back? I don't know why he would. She snores so loud that I barely got any sleep."

He grinned, "You may want to give her back after a few more nights." He handed her back to me. "Alexander does not like to lose, but he has no idea what he will face in Rossville."

"Do you know Alexander very well? I ask because I should like him, he saved Jacques, but I didn't feel comfortable around him."

"You will do well to trust your instincts. By the way, Carlos left during the night. Sir Jorge felt there were enough vampires in Rossville." He glanced to the east, started heading back to the barn as the sky began to turn a lighter gray. He turned and said, "Have a good day, Baroness."

The kids quickly fell in love with Lady Penelope, Jacques started calling her Piglet, and the nickname stuck. She would run in circles chasing her tail, and they would fall over laughing. Danuta would give the little beggar scraps from dinner. Batu started taking Piglet, and the kids for nature walks when I needed a nap. The pug would start off walking with them, but it didn't take long before she would fall behind, and Batu would end up carrying her the rest of the way. She wasn't particularly fond of stairs either and usually sat at the top or bottom of a flight of stairs whimpering until someone took pity and carried her up or down. Even Camo was getting attached to her and told me he wanted to find her a leather collar with spikes. I was amazed by how much chaos and happiness one little pug could bring into the household. The kids often watched cartoons with Piglet fast asleep on one of their laps. She brought some normalcy into our lives. My parents soon called her their grandpup.

Two months after the snake incident, my ankle, surprisingly, was still a bit tender, but it looked like there would only be a little scar to remind me of the bite. Still, there was no news about why I had been attacked. I hated to think it was Benedetto, but when they described a tall skinny Italian, he came to mind.

Having Batu around for extra security and help with the children was working out fine. His daily interactions with them made me realize how much they missed their dad. Batu and Jorge taught them to play soccer, and they loved it. They even got Camo to play, but he refused to wear tennis shoes. Biker boots seemed to give him an advantage when he kicked the ball but were hard to run in. I was glad the crazy soccer matches wore out the kids.

Early one evening just after sunset, I heard Piglet barking her head off in the yard. I came out on the porch and looked in the direction of the small wooded area behind the barn. I froze in my tracks and screamed, "Marie!"

My little girl was standing about a foot away from a giant wolf, and she held a dog treat in her tiny hand. Batu and Bart came out of the barn and slowly walked towards her. I started to run, but Jorge grabbed my arm. "No. We must not threaten the beast, let them handle it."

I realized Batu was carrying a bow and arrow. "Kill it!" I urged him.

"I could, but then we won't know her purpose," he stated calmly. "If she meant to harm Marie, we could not have stopped her. Look!"

I was trembling, Jorge put his arm about my shoulders. Marie placed the treat on the ground, and the vamp-wolf gobbled it up. She said, "Good doggy."

"Marie," Sir Bart, in a calm voice, told her. "Come here, and we'll see if we can find some other treats."

She turned and ran happily back to them. Batu picked her up, and I breathed deeply and leaned against Jorge. The vamp-wolf looked at me with glowing eyes like some creature from a Rudyard Kipling tale, then vanished in the trees. I began to sense something, something oddly familiar to me. I closed my eyes for a second thinking. "I know what it is. It's one of Lena's monsters. I can smell her."

"The only one that survived," Jorge replied.

I ran to Batu and grabbed Marie, yelling tearfully, "Never do that again!"

"The doggy was hungry mom." She did not understand why I was so upset.

Bart glanced at me then looked down at Marie, "I feed her, don't worry. Whenever she visits, I take care of her."

"Are you crazy?? Why would you do that? How long has this been going on?" I stared at him, confused, angry, upset, and relieved all at the same time.

"Let's go in the house to discuss this," Jorge said.

We all went back in the house, and Danuta took charge of Marie, and the siblings still glued to the window. She admonished Marie, "The next time I tell you to go wash your hands for dinner, do not go outside!" The housekeeper turned to me, "I'm so sorry Baroness."

"Danuta, it's not your fault. We'll all have to be more careful." Batu, Sir Bart, and Sir Jorge followed me into the living room.

I sat with my back to the fireplace and faced them. "When in the hell were you all going to tell me that what I thought was a big coyote was a vampire wolf that was stalking my family?" I struggled to not scream at them.

Jorge had known me the longest, our friendship made him brave enough to start, "Miranda, we have been carefully tracking her movements since she left Alaska five years ago. She spends time in Montana near your friend, and then comes here. She has never been aggressive to our kind, you and the kids or James."

"She is a powerful wild animal. You can't predict what she'll do. She could have killed Marie or any of the kids, or even James! And on top of that, she has Lena's blood!"

"Precisely," Sir Bart responded. "But she acted like Marie's pet, and she is the same with James. I have had the most contact with her, though she has never allowed me to get as close as the little Baroness. She has been eating the beef and chicken left for her at night and stayed hidden during the day."

"Why didn't you shoot or poison her?"

Sir Bart explained, "Because I don't sense a threat, to me or anyone in the household. Have you ever noticed when a dog is given a task, like retrieving a ball, it will continue to look for it until it can complete the task? Consider the difficult and long trek she has made. It is a miracle that she could track you. The wolf is compelled to watch us for some reason we don't understand."

"Yeah, maybe she's not looking for a ball, maybe it's someone's head."

"Whose?" Jorge asked.

"I first saw those eyes when I was pregnant, and since then, I'd just seen a glimmer and movement at a distance and thought it was a large coyote." I turned to Batu, "I assume my husband knows." Batu just nodded. "Bastard! He should have said something to me."

Bart responded, "We did not want to upset you, especially during the pregnancy. She usually makes an appearance near dawn when you're asleep. That's when I feed her."

"The other morning, when I was outside with the pug, you came out to check on me."

"I did not believe that she had not come back from Montana yet, but I wanted to be sure."

I looked at them all, "I don't give a fuck about her purpose. If she comes any closer, if she ever gets close to my kids again, kill her! Now leave me alone!" They left without an argument. Maybe they left without a word because I'm a Baroness, or maybe it was because they feared a pissed-off mom.

I grabbed my phone to call James. As soon as he picked up, I snapped, "Why didn't you tell me about the vamp-wolf! She got close to Marie, just walked right up to her!"

"Oh my God, Randie, is she okay?"

"Yes, she's fine. It didn't hurt her, but why didn't you tell me what was going on? Didn't you think that might be something I should know?"

"Your husband asked me not to. He said he was making sure that you and the kids were safe. She keeps her distance when she visits, just sort of hangs out and watches."

"Is there anything else you're not telling me that I should know?"

"Sarah and Ruben came by while the wolf was here to check on me. I think the snake attack has made them a little nervous about the F.O.V.'s well-being."

I suddenly feared for James, "I'm sorry I shouldn't have gotten mad at you. None of this is your fault. You must have had your hands full when they visited. Be careful with Lady Sarah. She is a very…enthusiastic…vampiress."

"Yeah, I noticed. Though I don't mind the company. She's not so arrogant around me. Ruben is always entertaining." He was not about to divulge how friendly Lady Sarah had been.

"When it comes to vampires, always look a gift horse in the mouth, twice."

"You're talking to a dentist," he chuckled.

"I'm serious! Borgia flew Al and Lolly home from the party. The undead don't do nice things without a bad reason."

"I think they're trying to protect us. Maybe they like to have regular folks to talk to, you know, get out of their weird bubble now and then."

I knew by his tone it was worse than I had thought, "Yeah, well, don't get too folksy with Sarah. I've seen her bloody."

"I will keep that in mind if she visits again. Go be with your kids. Give them all hugs for me. Goodnight, Randie."

"Stay safe, James."

After he hung up, he sent a text message to the Baron.

```
Your wife knows about the wolf.
Angry, I did not warn her.
Marie got close to it, but she is OK.
```

Tristan responded,

```
Thanks, I expected this
```

I had a growing sense of unease about all the plots that somehow involved my family. I knew the only person who could tell me what was going on was the Magus. Good luck getting anything out of him. Not even my husband would be privy to all the Haute Caste intrigues. I started to call Tristan, but I was so angry at him that I changed my mind. I was pretty pissed at all of them. The males, mortal and immortal, had retreated to Bart's place. I would let them handle the wolf, for now. Danuta and I hung out with the kids. Marie talked about the big dog. Her siblings were eager to give it treats too. I reminded them of the story of the three little pigs and the big, bad wolf. Jacques hugged Piglet. Danuta distracted them with chocolate cake. I gave the pug an extra dog treat for her bravery. I would never complain about her barking again. I mistakenly thought we had left all the intrigue of the undead and their machinations in L.A. and Chicago. The shadow of the vampire world was slowly creeping over our safe place in the cornfields. I laid in bed for a long time before I was finally able to fall asleep.

In Los Angeles, Sir Borgia knocked on the door of Al and Lolly's beautiful ranch home overlooking a canyon. Lolly greeted him warmly, "Sir Borgia, it is so nice of you to visit us." She wore a little red Dior cocktail dress that cost a small fortune.

"Cesare, please," he purred with a soft accent, took her hand and lightly kissed the back of her fingers. His thick, wavy hair framed his chiseled cheekbones and expressive brown eyes.

Al walked up to Borgia to greet him, "Welcome."

Lolly had Vivaldi playing in the background. She was hoping to impress the former Duke of Valentinois with her choice in music.

He understood the gesture, and his handsome features lit up, "Ah, Four Seasons." He looked at Al, "You appreciate beautiful women and beautiful music, as do I."

They went into the living room where Lolly had opened a bottle of the best Italian red wine she could find, Monfortino. "Please, have a seat," and poured them each a glass in their finest crystal.

Though Sir Borgia was thirsty for something much more substantial, he took a sip and praised the choice of wine. Lolly felt vindicated for spending so much and looked at Al, who tried to ignore her.

"Sir Borgia, I mean Cesare, I have so many questions, it is so amazing to have you as a guest in our home. I read that 'The Prince,' by Machiavelli, was based on you? Is that true?" Al knew that he was dealing with a narcissistic sociopath of the first order, but Sir Borgia was so charming and intelligent he did not care.

"Perhaps. It was so long ago, and now but a small moment in history. I would rather talk about you. I am curious about how you see my kind?"

Lolly responded, "Unbelievable. I mean you never age, you're all so attractive, and it seems effortless for you. As a model, the focus on physical perfection makes beauty a constant struggle."

He would go with her weakness. "Lolly, you are as beautiful as any vampiress I have ever encountered. It is true that our kind will always stay at the height of physical attractiveness. Our special chemistry causes our cells to rejuvenate and correct any imperfections constantly." Lolly was lost in his stare. He turned towards her husband as he realized her behavior was making Al uncomfortable.

"Al, I think receiving some of the Baron's blood to help heal your wounds after that unfortunate event, you must appreciate how that keeps us youthful," Cesare said with a smile.

Al replied, "Yes, after I was attacked in the attempted coup, I thought it was over for me. I got to feel the benefit of your blood elixir firsthand. I could describe it best as vital energy infused with euphoria."

Sir Borgia noted how Al's face brightened as he recalled the event. "Yes. Though you seem to have returned to normal, I'm sure you are aware of a residual effect. Even a small amount will cause the aging process to slow down, though unfortunately not stop it." He turned his gaze back to Lolly, "Only a transformation can accomplish that." He took another sip of wine.

"I noticed how Miranda has not really changed, even after having the babies," Lolly stated, sounding envious.

"Yes, her life has been touched by Haute Caste influence in many ways." Sir Borgia was not sure how much they knew about Miranda's history, so he stayed as vague as possible. He was ready to get to the point of his visit, "Because of your friendship with my kind, the Magus has asked that I offer you both a gift. A little something from the Haute Caste to enhance your well-being."

Al and Lolly leaned forward as Sir Borgia held his wrist over Al's wine glass and made a small cut on his wrist with a fingernail. A few drops of blood fell into the wine glass. Desire lit up Al's and Lolly's faces. Then he did the same with Lolly's glass, sat back, and smiled, "Enjoy!"

Chapter 15

Alexander the Great Vs. Connie the Mom

After the incident with Marie and the wolf, Tristan called me ten times, but I refused to answer. I was still so angry I didn't even listen to his voicemails. Over the next week, Jorge became a go-between, trying to calm the waters before my husband's normal monthly visit. There had been no word about Franco and Alexander's pursuit of the missing Pug. It seemed like Piglet had been part of the family for years. She started sleeping on Jacque's bed every night. She loved to lay in any lap that was available when they watched TV. The wolf had not come close to the house again. She stayed in the wooded area at the far end of the property, which bordered on a creek. Bart fed her regularly, which, I suppose, was why there were no reports of missing cattle. I was still more than a little uneasy about the whole thing.

Tristan flew into the Danville Airport in his private jet. Not having to drive down from Chicago allowed him to arrive about nine that night so he could have a little more time to visit with the kids. Batu drove his Camaro with the boys, and Bart drove the Jeep with Marie and Piglet to the airport to greet him. I stayed home to avoid ruining the moment. They loved to hang out with their dad. They convinced him to take them to the Custard Cup for hot fudge sundaes before heading home. I think Batu had brought up the idea.

I saw lights coming up the road and assumed it was my brood. I walked out on the porch and was surprised when a silver Rolls Royce pulled in the drive. I got on my phone to Bart, "We have company, and I think he's looking for Piglet."

Jorge came outside and told me to go in the house, but I refused, "This is my home."

I noticed that Jorge was wearing dress slacks with a matching vest over a tailored shirt.

His bergamot cologne smelled great. "You knew they were coming."

"I have been expecting them for a week," he replied.

First, Franco got out. "Baroness, please excuse us visiting without an invitation, but we seemed to have lost something." He took several steps towards us until Jorge gestured for him to stop. He was wearing a tropical shirt with Singapore printed over bright flowers. "Excuse my casual attire. We've been traveling."

The chauffeur opened the rear passenger door and Alexander stepped out dressed in a golden silk shirt and tan pants. His demeanor was arrogant, as he looked about our place with an expression of disappointment. "Good evening Baroness, so this is the rustic abode where you hide yourself and the children from our world. You deserve to live in a palace."

I knew that I should have invited them in, but I really did not want to. So, I did what no one ever did. I ignored Alexander the Great. "Franco, I'd love to invite you to stay, but we're full tonight."

Jorge chuckled, "You'll probably be able to find a hotel in Danville, but I don't think you'll find the accommodations that you're used to."

Alexander was not amused, "Lady Penelope! Now!"

Just then, my parents drove up. They were stopping by after closing the café to say hello to Tristan. The circus was getting better and better. Without a word, everyone adjusted their attitudes.

Mom got out of the truck and called out to Franco, "Hi there, Frankie, how are you?" She walked over and hugged him, and Dad shook his hand. "Who is your friend?"

I responded, "Mom, Dad, this is Alex. They were just passing through on their way to Chicago."

"Alex and Franco?" Mom asked, looking right at Jorge.

It took all my self-discipline not to laugh out loud. At that moment, the cavalry arrived. Bart came driving down the road like a vampire bat out of hell. He pulled into the drive and stopped the Jeep next to the Rolls.

My husband jumped out of the Jeep and slammed the door. Batu was keeping the Pug hidden in the Camaro with the help of Jacques and Marie while Sir Bart stood by my husband, staring down Alexander and Franco. My parents came up on the porch beside me. Dad asked, "What is going on?"

I whispered, "Piglet used to be Alexander's dog, and he wants her back."

"Franco used to be Jorge's; does he want him back too?" Mom whispered back.

Jorge said loudly, "No!"

My husband was pissed, "Alexander, Franco, you are here uninvited. You have come a long way for nothing. Please leave!"

Suddenly there was a commotion in the Camaro. Piglet had gotten away from Batu. She poked her head up in the window while the kids tried to grab her and barked at Alexander.

"Lady Penelope!" Alexander turned to the Baron, "Perhaps you did not know that Jorge and your wife conspired to steal Lady Penelope. Return her now, and we shall put this regrettable incident behind us." He crossed his arms.

Jorge spoke, "Alexander, no one cares about what you want."

Alexander stared daggers at Jorge, "Give me my dog! At once!"

Batu and the kids were heard talking loudly. They decided to take matters into their own hands. The door opened, and Batu helped them out of the car. Batu was holding Piglet, who snorted. He gave the Pug to Jacques, who stepped forward awkwardly, trying not to drop her. With tears running down his cheeks, he looked at Sir Alexander, "Please, can we keep her?" Then she scrambled out of his arms and ran to her former owner. Sir Alexander seemed to be touched by Jacque's plea. For a moment, everyone was silent. He stared at my son and started to reach out to him, but my husband picked up Jacques. Tomas and Desmon sniffled and hugged Batu's legs.

Marie glared at the unwanted visitors, "She's our dog!"

Sir Alexander appeared very uncomfortable, not at all victorious. He looked down at the Pug and started to bend over.

"No, you don't!" Mom swooped down the steps, grabbed the Pug, and scolded him, "What is wrong with you? You're a grown man. What kind of person takes a dog away from children?" She kissed Piglet's head and winked at the kids.

"You both need to leave!" Dad told them with all his "dad" intensity.

I added, "You heard him!"

Jorge smiled, "It's not like you're leaving empty-handed; you have Franco."

They got back in the Rolls and left without another word. We laughed long into the night about the look on Alexander's face when my mom confronted him. She had no idea who she had bested. She just referred to him as, "That rich jerk!" The rest of us knew that my mom and the kids had defeated Alexander the Great.

After my parents left, the kids were tucked in with Piglet. I went to bed in my room, leaving the Haute Caste men and Batu to discuss whatever was going on in their little undead minds. I was not in the mood to hear any bullshit from my husband about the wolf. That could wait until tomorrow night. I was almost asleep in my room when Tristan entered.

"Not tonight, I have a headache."

"I can make you feel better," he responded and sat on the edge of my bed. "Why are you sleeping in here?"

"I'm exhausted and still pissed at you."

He looked irritated, "Every decision I make is for the benefit of you and the children."

79

"You should tell me about all the threats. I must know. Keeping something like Lena's wolf from me is dangerous."

"She hasn't been aggressive towards any of us, or James. I did not want to cause you needless worry," he spoke in a very seductive soft voice. One hand gently slipped up my arm.

I looked into his intense blue eyes, inhaled his intoxicating phero-mones, and said, "Once I was a moth to your flame, but not anymore." I got a little louder, "And another thing, I'm not some delicate flower that needs to be protected and shielded from the world!"

He looked slightly amused and played with my hair. He leaned for-ward to kiss me, but to his surprise, I pushed him away.

"When you go to bed alone at the break of day, I hope you'll consider the fucking great sex you missed out on because you kept me in the dark. Goodnight!" I rolled away from him and pulled up the blanket.

He left in a huff. He could not understand how I could turn my mag-nificent lover down. It was getting easier.

I slept well and got up in the morning with a mission. I arranged for my mom to come over and help Danuta with the kids. It was a beautiful late summer day, with just a hint of Fall in the air. As I got into the Jeep, I heard someone calling me.

"Baroness, wait!" It was Batu, trying to button a denim shirt as he ran to the car. He jumped in the passenger side. "Where are you going?"

"Errands."

"You're not supposed to be alone," he pulled his long black hair back with an elastic band.

"I'm not," I quipped and headed for Danville.

"Where are we going? Does the Baron know about your plans?" He was catching on that I was not much of a team player.

"He rarely does," I smiled. "You smell nice."

Batu seemed uncomfortable with the compliment. "It's just soap."

"I have a vampire's sense of smell. It picks up everything, even blood type. I'm guessing you're Type B."

"Yes. I wish I were HH like you."

"Be glad you're not."

We arrived in town, and I parked the car in front of a beauty salon, next to a local coffee place, Mad Goat. "I'm going to get my hair cut. Would you do me a favor and get me a cappuccino?"

He nodded and watched me until I went into the salon. It was the kind of place where you did not need an appointment. There were lots of conversations between the staff and the regulars to keep you enter-tained while getting fussed over. The young woman with short, bright pink hair looked at my long curls and asked, "What can I do for you?"

"Chop it all off. I want something easy to manage."

She looked at my hair like it was a wrestling opponent.

"Just below the ear lobes," I told her.

Her eyes got a little wide, "Really?"

"Hell, yes! I want it all gone."

She smiled, "Challenge accepted!"

She was combing out my hair, getting ready to attack it when Batu brought me the coffee. The hairdresser took one look at him and asked, "He's with you? Nice!"

Batu turned about the shade of her hair and went outside. I laughed and told her not to worry that he was just shy. The hairdresser did a great job. I left looking a little like Peter Pan. It felt weird at first, but I liked it. I knew Tristan would hate it.

Batu looked at me and asked, "Are you okay?"

"Great. Really great." He looked skeptical.

Then we went downtown where they had a comic bookstore with lots of horror and Sci-fi items. I bought a mug and a wallet that had images of Bela Lugosi on them. I was disappointed they were out of vampire T-shirts and posters, but that might have been pushing it a little too far. Then I talked Batu into having lunch with me at a local café.

We sat down and the waitress, who used to work at my parent's café, asked all the personal questions I expected. I introduced Batu as my husband's cousin, who was helping with our horses. When she walked away, he looked irritated. "You lied to her. I'm not a ranch hand or a relative."

"Sometimes, close enough is better than the truth. If I said you were my bodyguard, the rumor mill would go viral." Then I whispered, "C'mon, I just told a white lie, I didn't suck anyone dry. Don't you ever do anything wrong?"

"I almost let you get away today. The Baron and the Princess would have had my head."

"Okay. I won't run away without taking you with me," I smiled.

"Pardon my being blunt, Baroness, but you're a pain in the ass." He took a bite of his burger, and I started laughing.

"I'm really starting to like you. How did you meet Princess Khunbish?"

"My parents had a small grocery store in her province. My father died trying to put out the fire that burnt it to the ground." Batu paused for a moment but remained stoic. "I was ten years old. I tried to help my mother, but I could not find work. The Princess heard of our difficulties, and she hired my mother as a housekeeper. She watched me grow and allowed me to train in the tradition of the Mongol warriors. The Princess knew I did well in school and with the help of the Magus, arranged for me to study at Stanford. One day I hope to have the honor to be one of the chosen." He looked down in his lap.

"Batu, thank you for letting me know about your life. I'm sorry about your father. I'm sure he would be proud of you. I have never seen anyone ride a horse like you."

"That's what she said." He broke out laughing.

"What's so funny?"

"I just made all that up." He looked at me with a Cheshire Cat grin. "You should have seen your face. My parents are professors of mathematics in London. I learned to ride while playing polo, and I added the bow and arrow to impress the Princess. I met her highness a couple of years ago when I went back to Mongolia to discover my roots. One night I was in an alley coming back from a night club and ran into her retinue. They thought I was a threat, but the Princess stopped them and saved my life. I've been trying to become one of them ever since. The only true thing I told you was that I went to Stanford. Now I am sure you will excuse me."

Before I could respond, he stood and went out to the car. I paid the check and walked out to the Jeep and got in. "Asshole! You've lived with us for months and barely said a word to me. I know you talk to the kids, Sir Bart, Danuta, and even Camo, but you constantly ignore me, and now you tell me some bullshit story about your life! Why?"

"You've met the Baron, right? No one in his right mind would want him to think they were flirting with you. Sir Bart tells him everything, I mean everything, and I would not be surprised if Danuta does too. I have to act distant and uninterested when anyone is around."

"Yeah, you're right to be careful. I thought you were just sort of unsocial, but Camo said you've been going to Urbana on weekends to see someone. I'm glad Bart isn't your only friend here."

"The daughter of friends of my parents goes to the University of Illinois, and I've been clubbing with her. Nothing serious, but I need a little recreation after a week with the offspring."

"Be honest with me, since you spend so much time with them do you think my kids are going to be okay?"

Batu looked at me with his soft brown eyes full of compassion, and he reached over and lightly touched my arm. "You're a good mom, and they are really bright and interesting. If I were a betting man, I'd put my money on your kids every time. I think we better be getting back."

"Thanks for saying that." I wished we had more time away from the others. His company helped my mood. I sighed a little too loudly and started the car.

As we drove home, he said, "Don't take offense if I continue to ignore you. It's just self-preservation."

Chapter 16

Bela Lugosi and the Offspring

Jeanne paced in the Magus' den, considering what to tell him. She looked quite plain with her hair pulled back and no makeup. Her gentle beauty was a stark contrast to the fashionable undead females the Magus was used to. The door swung open, and he entered with Dr. Kyoto. "Please, Jeanne, sit down and tell us what you have found."

Dr. Kyoto wore a kimono and had his hair pulled up in a topknot. He was normally in western clothes. She wondered what was up with the ancient vampire. Jeanne let the Haute Caste seat themselves first in two brown leather chairs, which faced the dark green velvet couch. She sat on the edge of the couch as though ready to spring up.

"Good evening, Magus and Dr. Kyoto. Will Lady Lily join us?" The Knight of the House of Cups was always at Kyoto's side.

"No," Kyoto replied brusquely.

Jeanne quickly gave her report, "I'm afraid I don't have much to tell you. The monk, Turlock, and his accomplice Benedetto have vanished. No sign in Rome. We believe they are in hiding together, that Turlock is in charge. I have been unable to find out where they went after the incident with the snake. The other monk, Grigoryi, was not involved and has no knowledge of their whereabouts. I am so sorry."

The Magus gave her a comforting smile, "My dear, I know you have tried. You are not the only one to have come up empty-handed. They have carefully covered their tracks. It is hard to believe they could have accomplished this without the help of at least one of our kind. It makes me wonder if the attack was more of an attempt to embarrass me than actually to harm the Baroness."

"They must have known the attack would not be lethal. The monk's funding has been cut off in Rome, but that has not stopped them. Father Rinaldi has promised to let me know if he hears anything more about them. I'm inclined to trust this priest."

Dr. Kyoto gazed at the graceful warrior, "You don't trust many. You pay him a great compliment."

"I find his deeds match his words and the oaths he has taken." She was uncomfortable with Dr. Kyoto's prying, afraid her fondness for the priest might be seen as folly or weakness.

The Magus smoothed over the awkward moment, "I find him to be meritorious and open-minded. Not something I've ever said about a member of the clergy before. The rogue monks seem to have an agenda that causes us to fear for our mortals."

"It is interesting how the birth of Miranda, and now her offspring, have brought us closer to the shorts," Dr. Kyoto mused, using the vampire society term for mortals or short-lived. "It has been centuries since I thought of them as anything other than useful tools to be manipulated or more than worthy targets that deserved to be a meal."

"Yes, the Baroness fondly refers to her friends as F.O.V., not mortal servants, and their numbers appear to be growing. Luckily, they seem loyal to the Haute Caste."

Dr. Kyoto smiled, "Even Lady Lockporte appears to be quite concerned with the well-being of that dentist in the wilderness."

Jeanne leaned forward, "Do tell!"

The Magus smiled, "We have requested that Lady Sarah get close to James, and that

Sir Borgia get to know Lolly and Al better. We encourage these relationships to ensure their loyalty."

Kyoto added, "These particular mortals seem very receptive to becoming better acquainted with our kind. Especially the actress and the psychiatrist." Dr. Kyoto stood and turned to the Magus and Jeanne, "Please excuse me. I have some lab work I must attend to."

The Magus gave a slight nod of his head, and Jeanne stood and bowed slightly, "Of course."

After Kyoto departed, the Magus commented, "He is adjusting to working alone. Lady Lily has taken her research in a different direction."

Jeanne responded, "I could sense that something was off about him. I hope you don't mind me saying that."

"My dear, your honesty has always been refreshing. Now let us discuss your next assignment."

My husband, as I expected, hated my hair cut. "You are being childish, but your neck displayed so openly is tantalizing." We shared his bed at times, but our relationship was in decline. The sexual urges were more

like reflexes than the passion I used to feel. Little disappointments were taking their toll. I once got him a Valentine's card, and he responded with, "That tragic saint has nothing to do with my feelings for you." My trust in Tristan already strained with his affairs was further eroded when he kept knowledge of the wolf from me. It was getting harder to imagine a future together.

When the kids were seven and eight, I was surprised to find a stack of red and pink envelopes on the kitchen counter when I came down for coffee before the hordes awakened. I glanced at the wall calendar, February 14th. I took a few sips of coffee to brace myself before opening them. The first one showed a queen on a throne, "To my Queen of Hearts!" inside there was a scribble which I recognized as Jacques's signature. The second had a drawing of Superman with a big heart on his chest, from Tomas. The third had a fire breathing dragon, with "I burn for you!" from Des. I almost spit out my coffee. Then there was a card with a basketful of puppies, from Marie. The last card showed a heart made of flowers and was signed, "Your special friend."

I was not prepared for sweet normalcy. I got choked up. Then I noticed Batu standing in the doorway. I smiled at him and said, "Thanks!"

"For what? I've got to feed the horses," he left for the barn.

I knew it was from him. The kids would spill the beans if I asked, but I didn't. Even years later, when the kids had outgrown giving me valentines, I still got an anonymous one. I never asked. I saved every one of them and locked them in a drawer of my desk.

Months turned into years, and the children stayed busy with the horses, soccer in summer, and hockey in winter. They started to help at the café after school. There were drama-free times that were amazing. I began to think we were out of the woods, though I was still hypervigilant when out with the kids. Our resident Mongol was, more or less, accepted in town. Batu and I engaged in friendly banter when we were running errands away from the house. He was funny, bright, and did not take any shit from me. We never spoke about our growing fondness for each other. I invented reasons to go to Champaign just to spend time alone with him.

My parent's café became the kid's hang out after school. They could see their buddies and not be bothered with questions about the guy in the barn who only came out at night. They learned to hold back in sports and to miss a question now and then on a test. Tomas, more than the others, wanted to be seen as normal and accepted. Des had a couple of friends who were obsessed with technology. Marie was aloof, she escaped to the world of books and spent hours learning how to care for animals from Bart. Jacques, to my surprise, was the kid brother everyone liked. He was genuinely nice to people and took teasing well. He had been born in Rossville, after all.

I thought the kids were so used to Tristan's side of the "family" they just accepted their weird behavior. Then one afternoon, when the kids were nine and ten, I heard Marie say, "Shhh! Mom's coming." I was in the hallway outside the game room.

Tomas said, "Children of the night!" then more laughter.

Des added, trying to sound like Bela Lugosi, "I want to suck your blood!" howling laughter.

"Shut up and watch the movie!" Marie told them.

I opened the door to see Dracula about to close in on a pale virgin. Jacques grabbed the remote and turned it off. They all looked at each other, guiltily.

"What's going on?"

Tomas said, "We're watching horror movies."

"Horrible movies!" Des laughed.

"Why did you turn it off?"

Marie became the spokesperson, "We thought you would get mad."

"Because?"

"Because of Dad and well, you know."

I knew better than to lie to my kids, or suggest they had overactive imaginations. They looked to me for the weird truth.

"When your dad gets up, we'll meet in the living room and talk about this. It's okay. You're not in trouble." I left before they could ask more questions. Crap! I knew this day would come, but they were so young. I should have been suspicious when they all wanted to be vampires last Halloween.

I went out on the front porch for some fresh air before Tristan woke up. Batu was sitting in the rocking chair reading Stephen King's Under the Dome. He said it reminded him of Rossville. "I've got some bad news," I told him, "The kids suspect the truth about their dad and company."

He looked up, "They figured it out a year ago."

"What? A year ago? Why didn't you say something to me?" I stood there, glaring at him.

"They asked about the blood supply that nobody else they know keeps at home. They were afraid that their Dad was sick. I reassured them that the Baron was very healthy because of his special diet. They are pretty smart kids, and it didn't take them long to figure out it was a normal diet for vampires, and that the Baron and the others are never up and about during daylight hours. They made me promise to keep our conversations a secret. They thought you might get upset. I've been waiting for them to tell you." He closed the book and looked at me with those warm brown eyes. I could not be pissed at him.

"What the fuck!" I let out a big exasperated sigh.

"I told them it had to stay between us, that none of their friends, their grandparents, or anyone else could know. They said they would not say anything to townies and would ask me before saying anything to anyone else. How did you find out?"

"I found them watching vampire movies and laughing their asses off. When I went in the room, they looked like they were hiding something."

He smiled, "They always think they are one step ahead of the adults, and unfortunately, they often are."

"Yeah, now tell me something I don't know. Now, I've got to take the news to his highness and figure out how we are going to handle this. I knew this day would come and have been dreading it. I guess I put off dealing with it thinking there was lots more time."

"I don't envy you. Good luck!" With that unhelpful comment, he got up and quickly retreated to the safety of the barn.

I needed more coffee! One cup of Sumatran later, I went upstairs and crawled into Tristan's bed. He smelled great and I wanted him to be in a good mood, so it seemed like a good excuse. I caressed his back, like I was stroking a cat. He turned and murmured, "My love," then began to use his magic touch to ignite my senses further. No one has ever kissed me so deeply, and we could still quickly unleash each other's passion. He could go from a dead sleep to deep thrusts in no time. We melted into each other's bodies, forgetting everything else for twenty precious minutes. I began to understand that great sex was not a good barometer of a relationship.

He sheltered me in his embrace with my head on his chest. "Tristan, it's time to have 'the talk' with the kids."

He sat up, dislodging me and pushing his mane back. "Don't they see enough farm animals? Do we have to explain it to them?"

I almost laughed, "Not that talk. I explained sex to them a while ago. They figured out that you, Bart and the others are more than just nocturnal Lithuanians on some kind of special diet."

"Did someone say something to them? They're too young! How do you know they figured it out?"

"They were watching Bela Lugosi movies and thought they were hilarious."

"How could you let them?" He responded like it was porn.

"How could I have married a vampire? I didn't let them. This day was going to happen sooner or later. I am surprised it took this long, so stop it! They know. So, what are you going to tell them? They are waiting in the living room."

It was probably good we had sex. It was not going to happen again for some time. He dressed in all black, which sort of added to the whole, "my dad the vampire" look. In a weird way, I thought it was kind of funny. The kids were on the couch and in the stuffed chairs, looking like they had been sent to the principal's office. I sat between Jacques and Marie. Tristan decided to stand by the fireplace under his family crest. They sat quietly, waiting for him to say something, which was very unusual.

"Your mother said you were watching wretched old vampire movies. Those films are nonsense."

Tomas blurted out, "What about you, don't you drink blood?"

"Yes. I am a vampire, but not like those bizarre characters," he said with disdain.

"Wow!" Jacques uttered.

"Since your dad really is from Lithuania, we adopted that as a code word for vampires. We have to continue to keep his true nature a secret. You can't tell anyone, not even Grandma and Grandpa. They would not understand."

Des turned to Tomas, "I told you they didn't know."

"Bart? He's one too, right?" Marie asked.

"Yes," Tristan affirmed. "He is a very respected, powerful vampire who has dedicated himself to watching after you."

"The Magus and all those people in Chicago, they are too?" Des was connecting the dots.

Tristan nodded, "Except for a few friends like James, Lolly, and Al. Also, some of the people that work for the Magus are mortals we trust."

Marie asked, "So, the same with Daunta and Batu?'

Tristan smiled at her and nodded, "Yes, that's right."

Tomas asked what was really on their minds, "Does that mean we're going to be vampires too?"

My husband shook his head with a slight smile, "No. The honor of becoming a vampire happens by choice when you are in your late twenties. Being related to me or bitten is not enough to become one of us. One must be selected and be willing. It involves a complex, beautiful ceremony."

"I think that's enough for now. You all get the idea." I did not want him to give them too many details.

"We figured this out a while ago," Des bragged, "We never see you or Bart in sunlight. It doesn't take a genius."

"That and the liquid diet," Tomas added. Tristan gave him a not very happy look. "Just saying," Tomas muttered.

Marie looked at her dad, wide-eyed, "Have you killed people?"

He looked at his daughter with apprehension, "Marie, rarely, and I have only taken the lives of very bad people to stop them from hurting others."

"Vigilante vampires!" Des blurted out.

"Cool!" Tomas exclaimed.

Marie did not look favorably impressed but said nothing.

Jacques jumped up from the couch and hugged Tristan, "I love you, Dad! Even if you're a vampire."

Des asked, "Do you have fangs?"

I held my breath, afraid my husband would do a vampire show and tell. Tristan replied, "There's more to share with you, but it will happen when you are all older."

"C'mon dad, we can handle it," Tomas protested.

Tristan replied with a very stern look.

"I already said, that's enough for now. It's time for dinner!" I announced.

They all stood up, looked from their dad to me, and back then trooped out of the room. I turned to my husband, "Well, that went better than expected." I resisted rolling my eyes.

"Yes, I supposed it did. I'll warn Bart. I'm sure they'll interrogate him next."

The kids were loading their plates with fish sticks, sweet potato fries, and greens. I heard Des sucking ketchup off a fry, saying, "I want to suck…" He cut himself off as soon as he saw me enter the kitchen. I gave him a little "mom" glare, and he just shrugged.

Tomas said, "Maybe I'll just have cereal." He went off to the kitchen and returned with a box of Count Chocula.

"All right, Knock…It…Off!" I demanded.

Jacques muttered under his breath, "Maybe we should start drinking tomato juice to prepare us." I decided that it would be best to ignore it and sat down to eat.

Marie watched me eat my veggie burger. "I want to be a vegetarian too."

Tomas just summed up his father's confession, "This explains everything!"

In Champaign, Batu was having drinks with some of the grad students he had met. They liked to gather at the Clark St. Bar, a club with great music and dancing. He watched some really fit women dance with Hula Hoops that glowed in the dark. He enjoyed the accepting ambiance and fun vibes of the club. "Too bad this place is an hour away from Rossville," he told a friend as he finished his beer.

One of the young women said, "Come over to my place Batu. It's only midnight!" As he spent more time with Miranda, it became harder for him to engage in casual sex.

"Tempting, but I've got a soccer match early in the morning." The soccer match was with the kids at home, not exactly a lie, but it helped make his leaving less awkward. He said his goodbyes and exited the bar. As he walked down the poorly lit street, he noticed someone breaking into his Camaro. "What the Fuck! Get away from my car!"

Two other young men with ball caps and sweats came out of an alley flanking him. "Give us your keys!"

The three punks jumped Batu pushing him against a storefront. Even though there were three of them, they didn't realize they were outmatched. Batu quickly gave a hard kick to the side of the knee of the closest one. There was a loud pop, and he fell to the ground disabled, howling in intense pain. He grabbed the second one and smashed his head against the thick glass of the store window, the window didn't break, but the assailant slid to the ground unconscious. The third man produced a gun and pointed it at Batu's head. The man on the ground holding his knee yelled, "Shoot him!"

Silently someone came out from the shadows of the alley and in a blur of speed, knocked the Glock out of the gunman's hand and kicked it out of reach. The now unarmed and only unharmed assailant wanted no more part of the action and ran away.

Bart stepped into the light of the streetlamp, looked at Batu, and said, "You need to go! Now! I'll deal with this!"

Batu did not hesitate and he quickly climbed into his car and sped off through the darkened streets and out of Champaign. He was never so glad to be back in the moonlit cornfields heading back to good old boring Rossville.

Bart stared at the men who wouldn't have thought twice about killing Batu for his Camaro. "Do you think you deserve to live?"

"More than you do! Freak!" the man Batu had disabled started to reach for the weapon still lying on the sidewalk.

Bart shook his head slowly, reached down, and grabbed him by the collar. "Wrong answer." He knocked him unconscious with one blow and dragged him into the dark alley. It had been a long time since he had tasted fresh blood. His fangs jutted out slightly from his upper lip. Every vampire instinct commanded him to take this life. He sighed and dropped the budding criminal to the ground hoping the beating would help change his ways. With all his self-restraint, Bart turned away.

A bullet whizzed past his head and ricocheted off into the alley. "Stupid bastard!" he exclaimed. The fool had come to and found the gun on the sidewalk. Bart now pushed beyond his patience, knocked the gun away, ripped into his throat, and drank deeply before the thug could react. The smell and taste of fresh blood was invigorating. He had no thought of stopping in time to spare this mortal's life. He felt the warmth of the living fill him. The badly aimed bullet had sealed the unfortunate, would be, car thief's fate. The rush from the kill filled him with memories of past bloodlettings, which overwhelmed his brain. He pulled himself up from the body and quickly looked around. He pulled a knife from a sheath on his belt and used it to camouflage the bite wound on the dead man's neck. He looked over at the other man on the ground, saw he was still unconscious, and quickly ran down to the far end of the alley, breathing heavily. He leaned against an old brick building to steady himself, removed his knee-length caftan, and wiped his beard. He pulled a bottle of hand sanitizer from his pocket to clean-up. The sanitizer left him smelling of pumpkin spice. He stood on the street half-naked. Some very drunk college students came out of a bar and dropped five dollars at his feet. The Hierophant picked it up, "Bless you!" he called after them. He made his way to the Jeep parked a block away and considered shaving his beard but realized the students would never be able to describe him in their drunken state, and he really liked his beard.

Chapter 17

May the Force Be with You

Several more years went by, and although the kids continued to ask questions about their "Lithuanian" relatives, they knew at least they were mortal, which seemed to make the strange family connection acceptable. Bart explained that in modern times, most vampires got their nutrition from blood banks, which also helped. They lost their interest in Lugosi movies and instead got caught up in Zombie movies and books, which were more acceptable to their father. One day when Tristan was visiting, we were all sitting watching TV, and out of nowhere, Marie asked me, "Who are we to judge the Lithuanians?" To my relief, all her siblings agreed. Although Tristan didn't say anything, I could tell he was pleased.

The kids were beginning to develop their own separate interests. Tomas played basketball in Middle School, and Des showed a flair for computers, Marie was a math whiz, and Jacques had a real talent for art. Tomas was the team's top scorer, Marie won first place in a state math competition, Des' computer knowledge soon surpassed the teacher's, and Jacques entered some drawings at the local Art in the Park show in Danville where he won second place. I was proud of them that they didn't feel the need to show up their competitors at every opportunity. They were growing up faster than I sometimes realized or maybe than I would have wanted. They found ways to get by in a small town where they had to hide the truth about their family and abilities. At times I wondered if they would have been happier in Los Angeles, but in my heart, I always knew that it was healthier to raise them here than amid the bizarre, nocturnal society.

One evening, when the kids where thirteen and fourteen, the "Emperor" of the Vampire world was greeted enthusiastically by them as he came downstairs.

"Dad! Dad! C'mon, we want to go see Star Wars!" Des yelled, grabbing Tristan's arm, pulling him toward the door.

The Baron was not enthusiastic. "Star Wars? That doesn't sound like my kind of movie. You run along; I'll see you after the film."

"But Dad, c'mon, you and Bart are like Jedi!" Jacques exclaimed.

"Yeah, and Bart is coming with us," Marie threw down the challenge.

"I told you he wouldn't go," Tomas added.

My husband felt verbally assaulted by his offspring before he was quite awake. He looked at me as though hoping I would intercede. No way. I picked up my purse and walked to the door.

Tristan responded, "Bart is going for your protection."

"Yeah," Jacques-Omar stated, "the Jedi protect the universe!"

Then the kids all ran out the door.

I saw his hesitation, "Would it be that much of a sacrifice? It would mean a lot to the kids, a fun memory of you."

"Fun?" he looked at me as though I was speaking a foreign language.

"Imagine having a good time without sex or killing someone."

He considered my words for a moment, "All right, I'll try."

This was our first normal family outing, if you ignore the Hierophant bodyguard. To be able to get me, all the kids, Batu and sometimes Tristan and Bart into one vehicle, I finally had to get a minivan. But I still kept my Jeep! Bart had already gotten the kids into the van and acted as our chauffeur. I climbed in front next to Bart. Tristan got in back with the kids who were thrilled. Bart, surprisingly, enjoyed the kids' taste in films. He started out watching Harry Potter movies with us at home, and eventually, we convinced him to go to the theater for the big screen and surround-sound experience. After that, he became quite the film buff.

When we got to the theater, I made the kids sit in the row in front of us. The vampires sat on either side of me, for protection or perhaps to make it easier to escape.

The kids had popcorn, which mysteriously seemed to land on their dad. "Stop throwing the popcorn."

Jacques called out, "It's not me. I didn't do it!"

"I don't care who is doing it. I'll take it away!" I warned.

There were snickers from the kids' row, but the popcorn rain ceased. "How long is the film?" Tristan inquired with a pained expression. I could tell he wanted to be almost anywhere but here.

"Two hours," Bart responded enthusiastically. "It got great reviews."

The movie started, and a hush fell over the crowd and thankfully, the kids. I watched Tristan's responses to the screen as he became engaged in the story.

Half-way into it, he whispered, "I can see the Jedi comparison." I tried not to laugh.

After the movie, we all trooped back to the van, and the kids excitedly talked about their favorite parts. When we got home, the kids made ice cream sundaes and discussed the possible origins of Porgs, the birdlike Star Wars creatures. Marie came up with puffins and pugs while holding Piglet.

"Dad, did you like it?" Jacques asked. The dining room became quiet.

"It was entertaining," my husband replied.

"Crap!" Tomas stated, and pulled a dollar bill out of his pocket, and gave it to Des.

"Thanks Dad, I knew the force would win you over," Des said grinning. "Hey, Marie, pay up."

Marie said, "Jerk! I'll give it to you later."

"Haven't you learned not to bet with Des?" I asked.

"I'm saving up for my own Lamborghini," Des responded with a self-satisfied smile.

"Do you often wager on me?" my husband asked the kids.

"It's how I made my first hundred," Des responded.

Marie threw her napkin at Des. I raised my voice, "That's it; its midnight, get to bed."

"Mom, c'mon, we want to hang out with Dad," Tomas pleaded.

"Obey your mother now!" my husband told them in his best command voice.

As they left, I heard Marie say, "Thanks for telling him about the bets!"

Des laughed, "Sore loser."

We went to Tristan's room, and he asked, "Do they know that our kind loves to place bets?"

"I try not to think about how much their behavior reminds me of you."

"Excuse me?" he grabbed me around the waist, and we fell on the bed. "I know where they get their disrespectful natures."

"Stop talking," I began kissing him.

He responded passionately, and soon our clothing was being shed. My body quickly responded to his touch. His lips lightly started tickling my neck as he traveled down my chest to my breasts, then he suddenly stopped. Tristan pulled away and looked at me as though I had done something wrong.

I sat up, pulling the sheet about me. "What is it?"

He stared at me, looking shocked. "I don't understand."

"What?"

"I'm not responding."

"You're not getting hard?"

"I was, but then my mind wandered…" He looked distressed.

"What were you thinking of?"

"Porgs. I just started seeing that little creature's face. I can't explain it."

"Tristan, it's okay." I tried not to chuckle as I reached out to him, but he pushed my hand away.

He stood and pulled on his pants. "What have you done to me?" He looked at me accusingly. "I must see Kyoto."

"I didn't do anything! This is just a guy thing. It's normal, sometimes the lightsaber malfunctions. It's temporary. You'll be fine."

"I'm glad you're amused, but I do not find this a joking matter. I'm leaving for Chicago to see Dr. Kyoto. Tell the children I'll return soon."

"Seriously? Right now?"

"This has never happened to me. Never!"

He got his keys and left the house. I heard, through my secret grapevine, that Kyoto, who sworn to secrecy, took the Magus' private jet to Chicago to meet with him the next night for a thorough exam. I had a feeling Tristan would never watch another Star Wars movie again.

It became apparent to me that our mortal world had unexpected effects on vampires who were close to us. Tristan's automatic sexual response had been impacted by human emotion. So much for being a superior being. Then there was Antoinella, who did not understand how my husband could favor me over his own kind. I think the Magus appeared the most effected by us, as he had executed vampires that were a threat to us, though I suspected that might have been an excuse to help him clean house. Perhaps the most surprising impact was the Haute Caste vampiresses raising their voices in support of me. When Tristan and I had a disagreement, they might try to explain my position to him. Of course, in a respectful Haute Caste way without the F-word. I'll never understand why they seldom cussed. I always found it quite satisfying. The undead were catalysts for many of my foul-mouth tirades. Perhaps they thought themselves too noble for such crude language.

Tristan did not return for three weeks, and when we talked on the phone, he would not answer my questions about his medical concern. The kids decided we must have had another argument about living in Rossville.

Bart came to the house as I sat by the fireplace on a cold fall evening before my husband's return and said, "Prepare for a visitor," then went back to the barn, leaving me puzzled as to how he knew someone was coming.

An hour later, an Escalade blaring rock n' roll came up the driveway. Danuta and Camo stared out of the kitchen windows, wondering if the visitor was welcome. Batu went out on the front porch. When Ruben stepped out of the car, they breathed a collective sigh of relief. I was still getting used to Bart's premonitions. Batu shook his hand then headed for the barn. A little Ruben went a long way.

I greeted him in the foyer. "Ruben, what are you doing here?"

He took off his long leather coat, "Gossip. I have to know from the horse's mouth what happened."

"Excuse me?"

"The vampire world is going crazy about rumors that you tried to kill your husband, and he was rushed to Chicago for Dr. Kyoto to heal him. So, was it poison? A knife to the heart?" he asked enthusiastically.

The kids had run down the stairs and were hanging on every word.

"None of the above. I didn't do anything to him." I responded and pointedly looked at the kids then back at him.

He caught my drift, turned, and smiled at them, "Greetings, royal offspring! I was just joking with your mom. Your father is fine."

"You'll see for yourselves tomorrow night. Now go back upstairs." I tried to sound as though everything was normal, as normal as it ever got in our house.

"Mom, c'mon, we wanna hang with Ruben," Des whined for all of them.

"Can't blame you," Ruben said with a smile, "Let me talk with your mom, and I'll be up in a few minutes."

"Let's go to my office."

We passed through the kitchen, where Ruben high-fived Camo. He had been helping Danuta with the dinner dishes.

"Long time no see Sir Ruben, how are you?" Camo asked.

"In trouble as always," he gestured towards me.

I grabbed a cup of coffee; it was going to be a long night. We settled into the small writing office off the kitchen. "Tell me what you know, not what you heard."

"No problem, Baroness, just the facts," he smiled, but I did not return it. "Dr. Kyoto gets called to come to Chicago to take care of your husband. A couple of nights later, they return to Bel Air, and the Baron seems perfect, with no sign of illness or injury. The weird thing was he immediately started hitting up every vampiress in town for a good time like he was trying to prove something or get back at you."

To his surprise and relief, I just started laughing, "That fucker! Unbelievable!"

"Well, yes, you could say that," he seemed a bit confused. "You're not mad or jealous?"

"No. It was probably what the good doctor ordered. Idiots!" I took a sip of coffee to give me time to come up with a response. "Ruben, I can't tell you what happened. It's between the Baron and me. All I can say is that I did not harm him."

"Okay, Baroness, if you say so. Whatever you did not do, the female immortals hope you don't do it again," he grinned.

"Are you sure you want to be here when his highness arrives tomorrow? He'll wonder about your visit."

"Will you keep it a secret?"

"Yes, but the kids won't. Try bribing them or letting them win."

"I like your criminal nature, yeah, I'll play for an hour or so then take off for Indianapolis. I haven't been to the Slippery Noodle Club in ages."

"Yeah, I'm sure they've missed you. Thanks for coming by. You're welcome to rat on my husband anytime."

He was good to his word. After about an hour, Ruben left for the oldest night club in Indy. I overheard the kids talking about earning an easy fifty bucks each. I really didn't want to know.

I went out to the barn to thank Bart for warning me. He and Batu were cleaning out a stall. I gave a carrot to each of the stallions. "You didn't greet Sir Ruben."

Bart glanced at me, "Talking to him hurts my brain. Following his thoughts is like tracking a ping pong ball during a tournament."

"I find him amusing," I replied. "Also, I find him generally good-hearted, just a bit immature."

"Jacques Omar is more mature than he is," Bart stated like it was a fact and returned to his work. Batu chuckled and kept cleaning.

Chapter 18

A Sad Day in the Small Town

Pete went to the café at five on Saturday morning to get the biscuits started. He enjoyed a little quiet time away from Connie when he could focus on food preparations without having to answer a thousand questions. The restaurant was his life's work, and he continued to get up six days a week even though Miranda had asked him to hire more help. He politely turned down her offers to help slow down a bit. He was proud of the café he and Connie had started when he got out of the Navy years ago. He was about to put the first tray in the oven when someone came to the back door. It was just starting to get light. Pete was not expecting a delivery. He cracked open the door and saw a thin man wearing baggy sweats with a large silver cross.

"Please, sir, my van broke down. May I use your phone to call for a tow? My phone isn't charged." He held up a twenty-dollar bill. "I can pay you for any inconvenience." He spoke with a foreign accent. He looked in need of a meal as well as a car mechanic. Something about him made Pete uneasy, it seemed odd that the man had pulled his van behind the café, but he could not bring himself to just shut the door on this stranger.

"Keep your money and stay out there, we're not open yet. I'll hand you my phone."

"Thank you. You're very kind."

As Pete held out the phone, the man grabbed his arm and jerked him hard onto the ground. Pete yelled and tried to stand, but he was silenced by a baseball bat hitting his head. He fell to the ground in a heap, and blood trickled onto the ground.

Turlock threw the bat down and barked commands at Benedetto, "Quickly, in the van!" He looked around. The neighboring gas station still had not opened, and behind them was nothing but dark cornfields. No traffic, no witnesses just as he had planned. "Tie him up and gag him!" Benedetto was breathing hard from the adrenaline rush. It brought back

98

memories of unsuccessfully trying to kidnap the Baroness years ago. They lifted the unconscious, bleeding man into the van. The monk was getting too old for vampire hunting. Pete mumbled, so Turlock smashed his head against the van. He started bleeding more. Benedetto tried to wipe the wound with a rag. "Leave him alone. Let's go!' Turlock yelled.

Turlock climbed into the driver's seat. As Benedetto closed the van doors, his hands trembled. He feared that their prisoner might not survive. No one was supposed to die. He started to come around to the passenger side when he heard a snarling sound. A chill went down his spine as he turned. The vamp-wolf stared with golden eyes that burned into his soul. Then with a blood-curdling growl, it leaped on him, pinning Benedetto to the van tearing into his neck and almost severing his spine. He died instantly. Turlock heard the eerie animal sound and was shocked to see the attack in the side view mirror. His hands shook, and his heart raced as he started the engine. The vamp-wolf smashed through the windshield, shattering it and impaling itself while slashing at Turlock's head, almost blinding him. He hit the gas, but the van just crashed into the side of the café. He was unable to move as his blood blended with the creature's and flowed down him and onto the seat.

A farmer coming by for breakfast fifteen minutes later found them and called the police. The local law enforcement department consisted of the full-time Chief and part-time Deputies. They were horrified by the terrible scene. A mutilated body lay in a pool of blood on the ground and another body covered in blood in the driver's seat of a van with a smashed windshield. When they found Pete badly beaten in the back, they were devastated. It made no sense. He was one of the nicest guys in Rossville. They noticed large bloody paw prints that led through the rear parking lot of the café to the cornfield behind it and then to the creek. They called for the ambulance, the coroner, and extra forensic help from the County Sherriff's Department and the State Police.

Our old family friend, the police chief, notified me, "Miranda, there was what we think was either an attempted abduction, or maybe a botched robbery at the café. Your dad was hurt and he's being taken to the Hoopeston ER. It looks like the assailants are dead."

"Is Dad hurt? What are you talking about? Is he going to be okay? Does my mom know?"

He stopped me before I could ask any more questions. "It might be better if you tell your mom and go to the ER right away. I'll find you, and we will talk later."

I told Danuta, Camo, and Batu to keep the kids safe at home. Batu did not want me to go alone, but I told him in no uncertain terms he had to protect the offspring until we knew what was going on. I made them promise not to wake my husband, and I wanted him to be at full strength to deal with this when he woke tonight. Besides, the sun had just come up, and he couldn't help right now. I drove the Lamborghini to my parent's house. I thought it would get me there faster. Mom was just about to leave for the café. The look of shock on her face made me even angrier at whoever was responsible. I tried to reassure her that he would be okay. She asked me what had happened, but all I could do was tell her what the chief had said. I drove 100 mph to the hospital; she was so worried she didn't even complain. When we got to the ER, the staff said he had severe head trauma and needed to be flown to a medical center in Urbana, and the helicopter was on the way. When we saw him, my heart broke, and Mom started sobbing. His head wrapped in bandages, his pallor was gray, and what we could see of his face and head was covered in large bruises. He was unconscious. He looked as though the IVs, and the oxygen mask were all that was keeping him alive.

I tried to keep my composure and helped my mother to a chair by his side. The doctor told us that due to hemorrhaging, he needed to be transported for surgery right away. The helicopter arrived and told us they only had room for the patient. Mom was beside herself. I called the house and told Camo to bring the Jeep and drive my mom to Urbana. I told my mom I had to go home to tell the kids what was going on, then I would join her at the hospital. By the time the helicopter left, Camo had arrived and took charge of my mother, and I raced back home.

I knew there was only one option to save my father. The house looked quiet, and only the kitchen light was on. I hoped the kids were still asleep. I did not wake my husband; I could get all the help I needed from Bart and be on my way. I pulled up behind the barn and knocked on Bart's door. The heavy curtains closed, but I could see that the lights were on. I was surprised when he opened the door quickly, staying behind it out of the light of the early morning. Normally vampires are in a deep sleep by this time. There was the stench of wet dog and blood in the air. Then I saw it in the backroom by his bed. The vamp-wolf lay on the floor with labored breathing covered in blood. Batu was gently cleaning her wounds. A surgery kit was next to her.

"Did she attack my father? What happened?" my anger flared.

"No, she didn't. She was badly cut when she attacked the assailants. She saved his life. The wolf is fighting to stay alive."

"So is my dad!" I snapped impatiently.

He pointed to a table. Bart already knew what I needed. On the table was a vial of blood from Bart and a large syringe. I would not waste time asking more questions. I grabbed them both. "Tell my husband what has happened if I'm not back by sunset. Thank you!" I ran out the door before he could reply.

Lena would have turned in her grave if she knew the monster, she had created to attack her enemies had tried to protect us. I drove like an Indy 500 driver on little backcountry roads where you never saw a police car. My mind was racing, trying to comprehend what had happened and who was responsible. I rushed into the ER with the precious vial of blood hidden in my coat pocket and wondered how I would be able to inject my dad secretly.

A triage nurse in the ER motioned to where he was. It was surprisingly quiet and still in his curtained area, all the monitors were turned off, I saw Mom's grief-stricken face and rushed to the bed.

"He's gone, Randie," she said softly, "They tried everything. I don't know if he ever knew I was here, but at least I was with him at the end." She sobbed softly and held onto his swollen hands.

I fell to my knees next to the bed. "No!" I shrieked: I knew the HH blood could not help him now. I buried my head in my hands. I couldn't believe I was too late. A few minutes passed, I stood and dried my tears. A sort of numbness began to set in as I tried to calm down. I began to focus on what to do next. I put my arms around my mother. I could hear voices in the next cubicle talking about a dying child who was the victim of a hit and run. A nurse entered to tell us the coroner would arrive shortly, and she asked about the name of a funeral home. With all her strength, my mother straightened up, took a deep breath, and stepped out to deal with the inevitable hospital paperwork. "Stay with him," she told me.

I heard a woman quietly sobbing in the next cubicle with the dying child. I peeked through a narrow gap in the curtains that separated the bed areas. The child was receiving a blood transfusion. The weak, fragile child looked to be about seven years old. His parents were oblivious of anything but their child. The father had his arm around his wife seemingly keeping her from collapsing to the floor. There was a look of utter devastation on both their faces. Even though I had just lost my father, I couldn't imagine the pain they were experiencing. Without thinking, I slipped my hand into my jacket pocket touched the vial of Bart's blood. I knew what I had to do. It might be too late for Dad but not too late for the little boy. I knew my dad would have wanted me to save him. I carefully filled the syringe with Bart's blood and reached through the gap in the curtain and carefully stuck it in the port of the IV bag, and I pushed in the plunger. I finished in an instant. The parents focused only on their son's face. I was never detected. I put the empty syringe and vial in a sharps container in my dad's cubicle.

I turned back to Dad, "I will miss you the rest of my days. No one can take your place," my voice cracked, and tears welled up in my eyes, "I will do what is right for mom and the kids. I'm sorry, I could not tell you the truth about my life."

When Mom returned with the nurse, there was a coldness about her. She said the coroner had arrived. "I can't see him like this anymore. That's not my Pete. He's gone, he's in a better place. I want to go home now."

As we walked down the hospital corridor, I heard the parents of the child call out, "It's a miracle he's waking up!" Medical staff went running by us. I knew the Haute Caste vampire blood hadn't gone to waste.

We slowly, silently walked out to the parking lot with our arms around each other. When we were getting into the car, she said, "I want to know about the bastards that did this. Have the Police Chief meet us at home." I texted him before we started home. I said little, so she would have the chance to talk, "Pete didn't have any problems with anyone. It's so senseless. He had been so happy with you and the kids here. How could this happen in Rossville? We used to worry about you in Los Angeles. This is so wrong!" When we got to her place, she got out of the car before I had it in park and slammed the car door. "This is a very impractical vehicle."

The news had already spread through town. The food had started to arrive. The porch of their small, late Victorian house had large baking pans and bowls of food that had been arriving since the news of the attack got out. I called it drive-by pot roasts. When someone died in our town, people would come by with food, even if they did not know the family well. I helped mom bring in a spaghetti casserole, chicken wings, meatloaf, and a pie. Some form of Jell-O was bound to come later. I got tearful over the outpouring of generosity from the town. It was somehow comforting to know things in Rossville had not changed. The Police Chief and the County Sheriff arrived a few minutes later. This was the most bizarre and violent crime ever to happen here. The Sheriff drove an official vehicle, and the Chief drove up in his golf cart. He lived on the next block.

They sat stiffly on the edge of the couch in her living room. Mom insisted on making coffee; it's what you did when someone came over. I started to stop her, but there was no point. Rituals help when you are in grief. The living room had been off-limits when I was growing up except for holidays and piano lessons. After today I didn't think I would ever want to be in that room again. They politely took the mugs of coffee from her. She had known the Chief, Ben Bryant, for twenty years. He was a bit overfed with a red-tinged beard and glasses. He was six foot three, so everyone called him Big Ben. I did not know the young Sheriff. He was smaller and thinner, with short blond hair. He almost spilled his coffee. He seemed nervous and excited about the case.

Big Ben took the lead, "Connie, I'm sorry to have to be here under these circumstances. Pete was a fine man, none better, and he will be missed." He looked at the younger officer, "This is George Fleming, from the Sheriff's department who helped at the scene."

"Ben, just tell me what the hell happened!"

"Judd Winston came by the café at six o'clock and found a van had crashed into the side of the building." There was a body on the ground by the van with his throat lacerated. Another body was found in the driver's seat. It looked like someone had broken the window to attack the driver."

The Sheriff added, "It couldn't have been your husband because he was tied up in the back of the van."

Big Ben seemed a bit irritated by the enthusiastic young Sherlock, "Pete was unconscious in the van, bleeding from a head injury..."

"We recovered two Italian passports which match the bodies at the scene," Fleming continued.

The Chief turned to the Sheriff and nodded. Fleming pulled out two plastic bags tagged with "Evidence" in red, each containing an open passport so I could see the names and photos.

"My God, it's Benedetto...," I blurted out without thinking. I did not recognize the other somewhat emaciated man.

"Randie, how do you know him?" Mom asked, stunned.

"Years ago, in Los Angeles..." I paused for a second to gather my thoughts. I knew I couldn't tell them the truth about how I knew him. "He and another Italian tried to rob me." I looked at the police, "My husband is very wealthy, and I was wearing a large ruby necklace. I could never forget their faces. They got away but were picked up on some other charges involving a dead drug dealer. I heard later they got off on a technicality." I told them enough information to let them check Benedetto's arrest record and come up with a motive.

The Chief asked, "Do you know the other man?" I shook my head no. "Probably tried to kidnap Pete for ransom," Big Ben looked as though he had solved the crime. He would sleep better now. "I'll contact the L.A. police department this afternoon." He started to get up.

"But Chief Bryant, who killed the assailants?" Fleming asked, "Mr. Ortega was tied up. There were bloody footprints that looked like they came from a large wild dog or a big coyote that went down to the river. It might have killed these men." He turned to my mother, "Did you and your husband have a guard dog?"

"No, we always felt safe here," Mom stated and began to cry.

Big Ben disliked Fleming upsetting my mom further, "Sheriff, you should report that to Animal Control in Danville. Connie, we'll leave you alone now. Father Martino called and said to let him know if you would like any of the women from the church to stay with you. I'll have someone watching the street as long as you're here." We all knew that would not be necessary

as the neighbors would be vigilant.

The Chief stood, and the Sheriff took the hint, though he seemed to have a lot more questions. He turned to me, "If you remember anything else about the Italians, please let me, I mean us, know."

The Chief stated, "Again, we are sorry for your loss."

My mother looked at the chief, "Thanks Ben, I'll probably stay at Miranda's for a while."

After they left, Mom turned to me and asked, "Is the wolf okay?"

WTF! How did she know? "The wolf?"

"The kids told me Bart has been taking care of some poor creature to keep it from starving and going after the horses or your neighbor's cattle. Marie said she gave it dog treats. I didn't tell the Chief because I don't want it to be killed. I think it tried to help my Pete."

"Bart is doing everything he can to save her," I hugged her. "Is it okay if I call Batu, have him come over and help you, he won't be intrusive, just come over when you're ready. I've got to talk to the kids."

She looked around the home they had shared for so many years, "Yes, honey, tell them I'll be over soon and to be strong." She began to cry again. "We had so many plans. We were going to take that cruise…"

I put my arm about her shoulders, "Do you think you could ever have gotten dad away from the Café for that long?"

She shook her head and smiled, "No, I suppose not." We sat there quietly for a few minutes, trying to absorb it all. I sent a text to Batu and asked him to come over.

"Mom, is there anything I can do for you right now?"

She took my hand in both of hers and said, "No, not right now. You go on. Batu can help me here. If I am going to stay with you, I better pack. I need a little time alone right now."

"Okay, mom, if you need anything, just call. I'll see you in a while." She walked me outside, and I hugged her. We stood there for a while, holding each other. She pulled away and told me to go home and see her grandbabies. I got in the car, drove to the end of the block, and pulled over. I banged on the steering wheel and cried out, "Fuck! Fuck! Fuck!" What did she know? Why hadn't she asked why Tristan was not with me? How could this have happened? The Haute Caste had told me for years that we were protected. Poor Dad, he did not have a clue, but I was starting to wonder about my mother, I sighed, frustrated not to have any answers.

I got a text from Batu,

```
On my way. Your dog is better.
```

Batu waved as we passed each other on the road. Mom would be glad he was not gabby. I couldn't believe it was already close to sunset when I pulled up in front of the house. Danuta came out on the porch with the kids and Piglet. Danuta's eyes were red from crying. She always enjoyed sharing recipes with my dad and laughed at his jokes. The kids were thirteen and fourteen now, almost as tall as she was. I guess it was time for them to grow up emotionally.

Des called out, "Mom, what happened?"

Then Marie asked, "Is Grandpa okay?"

I slowly walked up the step and hugged them, "Let's talk in the kitchen."

"Damn it!" Tomas exclaimed, "Just tell us."

Jacques responded, "Do what mom says."

They all fell silent and followed me into the house. Jacques took one hand and Marie the other, which made my tears well-up. When I sat at the kitchen table, exhaustion hit me. I started to talk but choked on my words. Danuta handed me a mug of coffee then put a box of Kleenex on the table. I put my hands around the warm cup and took a sip. I looked at my kid's faces full of confusion mixed with fear, sadness, and anger. I had to tell them the truth. "Your Grandpa Pete died early this morning." They all started talking at once.

"No! That can't be true!" Jacques blurted out.

"Did someone hurt him?" Marie asked through tears.

Des asked, "Did he have a heart attack?"

"Please, mom tell us what's going on!" Tomas pleaded.

I held my hand up, "Okay, okay, give me a chance." They all quieted down. "I will tell you what Chief Ben said, and you need to be very grown-up right now. Two strangers tried to kidnap your grandpa; they hit him and hurt him very badly. The kidnappers were killed before they could get away." They all started sobbing. Danuta passed the box of Kleenex around while holding one up to her face. "Grandma was with Grandpa when he passed away."

I could not hold back my tears. Jacques sobbed, "I want my grandma!" I reached over to hug him, and they all piled on me.

"Batu is with her, and he'll bring her over soon. She'll be staying with us." I gave them each a kiss somewhere on their heads, and we all had a big family hug. When we had all finished crying, for now, they went back to their chairs.

Tomas dried his eyes, "I can't believe anyone would hurt Grandpa."

There was a knock on the door. I told Danuta that unless it was the Chief, I did not want to talk to anyone. She returned with a strawberry dessert and a card from one of my mom's neighbors. I looked at the kids, "Good thing you like Jell-O. Thanks Danuta, there's going to be a lot more coming."

Des asked, "Does dad know?"

"Not yet. I'll tell him soon."

Tomas' eyes got big, "Lithuanians? Did they kill the guys that hurt Grandpa?"

"This has to remain between us. You cannot tell your friends, not anyone! We think it was the great wolf. She tried to protect Grandpa. She got hurt, and Bart is taking care of her."

They all jumped up and started to go for the door, "Stop!" I yelled so loudly they stopped in their tracks. "She is with Bart, he and Batu have been taking care of her. Leave them alone till Bart opens the barn door. Do you hear me?"

They looked at each other then, over at me, and one by one nodded and said okay. Their acceptance was mixed with sadness and anger that they had never experienced before. I told the kids to help Danuta get a room ready for my mother. I could not believe I would not be able to talk with my father again. The world was an emptier place. As the sun set, I went upstairs and crawled into my husband's bed. I was thankful this was his week to stay with us. I was beyond blaming him for bringing the violence of the vampire world into our lives. I knew it wasn't his fault. The crazed, fanatic monks were to blame. Their obsession with vampires made them vicious and twisted. I would no longer take the Magus' assurances of protection without question. I should have learned that after the snake attack. I just thought we were safe here. It was all so crazy and tragic.

I was used to the coolness of his body. His breathing increased as he came out of the deep slumber of the undead. He started to caress me, and it was almost an automatic behavior when he woke up. Then he realized I was fully dressed, "What is it?" he mumbled, sitting up.

I looked at his muscular body and the thick mane of blond hair that brushed his shoulders. I was touched by the intense gaze of his deep blue eyes and started crying. "My father..."

He held me, "I had a dream about Pete. He was fighting a hooded man, and he fell, that was all I remember. Was it a vision?"

"I think so. He was killed at the café this morning, murdered by monks. They were trying to abduct him. Benedetto was one of them."

He pulled away, "Is your mother okay?"

"Yes, he was at the café alone. She's at her house with Batu. She will be here soon. She is going to be staying with us." I dried my eyes with the sheet. "I don't know if she'll ever be okay again. She was with him when he died."

He started to dress, "I will hunt down those responsible!" He did not think to express comforting words, just vengeance. Somehow, I wasn't surprised.

"We found out what the wolf's purpose was. She killed them both as they tried to take my dad. I think they bled to death, that's justice. She was hurt in the attack. Bart is caring for her wounds." I sat with my arms about my knees, hugging myself tightly.

"I must call the Magus. We thought that you and the children would be the targets, not your parents. We had people watching the monks, but they disappeared when we took away their funding. Benedetto, you're sure?"

"Yes, and Turlock. The police have their passports."

"Cowardly bastards! Attacking your father."

When we opened the bedroom door, the kids could be heard running into their rooms. They had heard everything we had said. We went downstairs intending to go out to the barn, but Batu arrived with my mom. Batu whispered to me, "She has a lot to say to both of you."

We got her suitcases in the house, and Batu took them upstairs.

Tristan was quiet and respectful of her grief. He pulled out a chair for her to sit down at the kitchen table. I asked if she wanted some coffee or something to eat. She just said, "No." Then she looked at Tristan, "Pete never knew anything."

My surprised husband started to respond when there was a knock at the door. Danuta said it was a priest. Mom said to let Father Martino come in. He was a short, thin man with a receding hairline who took his calling very seriously. "Mrs. Ortega, please accept my condolences. Your husband will be greatly missed." Then he looked at Tristan and me, "Your father was a kind man." I gestured for him to take a seat. He pulled a sheet of paper out of his pocket. "I received a call from Rome. This has never happened before." He sat up straight and leaned towards my mom. "They emailed this letter for me to give to you, it's from the office of public affairs at the Vatican."

Tristan and I stood behind my mother to read it with her. It was a condemnation of the unholy acts by fanatic, rogue clergy, and a promise that any descendant of de Molay could seek the protection of the church.

It went on to say prayers would be offered in the holy city to honor Mr. Peter Ortega. Mom just stared at the sheet of paper.

I looked at Father Martino, "How did they hear about my father?"

"It is my understanding that the police contacted the State Department, who contacted the Italian embassy who contacted the Vatican."

"Wow, they sure got in front of this fast," I replied.

Mom said, "He wasn't even a de Molay."

"Mrs. Mordecai and Mrs. Ortega, we would like to have a special mass."

My mom looked at the well-meaning priest, "No, thanks. The church has done enough. We will have a private ceremony at the gravesite, just family."

I was not sure if Mom was being critical or appreciative of the Vatican.

My husband finally spoke. He looked at the priest and said, "I think we need some time alone. Please leave now." Mom nodded.

Father Martino left without another word. Mom said, "I'm probably going to hell."

My husband knelt and put his arms about her shoulders, "Connie, you and Pete have always been great parents and grandparents. You've contributed to this town. You fed hungry people who had been laid off from their jobs. No one will dare condemn you for how you choose to bury your husband."

We sat down beside her. She turned to Tristan, "Thank you. I did not think they would find us after all these years. I should have warned Pete. I should've told him about the crazy religious fanatics that had attacked my mother years ago. I thought it was just a random attack. My mother only told me about our history years later. She said that they were looking for Templar gold, but when they realized how poor we were, they left us alone, and we never saw any of them again. My mother was convinced your kind made them go away. I know you would have protected my husband if you had known. After all these years, I thought they had forgotten about us."

I was having a hard time accepting what she was revealing. I couldn't get my head around the fact that she knew about Tristan, not to mention the de Molay family history and the Templar gold.

She turned to me. "I always knew Tristan wasn't gay. I just said that, so you wouldn't wonder why I didn't ask questions about his eccentric behavior. Your father never knew, and I thought it best to keep it that way. It hasn't been easy pretending to be ignorant and blind." She started to cry, "At least now we don't have to lie to each other anymore."

"You knew? It doesn't bother you that he's a vampire?"

"If I cared, you wouldn't be here."

In an instant, years of deception melted away, and I just blurted out, "What the fuck Mom!"

"I never let on to your dad why I wasn't getting pregnant. I always knew that I could have a baby. I didn't have that much to drink that night in Chicago, and I somehow suspected who he might really be, not his name, of course, but..."

Almost on cue, the kids came scrambling into the kitchen, yelling, "Grandma!" They swarmed her, and she gave them all hugs and kisses. "I'm all right. It will be okay," she tried to soothe them with tears in her eyes. Jacques handed Piglet to her. The clueless dog licked her chin, and she managed a sad smile.

Tomas said, "We were afraid, something might happen to you too."

Marie added, "Why would someone hurt Grandpa?"

Before Jacques and Des could add to the discussion, she said, "Hush, enough now. I'll be okay. We'll talk later. Be good for your mom. I want to lay down for a few minutes."

They all got quiet and disappeared somewhere in the house. Mom went upstairs, and I told my husband to call the Magus. I went out on the porch for a few minutes to try and clear my head. My thoughts turned to the home I had grown up in, the kitchen painted in sunny yellow with rooster decorations on the walls. My mother had always tried to look like a typical Rossvillager. She wore boring, modest clothing from a local department store. Nothing exotic in the house, just maple furniture, a few antiques, family pictures, and University of Illinois Teams' sports memorabilia on the wall by the TV. No one would have guessed in a million years that for generations, her side of the family had been consorting with vampires. It must have been so hard to pretend to be normal all those years. I was glad she would be staying with us. Perhaps in time she would go back to the church, but some wounds take a long time to heal. She knew! The whole time, she knew but decided that it would make my life easier to keep the de Molay secret. I sat down, looking across the cold moonlit empty fields yet not seeing any of it.

Chapter 19

Sally the Wolf

I lost track of time, but after a while, Mom came out on the porch, flanked by the kids and Tristan.

"You should have let Grandma rest."

Des went to the end of the porch and peered around the corner then cried out, "Look, Bart opened the barn door!"

Before I could stop them, they went running down the stairs to see the wolf. I assumed she would still be too weak to pose a threat.

Mom looked at me and then Tristan and said, "I must see the wolf."

"Of course," Tristan replied, as we followed the kids into the barn.

The great wolf was on her side, lying on a bed of blankets that Bart had made for her. Batu was kneeling next to the wolf holding a jar of salve, applying it to her wounds. She looked weak and was barely able to lift her head. The kids all were wide-eyed and quiet as they stared at her.

Mom slowly walked over to the beast, hesitated, and looked down at Batu, who gave her a nod. She crouched down next to Batu and gently extended her hand toward the wolf. The wolf lifted her head; her golden eyes glistened; her breathing got louder, and she looked directly at Mom, who slowly reached out and gently rubbed the wolf's head like it was a beloved pet. She leaned down and whispered, "Thank you." She turned to Sir Bart, "Those cuts look deep; will she recover?"

He looked very solemn, "She is weak, but starting to improve. The bleeding has stopped, and she ate a little." Then with a tiny semblance of a grin, he said, "James named her Sally after a dog he had years ago."

My mother's voice started to crack, "She tried to protect Pete, we must protect her. I'm afraid that young Sheriff might try to find her."

Marie turned to her father, "We can't let anyone else hurt her!"

"She tried to save Grandpa!" Jacques cried.

"Dad, you have to do something!" Tomas added.

Des asked, "Can't we move her to a safe place?"

Tristan turned towards my mom, "Bart started making the arrangements this morning. James will arrive late tonight, then help us transport her to his home in Montana. A couple of trusted friends will assist him."

"Lithuanians?" Des asked.

Tristan looked at Des and gave a little smile, "Yes. Lithuanians."

"Mom, can we stay with Sally till she leaves?" Marie asked.

"Yeah, let us stay up tonight!" Jacques added.

Tomas joined in, "You have to let us help! We're old enough. We can help you can't we Batu?

Batu, seeing no protest, said, "I'll show you how to put salve on her wounds."

"You can help Bart and Batu, but you're not staying up all night." The kids decided not to argue their case anymore, which surprised me. Out of the corner of my eye, I noticed that Bart had raised his finger to his mouth to hush them.

Mom stood up, looked around, "I'm suddenly feeling hungry. I don't think I've eaten anything all day."

"We've got an amazing buffet in the kitchen from your neighbors. C'mon, let's all have dinner, then the kids can come back and help with Sally."

Tristan joined us. Danuta helped me set out the food in the dining room that we rarely used. The kids rushed in and grabbed plates, but my husband said, "Let your Grandmother go first."

Mom beamed at Tristan and said, "That is very gracious of you!" Mom always liked Tristan; now change that to adored. We all filled our plates and sat down to eat, except Tristan, of course. Mom said grace, just like when I was a kid, and we started eating. The mac n' cheese was comforting and helped settle my nerves. So much had happened in such a short amount of time. I had not begun to process my dad's murder. It was overwhelming, and I just tried to stay in the moment with my loved ones around me. Tristan sipped black coffee and looked at the children as though saving a sad but peaceful memory.

"I miss Grandpa. He should be here." Jacques sighed as he stared at his half-empty plate.

Mom touched his hand, "We all miss him, and it is so hard to believe he is gone." She looked around at each of her grandkids and continued, "He loved all of you and loved to spend time with you. Always remember that."

Everyone was tearing up. Through sniffles, Des said, "But he wouldn't love Mrs. Peterson's tuna casserole."

We started to laugh a little, wiping our eyes.

"Bill Benton's chili would not have been allowed in the house!" Mom added.

"But," Tomas replied, "He would have approved of Mrs. Ray's chocolate pie." He took a big slice and then passed it around.

"She would never give me the recipe," Mom grumbled.

"Try asking her now, you never know," I said. "You know that the whole town will help you in any way it can."

"I know, Randie, I'm just not ready for all that attention or pity. Tomorrow we have to make the funeral arrangements, but for now, I'm going to go unpack." She stood up and looked at the kids, "You take good care of that wolf and don't give your mother a hard time!" Then she headed up to her room. She had barely touched the food on her plate.

"Is Grandma going to be okay?' Marie asked.

"Yes. She is very strong and will surprise us all. Today your Grandma told us she knows all about the Lithuanian side of the family."

"Wow," Jacques replied.

"My sentiments exactly," Tristan stated.

"How did she know?" Des asked.

"We'll talk about it another time," Tristan replied. We finished our dessert in silence, each of us lost in our thoughts. After dinner, the kids cleared the dishes without being asked, then went with their father back to the barn to help care for the wolf.

I went upstairs to seek refuge in a long hot shower, put on a pair of old comfy blue jeans, and a Blackhawks sweatshirt my dad had given me. I went back downstairs and sat on the front steps. Piglet was sitting in my lap. It was a cool September evening, and I stared out into the darkness across the fields. My solitude was interrupted when a black Cadillac with shiny chrome wheels, matching trim, tinted windows, and Louisiana plates turned into the driveway. It was followed by a Triumph motorcycle. I did not remember seeing either that car or the bike around town. Piglet popped her head up but didn't bark which surprised me. The biker, a young man in his mid-twenties, wearing jeans, a brown leather jacket, and a WWI type helmet. Camo and Danuta were suddenly beside me. The biker dismounted, opened a saddlebag, and replaced his helmet with an old-fashioned bowler hat. He was about 5'8", clean-shaven, with shoulder-length light brown hair. I sensed he meant no harm and caught the scent of the Common Caste. Camo whispered, "It's okay; he's a friend of Ruben's."

"Howdy ma'am, I mean Baroness if I'm not mistaken." He came over, took my hand in a gallant gestured, and tipped his hat, and introduced himself with a distinctly western twang. "I'm William, Billy, to my friends."

Before I could respond, the Cadillac's door popped open, and a tall thin black man about the same age as William got out. He had short dreadlocks, was wearing a neatly pressed white dress shirt, gray slacks, and shiny black loafers. He walked over and greeted me in a similar fashion but sounded like a perfect southern gentleman, "Baroness, it's an honor. Sorry to meet under these circumstances. I'm Robert, at your service."

"I'm at a loss, I didn't know you were coming, but welcome."

Billy explained, "We're here to help with the transportation of a heroic canine," He patted Piglet's head. "My goodness, Lady Penelope, you really get around." She snorted her delight at seeing them. "She's better off with you, Baroness, than Sir Alexander."

"Thanks, the Baron is in the barn helping with the wolf, if you want to let him know you're here."

"We sure will," Robert replied, "And I'll tell him he's a lucky man."

"Thank you kindly," Billy added, tipping his bowler hat. They went off to the barn.

A cowboy and a Southern charmer, they had to be from the House of Plows. I probably should have joined them in the barn to find out what was going on and learn more about our visitors, but I was exhausted. I had tried running away from Tristan and his insane world. Unfortunately, the undead and their craziness always caught up with me. At a time like this, I wished I could be oblivious to the reality of the nocturnal world like my dad had been. Blissful ignorance sounded great to me right now.

I started to go back in the house when I noticed Tristan coming out of the barn, followed by Robert and Billy, Batu was leading two horses behind them. They walked over to the Cadillac and started pulling plastic gallon containers out of the trunk and tying them to the horses' saddles.

"What's in the jugs, and what are you doing now?" I called out.

William responded, "Making sure that Sheriff won't be able to track our furry friend."

Billy grinned, laid his hand on one of the jugs, and added, "What we have here is some of the finest wild pig stink this side of the Mississippi. It's an old cowboy trick to cover the scent."

Billy and Batu each got on a horse. Tristan handed out flashlights to Billy, Batu, and Robert then turned to me and said, "Sir Bart might need some help, the kids are washing Sally." Billy and Batu rode off in the direction of the small wooded area by the creek where the wolf had stayed. Robert and Tristan each took a jug apparently to cover the scent trail between the house and the wooded area.

"What the fuck!" I handed Piglet to Danuta. Camo and I went to the barn. Bart might be Haute Caste, but there was only one of him and four offspring.

"Mom, look, we're using organic lavender shampoo," Marie said excitedly while she gently rubbed Sally's back. The beast tried to stay standing with the help of Bart. Sally did not seem pleased but was either too weak to protest, or too fond of the kids. Jacques was washing her front legs, and Tomas had her back legs while Des started to rinse her off with a bucket.

"Be careful not to get soap in her eyes," I swear the creature looked at me with gratitude. Her wounds were less visible. She appeared to have the healing powers of the undead. I helped them gently dry her off with a big fluffy purple towel that must have belonged to Bart. He also had a hairdryer, which came in handy. The kids made a bed on the ground with some clean blankets. She slowly, tentatively laid down. The horse left behind, poked her head between the slats of the stall, and licked her head. After years of staring at each other from a distance, they had become friends.

Tomas announced, "Bart says we have to spray around the barn, inside and out to get rid of the wolf scent." Tomas handed spray bottles, filled with lavender-scented air freshener, to Marie, Des, and Jacques. He sniffed the bottle in his hand and added, "I don't want to smell like flowers." In a flash, Des began spraying Tomas, and then they were rolling in the straw beating on each other.

"Stop it!" I said, trying not to yell because of the wolf.

"I can't believe we're related," Marie said and picked up her bottle.

She and Jacques did a good job of spraying the ground around the barn while Des and Tomas sprayed each other as much as the ground. Bart and I cleaned up inside and sprayed the sweet flowery scent everywhere. The next day, Des and Tomas found their bikes had been soaked with the lavender spray, the smell lasted for weeks. I suspected it was Marie, but with those four, you never know. I was just glad they had not been given Eau de wild pig. I think doing something for Sally helped us feel less lost in grief and was glad the kids were so resilient. I started a fire in the firepit behind the house and burned all the bloody bedding and dressings. I sent the kids back to the house to get ready for bed in case they fell asleep, but that was doubtful.

I sat alone in the kitchen with the last piece of chocolate pie. "Damn monks!" I muttered and pushed the plate away. Dad should never have had to suffer at their hands. The Magus was losing control of his empire; the beheadings of the rebels the year Tristan and I had married, the kidnapping of James, the abduction of Marie when she was an infant, the snake attack, and now this. Destroying Lena had not ended the threat. I did not believe the monks acted alone. They were just willing pawns. Fortunately, they had not counted on the vamp-wolf. Yelling at the back door halted my thoughts.

"No, Baron Mordecai! Please!" Danuta pleaded, trying to block them before they made it into the house.

"Oh, my God!" I could smell them before I could see them. The mac n' cheese from dinner started to come back up. My husband, Batu, Billy and Robert were standing in the mudroom, Danuta stopping them from entering the house. "You all smell like a rotten carcass the horses pissed on! Leave your clothes and shoes outside. We'll have to burn them too."

They stared at me, a little taken back by my description. Then Billy asked, "Yes ma'am, but may we keep our undergarments on?"

"I suppose you better!" I laughed, "Go back outside. Now!"

A few minutes later, the four well-built, handsome, almost naked males paraded past Danuta and me. I think I succeeded in suppressing my laugh at seeing Billy in his underwear and his bowler hat. My husband turned to the housekeeper who was trying to keep her eyes at face level and said, "Please have our guests' luggage brought to the guest room."

We all headed upstairs. Mom was coming out of her room with swollen red eyes as we entered the hallway. She saw the guests first. Billy removed his hat and held it in front of himself. "Please excuse our current state of attire, ma'am."

"The Baroness insisted we disrobe," Robert added.

There was an uncomfortable pause, then my mom said, "I don't even want to know," shaking her head she turned around, went back in her room and closed the door. I heard her chuckle.

"That's my mother."

"Fine looking woman, if you don't mind me saying so," Robert replied.

I turned and glared at him, "Baroness, no offense meant," Robert stated.

"Not to seem ungrateful, but when are you all leaving? No offense meant, of course," I replied.

"And no offense taken," Billy replied.

"James will be arriving about midnight. They'll get provisions, load the wolf, and be on the road while it is still dark." Tristan said.

"He'll be here by midnight? That's quick."

"He flew into Chicago and is driving the Magus' RV down."

Billy looked uncomfortable, "Not to be too critical of your hospitality, but might we get more respectable before discussing our plans further?"

"Of course," my husband responded and pointed to the unoccupied guest room. Billy and Robert quickly went inside. Camo followed behind with two leather satchels. Batu went to his room.

With our guests taken care of, I checked on my mother. I quietly knocked on her door, "Mom, it's me, can I come in?"

"Of course!" I went in and found her sitting up in bed, staring out the window into the darkness. "You probably heard about James. He and the guests will be leaving during the night to take the wolf to safety at James' ranch. Do you want me to wake you when he comes?"

"I don't think I'll get much sleep tonight, anyway I want to thank him. He'll take good care of her. He's a kind man. I'll be down later."

I gave her a hug and slipped out of the room. Piglet, looking lost, was wandering around the upstairs hallway. I headed downstairs, and she followed me to the kitchen.

I thought of my poor friend James, caught in the middle of vampire drama one more time. We would always be fond of each other, but it was like someone you had a crush on in high school. Simplistic romantic affection would not be possible again. My husband trusted us to keep appropriate boundaries. That was why James could remain a F.O.V.

Even though neighbors had brought a ton of baked goods, I started baking chocolate chip cookies, James could take on the road trip. I hoped the smell of the cookies baking would help get rid of the lingering scent of pig stink. Baking seemed like a good distraction for my brain until I started remembering how my dad would tell me to add more butter and less sugar, etc. He could never cook or bake with anyone without taking control. My hands trembled, and a few tears fell on the dough. "What the fuck!"

"Miranda, let Danuta do this." Tristan had walked up behind me. He gently started rubbing my shoulders. I turned and buried my head in his chest. His strong arms provided comfort.

"I already miss him so much!" I sobbed. We stood in a sweet embrace for a few minutes. He softly rubbed my back as the tears subsided. I heard bluesy guitar music coming from the front porch. I dried my eyes with a napkin.

Danuta said, "I'll finish the cookies. They'll be good just like your father showed me." He had touched so many lives.

"Thanks Danuta, I know you miss him too."

Tristan took my hand and led me outside. Robert was playing a sad beautiful tune. The song ended as we walked outside.

"This one is just for you, Baroness." Robert started playing, 'Sweet Home Chicago,' joined by Billy on his harmonica. Suddenly I realized he was the famous delta blues musician, thought to have died almost eighty years ago. "Holy crap! You're Robert Leroy Johnson! Unbelievable!" There was a legend that he sold his soul to the devil so that he could play better.

He smiled, nodded, and never missed a note and did not stop until the song was over. "I hope we're not playing too loud. Don't mean to disturb your poor mama."

"No, you're fine. I mean great. So, I have to ask, was it the devil?"

He and Billy laughed, "Some might call him that, I just call him the Magus. He saved my sorry ass when I got poisoned."

Billy added, "Robert is not the best judge of character when it comes to the finer sex."

"I can't help it if you're more at ease with horses than beautiful women."

The banter amused my husband, but I knew I was missing something. "Billy, how did you meet the Magus and end up partnered with Robert?"

"I was working in my capacity as daytime security for the Magus when the Sheriff endeavored to cause my untimely demise. His highness came to my rescue. Just as I was fading from this world, he gave me some of his elixir of life, and then later invited me to transform. When Robert joined our gang, I was assigned to look after the greenhorn. It hasn't been easy listening to him every night, so I started playing the harmonica in self-defense."

"Wait! Billy? As in Billy The Kid?"

"At your service, ma'am. We call ourselves the House of Plows' gang, but don't let Lady Sarah know I said that she's kind of touchy."

I noticed the children had snuck down and were listening by the door. I motioned to them to come out.

Des said, "Billy the Kid is a gunslinger and a musician?"

"Harmonica player," Robert corrected him.

"Yeah, I just thought you were a good shot," Tomas added.

"Great shot," Billy corrected.

Robert rolled his eyes. The kids sat on the steps by the guests. If I had not been emotionally drained, I probably would have figured this one out sooner. I knew better than to question if it was true. If a vampire tells you something fantastic, you learn to accept it.

"It always seems to come back to the Magus," I stated.

"He ever come 'round here?" Billy asked.

"Mom won't let him," Jacques blurted out, looked at me, then regretted it.

Tristan cleared his throat, "The Magus will attend your Grandfather's funeral."

I stared at my husband, "You didn't even ask Mom or me!"

To everyone's relief the awkward moment was interrupted when an RV pulled into the drive and parked by the house.

"Uncle James!" Marie called out.

The kids ran to greet him. I gave my husband a dirty look, deciding to leave the issue of the Magus for another time and went to greet James; it was good to see my old friend, even under sad circumstances. His tan face was showing signs of aging, smile wrinkles, and a furrowed brow testified to his normalcy. He gave me a big warm hug then asked, "How is your mom doing? I'm so sorry about your father. How are you both holding up?"

I started tearing up, "She's doing better than I could have imagined, I'm still in shock. Sally is starting to improve but is still weak. Do you want to see her?"

"Yeah, poor Sally. Taking on the vampire hunters. Glad she's on our side."

Tristan came over and shook James' hand, a rare privilege for a mortal. "Thank you for helping us with the wolf."

I turned to Robert and Billy and introduced them to James. "They'll help with the driving at night and taking care of Sally."

"I'll be glad to have the company. Nice boots he said to Billy."

They did the manly nod. I said to James, "If you're lucky, Robert will play for you."

"You can't mean the 'deal with the devil' Robert Johnson?"

Robert responded, "Well, that's a long story, and my friend here is also called the Kid."

James' eyes got big. "No way! Seriously? Outlaw vampires, I never saw that coming," he just shook his head. "Anything else I should know?" I just smiled and showed him the way to the barn. Sally lifted her head and sniffed in James' direction. For a moment, I felt afraid, then James walked over and patted her head. She rubbed her muzzle against his leg. I caught my breath and relaxed. Bart and James began discussing how to transport and care for her. It amazed me how easily James interacted with the undead. I mean, once you got over the initial shock, you realize they're just like the mafia except they have superpowers and a weird diet. No big thing, human beings can normalize anything.

Tristan then turned to me, "I have to go to Danville with Robert and Billy. We won't be long." They all climbed into my Jeep and headed off into the night. Normally I would ask what they were up to but tonight I didn't even want to know.

Tristan and company arrived at the Medical Center in Danville on a mission. They located the morgue in the basement and found it easy to get past the minimal security. At that time of night, it was deserted.

Tristan quickly located Benedetto's remains. Though his neck was ripped open, his face was eerily intact. "Bastard priest! Look for Turlock." They looked under the sheets covering the two other bodies, but Pete's killer was not there. "He was here. I can smell his putrid blood tainted by our kind."

They began searching all the floors of the hospital. When a nurse sent security to question them, they just told him that a friend, Pete Ortega, had been hospitalized. The security guard checked with admissions and told them to check with the hospitals in Urbana. It was lucky he was helpful; my husband was getting hungry and impatient. They went back to the parking lot.

The trio stood by the Jeep. "There's a lingering scent here, I detect Common Caste and heavy perfume to disguise their scent," Robert observed.

Billy agreed, "Yeah, I smelled it too. Whoever the monk was working for came and got him. Apparently, they are not done with him yet. For Turlock to survive, he would have needed another shot of our blood."

"Despicable traitors!" The darkness and contempt in Tristan's voice made his comrades uncomfortable. "I must get back to the Baroness and our children. I will discuss this matter with the Magus. Tell no one."

Robert replied. "Hard to believe anyone would be so disloyal and stupid."

"We will deal with them in time," Tristan stated. "The priority is to keep my family safe."

When they got back, Tristan asked me to come with him to my office. Tristan closed the door and started dialing. "I am calling the Magus, and I want you to hear everything. I will not keep any secrets involving this matter from you." He put the Magus on speakerphone.

"Magus, I have to report our worst suspicions are true. A fresh infusion has revived Turlock. It was Common Caste blood."

"No!" I gasped.

"Miranda is here, and she must know what we are dealing with." He put his hand on my shoulder.

"Of course. We will hunt down those responsible for this tragic offense. Lady Sarah and Sir Ruben will arrive in Chicago tomorrow night. How are you, Baroness, and how are your mother and the children holding up?"

"I don't think it has hit us yet. We are just trying to cope minute by minute. Do you know who is behind this?

"He was cast out of the Vatican, and his contacts in Rome now shun him. His only support is coming from rogue vampires. It is my fault. I underestimated to what lengths they would go. We will not let our guard down again."

It was not like the Magus to admit a mistake. I wanted to scream at him, but that would not have brought my father back.

"Magus," Tristan responded, "I shall stay with my family for now."

"Good. I am bringing someone recommended by Lady Pauline for additional daytime security."

"When Turlock is located, I want to be the one who ends his miserable existence," Tristan stated flatly.

"I personally want to cut off his head!" I exclaimed.

The Magus replied, "Sir Omar has also requested to be the executioner."

Tristan smiled, "Like father, like daughter."

Then it hit me. I still had a dad in this world. My biological father was still available to the kids and me. One day I would tell them the truth. I just wasn't sure when.

"I understand the desire for an immediate response, but we must investigate this crime to find the head of the serpent. The extent of the Haute Caste involvement has been carefully concealed. We shall talk more after the funeral. Goodnight." He hung up before I could ask more questions.

"What the fuck, so who can we trust?"

"No one with anything to gain," my husband replied. "Not even your friends. Lolly contacted me recently to ask about how one becomes a vampire. She asked me not to tell you. I refused to enlighten her."

It felt like my world was crashing down around me. "Lolly!" I started crying. Tristan pulled up a chair and held my hands.

"Contact with our kind tends to accentuate qualities of mortals, good and bad. Your friend James has become heroic. Lolly and Al are struggling. For them, like for many mortals, it is hard to resist the lure of immortality." He handed me a tissue and stood, "Come, we must see to the wolf."

When we came down the front steps, everyone was standing by the RV. The kids were listening to Billy tell some story about robbing a bank. They got quiet as we approached. "It's time," Tristan said. Bart and Batu went to the barn and slowly walked back with the limping wolf. It was amazing how much she had healed since I last saw her. Des and Tomas put boards over the RV's steps to make a ramp. Bart and Batu had taken out the dining table to make room for a bed for her. Foam rubber was cut to fit the space and covered with blankets to cushion Sally from the bumps in the road. When she was settled, I came inside with the kids. We were indebted to her. Marie gave her a handful of Piglet's dog biscuits. The boys gently scratched her ears.

Mom entered the RV, knelt beside the great beast, put her arms about Sally's neck, and kissed her head, "I know you tried your best." The wolf rubbed her muzzle against my mom's arms. When Mom was stepping out of the RV, she turned to James, "Thanks, James! Sally likes cheeseburgers; I used to sneak them to her at night when I was emptying the trash at the café."

You could have knocked us over with a feather. How many more things had she been keeping from me? Then my mom went back in the house and went to bed.

Chapter 20

Full House at the Mansion

The R.V. fridge was stocked with sirloin cut up into chunks. James could cook some for himself, while the wolf and her nocturnal caretakers would eat it raw. Danuta also packed a few peanut butter sandwiches, cookies, apples, and a large thermos of coffee.

Robert parked his Cadillac by the house. Billy left his Triumph under the overhang from the barn. They both gave their keys to Batu. "Take care of my baby till I get back," Billy told him.

James looked at the vintage chopper, "Shame, you can't bring it. Lots of open country around me."

Billy sighed, "There'll be time for riding the big country after we figure out who these treasonous vampires are." He took off his hat and scratched his head. "I just can't imagine anyone being stupid enough to cross the Magus."

"I met a few of those folks, it didn't end well for them," James responded.

Billy and Robert looked surprised. Robert asked, "You witnessed the West Coast massacre?" James nodded. "Wait a minute, are you the guy the Baroness…"

James interrupted him, "We were just friends."

Billy looked eager to get started, "You can tell us all about it on the road, and don't spare any of the grisly details."

James suddenly felt a bit of pride, knowing he had impressed Billy the Kid.

Billy looked around at the assembled group seeing them off, turned to James, and said, "I guess we better hit the road." After a round of hugs and expressions of gratitude, there was barely a dry eye as they climbed into the RV and drove off into the night.

As the RV left Rossville, in downtown Indianapolis, a Mercedes sedan with darkened windows pulled up behind a limousine parked under a poorly lit underpass. A woman wearing a designer hoodie, tight black jeans, and high heels got out on the passenger side of the Mercedes. She took a deep breath of fresh air, then walked around to the driver's side. The driver, a young Chinese Common Caste vampire, lowered his window and looked back over the front seat. Turlock lay in a fetal position, covered by blood-stained sheets. The driver asked, "Lady Antoinella, what do you wish me to do with him?"

"Take him to the address in the GPS. Get him inside without being seen, then clean the car thoroughly. You may keep the car as a reward for your service. Keep him in the hotel out of sight until you hear from me." Then she looked at Turlock, "We may still have use for you, you fool, but for now, you must go into deep hiding."

Turlock croaked out a whisper, "Thank you!"

Antoinella got into the limousine and looked at her Haute Caste companion, "What a disaster. We must be much more careful now."

I did not join my husband when he retired at dawn. It was not intentional. I had fallen asleep on the couch, watching the weather channel to calm down my brain. I noticed a throw had been placed over me. At about ten in the morning, Piglet started barking. Since she had not been upset by the great wolf or vampires, I thought it must be important. Then I heard some howls in the distance as I walked out on the porch. The young Sheriff and another officer were walking towards the barn from the creek in waders with a couple bloodhounds that were sniffing the ground. "Hello, Mrs. Mordecai!" he waved.

I scrambled to get to the barn before they did. "What are you doing here?"

"Just following up on the investigation. I hope you don't mind if we check out the area, make sure no vicious wild dog has been near your place."

Piglet was jumping up in the window and barking her head off. "Just a vicious wild pug. You're welcome to look around but keep away from the barn. I don't want the horses to get spooked."

The young Sheriff was eager to make some important find in the first murder case that had come his way. "OK. We'll stay clear of the barn. Thank you, ma'am." They started to walk back towards the creek when a loud motorcycle came up the road and turned into the drive. As Camo rolled up to the house, he saw the two officers and tensed up. I noticed

Sheriff Fleming had put his hand on his holster.

"It's okay!" I called out to Fleming, "He works for me."

The Sheriff and the biker relaxed. Fleming and the other officer turned away and continued to search the grounds. The red Mohawk, and black widow tattoo on his neck made people a little judgmental. Good thing he wasn't wearing his vest.

"What in the hell are they doing here?" he asked as he continued to watch them.

"Investigating my dad's murder. I think they'll leave soon."

"If you need anything, just let me know. I mean anything," he stated quietly.

I knew what he meant. There seemed to be no shortage of people around me, alive or undead, willing, and able to make anyone disappear. I realized I would have to be more careful about what I said around them. "Just keep the kids safe."

"I hate to put such a nice ride by his pile of crap with wheels," Camo muttered as he parked next to Billy's Triumph and pulled a bag with some groceries out of a leather saddlebag.

"Good thing he isn't here," I replied.

"That was Ruben's bike before he gave it to Billy. A few years ago, back in Peoria, I pulled up to a bar, and "that" was parked outside. I went in and asked the bartender who was the wannabe biker with the piece of shit Triumph outside. Well, that's how the fight started. When I turned around and first saw him, I thought, 'This is going to be too easy!' I was amazed how strong that little sucker is. We both took some pretty good licks, and we've been bros ever since. After we were friends for a while, he let me in on his secret. He even saved my life once."

We went into the kitchen, Batu handed me a cup of coffee and Danuta put a plate of fresh biscuits on the table with butter and jam. "Comfort food, you need it," she gave me a sad smile.

Maybe it was lack of sleep, but I started to tear up. Batu and Camo looked uncomfortable. Luckily my mom broke the tension by walking into the kitchen.

"It's going to be a difficult day, what about some bacon and eggs?" She looked over at Danuta and asked, "Would you mind if I make some breakfast?" Danuta smiled and replied, "Of course, just let me know if I can help." She made not only bacon and eggs but also pancakes. I think there was enough food to feed half the town. The kids came down, and we all dug in. I ate bacon that morning, forgive me pigs, but Mom was determined to feed us.

After breakfast, Batu pulled me aside. He stood silently for a moment, looking down at the floor. "I know I failed you all. I'm sorry I did not protect your father. I will understand if you want me to leave." The sadness in his gaze went straight to my pain.

"Batu," I put my hand on his cheek, "We all feel somehow responsible for what happened, but it's not the fault of any one of us. It was the sick twisted vampire hunters who thought they were on a mission from God. They did this." I stared into his soft brown eyes, "You are a comfort to all of us. Please don't leave!"

I wanted to say more, but the kids, with their usual uncanny sense of timing, came barging in, "Batu, can we help you feed the horses?"

He smiled at me, "Sure." They all headed out to the barn. I sighed and thought about everything that we still had to do.

I spent much of the day making arrangements for the funeral. Then I hired a clean-up crew to erase the signs of the bloody struggle outside the café once the police were done with the crime scene. Mom could take her time deciding what she wanted to do with the café, and with her life. So many options that she never wanted.

That evening the Magus' jet landed at the Danville airport. Although it was expected, I did not go to the airport to greet him. My relationship with him was complicated, and he gave the term control-freak a whole new meaning. He knew a lot about survival, which is why he had reigned over the vampire world since he founded it many centuries ago. I suppose there was a lot I could learn from him if I could better control my temper. My life and my children's lives were just subplots in his grand plan. We did not always go along with his script, and I knew that frustrated him to no end. His inability to keep my dad safe only increased my distrust of his authority and control over the undead world. I always needed a reason to be obedient. Still, he had made moving to Rossville easier by supporting my decision despite Tristan's protests. I wondered why he put up with my disrespect. He usually dealt quickly and harshly with anyone rebelling against his authority. I needed to figure out what his end game was.

Bart and Tristan waited as the Magus descended from the jet. He always looked like a model for a clothing designer. He was followed by a petite woman with short dark hair, dressed in tight black exercise clothes. "My dear Baron and Sir Bart, so good of you to meet me. This is Teri, a renowned martial artist recommended by Lady Pauline to help with your daytime security."

The young woman smiled, "Glad to be able to help." She spoke quietly with a SoCal accent.

The pilot loaded the Magus' leather luggage into the Jeep then returned to the jet. Tristan took the Magus to Rossville in the Lamborghini, followed by Bart and Teri in the Jeep. He patiently waited for the Magus to start what he knew would be an awkward conversation.

"I assume that Mr. Ortega was supposed to have been a hostage. This reckless, poorly managed attack resulted in his death. Any violence towards any member of your family is an affront to me personally and to the Haute Caste. There will not be an immediate response. I know this will be difficult for Miranda, but we must carefully uncover all those who were behind this heinous act. Let them think we are satisfied that the deranged monks acted without assistance from any of our kind. I can assure you and the Baroness that I will use all my powers and resources to find and punish Turlock and his benefactors."

"Of course. I am sure you will keep me abreast of any information you uncover."

The Magus looked at Tristan's noble profile. "I know you personally want to administer justice to these traitorous criminals. I have asked the Haute Caste of the House of Plows and the House of Swords to apprehend Turlock alive. He has information that is crucial to stopping this attack on our social order. After he has been interrogated, he will pay for his crime."

"You do not trust the Haute Caste of the other Houses?"

"No. This must stay between us. I have heard rumors of alliances between traitorous members of the Haute Caste and Common Caste. I will not disclose more until I know the whole truth."

"Surely you don't suspect Sir Jorge or the other heads of the Houses." Tristan was upset by this possibility.

"I do not wish to cast doubt on those that are loyal in the Haute Caste, but there may be rebellious members in all the Houses. This is a regrettable situation, but it has been years in the making. I fear that communications with anyone in those Houses might be compromised. I am sorry this rebellion has had such tragic consequences for your family."

The kids were excited when the cars pulled up to the house. They ran down the stairs and out to the drive to greet the only person of which their father was in awe. He was tall, though not as tall as Tristan and handsome with a touch of mystery veiled in wealth. His straight black hair cut at a complimentary angle to his cheekbones. Jacques got to him first and formally extended a hand, the Magus shook it and proceeded to greet Tomas and Des in the same formal manner. Marie stood back, clearly not willing to seem that impressed. "Baroness," he nodded, and she returned the nod. He turned to me, "I am so sorry for your loss."

I looked him straight in the eye, "I don't want sympathy! I want Turlock and anyone that helped him dead!"

"Yes, of course!" he replied and walked up the steps to my mother, "No words can diminish your loss. If you need or desire anything, you've but to ask."

"Keep us in the loop," she stated plainly. "I'm done pretending vampires don't exist."

The Magus looked surprised by her response, "Whatever you wish."

"Mom," Jacques called out, "This is Teri. She's a ninja!"

"Cool!" Des added.

Bart was introducing Teri to Batu and Camo. The biker was skeptical that she could do much damage to anyone, but then that was what he had thought about Ruben. Batu and Camo had been throwing knives at a target on the side of the barn. Before I could walk over to introduce myself, she produced a throwing star and threw with such speed and accuracy it split the handle of a knife stuck in the wall.

Batu smiled, obviously impressed, "Welcome, Teri!"

"A ninja, a biker, and one of the Mongol horde. Who would mess with us now?" I shook her hand. "Welcome, Teri, there's a room off the kitchen for you. Danuta, our housekeeper, will get it ready for you."

"I'm sorry to arrive at such a sad time."

"Thanks. Still, I appreciate more security."

She smiled and said, "I'm not a ninja, just proficient in a few of the martial arts. I'm a friend of Lady Pauline. I also went to U.C.L.A. Go Bruins!"

"You know all about us?"

"Yeah. Sworn to secrecy by Lady Pauline. I took leave from my private security gig to help out. I'll stay as long as you need me."

Teri looked past me and saw Des hit Tomas with a set of nunchucks. "Oh shit! Stop that!" She ran over and grabbed the weapon out of Des' hand, turned to me, looking embarrassed, and said, "I'm so sorry, I'm not used to being around children."

"You might want to keep your weapons away from the kids. They are dangerous enough, unarmed," I warned her with a smile.

She noticed Mom staring at her, "Sorry, I'll watch my language."

Mom replied, "Hon, they've heard it before. If I were you, I wouldn't turn my back on my grandchildren."

Teri looked surprised. I added, "Welcome to Rossville."

It was good that Billy and Robert were on their way to Montana; even a mansion has a limited amount of space. Between my mom, Batu, Camo, the Magus, and Teri, our guestrooms were almost full. Danuta and Batu helped with the most recent arrivals' luggage. Mom invited anyone who wanted dinner to join us but insisted everyone gather in the living room later. As I was setting the table, she asked, "Have you called Lolly and Al?"

I was not ready to discuss my fears about my best friends growing fondness for the undead. The last thing I wanted was to have them anywhere near the Magus right now. "Not yet, I'll call them in a few days. You know how Lolly is, she'd be flying out on the next plane. I think we have enough support right now."

My phone rang. It was my biological father. I wanted a little privacy, so I went out on the front porch.

"Good evening Miranda, Anastasia is here with me." His soft, deep voice was comforting. I could picture his perfectly trimmed beard and white cloak.

"I cannot adequately express my sadness and regret that this happened. Anastasia and I are ready to help any way we can. How is your mother? How are the children?"

"She is strong. The kids are resilient. We're just coping an hour at a time," I started to get choked up.

"I'm sorry, I can't be there. It does not seem appropriate."

"You're right. Not yet, but Mom told me today she knows all about Tristan's side of the family. She has been feigning ignorance for years."

"She is very good at keeping secrets," he replied. "Did she mention me?"

"I want to have a long talk with her, but now doesn't seem like the right time."

"I'll abide by whatever you think best. The Magus has requested we help find those who are responsible. We feel it is our duty."

"Thanks. It helps to hear from you and know you're doing what I wish I could do."

Anastasia finally spoke, "Dear Miranda, you must leave the pursuit of justice to us. You must take care of yourself and help your loved ones heal. Hug your children for us."

"I will. Love you both!"

"Stay well, dear daughter," and we hung up.

I have never met anyone more stoic than Omar. Even though he appeared a bit younger than me, he gave the impression of great wisdom and maturity. He showed his dedication once by beheading two vampires who tried to harm me during the Common Caste attempted coup.

Anastasia used graceful gestures and spoke with a royal Russian purr, but if crossed, she could be scarier than Omar. They could not have seemed more opposite except that they took pride in their assassin skills. Anastasia took it personally that someone had killed a family member. They had my back.

I went upstairs to take a shower and change for dinner. On the wall of my bedroom was a framed Tarot card, the Empress, given to me by the Magus. I was not feeling very royal. The Haute Caste invented Tarot cards as a way for the undead to send coded messages. Common Caste could make a living using them to tell fortunes. In some cases, vampires could make the fortunes they were telling come true. "Your husband who beats you will not live long." The traditional Tarot decks did not include North America's House of Plows, or Central and South America's House of Arrows. The vampires periodically modified the traditional decks to suit their needs over the centuries.

The House of Pentacles in Europe had become involved in a plot to usurp power from the Magus, using Common Caste rebels, heads rolled as a result, literally. The Death card was used by the Magus when he announced his response to their misdeeds. Despite their amazing healing abilities, decapitation will destroy a vampire. The Magus was the actual inventor of what came to be called the guillotine. It was just another way vampires decided to "help" humankind. Though I could understand that the Common Caste rebels felt relegated to second class status, they had lost any chance of my support when they killed my father. Their desire for power and status had risen to lethal stupidity. I would use all the power of my position as the Baroness to protect my loved ones. My husband's Tarot card was the Emperor. He preferred going by Baron, as it could be used around mortals. Besides, he was the bastard son of a Lithuanian Baroness back in the day. Perhaps a time would come when I would turn in my Empress card and separate myself totally from the Magus, but I needed that authority now.

Chapter 21

Mom vs. the Magus

I put on a black sweater and black jeans. Though I hadn't planned it, it seemed appropriate wearing all black. As I came down the stairs, I was greeted by a familiar smell. Mom had helped Danuta cook a large pot of chicken and noodles, comfort food from my childhood. I continued to give up my vegetarian diet to avoid insulting Mom's cooking. Okay, so I was enjoying my expanded diet a little. We had quite a gathering at the table: Teri, Camo, Batu, Danuta, my mom, the kids, and me. The undead took a pass as there was no reason for the vampires to show up and pretend to be on a liquid diet.

Everyone ate except for Mom; she just played with the food on her plate. My parents had been together for thirty-seven years. I could have strangled Turlock with my bare hands at that moment. My biological father's darker side DNA was slowly but surely asserting itself. I was aware that I had become much stronger, with faster reactions and an increased ability to read people. I also found my hearing and vision sharper and my sense of smell greatly strengthened. I could even detect the blood types of the people around me. The scents of my children comforted me. I walked around the table, going for another helping of noodles but lingered near Teri. I became aware someone else in the room was HH. I wondered how much Pauline had told her about the Haute Caste obsession with her rare blood type. Tristan walked into the dining room and requested that the family meet with him, the Magus, and Bart.

I looked at Mom. She cleared her throat and said, "At ten o'clock in the living room. I need a little time to prepare."

"Of course," Tristan stated and turned around.

My mother went up to her room while the kids and I helped Danuta clean up after dinner. Teri, Camo, and Batu walked around outside to make what would become a nightly security check. Then the kids went off to the game room, and I hid in my office for an hour. The people who had harmed us were patient. The snake attack had been several years ago. I could not believe they wanted to kill my father. It made no sense. The monks had probably overreacted when my dad fought back. For an instant, I saw a vision of him struggle for his life. "No!" I cried. Tears streamed down my face. It took half an hour for me to recover from the avalanche of emotion. I laid my head on the desk and closed my eyes. I focused on my breathing and slowed down my heart rate. By the time we were ready for the meeting, I had recovered, but my eyes were red.

At ten o'clock, the family, the Magus, and Bart gathered in the living room. Our mortal protectors stayed out on the porch. An uncomfortable silence filled the room as everyone waited for someone to break the ice. Mom sat in an overstuffed chair across from the Magus, who was sitting in a matching chair. Tristan sat at his right side in his antique carved chair with gold upholstery that I called his throne. Bart was next to me on the love seat, and all the kids had crammed in on the sofa facing us. Mom stared at the Magus, who looked back at her with his usual unflappable calm demeanor.

Finally, she started, "I have a lot of questions, but I won't try and get them all answered tonight. What I must know now is how you're going to make this right. A long time ago, a promise was made to protect the de Molay descendants. In the past, your kind has always protected us. Are you going to keep your promise now? How will you guarantee my family's safety since you and your lords of the night couldn't stop a crazy fanatic from killing my husband?" Then in typical Midwest politeness, she added, "That being said, I do want to thank you for coming for the funeral. It will be just after sunset tomorrow."

My husband was visibly mortified that my mother had taken the Magus to task and insulted the head of the vampire world. I was amused and wanted to applaud but restrained myself. The kids kept looking from Mom to the Magus as if they were keeping score.

"Mrs. Ortega," he spoke with a solemn expression, "Let me start by saying that I take personal responsibility for what has happened. Over time we focused our efforts on safeguarding your daughter and grandchildren. To my deep regret, we did not consider an appalling daytime attack on you or your husband as a possibility. We are now providing more protection for all of you and your close friends. We are also in pursuit of those responsible, and we will not stop until they are brought to justice. I would strongly urge all of you to return to Bel Air with the Baron, where we can provide a much higher level of security."

"That's not going to happen," I glared at the Magus.

Tristan cleared his throat, "The children would have excellent private schools there, and they would begin to assimilate with our greater community, forging relationships that could help protect them."

I turned to Tristan, "At the Narcissus Club? They are too young to be hanging out in your macabre, vampire nightclub."

He tried another tack. Tristan turned to the children crowded together on the velvet couch. "I would like to know your preferences. What do you want?"

"Ice cream!" Mom said as she turned and glared at Tristan before the kids could say anything, "They would want a gallon of chocolate chip ice cream each and eat so much they'd get sick. Why would you ask them that? They aren't old enough to choose what is good for them."

"I like Bel Air," Des called out, Marie elbowed him in the ribs.

My husband knew the kids would choose the big city over Rossville. I feared all that exposure to vampire culture at such an impressionable age would make it difficult to make an independent decision about transforming when they grew up. The Haute Caste could be very cool and attractive to adults, let alone preteens and teens.

The Magus tried to calm things down. "Perhaps we should defer the discussion to another time. Mrs. Ortega, could you kindly tell us about the funeral arrangements?"

She sat up straight, and her eyes began to well with tears. "There will not be a viewing of his body. At sunset, we will lay his remains to rest by the grove at the west end of the property." She dabbed her eyes.

Jacques responded, "Grandpa used to help us find arrowheads there, by the creek."

Mom smiled, "I told the priest he would not be needed. I want a small private service for the family. We didn't invite anyone from the community except Katy and Josh. For those of you that don't know, Pete was an only child, and his parents died when he was very young. He barely remembered them, except memories of lots of hugs, and loud laughter during the tamale-making around Christmas. He was raised by a doting grandmother who passed away while he was in the navy. Sadly, his parents were also only children, and his grandmother was the last of his family. I have changed my mind and asked Father Martino to honor Pete at mass on Sunday."

"May I order flowers?" the Magus asked. It was strange to hear him ask permission of a mortal.

"Yes. That would be nice. Pete liked roses and lilies." She was starting to cry, "Randie, will you explain the ceremony?" She stood and went to the kitchen.

The kids looked at each other, and almost in unison said, "I'm gonna go help grandma." They took off with Piglet.

I was fighting back tears. The kid's actions gave me hope for their futures. The Magus, Bart, and my husband sat in an uncomfortable silence broken only by Mom's muffled sobs from the kitchen. I got choked up as tears welled up in my eyes. The Magus handed me a black silk handkerchief that smelled faintly of spice. They waited as I regained my composure.

"Thanks," I started to hand it back, but he waved it off. "Tristan, my mom asked if you would start by saying a few words tomorrow. Then she will speak. The kids will take turns reading parts of the Lord's Prayer. I'll finish with a passage from a book."

"Yes. Of course. Is there anything else you will need?" the Magus asked.

"Tell me when Turlock is in hell. Now, I'm going to check on Mom and supervise the kids as they pretend to go to bed." My husband stood and kissed my cheek as I left the room.

Bart finally spoke, "If the rebels knew the Baroness or her mother, they would never have attacked."

Tristan replied, "I think I liked it better when Connie acted like we were eccentric mortals." He sat back down in his chair and faced the others, "I never realized how much Miranda is like her mother."

"They are wounded," the Magus stated. "Wounded animals are very dangerous. Our opponents know they made a grave error in putting their faith in Turlock's ability to carry out their plan. It will be some time before they strike again while they plot their next move. I thought destroying Lena, and her conspirators would be enough to stop the uprisings. Unfortunately, it seems to have made them bolder."

Tristan responded, "Surely, the loyal members of the Common Caste will aid us in finding Turlock."

The Magus looked pensive, "How many of the Common Caste do you know well? How many have you spent time in serious conversation with?"

"Truthfully not many, Sergio comes to mind, but we beheaded him," Tristan struggled to answer the question. He stood and walked to the window that looked out. "Are we that out of touch?"

"I don't spend much time in conversation with many Haute Caste either, except for the Baroness and your children. They are fascinating," Bart responded. "However, I have a dear Common Caste acquaintance, Jeanne."

The Magus responded, "Yes. I have spoken with her; she was helpful with the Vatican. She was not happy about the snake attack on the Baroness. When Jeanne hears about Mr. Ortega, I'm sure she will be willing to do whatever she can to protect the children. We must develop closer relationships with the loyal Common Caste to keep them from turning against us. Lady Anastasia had warned me to consider their complaints. I thought she was reacting to her own family's tragedy, but I was mistaken. The dissent is more widespread than the Common Caste of the House of Pentacles."

Bart continued, "I must speak plainly, the last time I was near Sir Alexander I picked up thoughts of unrequited ambition."

The Magus nodded, "I have been tracking some of his activities, but he has carefully hidden his intentions from me. There have been some reports of unsanctioned transformations, but I have not been able to prove this. Tristan, I know that you had a falling out with Antoinella, but she is back in Los Angeles asking about your return. I believe she is involved with those of the Common Caste harboring resentment. I do not wish to upset the Baroness, but you might be able to persuade her to cooperate with us."

"My tolerance for Antoinella's demanding nature and petulant behavior has significantly decreased."

"Perhaps just focus on her sexual prowess."

Bart shook his head, "Be prepared for your wife to find out. She is allowing her telepathic abilities to grow stronger. She hopes it will help her protect the children."

Tristan shook his head, "I believe my next encounter with Antoinella will involve instilling fear of the Haute Caste. The Baroness will not object to that."

The Magus mused, "That might be a better approach." The Magus turned to Bart, "I believe you have some contacts in the Far East who may have information about the rumors of unsanctioned transformations, would you look into this? Bart nodded. I will ask Batu for his assistance as well."

Bart and Tristan looked surprised. Bart responded, "The House of Cups?"

"I have made several inquiries but have not been able to find out who is involved. This is too serious for baseless accusations. I give you this task because I trust your ability to remain discrete."

"Of course," Bart stated solemnly.

Tristan shook his head, "I don't understand. They chose to become vampires knowing they had a lesser blood type. They chose to become Common Caste. They are all wealthy, and they are immortal, they want for nothing."

"Except respect," Bart stated. "The HH blood indeed gives us certain gifts, but perhaps it is time to admit the Common Caste have unique abilities as well."

"Pray, tell us what they are," The Magus responded with a touch of sarcasm.

Bart smiled, "They are quite good at going unnoticed, using our self-importance to their advantage. Our current crisis comes from centuries of ignoring the desires of most of the vampires in existence. Dear Magus, we are in the minority. They know so much about us, yet their existence is invisible to us. Who are the Common Caste leaders?"

"Who are their leaders?" Tristan exclaimed, "We are!"

The Magus held up his hand to silence Tristan. He sat quietly for a moment, considering what Bart had said. "There are a few tiers of power in our society. Some of the Common Caste have more social influence than we have realized. I will consider your input, but at the moment, they have used their stealth to kill an innocent. They broke our code of conduct."

Tristan said, "I believe that was an abduction that went terribly wrong. I think they wanted a hostage, not a kill."

The Magus continued, "They want me to look vulnerable. I must question Turlock! I will not ignore the threats to our society. Bart, thank you for your honesty. Tristan, once again, I extend my condolences. Excuse me as I have to attend to some business. Good evening."

They bowed as the Magus left. Tristan walked over and stared into the fireplace. "I thought that Lena, the second most ancient vampire, would be the only one ever to challenge him. I was sure this insanity would stop after the Magus disposed of her. If they had any idea of his powers, they would be loyal. I have seen him make a beating heart burst by merely holding his hand over a traitorous vampire's chest."

Bart touched Tristan's shoulder, "I have some sense of his great abilities, but for me, it is about honor, respect, and gratitude. He passed on the gift of immortality to us all. I am forever in his debt." He went to the door, "Excuse me, I must contact Jeanne and renew some old friendships in the East."

Tristan sighed, "Now I must write a eulogy, a task I am ill-equipped to undertake. It will be my first funeral."

The vampires were busy contacting their trusted sources all over the world to find out more about the threats to the Haute Caste. Odd that the demise of a mere mortal bothered them so much. Their rules insisted that a meeting would be called to determine if a mortal was so despicable, they should be removed from the general population. There were exceptions for the Haute Caste like Jorge taking out a terrorist, but never for the Common Caste. It was more difficult for them to get permission. They were not given the same respect and freedom as the Haute Caste.

The Magus reminded me of the French king during the revolution. It did not end well for him. I could not blindly trust the Magus' ability to make sure we were safe. I had to protect my family better. I was sure the vampire class war was connected to my father's murder. I had seen the Haute Caste flip a coin to see who would have the honor to be the assassin once a 'Worthy Target,' as they called their victims, was chosen. Turlock was the Most 'Worthy Target' in my book.

Later that night, sitting alone in the kitchen, I heard a car coming up the driveway. I was not concerned knowing the Magus, Tristan, and Bart were awake. A Mustang Shelby parked in front of the house. As it pulled up, Camo, Batu, and Teri came around the house and approached the car. Ruben got out and gave high fives to them. He came into the kitchen. "Why are you sitting here alone? Where are the most powerful hanging out?" He stood in the doorway, dressed like a rock band roadie and dropped his leather backpack on the floor, and smiled at me. "Did I miss the funeral?"

"I guess my mom forgot to call you before she made arrangements."

Rare self-awareness swept over him, "I'm sorry, Miranda."

I had to smile, though tears were in my eyes. I walked over and gave him a big hug. "Thanks for coming. It's tomorrow at sunset. Is Sarah coming?"

"Um, well," he lowered his voice, "She thought your mom might recognize her. She used to flirt with your dad when she was working undercover as a waitress to cause some friction between your parents, you know, so your mom might get involved with Sir Omar."

"Good point. I'd forgotten about her role in all of this. My mom knows a lot more than any of us ever suspected. She said she has known you all were vamps from the beginning and just pretended ignorance for my dad's sake."

"Wow! That was a seriously good job of seeming clueless. What do you mean, you all, Ms. Half-blood member of the House of Swords?"

"I'm still a mere mortal," I took a bite of a brownie.

"There's a solution for that," he opened the fridge and pulled out a chunk of raw steak. "Yum!" We both sat at the kitchen table. "Your hair is really short, that must have pissed off the Baron."

I loved his lack of tact. "You think? He'll adjust. I like it this way because it's easy to deal with."

"I'm glad you have at least one thing in your life that's easy to deal with. Where's the Magus?"

"They're all trying to figure out how the fuck they didn't see this coming."

"Yeah, Sarah is hunting down Turlock. Maybe apprehending him might help her get in your mom's good graces."

"Fat chance. We're not big on forgiveness."

"That's true," Mom said from the doorway. "I remember you. You were the drifter who took odd jobs."

"Ruben," he stood and bowed to her, "at your service." He ran his fingers through his unruly auburn curls. "My condolences."

"Thank you," she replied with a grim smile.

"Sir Ruben," I added. "He looked after me at UCLA."

"May I attend the funeral? I admired your husband's kindness."

"Yes, but what were you saying about forgiveness?" she asked me.

"I was talking about Turlock, Mom, no one will forgive him."

She walked over to the stove, "I'm not hungry, but I'm going to fix some eggs because I have to eat to take care of my family." She looked over at Ruben, "Why don't you go help my son-in-law figure out what the hell can be done to protect us."

"Yes, ma'am," without another word, Ruben took his backpack and went upstairs.

The mortal guardians came into the kitchen. Danuta tried to help my mom, but she waved her off. "Go get some rest while you can."

They all left except Batu. "Baroness, I locked the gates. Here are the keys to the Cadillac," as he placed them on the table.

I handed them back to him. "You can give them to Teri to use until Robert comes back. You might want to clean out the trunk, it probably still stinks from the pig stuff."

"I'll get the kids on it," he smiled. "Goodnight." His gaze lingered on me for a moment like he wanted to say more, but he changed his mind and went to bed.

Mom turned to me. "There's something special about him."

"That's the truth." I kissed her cheek, "I have to go to bed. Wake me if you need anything."

I went straight to my room. I was beyond being polite to my husband. I fell asleep as soon as my head hit the pillow. A few hours later, Tristan came to my bed. I felt him lay beside me naked. I've been told all undead like to sleep naked. He gently rubbed my back. I turned away on my side. The normal sequence of events did not follow.

"Go away."

"I want to comfort you."

"You just want to get laid. Go away."

He stopped rubbing my back and sat up. "I'm also experiencing loss. I just want to hold you."

"Fucking won't bring him back. Leave me alone."

He stood up and quickly got dressed. "As you wish."

I hoped he would control his temper. I knew he was close to breaking things. I heard a door slam. He would not raise a hand to the kids or me, but I had seen him throw a desk across a room. I breathed a sigh of relief. I had done it. I had refused him. I loved him but could not stand him at the moment. Aging and emotional maturity went hand in hand, which explained a lot about vampires. It would be hard to get back to sleep. Soon we would bury my father.

Chapter 22

The Funeral

The day passed quickly because I stayed busy. I coached the kids with their parts and gave them emotional support, helped Danuta make Barbacoa tacos for our gathering after the funeral, and Mom and I made some final decisions for the ceremony. All day people were coming and going, the staff from the funeral home came to prepare the gravesite, the Magus had two dozen large containers of assorted hues of roses and lilies delivered. The garden center staff planted them around the empty waiting grave while we hung lanterns from the trees. Everyone quietly went about the sad day's tasks with little conversation.

I was pleased to see Batu and Camo helping the kids exercise the horses. It was a good distraction for them, and for a change, they were all getting along well. Everyone needed a little distraction today. The kids were bonded with their horses, and Marie shared her stallion with Jacques since he didn't yet have his own. The amazing steeds that Sir Omar had given us would nuzzle the kids and almost knock them over at times. Tristan would never experience these every day, simple daytime joys with his children.

As sunset drew closer, the kids and I went in the house to get cleaned up and change. An hour later, the Haute Caste emerged from their rooms dressed in their finest, even Bart and Camo had cleaned up nicely. The boys looked stiff and uncomfortable in their rarely worn dress clothes. Marie had insisted on wearing black pants and a jacket too. Mom wore a lavender dress last worn on their wedding anniversary, and a single strand of pearls. I chose a gray sweater and gray slacks with no jewelry which suited my mood. Danuta wore a simple black dress, and Batu wore a buttoned-up black shirt and black pants with his hair tied back, reminding me of an Amish farmer. Batu stared at me for a long moment, and then he looked over at Tristan. Tristan noticed, and Batu tried to look anywhere but at Tristan or me.

Earlier, the hearse carrying my dad arrived as the prairie was starting to darken. Batu had directed them to the stand of trees where dad would be buried. Funeral staff had done their best to accommodate our wishes. They had never arranged a funeral quite like this one. By the time everyone began to walk to the gravesite, all the lanterns were lit, the casket in place, and the chairs arranged. They stood quietly at a discrete distance to give us privacy. Josh and Katy arrived, and their hugs started tears flowing. Teri, Camo, and Batu positioned themselves around the perimeter of the assembly so they could keep watch over us.

Just as we assembled, a limousine with dark tinted windows came racing down the driveway. It came to a sudden stop in front of the house. Teri, Camo, and Batu quickly moved to the driveway and surrounded the unexpected vehicle. A chauffeur got out and opened the passenger door.

Tristan, Bart, and I walked towards the visitor. Jorge waved to us as he stepped out of the limo. Everyone relaxed. Then to my added surprise, Franco climbed out after him. Both were wearing sunglasses and fedoras; they reminded me of the Blues Brothers.

"I told you Jorge. You should have given me a chance to change. I'm just not dressed..."

"Franco, not now! Miranda's father won't care what you're wearing. It's not about you. We are already late."

Shaking my head, I went over and hugged them both. "You're back together?"

"Jorge called me about Pete. I felt I had to come. I'm so sorry. It made me think about what I had lost. I left Alex." He removed his hat and smoothed his short black hair. Piglet came running up to Franco. He picked her up despite her muddy paws, "Penelope, you little slut." He scratched her head.

Jorge continued. "It's complicated. Miranda, we were so sad to hear of this tragedy." Then he turned to Tristan, "My sincere condolences. We have much to talk about later."

We walked back to the grave in silence. I sat next to Mom, and she took my hand. Everyone else got settled. My husband looked to my mother for permission to start. It was strange to see the Haute Caste waiting on a mortal. She nodded to begin. Tristan moved next to the casket and faced the mourners. "It is with sadness that I say goodbye to a man who taught me about the greatness and joy of being a father. He raised my wife with love, kindness, patience, and unselfish devotion. I will try and do the same for his grandchildren. Every attempt will be made to find a just resolution to this untimely loss. Pete, you will be dearly missed." He came over and stood in front of my mother, clearly uncomfortable and not knowing what to do now. Mom stood up and thanked him for his kind words, and he sat down next to me. Not a dry eye in the crowd, except for the Magus, who bore a grim expression.

Mom took a couple of steps toward the casket and began, "You were not supposed to leave me this way. You were not supposed to leave me so soon. I know in my heart you are watching us from a better place. We went through heaven and hell together, and still, our love thrived. You were so trusting, always wanting to see the best in people. Sometimes your optimism was too much for me, but it gave you strength, and you gave me strength. When you decided that you wanted to open a café and the bank would not give you a loan, you worked double shifts to save up for the café. I was so proud of you when the café succeeded. You supported Miranda's dreams of being a writer instead of staying here and managing the café. Even though I knew you were right, I never told you that. I have a lot more to say, my sweet Pete, but as you often harped on having to wait for me, you'll have to wait one last time to hear the rest."

She reached out and put her hand on the casket, and we all sat in silence for a moment. I went over to her and put my arm around Mom's shoulders, she turned to me, and we hugged, I think we were holding each other up. We walked back and sat down, still holding each other's hands.

The kids each read part of the Lord's Prayer. Their voices cracked at times, but they all managed to get through their parts. Sadly, coping with their first big loss made them grow up that night.

The House at Pooh Corner was a favorite book of mine. Dad had read it to me, and I read it many times over the years to the kids when they were younger. "If ever there is a tomorrow when we're not together… there is something you must remember." I paused to wipe tears away. "You are braver than you believe, stronger than you seem, and smarter than you think. But the most important thing is…I'll always be with you." I looked at my mom and the kids through tears. "We will miss him terribly, but his memory will always comfort us."

Mom and the kids ran up to me for a group hug, Tristan stood nearby and seemed to be fighting back tears. Jacques turned and ran to his father, hugged him fiercely. My husband picked him up and held him tightly, and the other siblings hugged Mom. Tristan put Jacques down and held me. I welcomed his embrace. This was the comfort from him that I needed. I saw Bart turn away, so no one would see him cry. For a few minutes, there was only the sound of the night and a few sniffles to be heard. Mom looked at the kids and said, "Let's go back to the house; it's getting chilly." She walked back, surrounded by her grandchildren. Josh and Katy followed them to the house. Jorge and Franco walked behind the others, talking quietly with the Magus. I told Tristan to go back to the house. I'd join them all soon.

I stood alone by the grave while the funeral home staff waited patiently at a discrete distance. The lanterns were burning low. The cold air that I had ignored now engulfed me. A sudden chill made me shudder. I placed a single yellow rose on the coffin. "Damn it!" It was my dad's favorite curse. "I'll miss you, Dad!" I walked slowly back to the house.

Josh and Katy were waiting on the back deck. Josh asked, "How are you holding up?"

"I don't know, ask me again tomorrow. Thanks for coming."

Katy said, "Everyone in town loved your father. Don't be a stranger, call me next week and we'll go for coffee."

"I will. Thanks." I watched them drive away and wished I could leave too. I was not surprised they did not stay. Sometimes there was something about vampires that was off-putting even when you didn't know what they were. Maybe it was the lack of warmth. Batu, Teri, and Camo were going to stay outside watching, but I insisted they join us. I told them that with all the assembled undead around I was sure we would be safe. We brought more chairs from other rooms to the dining table. The vampires had silver goblets and waited for the rest of us to get drinks. Jacques raised a glass of ginger ale, "To the best Grandpa!"

We all took a sip. Tomas chimed in, "To Grandma too!"

We all took another sip. Marie added, "And all our family and friends!"

Then before we drank again, Des said, "And Grandpa's tacos that we'll eat soon!"

The mood lifted as I helped Danuta bring platters of tacos to the table. The kids helped by putting bowls of guacamole, salsa, and frijoles near the mortals and plates of small pieces of raw beef for the undead. Tristan sat beside me, gently touched my hand, and whispered, "After being abandoned as a child, I never had a real family, but you have taught me what a family feels like." I wished he was not so damned handsome and did not smell so good. I had been trying to distance myself from him. Showing his human side was not making it easier for me.

Franco and Ruben did their best to distract Mom by telling her of their 'horrible' trips to Rossville when I was growing up. The Magus and Jorge were deep in quiet conversation at the far end of the table. I don't think they meant me to hear, but apparently among other heightened senses, my hearing had improved.

Jorge whispered to the Magus, "Franco wants to come back. He said that Pete's death was not part of the plan. He does not know of Turlock's location, but he is ready to tell us what Alexander has been up to."

The Magus looked around the table then whispered, "You and

Franco will come to see me in L.A. when you return. You may tell him I will forgive any association with rogue vampires if he cooperates fully."

"Of course. Thank you, dear Magus. He does not deserve your kindness."

The Magus responded, "He may yet earn it."

The Magus drained his goblet and stood. "Please excuse me. I must be going." He came over to Mom and me, "No matter how long it takes, I will make sure that all those involved will be found and dealt with harshly. You have my word." The Magus did something I had never seen before; he gave a small bow to my mortal mother. When I saw the look of surprise on the other vampire's faces, I realized this was indeed a rare event. Then he leaned down and kissed her cheek. Even she knew this was an unusual show of affection from the head of the vampire world, looked at him for a moment then said, "I appreciate your support on this very sad night."

The Magus turned from the table and left the house without another word. Tristan and Bart excused themselves to accompany him to the airport.

Mom turned to Danuta, "Perhaps we could have some cake now."

Later, Mom and I sat in the living room while the kids went to their game room. Batu, Teri, and Camo helped Danuta in the kitchen. Jorge, Franco, and Ruben went upstairs to check on the vampire world online.

We looked at the fire burning brightly. My mother spoke first, "I knew he was the Magus that day we met him at Tristan's, years ago. My grandmother had told me about him. That pompous ass better find the killer."

"Mom!" I took a breath, surprised at her lack of tact. "I'm glad you didn't call him that to his face. Not that I disagree. He is the most powerful vampire. I can't believe he bowed to you and kissed your cheek."

"I was more surprised when I saw your husband cry. That was good for the children to see. Give him a chance, Miranda. I know things between you two are strained. Your dad always liked 'Stan.' He is not used to dealing with the emotions of us mortals. He isn't responsible for what happened. He's trying to figure out how to protect us and get justice for Pete."

"I hear you, but I'm not going to talk about my marriage tonight. I want to talk about you. Do you want to keep the café going? Will you let us help with it? Batu, Camo, Teri, and Danuta want to pitch in, and even the kids want to help."

She touched my hands. "I don't think I want to let it stay closed for long. Your dad loved that place so much. Danuta's a good cook, but what are the others going to do?"

"We'll figure it out. Camo likes to bake bread, Batu would make a great waiter Teri could run the cash register and help at the counter. The kids could hang out after school and help with the dishes. I think it would be good for all of us. You still have your part-time help from town."

"It will take a small army to replace your father, but we'll try. Give me a little time to figure it out."

"Mom, take as long as you want."

I left Rossville years ago because I did not want to spend my life working in the café. Now I welcomed the normalcy it would bring to our lives. Having the café reopen might help the town get over their fears after the murder. It did not have to make money. It just had to help Mom heal. We went to check on the kids, and after lots of teary hugs, she went to her room.

"Hey guys, I have to tell you something."

Tomas switched off the game, and Des looked at his brother, "Sure, you did that 'cause you're losing."

Tomas poked him, "Shut up and listen to Mom!"

It made me smile to see how quickly they were returning to normal. "I just want to say that you all did great today." I wiped my eyes with my sleeve. "I'm proud of you all, and Grandpa would have been proud of you too."

Marie asked, "We heard that one of the killers got away. Is that true?"

"Who said that?"

"We heard Dad talking to Bart about going after some guy called Turlock."

I sighed and realized that I couldn't keep the truth from them. They were always a step ahead. "Yes, it's true, he escaped. Until we catch him, you have to listen to Batu, Camo, and Teri. They are doing everything they can to keep us all safe. So do what they say."

Jacques spoke up, "The Magus and Dad will get him, right?"

"Yes, they will, and the others will help. Omar, Anastasia, Sarah, Jorge, and all the rest are doing everything they can."

"We don't know what to tell our friends about it," Tomas said.

"Just tell them someone tried to kidnap your Grandpa because your dad is rich, and it went wrong. That is the truth. It went terribly wrong."

"Nothing will be the same," Des quietly said, looking at the floor.

Tomas asked, "Will grandma be ok?"

"She is stronger than we all think. We talked about the café, and I volunteered all of you to wash dishes. That made her smile."

"I'll help grandma!" Jacques said.

Des responded, "Maybe I can be a food taster instead."

I told them they had half an hour before they had to go to bed and left them to their own devices. I thanked God for my kids.

At midnight I made the rounds to say goodnight to all the guests. The mortals had already turned in. My husband was on the front porch speaking with Jorge, Franco, and Ruben.

I smiled at Franco, "I'm glad you're back in the family. One good thing has come from this tragedy."

"Miranda, I was shocked when I heard the news. I'm so sorry that was what it took to see I needed to leave that egomaniac Alexander."

Tristan said, "I need to talk with my wife. We'll make plans to gather in Los Angeles later."

"Of course," Jorge said, and they went into the house.

"I'm freezing." I went inside and started to go to the kitchen for a hot cup of decaf, but Tristan insisted we go up to his suite for privacy.

He sat on the four-poster bed and motioned for me. I sat in the stuffed chair facing him. "Jorge is not the forgiving type."

Tristan shook his head, "He's the 'make you pay for years type.' What about you? Do you still refuse my touch? Do you hold me responsible?"

"My father was murdered! This is not about you. I'm in too much pain to want to fuck. Don't you understand?"

He laid on the bed on his side. It was a very seductive pose. "At least let me hold you."

"You're such an asshole. You just don't get it. I want a separation. I'm not saying a divorce, but I don't want full contact either. It's not just my father's death. I've been struggling with my feelings for a while now. You can still be here for the kids, but I need space."

"You speak as though I have no say in this!" He was getting louder. "What about my feelings?"

"Let Antoinella or some other vampiress take care of them!"

He sat up, "This is about petty jealousy? You're still trying to punish me for having sexual relationships when you abandoned me to move here?"

"First of all, keep your voice down. I left you to raise the kids away from your insane lifestyle. I did it to protect our children. I did not do it to create an excuse for you to be unfaithful. You have no clue all the ways you have impacted my life. I need some time to clear my mind and grieve. Is that too much to ask?"

He stood and faced me, "Perhaps you'll allow Batu to comfort you. Maybe you shouldn't transform so I can have some peace of mind when your mortal life span has ended!"

"How could you!" I threw a glass vase, and it just missed his head before it crashed against the wall.

Mom opened the door, "Quiet! Both of you before your children realize what self-centered fools you both are being!"

One of the kids yelled from down the hall, "Tell 'em, grandma!" Muted laughter followed.

Ruben appeared in the hall.

"Not to mention the guests," she added.

"We already know," he looked at Tristan and immediately regretted his remark. He held out a phone and said, "Baron, there's a phone call about Turlock."

Nothing could have taken the focus off that awkward moment more than news about my Dad's killer. My mother and I were ushered out while Ruben handed him the phone and closed the door, promising an update.

Chapter 23

Turlock is Found

I wanted to stay in the room and hear the phone call about Turlock, but I decided not to start another argument. Mom and I went down to the kitchen to wait for news.

"I'm sorry, Mom. The last thing you needed tonight was more drama. I tried to avoid him, but that was fairly pointless." I made myself a rare cup of decaf. My hands were trembling.

"How long have you been married? Fifteen years? I threw a coffee mug at Pete after six months." She started making a cup of tea.

I almost said that Dad never deserved it but remembered his affair. "It's not the first time. I threw something at him right after we met, but he has great reactions."

"Randie, that man may be brilliant, but he is clueless. Vampires are self-centered teenagers forever. Not all that different than when they were mortals, I guess. After all those centuries, I bet you and the kids are the only people he has ever really cared about." She sat down and began dunking her tea bag. I knew she was anxious about the phone call.

"They're strong, lethal, weird, and wealthy egomaniacs." I poured my coffee and sat next to her. "You know I do love him, but being in love, that's another matter."

"Right now, he is trying to help find Pete's killer. I hope he succeeds. I'll sleep better when that happens. Like it or not, we need them."

Jorge and Franco came into the kitchen, and Jorge asked. "Any news?"

Franco sighed, "I will do anything I can to help. Your family shouldn't be caught up in our spats. He was such a fine man."

Tristan quietly entered, followed by Ruben, "They found him in Memphis. Lady Sarah and other members of the House of Plows have located him. They are aware the Magus wishes he be taken alive for questioning. They have been watching and waiting for direction from the Magus."

147

Mom sighed and clutched my hand. I asked, "Is he alone?"

Ruben replied, "No, he is with a Common Caste we don't recognize and a short. As soon as the Magus gives them the go-ahead, they will move in."

Lady Sarah looked out of the windshield of their large black van at the old, dilapidated hotel, not far from Beale Street, where Turlock was hiding. Her crew included Sir Steve, Lady Pauline, and two former special ops members of the Magus' security staff. They were all dressed completely in black. They were monitoring a listening device that had been planted in the room by a bribed hotel maid.

Turlock coughed, "I must talk to Antoinella. I need to know what happens next."

"That's Lady Antoinella," someone with a Chinese accent replied.

"Yes, yes. She has promised me more blood, so I can regain my strength and continue to help her."

A voice with a Southern accent was heard saying, "I was promised some of that extreme energy drink too."

The Chinese Common Caste vampire snapped, "You will be taken care of in due time."

"What if we just take some now!" Turlock yelled, and they heard the sounds of a scuffle.

"Go! Now!" Sarah ordered her team.

They quickly and quietly slipped out of the back of the van, each having their assignment. They entered the hotel rear door and silently ran up the stairs to the second floor. The two special ops guys guarded each end of the long, dimly lit hallway. Sir Steve and Lady Pauline took up positions on each side of the door to the hotel room. Lady Sarah checked to make sure everyone was ready. She held up three fingers, two, one, and then kicked in the door.

They quickly entered the room, and each member went after their assigned targets. The three in the room were still fighting. Turlock and the mortal were on top of the Common Caste vampire. The scent of mortal and immortal blood was in the air. Steve grabbed Turlock, who looked like a Halloween skeleton with flailing arms. He lifted him in the air as if he were an empty sack. Turlock, wide-eyed, looking deranged, slashed Steve's cheek with his long nails. Steve grabbed him by the wrists and with little effort, broke both of Turlock's wrists, then gagged and handcuffed him as he writhed and wailed in pain.

Lady Pauline surprised the Southerner, who looked like a body-builder, picked him up and threw him against the wall. He got to his feet and tried to head-butt her, Lady Pauline kicked him in the groin, and he dropped to his knees, gasping for breath. Lady Pauline gave him a sharp kick to the head rendering him unconscious.

Lady Sarah knocked the Common Caste vampire to the floor, stood over him with her boot on his neck, and in perfect Cantonese, asked, "Do you yield?"

He nodded, and replied in perfect English, "I do, I am your prisoner." She allowed him to stand. He straightened his suit, bowed, and added, "I am Jung Lee."

The Southerner came to, rubbed his head, looked up at Lady Pauline, and called out from the floor, "You ain't shit!"

Lady Sarah looked down at him and silenced him with another kick to the head. "Search Turlock and Lee and get them to the van. Leave the mortal!" Sarah commanded.

They found a couple of knives and a burner phone on Jung Lee. Turlock was moaning through his gag as the security guards carried him down the stairs and threw him in the back of the van. Jung Lee flanked by Sir Steve, and Lady Pauline quietly climbed into the van and sat staring straight ahead without a word. A moment later, Sarah joined them with reddened lips. As they drove away, they heard police sirens at the front of the hotel. Turlock was shoved down on the floor of the van. Lady Pauline covered him with a blanket. Jung Lee was cuffed, but it did not seem necessary as he was true to his word and did not resist. He asked, "Which member of the esteemed Haute Caste has captured me?"

"Shut up! You'll find out what you need to know soon enough!" Sir Steve responded. They headed for the airport, where a jet waited to take them to Los Angeles.

The Baron put down his phone.

"Did they get him?" Mom asked.

"Yes. Lady Sarah, Sir Steve, and Lady Pauline captured him."

"Thank God," she replied.

I put my arm around her. "The Magus will find out who is behind this." I looked at my husband. I could tell he was hiding something. "What else? What else do you know?"

"They captured an unsanctioned member of the Common Caste from China."

Sir Jorge responded, "Surely the House of Cups would know."

"He could have been transformed anywhere. I ask that this knowledge be kept secret for now," Tristan admonished him.

"Alexander has to be mixed up in this, I'm sure of it!" Franco stated. "He kept so much hidden from me, but I did see a couple of young Chinese Common Caste bring him a message one day. I didn't know what it was about or who they were."

"To rise up against the Magus is foolish. They can't imagine the danger they bring on themselves," Jorge said, shaking his head.

"But they can imagine the harm they can cause us! This won't be the end of it. How do we stop them?" I asked.

The sun had just set on a tea plantation near Darjeeling, India. Alexander stretched and rose from his bed in a good mood, but that was about to change. An unsanctioned vampire helped him bathe and dress. He looked out on the last of the fading light reflected by the river. He told his servant, "The Magus thought I would be content to simply be a member of his court. That time passed long ago. Alexander the Great will not be just another sycophant in his court!" The servant remained silent, knowing Alexander expected no reply.

Another servant entered the room and bowed, "Sir Alexander, a visitor has just arrived from the House of Wands, Lady Kabedi."

He was not expecting this and wondered how they had found him. He was not sure what to make of this unexpected visit.

"Show her to the audience room." It was what Alexander arrogantly called the living room. He purposefully kept his guest waiting ten minutes before entering.

Kabedi rose, pushed back her long braids, and straightened her black Chanel dress when she heard Alexander enter. She noticed the faint scent of roses with a touch of musk that emanated from him. His brown hair fell loose, framing his cheekbones. She had been warned to look beneath his charming façade.

"What a pleasant surprise," Alexander purred and clasped her hands. She gently pulled away from him. "Please sit down and tell me the news from your House."

Kabedi remained standing. He reclined, arms outstretched, seemingly without a care in the world, on a blue velvet couch with brightly colored embroidered pillows.

"I bring a message from Lady Kananga. You have gone too far. Lady Kananga could ignore your plan to establish a new House as long as it did not negatively impact the royals. The Baroness Mordecai, her children, her mother, and her friends are not to be harmed. Our code protects the innocent. The House of Wands may now be compelled to enter this battle."

He attempted to look unimpressed, but she could feel his discomfort. "Sometimes, in war, there is collateral damage. It is regrettable, but mortals being mortal do die." He rose and looked in her eyes, "You are an exquisite vampiress. Surely you desire to be more than Lady Kananga's messenger."

Her smile was disarming. He thought he was detecting a change of attitude. Perhaps he was about to turn another vampire to his side.

"As the Baroness would say, Fuck-off!" Kabedi turned, walked away, then paused.

She looked back at Alexander. "You have been warned."

Alexander watched her depart then sent a text message to Antoinella,

    The guest in Memphis has outworn his welcome

He nervously waited for a response. Normally any time of day or night, she would quickly respond. Finally, his phone pinged,

    He has been captured and taken to Paradise Cove with the Asian

He sent the phone crashing against a wall.

Chapter 24

The Letters

Tristan left for the Danville airport during the night with Jorge and Franco. A jet was waiting to fly them to Los Angeles to help with the investigation. I had difficulty sleeping, got up about six, and decided to eat something healthy. An apple dipped in caramel. I was slicing the apple and cut my finger, "Ouch! Shit!" I held my finger over the sink. Blood dripped onto the pristine white surface Danuta had cleaned until it shined.

"My father died because of you," I muttered to the blood. Tears ran down my cheeks. I did not try to stop the bleeding. "God damn special blood!"

Strong arms reached around me and wrapped my hand in a kitchen towel. I turned and buried my head in Batu's warm chest. "You should just let me bleed."

"No, Miranda, your dad would not want that."

I looked up into his kind, concerned face, "What about you?"

He kissed my forehead, "Live long and prosper, my friend." It was the perfect response to save me from embarrassing myself further.

I managed a weak smile, "Thanks, Spock."

Danuta came into the kitchen, and he released me. "What happened?" She ignored Batu and looked at the bloody towel around my hand. "You should never be allowed in the kitchen."

"I'll be in the barn," Batu said and quickly left.

Danuta pulled a first aid kit out of a drawer and shook her head, "The kids are just like you. I'm almost out of bandages." She cleaned my cut and applied a gauze dressing. Then she hugged me, "Now sit down while I clean up, then I'll fix you some breakfast."

She was right. I did not belong in a kitchen. Maybe I'd just help run the cash register at the café.

Alexander paced in his mansion, waiting for a call from the Red Lotus. He had expected a contrite apology, but that was not forthcoming.

"Good evening Alexander. We must act sooner than we planned."

"Because of your mistakes."

The Red Lotus responded, "That will not happen again. I'll be in charge of all aspects this time, not Antoinella. You are the one that insisted on giving the Common Cast a leadership role."

"We need them to believe their status will change if they do our bidding. Engaging the Common Caste is key to our success. Antoinella has been critical to our efforts."

"Hannibal cared about his warriors; you care only about victory. In time the Common Caste could realize you do not take their aspirations seriously."

"Hannibal! The elephant whisperer? You dare compare us?" Alexander was not used to such disrespect. "I have gained the confidence of the young vampires in my army. They owe allegiance to me!"

The Red Lotus was not impressed, "Spare me the details of your greatness. Are the daytime personnel in place?"

Alexander replied in an irritated tone, "Yes. The equipment was delivered this week.

They are trained, in place, and ready for your instructions."

"Good, and the young vampires?"

"They will assemble in three nights. Antoinella and Chang have recruited them. She assures me they are ready to obey my orders."

The Red Lotus paused before responding, "Like Jung Lee? He is now cooperating with the Magus."

Alexander was losing his patience, "Do you think I waited hundreds of years because I'm careless? My time has come. I won't make the same mistakes as Lena did. I kept Turlock, and Jung Lee in the dark about my plans. When I strike, it will be a two-pronged attack that will bring them to their knees. My one concern is Lady Kananga. She sent an emissary, Lady Kabedi, to warn me to stay away from the royal family. We cannot afford any more mistakes. When I establish my great House of Alexander, it will be the foundation of a new empire. The Magus' time will be over. The other Houses will respect me, even the House of Wands."

"The news about Lady Kananga makes it imperative that we act quickly before her spies learn the extent of our plans. There are rumors the Baroness is distancing herself from her husband. She seems to want a mortal life," the Red Lotus said.

"It will be your job to convince her of the importance of transforming. She could be a magnificent ally or a dangerous enemy. I trust that she will cooperate when you explain what is at stake," Alexander sounded like he was trying to convince himself his plan would work. His two encounters, at the Magus' mansion and in Rossville with Miranda, left him unsure of what she was capable of or what she might do.

"When will you reveal your secret to her?" the Red Lotus asked.

"When it will benefit me the most."

After Tristan left for Los Angeles, I found a letter in an envelope with my name written in scarlet ink in Tristan's bold hand on the desk in my office.

> *Miranda, my only love,*
>
> *I have never truly and honestly spoken of my deep and abiding passion for you. In the past, I was always amused by lovers who vowed to die rather than be apart, like Romeo and Juliet. I had yet to feel the pain of longing, the fear of losing someone, the joy of beholding my love. With you, I experience desire for a woman beyond the flesh. It is because of love that I continue to hope you will transform.*
>
> *My childhood, as a bastard and orphan, did not allow familial relationships to develop. What I have with you and the children brings delight to my heart that is beyond words. It is a new and unexpected experience for me. I feel intense anxiety and anger when you are in danger. I have also felt great pride when you fended off rogue vampires. That was an amazing feat for a mortal, but you are no mere mortal. Beneath your warm-blooded countenance, a magnificent vampiress is stirring. When the Magus granted me the honor to court you, I had my doubts that we would be compatible. I thought I might be bored by you as I would by any mortal. As I watched over you from a distance, my desire to protect you grew. When I finally came to know you as an adult, your strong will, passionate writing, stubborn nature, undaunted spirit, intelligence, and seemingly infinite creative uses of the word, 'fuck' captivated me. You are often challenging, exciting, and never predictable. I knew I had met my match. There is a chemistry between us I don't understand and can't explain. The way you see into the depth of my being, and your response to my touch tells me that we belong together.*

I want to share my nights with you forever. You have taught me the meaning of family and love. Please let the lessons continue.

Your true lover,
Tristan

My hand trembled as I placed his disturbing letter in a drawer and slammed it shut. How could he do this to me! Pressure me with undying love! I imagined a lot of women would have been calling him at that moment, pledging devotion, but I was pissed! He had not even mentioned my dad's death. I was angry at myself for loving him so much that I had not yet refused to transform. I wanted the fate that had brought us together to take this decision out of my hands.

My father's death only complicated and confused my situation. Could I offer better protection for my mom and the kids as a vampire? Was staying mortal the moral choice? Was it the right choice?

Could the intense love we felt for each other ever happen with another? Perhaps that would be a welcome relief from the highs and lows of our marital tempest. I still remembered the way Tristan looked at me the night he revealed he was a vampire, and I had fainted. I came to with him hovering over me protectively. His look of love and concern was incredibly seductive. His world is incredibly enticing. The best of the material world, no illness, eternal youth, Tristan's devoted passion, and all the bags of blood you could want. Still, somehow, I have held onto my mortal nature. He was right about the vampiress beneath the surface, how long could I keep my bloody nature in check? Before my anger cooled, I pulled out a pen and paper and began to write.

Dear Tristan,

It's not easy loving an unfaithful, blood-sucking nocturnal vigilante who is keenly aware that he is charming, handsome, wealthy, excellent in bed, and brilliant, but I try. With just a glance, you still touch my depths with desire. I believe that you love me. I also appreciate your devotion to our children.

All in all, you're fucking amazing. Still, the wall between your immortal existence and my mortal life stands. Shall I choose to go through the door of no return to your vampire realm? Or will I choose to allow the ravages of time to slowly break down my body? Sunlight versus moonlight. I have not yet made up my mind.

It seems cowardly, but I am waiting for a bright flashing neon sign from the universe, which tells me which way to go. You'll be the first to know when that happens.

Your conflicted lover, Miranda.

The next night he texted:

`That would be such a waste of your exquisite body`

I started running that week. I was not allowed to run alone, so Batu or Teri would accompany me. I would wait until Camo had taken the kids to school. I guess it was symbolic, this need to run away from or towards something, but it helped my mood. When I was stressed I would go twice a day. I ran past the rows of corn and soybeans, past the old barns, and back again. Sometimes as I passed our corral, the horses would look up from their grazing as though asking, "What is wrong with that girl?"

In my head, I would answer, "Fucking crazy vampires."

Bart told me not to expect any answers from the Magus or Tristan until they had thoroughly questioned Turlock and the Common Caste vampire. The kids liked Teri. They thought it was cool to have a ninja around. My mother made plans to reopen the café. She was renaming it, *Pete's Café*.

I called my old friend, "Hi James, how is everything?"

"Okay. Sally has become a friendly gal and seems stronger every day. It will take a little getting used to. I was doing my best to keep Gracie away from Sally, but that damned dog got out of the yard. I found her in Sally's spot under the trees, licking her wounds. Now they're inseparable! I never expected that. How are all of you holding up?"

"Wow, I'm glad Gracie is okay. Vaccinating her with Lena's blood worked. Roller coaster days here, but it's to be expected."

"I hear you," he paused, "Robert and Billy send greetings. I have to say I'm really appreciating their music, but I do have to keep them out of the local bars. I had to bail them out once already."

"What did they do?"

"Robert was flirting with a waitress, and they both got into it with her boyfriend, who ended up with a black eye. I talked the boyfriend out of assault charges by promising him free dental work. It was tricky getting them released in the middle of the night and getting them back here before sunrise."

"Wow. Thank you! But I don't think any jail could hold them for long."

James laughed, "Yeah, they assured me of that, but we don't want to attract that kind of attention. Well, at least they aren't boring."

"James," I started laughing. "Tell them I'll personally assault them if they cause you any more problems."

"That just might work."

"You probably heard; they got the guy. Picked him up in Memphis. We should have some more answers soon."

"Whatever happens, just take good care of yourself, your mom, and the kids."

"I will. Thanks, James!"

Turlock lay on a thin mattress in a small dark, dank, basement room below the Magus' mansion. There was nothing else besides a bucket, a cup of water, and some bread. He had tried to take a bite of the bread, but some of his teeth had been knocked out. He dipped it in the water and gummed the bread. Even Turlock was offended by his own body odor, but there would be no efforts to ease his sorry state until he cooperated. "Damn Benedetto," he thought, "He was worse than useless."

The heavy lock in the steel door turned, and the Magus entered. Turlock cowered, not solely out of fear but to show respect. Tristan came in behind him and said with utter disdain, "What a foul stench!"

"His blood is spoiling. He was injected with a specially prepared bacteria that is eating him alive," the Magus replied without a trace of pity.

Tristan demanded, "Tell us which member of the Haute Caste has helped you."

"I keep telling you. I don't know. Everything came through Antoinella, even when I was in Rome."

Tristan continued, "Did she tell you to kill Pete?"

Turlock wanted to say yes to get the vampiress in more trouble, but he knew they could detect if he were lying. "No, the plan was to kidnap him, but Benedetto screwed up." He tried to raise himself on his mangled wrists and gasped in pain.

The Magus stated, "The dead monk's punishment is over. Your suffering has only begun." They started to leave.

"The Chinese, I can tell you about them!"

"No need," Tristan responded.

"I was given Haute Caste blood!" Turlock cried out.

They turned back to him. The Magus spoke, "Who gave it to you? Whose blood?"

"At first, I thought it was just from one of Antoinella's Chinese Common Caste when she handed me the vial a week before we went after Pete. I knew right away it was Haute Caste, much more powerful than Simone's blood that I had been given before. I was dying, and it gave me the strength to go after Miranda's father."

"Could you recognize her?" Tristan asked.

"The room was dark, and she wore a demonic mask. That's all I remember." Turlock was desperately bargaining for his life.

The Magus clapped his hands. A servant brought Turlock a cup of broth. "Drink it, and it will keep you from dying tonight. Maybe your memory will improve."

Chapter 25

The Inquisition

Sir Omar and Lady Anastasia arrived at the Baron's mansion. Lady Anastasia paced in the dining room. "They should let me talk to Antoinella!"

Sir Omar sat still and replied, "You mean torture. If you destroy her, it will be much more difficult to discover the forces at work. Come," he said. She sat beside him and rested her head on his shoulder. He pulled his cloak about her. "We will protect Miranda and the children. Hopefully, we will come to understand the Common Caste grievances and find a way to stop this abhorrent uprising."

She looked into his calm dark eyes, "And annihilate those responsible for Pete's death."

He merely nodded.

The Baron entered, "Good evening Lady Anastasia, and Sir Omar."

"Is Turlock still alive?" Omar asked.

"Have you captured Antoinella?" Anastasia asked.

"Yes, he barely clings to life, and I will apprehend Antoinella later tonight."

"She must know you have that cursed monk," Anastasia said. "She will try to disappear."

"She just texted about our rendezvous here at two."

"You know you can't trust her," Anastasia warned.

"I never did! The Magus has been tracking her. Turlock's burner phone has a number she has been using. Wait at the guest house, and I'll signal you when you may have access to her." He pulled a plastic baggie out of his jacket pocket. "This bit of cloth is soiled by Turlock's blood. He stated he had been given HH blood prior to the attack on Pete. Anastasia, you might be able to identify the scent."

She carefully opened the bag then barely inhaled before she started coughing. "Putrid! What a repulsive smell."

"I'm sorry to have put you through this. Do you recognize the underlying scent?" Tristan asked.

She looked surprised, "This can't be right, it reeks of Lena!"

"You have confirmed what the Magus suspected."

"This makes no sense," Anastasia shook her head.

Tristan sent a text to the Magus, saying that his suspicions were validated. Then he looked at his trusted friends. "She was destroyed, but we preserved some of her blood to inoculate Miranda, the kids, and the F.O.V. to protect them from Lena's wolf pack. Some was stolen from the Magus' lab."

"The unsanctioned Common Caste we picked up with Turlock, indicated a great ruler had allowed Turlock to be given HH blood, though it was done by Antoinella."

"Alexander!" Omar said.

"Strange alliances," Anastasia stated. "What of Sir Borgia?"

"The Magus and I are only truly certain of the loyalty of a handful of our kind. Sir Franco is back with Sir Jorge, and he has given us some information about Alexander's plans."

"So, Sir Franco's affair may help us." Omar pondered. "I never thought of him as a spy."

"The Magus did," Tristan stated.

A couple of hours later, Antoinella arrived at the Mansion. Tillie, the housekeeper, loyal to the Baroness, was not happy to see her. The vampiress wore a tight red dress and killer heels. When she got to the grand entryway and started to take the stairs up to the Baron's suite, Tillie stepped in front of her and said rather curtly, "In there!" pointing to the library.

The hair on the back of Antoinella's neck stood up. She felt like she was being watched and looked up to see the Baron's black panther staring down at her from the grand staircase landing. It took every ounce of her composure to act at ease as she slowly walked into the library. Tristan was seated in a high back velvet chair, reading a book. When she entered, he continued to read for a moment, then looked up but said nothing. She was counting on the Baron taking her word over some deranged monk.

"Good evening Baron, what are your reading." She advanced, trying to look nonchalant and bent down to kiss his cheek.

He turned his head away as he answered, "Crime and Punishment."

Undaunted, she touched his sleeve, "Wouldn't we be more comfortable upstairs?"

He brushed off her advance and stood. "Not tonight." Tristan looked at Tillie by the door. "Thank you. That will be all."

She closed the door and walked away.

"She is very loyal," Antoinella said as she sat on the couch.

"Do you even know the meaning of the word?"

"I've returned to you even after you embarrassed me, sent me away." She said with mock indignation.

"Put your weapons on the table." He eyed her coldly.

She hesitated but then slowly pulled a dagger out of her thigh stocking. Her seductive gesture was lost on the Baron. She also pulled a razor disguised as a barrette from her hair.

"And the gun."

She put her hand between her breasts and brought out a tiny derringer. He continued to stare at her, obviously displeased. Antoinella sighed and said, "All right." She pulled on the waist of her dress, and a silver wire used as a garotte appeared. She placed it beside the other weapons on the end table next to her. "What is this about? Are you suddenly afraid of me?"

Tristan stood and gathered up her weapons. "No. I don't want you to harm yourself during questioning."

He sent a text to Anastasia and Omar. The Magus entered, Antoinella cringed.

"I have to admit that I greatly underestimated you," The Magus stated.

"You never really see the Common Caste."

"I see you clearly now," he responded.

Lady Anastasia and Sir Omar entered silently and sat in chairs facing Antoinella.

She turned to Tristan, "Harming me will not help your precious Miranda or your brats."

A dagger flew through the air, grazing Antoinella's ear. "But it will make me feel better." Lady Anastasia smiled at her.

The Magus handed a handkerchief to the wounded vampiress, and she dabbed her ear. "I've always loved that painting," he said, looking past her at Van Gogh's self-portrait that hung just behind Antoinella. "Life imitating art."

Omar stared at her and asked, "Why Pete?"

She did not like the way his eyes drilled holes in her. "To pressure the Baroness to transform."

Tristan asked, "Why do you want her to be immortal?"

"I don't. I could not care less what she does."

"Who are you working for?" the Magus asked.

"I forgot and cutting off my ear won't improve my memory. I've told you enough." She called their bluff, thinking they might try bribery to win her cooperation.

The Magus stood before her and merely pointed a finger at the side of her neck. As he slowly started to move it a bloody razor-thin line began to show on her neck.

"Stop!" Antoinella shrieked as she pressed the handkerchief to her neck.

"A name!"

."Never!" she sneered at the Magus.

He said nothing, but as he continued to point at her the wound in her neck, it began to get deeper.

"Fine! Stop! It was Alexander," she spat at him while trying to stop the bleeding.

"Are any other Haute Caste involved?"

"Sir Borgia and one other called the Red Lotus, but I don't know anything else."

At five in the morning, Batu knocked on my bedroom door. I jumped up out of bed, afraid something had happened to the kids.

I pulled the door open and asked, "What's wrong?"

"Miranda," he whispered so as not to wake anyone else, "Bart is downstairs. He has some news from your husband and the Magus that he wants us both to hear."

We went downstairs and found Bart in the living room. He looked sad.

"Is Tristan hurt?" I surprised myself by worrying about him.

"He is fine. The Magus, your husband, Sir Omar, and Lady Anastasia thoroughly questioned Antoinella and Turlock."

"Are they dead?"

"No. Turlock is barely alive and Antoinella is only slightly injured."

"Too bad," I stated.

"The threat seems to be centered in the Far East. Unsanctioned Chinese Common Caste vampires are following Sir Alexander, and another called the Red Lotus." He paused before telling them the worst of it. "Please sit down." I sat on the couch, and Batu chose a chair. "Lena's blood was given to Turlock before the attack on your father."

"No! That can't be!" I cried.

"A sample of her blood was stolen from Dr. Kyoto's lab."

"Who is the Red Lotus?" Batu asked.

"A masked figure called the Red Lotus gave the stolen blood to Turlock. No one knows their identity." Bart answered.

Batu asked, "Is the Magus sure that Alexander had a part in Pete's death?"

"He does not know for certain who was behind it or the nature of the relationship between Sir Alexander and the Red Lotus. One would assume Sir Alexander is in charge, but we just don't know. Alexander has never been sloppy about his military operations, which makes you wonder about who really hired Turlock and Benedetto."

"I would like to talk with the Chinese prisoner," Batu stated.

"Give me five minutes with Antoinella!" I said angrily. "Where is Alexander now?" I asked.

"He has several residences and Franco only had access to the one in Hong Kong. We have spies watching it, but there has been no sign of him or any other Haute Caste. Sir Borgia is also implicated but we have no proof." Sir Bart answered.

"What about Common Caste? Is anyone watching them?" I asked irritated.

Bart considered my question. "I don't know."

"It's foolish and arrogant to forget that the Common Caste are at the center of this whole mess. You should tell the Magus he needs to start tracking the Common Caste."

Chapter 26

Antoinella's Excellent Adventure

I walked into the kitchen after my morning run with Teri and noticed an interesting smell. Batu was busy cooking. I glanced at what he was doing while I filled a bowl with granola.

"Wait, don't eat that!" he took my bowl and steered me to the dining room table, "Here! Try this." he put a plate of steamed dumplings before me. "It's Buuz. You're getting too skinny. The crows won't even bother with you."

I had been losing weight since Dad died. It was a combination of exercise and loss of appetite. I appreciated the gesture, but I could smell it contained some kind of meat. "Thanks, but it's not vegetarian."

"You can be a vegetable lover again when you get fat. Eat!"

"All right." I bit one of the savory dumplings. It was delicious. "This is really good. What's in it?" I asked then instantly regretted asking the question.

"Mutton. The traditional Mongolian diet is high in meat and dairy. It's what you need right now."

I got teary-eyed, "Thanks!" Batu was getting to me, which was not good.

Most vampires, like my husband, had graceful, strong, and lean builds like an ice skater. Batu was more muscular, like a weightlifter. His facial features were softer, and his eyes were kinder. I was glad that Bart could not read my thoughts at that moment.

That evening the Magus made a rare call to me and told me that Batu and I would be allowed to question the prisoners. The Magus had sent his jet to Danville airport to pick us up. The kids were excited about returning to Bel Air. I think they loved seeing the panther as much as seeing their dad.

Returning to the Stone Canyon mansion was a bit of a sad circus. Tillie, Clive, the butler, and his brother Jasper, the chauffeur, had all bravely protected the kids and me during the last Common Caste uprising at the time Tristan and I were married. The rogue vampires were not pleased with a mortal given Haute Caste status. Tristan came down the grand staircase like a rich rock star, followed by Delilah. She ran past him and tried to knock over the kids. This time they were ready. They moved out of the way at the last minute, and then they fell on top of her as she turned back.

My husband kissed me on the cheek, then moved on to the kids. He was not sure what kind of response I would give him. I turned to him and asked, "When will we get to question Turlock?"

"Tomorrow night. The Magus thought you might want to rest after the flight."

I still had my own bedroom here. I stayed there when I first came to Tristan's home as a guest protected from a jealous vampiress. The lavish furnishings, vases of fresh flowers, and marble floors with Persian rugs were lovely. It was a kingdom built on blood. For a moment, I wanted to grab the kids and run. I knew that was not the answer. One day the kids and I would have to come to terms with our heritage.

Tillie said, "Baroness you look thin as a rail, must be those precious children wearing you out. Come, dinner is ready." I glanced at Batu's amused expression.

"Thanks Tillie, in a little while."

The kids ran upstairs laughing with Delilah leaping ahead of them. I had to smile. They brought out the good in every situation. The adults went into the library to talk, and I made sure Batu was included.

Antoinella paced in a windowless room that served as her cell. It was significantly more comfortable then the basement cell Turlock was confined in. Suddenly she fell to the floor, clutching her side and yelled, "Poison!" Two servants posted outside her door rushed inside. They hesitated to touch her. She moaned, "Help me." They went to her and started to lift her off the floor. In a flash, she knocked them both to the ground, then gave each a kick to the head, rendering them unconscious. Their mortal abilities couldn't compete with her speed and strength. She silently went to the nearest room with a window, opened it, then lowered herself into the garden. As soon as the window opened, she heard alarms and shouting. She made it over the fence and onto the highway carrying her heels in one hand. She quickly flagged down a ride with two surfers in a Jeep who smelled of burgers and pot.

"We're going to Topanga, where are you headed?"

"Topanga's fine, just get me out of here."

"Rough night?" the driver asked as they sped away. Her hair was messed up, and her dress torn at the shoulder.

"I got in a fight with my boyfriend," she said, putting on her heels.

"Cool, no problem. Here," the passenger handed her a joint.

She took a puff, knowing it would have little effect on her. However, the smell of the young men's blood was intoxicating. She tried to focus on her situation. Her escape seemed too easy; something was wrong.

"Can I borrow your phone? I left everything behind."

"Sure," he handed her his cell phone.

She sent a text message. A minute later she got a reply. Then she deleted the messages.

She saw a deserted lookout point. "Can you pull in there for a moment, I feel a little sick." Not wanting her to hurl in their car they parked. She knocked the driver out first, then the passenger who was too stoned to react quickly enough to escape. She pulled them from the Jeep and carried them behind a low stone wall. She feasted on them, noticing the salty taste of the sea on their skin. Perhaps the joint made her a little more merciful than she would normally be. Antoinella left the stoners enough blood to recover. She pulled the baggie of joints out of the glove compartment and threw it on top of one of them then drove the Jeep to the San Pedro harbor.

I sat in a velvet chair in one corner, so I could see and read all the faces in the room. Tristan sat in the matching chair. Batu stood to his left out of his view, and Omar and Anastasia settled on the couch.

"Something's been bugging me. I don't get why the wolf attacked Turlock when he must have had the scent from Lena's blood."

A voice answered from the doorway, "Because the vamp-wolf detected the blood was tainted with the blood of a Common Caste vampire. Only I have the pure vials of her blood." The Magus entered, and everyone stood.

He came over to me first and took my hand, "Miranda, how are you?" He did look sincerely concerned.

"Pissed-off."

"Unfortunately, what I'm about to tell you will not make you any happier."

"She's gone!" I uttered.

The Magus looked pleased. "Your abilities are increasing. Yes, Antoinella has escaped, but I allowed it so she could be followed and lead us to those she is conspiring with."

"I wanted to confront her!"

Omar responded, "I'm sure that will happen in time."

"Letting her escape will only make us less safe," I replied.

Tristan stood and walked over to the polished stone chessboard. He barely contained his rage toward the traitorous vampires. He picked up one of the kings and crushed in in his fist. Tiny pieces of rock fell to the carpet. "Alexander and everyone else involved will pay."

Anastasia spoke, "I desire revenge as well, but we are dealing with a genius who exists for conquest. Consider how long he has been plotting against the Magus. We suspect he was secretly in league with Lena. Miranda, there will be no swift end to this uprising. Omar has helped me understand that we must work with the Common Caste, win them over to our side."

This was a pivotal moment in vampire history, though I did not realize it at the time. The Magus asked a mortal for his opinion. "Batu, as someone who desires to become Common Caste, how can the Haute Caste win them over?"

He looked at the floor, running a hand over his long dark hair. Batu raised his eyes to look squarely at the Magus, "I appreciate the honor, but I won't speak for the Common Caste. I'm just an ignorant mortal hoping to be transformed."

Anastasia glared at Batu. I tried not to chuckle, and my husband was clearly irritated. Omar seemed surprised, but the Magus looked amused, "Sir Bart speaks highly of you."

"I am privileged to spend time with him. Other than those in this room, he is the only Haute Caste vampire to ever speak with me. Even the Princess uses a Common Caste messenger. I am sorry I can't be of more help. May I be excused to look after the children?"

"Yes. Thanks, Batu," I answered before anyone else could detain him. He bowed toward the Magus and quickly left the room.

The Magus sat down on the end of the couch near me, "Do you still wish to see Turlock?"

"I have so many unanswered questions. I want to see him soon before someone kills him."

"Of course, tomorrow night then," he touched my hand, he was a little cool. His scent had a hint of cardamom. Despite my paranoia about him, I had a sudden desire to draw closer. His dark eyes pulled me in.

"Stop it! You want me to forgive you, to say it isn't your fault." I stood and walked to the windows which looked out on the rose garden. I turned towards the Magus, "You'll always be responsible for the madness the undead unleash."

"Miranda," Omar responded, "your grief speaks loudly."

Anastasia came to my side almost as a warning for the others to say nothing. To my astonishment, the Magus stood, gave a small bow, then left the room followed by my husband and Omar.

I looked at Anastasia's beautiful face. She had experienced much greater losses than me. "Thank you."

"They don't understand loss, just vengeance. They all want to kill Turlock personally. They have shown much restraint, so the mastermind behind all this may be caught."

"You know," I started to choke up, "It's not only about justice. I can't wrap my mind around anyone hurting my dad. I want to find some way to resolve this and move on so I can take care of my family."

"I chose immortality to survive my losses. It has given me the time I needed to accept humanity. The nightmares stopped, but it took a very long time." She displayed a sad smile and handed me a lace handkerchief.

"Thanks, but I think I have options that you didn't have." I left to gather the kids for dinner. I did not want to seem ungrateful for her advice, but becoming a vampire is not a cure for grief. I still could not shake the feeling of tenderness when the Magus touched me. It was the second time I had experienced his charismatic pull. He was as seductive as Tristan. I wondered if anyone else in the room felt it, or they just looked the other way. He should use it on the Common Caste.

Batu did not join us for dinner. I sent my mom a pic of the kids being served lemon meringue pie with fresh strawberries Tillie had made. She texted me back and her reply made me smile,

        Danuta is not impressed

I told her I would get some questions answered tomorrow. The kids started arguing about how late they could stay up and if they could go to the beach instead of playing ice hockey. It was nice to see a little bit of normalcy again. Batu stopped me in the hallway.

"It's my mom's birthday. The Mongol hordes are descending on London. I will be leaving in a few hours after I question the Chinese prisoner."

"Is this because of the Magus or my husband?"

"No," he smiled, "I had already planned the trip, but waited to make sure you'd be safe here, before finalizing it."

"After living with us in Rossville you deserve a break! But I will miss your sarcasm." I wanted to add, *and your fine ass* but thought better of it.

He had no response and just looked sad. Batu raised one finger to his lips, then gently touched my lips. It happened so quickly I was stunned. Then he walked away. I took a deep breath, looked up and down the hall, and hoped his gesture had not been picked up by the security system.

The rest of the evening was a blur. I remember Omar and Anastasia leaving to communicate with their contacts about Alexander. Tristan went off with the Magus to investigate where Antoinella had gone. Tillie and Clive kept an eye on what the kids were doing. They were eating pizza and playing video games when I went off to bed. I tried to sleep but kept seeing Batu's look of longing. It took a bubble bath and a couple episodes of War and Peace on BBC to finally knock me out.

Tristan's chauffeur drove to the Magus' mansion before taking Batu to the airport. He was taken to a small room behind the kitchen, which served as a temporary cell. The room was comfortably furnished, but it had steel bars across the window covered with heavy curtains; he had been warned that the bars were electrified. Being electrocuted wouldn't kill vampires, but they really hated it.

The Magus and Tristan were seated at a table having tea with Jung Lee when Batu entered.

When Jung Lee realized he was in the presence of a Mongol, mortal or not, he stood and prepared to fight. Batu remained standing, "I just want to talk to you."

Jung Lee nodded, "What do you want to know?"

In Chinese, Batu proceeded to grill him about the number of the unsanctioned and their hierarchy. At one point, Jung Lee stated that he feared revealing more. Batu assured him that the Magus and Tristan were members of the Haute Caste he could trust, and he would be protected. Jung Lee reported that scores of young unemployed Chinese had been recruited, and two dozen already transformed. Antoinella was their Common Caste leader. Then Jung Lee told them that he did not know if the Red Lotus was Chinese or not. She never spoke directly to the unsanctioned.

The Magus surprised Jung Lee by asking in Chinese, "How tall was the Red Lotus?"

"About your height sir."

The Magus turned to Batu, "Thank you. I won't keep you any longer."

Tristan walked him out, "Your service to my children is appreciated. I think he fears you more than me. Interesting."

"It is my honor. He expected civility from the Haute Caste, but not a Mongol." Batu got in the Bentley and wiped the perspiration off his forehead. No mention of taking care of the Baroness, he got the hint. He took a deep breath and mentally prepared for London. He felt relieved he had not said anything in Chinese that might have offended the Magus. He regretted not being able to tell Miranda what he was about to do. He hated being away from her.

Chapter 27

The Offspring Meet the Barbarian

Tristan and I drove in silence to the Magus' mansion to question Turlock. I was not sure what I was going to ask him. Nothing he could say could remove my grief. I held out the hope he might give away something about those giving the orders. In all honesty, I wanted to see him suffer.

We turned into the long, curved driveway from Pacific Coast Highway, and drove through the gardens, past the entrance to the main house, to a brick gardener's shack in the back. Turlock had been cleaned up and moved to this location for his questioning. Pauline was standing guard with Angel.

I gave her a hug. She had helped take down Lena when she was still a new vampire. I never forget my friends.

She brushed her blond hair back and smiled, "I'm happy to see you too. I am very sorry about your father. Angel has been guarding the prisoner since he arrived."

My husband nodded to her. I extended my hand to Angel, "You have my thanks." Angel reminded me a bit of Jorge, but taller. "Anytime Baroness, whatever I can do to help."

Pauline asked, "Do you wish us to go in with you?"

"No, we will be fine," Tristan responded.

They unlocked the wooden door. I was shocked by what I saw. A hunched over skeleton of a man resembling Gollum peered at us from a corner. He had pulled a blanket over his shoulders. His eyes grew large, "Satan's spawn!" He spat on the floor. "Have you come to kill me?"

I tried to ignore the smell of rotting flesh that they could not completely wash away. I took a step closer with Tristan at my side and glared at him. "Who ordered my father's death?"

He grinned like a jack-o-lantern, "No one. We were supposed to kidnap him, but he fought us. It was his own fault."

Tristan put his hand on my arm to stop me from stepping closer and warned him, "Turlock, your death can be swift or prolonged."

"I want to know who was behind this?"

"I told them already. It was Antoinella and the Red Lotus. They contacted me, gave me money, orders and blood." He looked at my husband then back to me, "It was to get you to transform! Such a waste! You don't even want the gift. I would have made a great vampire, a holy vampire!"

I stared back into his yellowed eyes, "Which House is behind this?"

He chuckled, "You mean Houses."

"Which ones?"

"The Common Caste belong to every House and they are angry that you were given Haute Caste Status just because you married the Great and Powerful Baron. Off with your head!" he cackled.

I started to move towards him, but Tristan grabbed me and carried me outside. I took a deep breath of fresh air. He asked, "Have you heard enough?" I nodded. "Tell your mother that I executed Turlock." Then he and Pauline went inside while Angel stayed outside with me.

"His blood is not clean," Tristan stated. He pulled surgical gloves out of his pocket and handed a pair to Pauline. Turlock's eyes widened as Tristan pulled a long knife out of his boot. The blade gleamed as he stretched out his arm towards the prisoner.

"I can tell you more…"

Tristan grabbed the struggling remnants of the man by his neck with one hand, lifting him to his feet. With one deep slice, his knife silenced him forever. His body dropped into the growing pool of blood. In a rage, Tristan tore the head from the corpse and smashed Turlock's skull against a wall. The shack filled with his putrid stench. Tristan pulled off the gloves, tossed them on Turlock's body. They walked out slamming the door behind them.

He turned to me, "It is done." He looked at Pauline and Angel, "Feed his remains to the Komodo Dragon, Dorcus, and incinerate anything he touched."

"Of course," Pauline replied. They went back into the shack and we walked to the mansion.

"Won't he make Dorcus sick?" I suddenly felt sorry for the beast.

"No, the bacteria that was killing him came from her mouth."

The Magus was waiting for us in his living room. To my surprise, Anastasia and Omar were there with the kids. I hugged them and began crying. "The person who killed Grandpa is dead. Your dad made sure he wouldn't hurt anyone else."

They rushed over to hug their dad. He was still in killer mode, transitioning to a loving father would take a minute. "Not now," he brushed them off.

The Magus' butler wheeled in a cart with a silver coffee service, and a pot of hot chocolate; I didn't wait to be served, I filled a cup and drank the heavenly dark roasted brew. I was glad they had not served food; I could not have kept it down. I could still smell Turlock's stench. My hands were trembling a little, the Magus noticed. The butler served the kids hot chocolate. It was surreal, like celebrating a hanging in the Wild West. It was about to get even weirder.

The Magus announced, "I had some clothing packed for you and the children. I think you're all overdue for a little adventure. You're going to visit some friends who live near Twentynine Palms for a few days."

My husband added, "It will be good for the children. It's an animal refuge."

"Are you saying our kids are animals?"

He didn't respond, apparently not getting the joke. I could see the kids were excited and I did need a break. For once I did not complain about him not consulting me first. I wanted to get us far away from the Magus' home. We set off in two Range Rovers. Marie and Jacques rode with us. Des and Tomas rode with Anastasia and Omar. I rolled down the window, and it felt good to feel the fresh air on my face. It was not over, not by a long shot, but one threat was gone. I turned to Tristan, placed my hand over his hand on the steering wheel and said, "Thank you."

"It was my pleasure," he responded.

I heard the kids chuckling in the backseat, so I turned and said, "Try to get a little sleep, it's going to be a long night." Sometimes you forget that they are always watching.

"Dad, how did you kill him?" Jacques asked.

I cringed, not wanting them to know the details. Tristan answered, "With a knife. It was merciful."

To my surprise Marie added, "He didn't deserve mercy."

My husband smiled, "We must be better than they are."

I wasn't so sure we were, but the kids seemed to like that answer and moved on to more normal road trip banter, "How much longer? Are we there yet?" Luckily, soon, they nodded off and slept most of the way. It seemed that Tristan wanted to distance himself from the whole sordid mess as much as I did.

It was after midnight when we drove up to a gate on a dirt road about fifteen miles past Twentynine Palms. We stopped so that Tristan could open the gate. He drove through, got out of the car then closed the gate after the second car pulled through. I noticed the tall chain-link fence that seemed to go on forever, had electric fence warnings. I could imagine the kids wanting to test it out.

We drove about half a mile when we came up to the sprawling house with a large Spanish style fountain in front of the entrance. The kids rubbed their eyes as they stumbled out of the cars. Then we heard it. A low, long, trumpet, yodel sound echoed a dozen times, which woke everyone up.

"What was that?" Tomas asked.

Des uttered, "What the hell?"

Marie smiled broadly, "Elephants!"

"You're right!" A small woman wearing an Oakland Raider's jersey and jeans approached. She had long brown hair in braids and smiling brown eyes. "I'm Cassie," she extended her hand.

"Miranda," I read her scent. She was Haute Caste. "Elephants?"

There was another Haute Caste vampire with a well-trimmed beard who appeared older than most of the undead. He had brown curly hair to his shoulders. He was shorter than my husband and broader in the chest. They shook hands. My husband was showing respect to another ancient vampire.

"Welcome my old friend, so I finally get to meet this woman who was foolish enough to marry you!" He turned towards the children and me, "I'm Hann, please allow my humble home to be your oasis."

Jacques said, "Can we see the elephants?"

"Please!" Marie added.

Hann looked at me, I nodded. "Right this way!"

Anastasia and Omar stayed behind to talk with Cassie. There were ten large barns located behind the house. I whispered to my husband, "He looks like he's in his late 40's."

He smiled, "He is a dear friend of the Magus who can be trusted without question. Yes, he is the oldest ever to be transformed."

"Why? Who is he?"

"Because he is very stubborn and refused for years until he almost died. Are your wits dulled? You usually put facts together quicker than this?"

"Wait…Hann and Elephants? You mean…"

My husband nodded, "Sir Hannibal felt guilty about the elephants who died in his service, so he started this refuge."

"Hannibal the Barbarian and our kids? You think this is showing good parenting skills?"

"He's fine with women and children, but adult men were another thing, but that's ancient history now."

"So, who is Cassie?" I had to ask.

We stopped in front of the first barn, and the kids helped Hann roll open the door.

"Lady Cassandra was one of the original Oracles at Delphi."

Before I could begin to process that information, my senses were overwhelmed as we entered the barn. There were seven huge African elephants inside. The baby was kept back by its' mom until she decided it was safe. Hann showed the kids how to hand treats to the great beasts. I grabbed Jacques' arm as a trunk almost knocked him over. To be so close to such enormous and magnificent creatures was incredible. Marie stared at them speechless. Des was trying to figure out how to climb on one of the smaller ones and ended up headfirst in the straw, while Tomas was trying to win the confidence of the mother elephant.

I try not to like the Magus; I was still pissed that he let Antoinella go, but at that moment I felt grateful. The kids and I really needed this. An African man named Dr. Mayi, joined us. He explained he had worked at the Virunga National Park in the Congo before coming to work for Hann. He was mortal, though I detected enhanced blood. He was the supervisor of the veterinary students that came during the day to care for the herd. He was short and muscular like a wrestler. He shook my hand and said, "I'm Kalonji Mayi. I'll give you, and your fine children a tour tomorrow."

"Thanks! That would be great."

It was about 2 a.m. when we got the kids settled in their rooms. There was an alarm on the outside doors that would sound in our room if they got up before me and tried to leave the house to visit the animals. They were warned by Hann in a very stern voice, "You must wait for Dr. Mayi to come to get you tomorrow."

I excused myself from social time with our hosts as exhaustion was setting in. I was still feeling emotionally and physically drained from interrogating Turlock. I told them I looked forward to talking with them tomorrow night, and they seemed to understand. Our suite was anything but rustic. As soon as I collapsed onto a king-sized bed, there was a knock on the door. A young woman from town, who worked as a maid, came in with fresh towels and went into the large bathroom. Soon I heard the buzz of the hot tub jets. After she left, I wandered into the bathroom, a plate of chocolate-covered strawberries, and a bottle of wine were near the tub. I ate the strawberries but left the wine. Even after all I had been through, I did not want to drink. I climbed into the tub and melted into the frothing hot water. It felt great, but I was not alone for long. Tristan in all his unnatural naked glory came into the bathroom and got into the tub with me. He gazed at me and asked, "How can I win back your

175

love?" His intense blue stare, the handsome features that gave him a look of haughty self-confidence were overwhelming me. "Tristan, I've never stopped loving you." After a few minutes I got out of the tub and wrapped a plush white towel around me. Then I turned back towards him. "Do us both a favor, and just for tonight, shut-up."

I lit a candle, turned off the other lights and climbed into bed. He was soon beside me, warmed by the hot tub. We slowly, meticulously explored erogenous zones savoring each sensual delight. He was a patient lover, waiting for me to be fully ready to receive him. There was no urgency. His hands worked their magic. His lips kissed me passionately, I responded in kind. The exquisite tension increased, and just when it seemed impossible to continue blissful release. My pounding heart started to slow down. His arm lay across me assuring our connection, and I fell asleep.

The kids each had separate rooms but were texting. At about three in the morning, they met in the hallway and found their way to the living room where the Haute Caste were talking. Sir Omar smiled, and Lady Anastasia tried to appear upset with them. "What are you doing out of bed?" she inquired.

Tomas appeared to be the spokesperson, "We have a question."

Omar spoke, "What is it children?"

"It's for Sir Hann," Des responded.

Marie stepped forward, "Is your name Hannibal?"

Hann attempted to look stern, "Do you know my whole name?"

Jacques responded, "Hannibal Barca. We figured it out earlier."

Des smiled and poked Tomas, "C'mon, pay up!"

Tomas did not look happy. He was the only one who could not believe that they were in the presence of the great military commander. "So, all you do now is take care of elephants?"

He furrowed his brow, which made Tomas squirm a little, "It is a worthy endeavor. They are the noblest creatures on the planet. Now off to bed with you all."

Lady Cassie turned to Lady Anastasia, "Interesting children."

She replied, "We may need to protect Sir Hannibal from them."

Chapter 28

Batu Undercover

Batu pulled his coat around him as he walked to London's Sloane Square. He had excused himself from dinner with his parents telling them he was going to see a friend. It was not his mom's birthday. He had told Miranda that to cover his departure for a mission the Magus had given him. Like a scene from the Godfather, it was an offer he could not refuse. If all went well, the Magus would recommend to the Princess that he be transformed.

He had checked in with the House of Pentacles when he arrived as protocol demanded. It also made his visit seem less suspicious. As merely an aide to the Princess, he was pretty much ignored, which helped him eavesdrop on the Common Caste. He had heard about a party at the Sloane Square Boutique Hotel that used to belong to Lady Lena. He invited himself. He stepped through the doors and was surprised by the number of undead who had shown up. A blonde vampire with a scar on his face sniffed in his direction and licked his lips. A woman in a short red dress said, "He's protected." It was Scheherazade.

Johann nervously touched his scar, "By whom?"

"The Baroness," she responded and gave Batu a flirtatious smile.

Johann scurried away. Scheherazade approached Batu. "Don't mind, Johann. He had an unfortunate encounter with the Baroness once."

Batu remembered the Baroness had once sliced off the nose of an assailant. "She is someone to be respected."

"I've heard you're privy to the intimate details of the household. Come and tell me all about it." She guided him past Common Caste dancing and flirting in their finest designer threads. She led him into a small room with a plush sofa in front of a fireplace.

He could not help but admire her beauty, but the danger beneath the surface of her beguiling gaze was palpable. Her long dark hair cascaded over the low-cut dress. As she sat on the sofa, he felt like a venomous snake was starting to curl up, ready to strike. He decided it would be safer to remain standing. Her phone rang, with a sigh of obvious annoyance she answered with a curt "Yes?" Then simply said, "I'll talk to Antoinella later," and hung up. Her eyes had never left Batu. "Now, you were about to tell me about the royal family."

He took a step back and leaned against the fireplace mantel, "I'm just a glorified nanny to the kids and a gofer for the Baroness, it's a boring existence, but I do what the Princess commands."

"Don't you want more?"

"Of course. I'm just kissing Haute Caste ass until I can be transformed."

"Perhaps you will not have to wait as long as you think. Would you consider serving another?"

"I don't know. It would be hard to find someone more powerful than the Princess."

She chuckled, but not in a good way. "I don't mean to disrespect her, but others like Sir Borgia are more powerful, command more Common Caste, and grant us more freedom. If I wanted, he would allow me to transform you now."

The hair on the back of his neck stood up, but he continued. "If I were to change loyalty it would have to be for someone more ancient and powerful than Sir Borgia."

With a smile more sinister than friendly, she replied, "So you aren't rejecting my offer, just asking for more. You are a greedy, ambitious mortal; I can see why the Princess likes you. Why don't you give me a little taste while I consider your request?"

Batu's heart pounded in his chest. He knew she had detected his lie. Just then, Johann walked in and said that Sir Borgia had arrived. Batu seized on the distraction to run for his life. He bolted out of the room past Johann and down the stairs to the exit. He almost ran over Sir Borgia, dodged around him and out the door. He continued at top speed until he was three blocks away. He breathed a sigh of relief. That had been close. He could not have fended off Scheherazade, Johann, or any of the undead for that matter. He leaned against a building winded.

"It's not polite to leave without saying goodbye," Johann, appeared seemingly out of nowhere before him, almost salivating.

Batu turned and tried to escape the other way.

In an instant, Johann leaped on him and pulled him into an old brick alley. He threw Batu against the wall. Batu stunned by the impact crumbled to the ground. Johann's bared his fangs as he pulled Batu up by his throat. "I wish you were the Baroness," he said. Batu struck out at him, but Johann barely noticed.

Batu struggled to get free. Johann savagely bit into his throat. The pain was unspeakable and he fell to the ground clutching his neck. Looking up, he saw Johann teetering above him in agony. He had been pierced through by a short sword. Batu looked up to see Lady Kananga bite into Johann's throat. Her eyes shut as she felt the rush from his blood. Her Knight, Samuel, leaned down and began bandaging Batu's neck. Lady Kananga dropped Johann to the ground. She reached down and pulled the sword out and cut off his head. It went rolling past Batu with a look of shock frozen on his face. Samuel retrieved the head and put it in a sack. Kananga managed to get some of the blood gurgling from Johanns's neck into a cup and handed it to Samuel, who took a sip then gave the rest to Batu, "You'll need this. Drink it all!"

Batu looked in the cup, then up at Samuel, and did as he had been told. Somehow Batu kept it down. He felt heat curse through his body, then a rush of energy. He was able to stand without assistance, but his neck still hurt as he touched the bandage as they walked to a limousine.

"Stop whining!" Lady Kananga commanded. They looked up and down the deserted street, but there were no signs of other members of the House of Pentacles or anyone else for that matter. "We must be on our way. Take the head, leave the body!"

Once in the limo, she declared, "They did not see you as enough of a threat to send more than that miserable fool Johann."

"Thank you both. I thought it was the end for me. Who sent you to help me?"

"No one sends me anywhere! The Magus mentioned your mission and I offered to keep an eye on you."

Batu realized he was in the presence of one of the ancients and bowed his head. "Yes, of course, I'm grateful."

"Sending a mortal into that pit of undead vipers was too risky. We must all be more careful. Did you find out anything useful?"

There was no way he would hold anything back from her. "Antoinella and Scheherazade are in communication. Scheherazade told me Sir Borgia would allow her to transform me. I wasn't able to get the identity of any other Haute Caste who are involved. I think the only reason she spoke to me was to get information about the Baron's family."

"Scheherazade is clever, always involved in some plot or other but never caught. You were brave to take this mission," Lady Kananga said.

Batu looked at the sack containing Johann's head. "Who is Scheherazade? I thought she was just a character from a story."

Kananga sighed, "Someone who caught the eye of the Magus and Tristan a great many years ago in London. The name she adopted, and her seductive behavior are just an act to further her ambition."

The limo stopped at an isolated spot along the Thames and Samuel disposed of the weighted sack in the dark waters of the river. The limo continued to a private airfield where a jet was waiting to fly them to Los Angeles. Batu texted his parents that an emergency had arisen back in Rossville and he had to return immediately. He promised to call them as soon as he could.

Antoinella paced on the deck of a freighter headed to China. Her ability to communicate with the House of Pentacles on secure channels was fading with each additional mile they sailed. At least she was free. She knew that by now Turlock had been destroyed. She felt no pity for him. He had been kept in the dark about her plans and would not have been able to tell them much. The identity of the Red Lotus would not be compromised. The Magus could have been much more brutal, and she wondered why he spared her. She thought her escape had been too easy but decided, in her arrogance, they had underestimated her. The Magus and the Baron would be wasting their time tracking her. The others were setting up the next trap. She noticed a lone sailor coiling a line. The blood from the stoners had not been sufficient. Antoinella silently came up behind him. His O positive scent was captivating. She reached out for him.

"Tsk, tsk."

She turned, Franco had appeared behind her and was giving her a disapproving look.

The sailor, startled that they had come up behind him without a sound, took the opportunity and ran to the nearest hatch and disappeared below. The crew had been warned to steer clear of the passengers. Franco shook his head. "You know we aren't supposed to dine on the crew. How will we ever get to China if they start disappearing?"

With a sly smile she replied, "Maybe we don't really need to get to China at all."

Lady Lily and Sir Kyoto met with the Magus that night. They had traveled together even though they were no longer sharing an intimate relationship. Sir Kyoto had his hair up in a Samurai topknot. Lady Lily's clothing and appearance had become much more modern and casual. The Magus could feel the tension between them as they joined him in his office. He turned off his worldwide surveillance screens as he turned to them. This surprised them as he normally kept them on with his trusted friends.

"How are you both?' he asked.

Kyoto bristled, "Fed up with this nonsense. How could Antoinella get away?"

Lily was more poised, "Good evening Magus. I'm fine, and you look well. Have you disposed of that wretch Turlock?"

"Thank you, Lily." He turned to Kyoto, obviously not pleased at Kyoto's rudeness. "Antoinella has an important part to play, so I chose to release her rather than break her spirit. The deplorable monk met a fitting end." The Magus continued, "Tell me about the Red Lotus."

Kyoto spoke first, "My sources have heard rumors, but no one knows her identity."

Lily, "I can't even determine if she is Haute Caste. They say a mask always hides her face."

"I believe she is in league with Alexander." The Magus stood and walked to his Victorian desk and pulled a small vial containing blood out of a drawer. He handed it to Kyoto. "I would appreciate it if you would both examine this specimen of Turlock's blood. I want to know who shared their blood with that wretch. There will be traces of Lena and Simone, but there may be another traitor."

"Of course," Lily bowed her head slightly.

Kyoto looked at the vial then back at the Magus. "May we work in separate labs? I can work from my home, and perhaps Dr. Lily could use the equipment at the Baron's home. It would be a way to double-check the results."

Nodding, the Magus, pulled a second vial out of the drawer and handed it to Lily. "I thought you might request that.

Kyoto stood and bowed, "I shall begin tonight. Excuse me." He left before the Magus could respond.

Lily appeared embarrassed by Kyoto's behavior. "I'm sorry dear Magus. Our personal issues should not impact this important task. I shall find out everything I can about Turlock."

"Thank you. I know you wish to protect Miranda and the children. A suite will be prepared for you at the Baron's home.

After Lily left, the Magus sat alone, considering Kyoto's behavior. He knew The Head of the House of Cups had been deeply wounded when Lily left him for Ruben. It was not a drama that the Magus had foreseen. When his old acquaintance recently discussed not experiencing love, he was in the midst of a heartbreaking crisis. "How blind can one be? I should have seen it." he mused. Introspection made the Magus wonder about the obvious signs of growing unrest amongst the Common Caste that he had ignored. "I have been blind to that as well."

To his chauffeur's surprise, the Magus requested the keys to his Prius. It wasn't often that the Magus would drive himself, but when he did, it was always one of his luxury cars. Only the staff had ever used the Prius. Seeing the look on the chauffeur's face, the Magus simply said, "I would like to see the city in a different light." He took the keys and drove the baby blue car to the Narcissus Club and parked across the street. He had put on a black hoodie before leaving the mansion and as he walked slowly towards the small group of Common Caste in front of the entrance, he put up the hood. He knew they were keeping watch. The tallest male called out, "Private Club, get out of here!"

He stopped fifty feet away. "Angel, may I speak to you."

Angel caught the scent of a Haute Caste vampire. Everyone was on edge, not knowing where a vampire's loyalties might lie. He whispered to one of the others, "Watch my back." Then walked over to the hooded figure.

"Good evening," the Magus said quietly.

As soon as he recognized the Magus, his eyes grew wide. "What the hell!" he blurted out. "I mean, good evening, your highness!"

"Shh. I don't want them to know I'm here."

Angel looked behind him at the car, "Your wheels sure didn't give you away. How can I serve you?"

"I wish to hear about your Common Caste world view. I have been away from the streets for too long."

Angel felt uneasy, "You want to hear my opinion?"

"You were helpful with Turlock. Sir Steve and Lady Pauline have spoken well of you. You're the only Common Caste I can remember them mentioning."

"Dorothy's friends!" Angel smiled.

"Dorothy?"

"Yeah, you know, the movie, The Wizard of Oz." Seeing the Magus still wasn't following, he explained. "Dorothy took out the wicked witch, like the Baroness taking out Lady Lena. It's our way of identifying loyal vampires."

The Magus knew it had taken him and several Haute Caste to accomplish Lady Lena's demise, but he let that go. No reason to take away from the legend of the Baroness. "Are there many who voice their displeasure with her?"

"Magus, your Excellency, I am not sure you will want to hear this."

"Please do not worry; you shall suffer no negative consequences for obliging me."

"Okay, if you insist. You would know if I lied anyway, so here it is. A lot of us are unhappy about not having more privileges and rights. The

Baroness and her kids being given Haute Caste status just rubbed salt in the wounds. It makes us feel like second class citizens of our society."

"And you? What would you like to see done differently?"

"The Friends of Dorothy would like to be represented when the Parliament meets. We would appreciate our role in the vampire world be recognized, but we don't want to see the Haute Caste attacked to get more respect."

The Magus was surprised by his audacity, but not angered. "You wish to have your station elevated?"

"Yes, we want a voice in our affairs" Angel started to feel more confident, "No one I know thought that hit on her father was right. You don't involve innocent mortals in our disputes!" He drew a nervous breath, afraid he might have gone too far. "Am I in trouble? My mother always said I talked too much."

"Not at all. Goodnight." As the Magus walked away Angel sighed with relief. It had gone better than he might have thought. When he returned to his friends, they asked about the visitor. Angel replied, "He's from out of town, someone in the valley gave him my name. I said we were closed. You can't just let any vampire into the Narcissus."

One of the others added, "No self-respecting vampire would be seen in that car!"

The next night a Porsche was waiting for Angel when he got to the club.

Chapter 29

Connie, the Saint and the Monk

A lot was happening in the vampire world while we were visiting the elephants. Eventually, I heard about Batu in London and the Magus talking with Angel. But that was not all. My first morning at the refuge I got a call from my mom.

"Honey, you won't believe it," she said.

"What? Is everyone okay?"

"Yes, of course, we're fine. Bart has a visitor. Her name is Jeanne, and she's French, and you know she's a night owl."

"Jeanne's there? Tristan had mentioned her."

"Yes. She's a sweetie. She's helping out with security, and she's really good with the horses. Bart has been smiling since she got here, can you believe it?"

I wondered how long it would take Mom to figure out her guest wasn't simply good with horses; Jeanne d'Arc had ridden into battle on them. Who but my mom would call a vampiress a 'sweetie'?

"Bart smiling, that must take a little getting used to. I'm glad you have more help. We'll be home soon."

"That's fine honey. Are you enjoying the beach with the kids?"

I didn't think it would be a good idea to tell her I was more worried about being trampled by elephants in the desert than sunburn. It was too much to explain before my first cup of coffee. "Yeah, they're having a good time."

"I almost forgot. Sheesh! I'm getting old. There's someone else visiting us. Remember that nice retired priest that you introduced me to. He was working in that deli in L.A.?"

"Grigoryi? He's there too?"

"Yes. I figured it was okay because Bart checked him out. Greg said he felt bad when he heard about Pete, and he wants to help out at the café."

I got a little choked up. I had saved Grigoryi from being a midnight

184

snack after being drawn into the Common Caste uprising in L.A. "Mom, he came from Rome to look after you."

"Yes, I know, and Jeanne came from Paris. I think the menu at the café is going to change. Camo and Greg got in a little tiff about who bakes the best bread. Can you imagine that?"

I could imagine a great deal since getting in bed with the undead. "Give my thanks to Grigoryi. I'm really glad you have so much support."

"Take care, honey, and tell Stan thanks for sending the extra help."

'Stan' had never mentioned it to me. I was grateful and irritated at the same time. Tristan had a way of inciting conflicting emotions.

I needed a really big mug of coffee. The veterinary students were having bagels and coffee in the kitchen. "Hi!" I could smell their mortal blood scents. I was still getting used to how my sense of smell had evolved. I found my fav caffeinated beverage and poured a mugful.

"Who are you?" one of the young students asked.

"I'm Miranda. Our family are guests of Hann and Cassie. Are you working with Mayi?"

"Yes, Dr. Mayi," a young man responded, correcting my familiarity, "is going to show us how to read the elephant scat for indications of illness."

"Great! If you happen to see my kids, just try to keep them away from your research." I grabbed a bagel and wandered into the dining room. As I sat down, I got a text from James.

> Billy and Robert are on their way to L.A. Billy shot a guy for kicking a dog. The good news is the guy will survive. Can't say I blame Billy, but they had to leave before the police found him. Ruben and Sarah will be here tonight.

I texted back,

> Give my thanks to Sarah for finding Turlock. I hope the dog is okay. I bet that guy won't hurt any more dogs. Stay safe old friend.

I sipped my coffee and savored the moment. As usual, there was too much drama in my life. I was sure Tristan probably assumed last night's passion had healed our relationship. I was also sure that he and the Magus were keeping me in the dark about their plans to counter the rebellious vampires. I knew the elephant refuge was good for the children, but sending us here was more than just for our safety it was meant to be a distraction. Sending Jeanne and Grigoryi to Rossville meant they had no idea where the opposition would strike next.

Grigoryi must have been sad to hear about Benedetto's involvement in Dad's death. There was goodness in that little Italian baker that was as powerful as any Haute Caste bite. When Lena tried to use him to poison me, he risked his life by defying her to protect me. His simple desire to do the right thing was inspiring. He had given up his quiet, safe life at a bakery in Rome to help my mom. An ex-monk and an ex-saint. I wished I could be there to see his face when Grigoryi figures out who Jeanne really is.

On the other side of the world, Alexander was examining a map of Nevada. He had acquired some acreage near Las Vegas. His new palace was almost complete. It was an ambitious estate with a deep ditch along the outside of the steel fence encircling it. He had wanted a moat. The architect he hired had difficulty convincing him that a water-filled moat was not feasible in the middle of a desert. He had some difficulty meeting his demands for two black marble columns, each topped with a gold hawk to 'guard' the entrance. That is until he understood that money was no object. A three-story tower was at each corner of the building, which resembled an ancient temple. A larger than life-size statue of his favorite horse stood at the bottom of the steps in the middle of a fountain. A troop of Chinese dancers had arrived in Las Vegas and went directly to his oasis. It turned out their dancing skills were nothing compared to their martial art skills. Alexander got a text from the Red Lotus.

> The day shift has been trained with the equipment.
> They are ready

He responded

> Soon

Franco was awakened by pounding on his cabin door. Fear seized him as he imagined only a maritime emergency would cause the crew to wake him during the day. In the hallway, Antoinella yelled, "Time to get up! We'll dock soon."

"Where are we?" Franco asked nervously.

"San Diego, the Magus could not get rid of me that easily."

"I was supposed to join Sir Alexander." He quickly composed himself.

She smiled, "He'll have a limo waiting for you." She threw him a bag, "There's your sun-proof clothing and mask. You'll be taken to Las Vegas. Don't ask me why he still wants you."

"It's my fashion sense," he quipped. "You might try a little color. All that black makes you look tired. You're not going to Vegas?"

"No. You ask too many questions. You're lucky Sir Alexander said you were protected."

Franco laughed, "You have no idea of the power of the Haute Caste. You would have lost your pretty head before you ever touched me."

Chapter 30

The Oracle's Vision

As I finished my first cup of coffee a truck full of produce arrived at the refuge. The students went out to help with unloading the elephant's buffet. The kids came running down the hall pulling on their clothes.

"Mom," Des cried, "why didn't you wake us up?" This was from the child I practically had to drag out of bed to get up for school.

"No elephants till you've all eaten!"

"Ah Mom, I'm not hungry," Marie complained.

"Eat!" I stood with my arms crossed while they hurriedly ate their breakfast. The triplets stared down Jacques as he was the slowest eater.

We found Dr. Mayi by the barn we had been in yesterday. "Hello Baroness, hello, children!" The students did a double-take after hearing my title. "I will assign each of you to help one of the students. You must do as they tell you if you want to be allowed to care for the elephants. Agreed?"

The kids all nodded. I knew it was the calm before the storm. I started to ask if anyone had medical training then remembered I was amid aspiring veterinarians. All but one of the barns had female elephants and their offspring. The last barn had four males, huge amazing creatures that greeted Dr. Mayi with gentle prods with their trunks. He explained the females excluded them unless it was time to mate. "I should try that," I joked. Dr. Mayi did not laugh.

"They are all African elephants rescued from poachers Dr. Mayi explained, "I would have taken the poachers to the authorities, but Hann always goes on these trips, and he is fond of swifter, more permanent forms of justice."

We walked out onto the acres of elephant parkland and a familiar voice yelled, "Asshat!" followed by a loud splash. We turned and walked toward a small muddy pond that elephants used to take mud baths to protect their skin from the sun. A student rushed over to pull Tomas out of the mud, but Des somehow managed to trip him and send him into the mud with Tomas. Then Marie ran up behind Des, and chaos ensued. Marie was pulled in by both her brothers while Jacques stood with the students on the bank who were laughing and pointing at their friend in the mud with the triplets. Then an amazing thing happened. A female elephant walked over to the muddy mess and reached out her trunk to help Tomas climb out. She did the same for the others. "She gets the mother of the year award. I certainly wasn't going to help them and end up in the mud too," I commented.

I marched the triplets to the house to get cleaned up. They had lasted a whole five minutes. Jacques stayed behind. As I was hosing the mud off the three of them, Jacques slowly rode by on the back of one of the smaller females guided by Dr. Mayi. His siblings were not happy, but he had a broad smile and waved to us as he went by.

It took two showers to finally get all the mud out of their hair and ears. Eventually, all the kids got to ride the great beasts. The elephants were curious about the new teenage humans and seemed to enjoy having them around. The rest of the visit the kids were banned from going near the mud ponds. When Jacques put on his shoes the next day, he found them full of mud.

In the evening, Dr. Mayi told the children tales of the Congo around a campfire. The Haute Caste and I sat in the plush leather furniture in the living room. I finished a bowl of chili while they politely sipped small ornate glasses of O positive.

"Cassie and I would like to offer our services to the Magus and your family."

Tristan responded, "I value your support. The enemy has retreated after their plans failed. They no longer have any mortal agents from Rome, but we believe Sir Alexander has a small guerilla army in the Far East of unsanctioned Common Caste. He has an ally we have not been able to identify, the Red Lotus. She is the one that gave the crazed monk some of Lena's blood."

Cassie mused, "They must have stolen a sample from Dr. Kyoto's lab in Tokyo. No one would have been able to steal from the Magus' home." I thought it was interesting that she knew the only places where samples of Lena's blood were stored, but then she was an oracle.

I was not as certain that the Magus had impenetrable security. "She could be anyone. A lot of vampires resent us, not just in the Far East." I commented.

Hann nodded in agreement, then changed the subject, "We are glad to be your friends. While you are here, I would like to show you some artifacts I have collected. The others have seen them before, but you all are welcome to join us."

"Sure, I would love that," I replied

Omar stood, "I would enjoy seeing them again."

I followed the ancient warrior and Omar outside to a building I had thought stored equipment. When we entered, I realized it was a museum. There were carved marble busts of my host, and framed quotes on the wall. Military maps that I assumed showed his campaigns lay on a table. Books about Hannibal were stacked on a desk. At the far end was a wooden structure covered with a replica of the armor his elephants had worn into battle. Above a mannequin with Hann's breastplate and a helmet hung a plaque that read, "Hannibal ad Portas!"

I pointed at the sign and asked, "What does the sign say?"

He smiled, "Hannibal is at the gate!"

Omar was looking at a map of the battle of Zama, where the Romans defeated Hannibal. "How did they ever beat you? It was a magnificent campaign."

"Treachery. I've warned the Magus never to trust Romans."

"Romans?" I asked, wondering if Hann was slipping back into time.

"Sir Hann means the House of Pentacles."

"I've always been uneasy around Borgia."

"Trust your instincts, Baroness!" Hann replied.

My fondness for Hannibal was growing. Our tour complete, I followed them back outside. "Thank you for your hospitality. I think we'll be heading home at sunset tomorrow."

While we were in the museum, Cassie was back at the house, giving my husband an earful. She had kept her distance from me, afraid that I might glimpse her thoughts.

"I had a vision; it was a masked figure with a long knife. I could not tell who it was. Then I saw your youngest child standing over a flaming crack in the ground. It became larger and he struggled to determine which side to jump on. I heard your wife scream, and then all went black." She was trembling.

Tristan lightly touched her hands. His reassuring touch helped her calm down. "Thank you. I will not tell my wife at this point. I fear it would cause her much distress. I shall share your vision with the Magus."

All I saw when we walked back in was Tristan holding Cassie's hands. I assumed she was distant from me because she had feelings for my husband. They broke apart when they saw me and she retired. Without comment, I turned from Tristan and joined the children. The fire was down to the last embers. Dr. Mayi greeted me warmly, "Dear Baroness, your children are very curious and bright. I have enjoyed sharing stories of my homeland with them."

"C'mon, it's late, off to bed. Tell Dr. Mayi thanks."

They all hugged him. Marie said, "One day I'll be a veterinarian too, then I can help you with the elephants."

"I look forward to that day!"

I love my kids, but their father, well, that was another very complicated matter. I was sound asleep by the time he retired, and I did not respond to his presence, the sight of him with Cassie diminished my libido. He fell asleep with one hand resting on my thigh.

The next day the children were more attentive to the students and seemed fascinated with the study of elephant scat. That evening we said our goodbyes, climbed back in the Range Rovers and headed back to Bel Air.

Chapter 31

The Sign

When we got back to L.A. from the elephant refuge, Tillie had dinner waiting for us mortals. After dinner, I got the kids off to bed without a protest. Two days with the elephants had exhausted them. Tristan left to meet with the Magus. I went to sit in the garden after a few minutes Batu came up the garden path. He stopped in his tracks, surprised to see me. "Baroness!"

I noticed the bandage on his neck. "Are you okay?" I caught the faint scent of vampire blood almost covered up by his mortal smell.

"I've been better, but I'll mend. Had a disagreement with a fellow in London."

For an instant, an image came to me, "Johann!"

"Yes, how did you... Well, he won't be a problem again. Lady Kananga made sure of that."

"You lied to me. You're as bad as the others."

"Thanks for your concern. Good to be back," he went inside clearly irritated.

I heard a commotion in the house and wondered "Now what?" I turned and saw Robert and Billy with their luggage. I caught up with them at the foot of the grand staircase. "Amigos!"

"Baroness," Robert took my hand and lightly kissed it. He smiled, "I heard the Baron is meeting with the Magus."

"You want to run away with me tonight?" I joked.

Billy grinned, "Anytime! But your situation can't be that desperate."

"I'm just pissed off tonight."

They looked at each other and were clearly at a loss.

Robert added, "I've heard the Baron sometimes hits hockey pucks to reduce stress. You might try that. Goodnight Baroness." They tipped their hats to me and went upstairs.

I could use an outlet. I went out to the small hockey rink in a building behind the house and lined up several pucks.

"Tristan!" I yelled and hit the puck as hard as I could. I heard it bounce off the wall. "Magus!" "Antoinella!" "Batu!" and finally, "Alexander!" I hit the last one so hard I lost my balance and fell on my butt.

Tristan and the Magus were watching the hockey rink on one of the screens in the Magus' office.

"See what I'm dealing with! How can I reason with her?" Tristan asked as he paced.

The Magus chuckled, "Be relieved she took her anger out on the pucks." "We failed Miranda by not stopping Turlock. You must acknowledge that if you want to repair your relationship."

"But she knows I killed him, isn't that enough?" He stopped pacing and stared at the Magus. "Why do you take her side?"

"Because she is right. Go to her, apologize and try to convince her to remain here with the children."

Tristan left the Magus' mansion in a foul mood. When he arrived back at the house, I was taking a shower. Normally he would join me then foreplay would begin, but not tonight. I was surprised to find him sitting on the bed. "What did the Magus have to say?" I asked.

"That I should apologize to you."

I laughed, "Wow! This must be painful."

"Miranda, you have no idea." The coldness in his voice stopped me. "You are ungrateful and disrespectful. You are moody. You are passionate one night, and the next refuse my touch. I am supposed to apologize to you for your father's murder. I had nothing to do with it, except that I executed his killer. I have no idea why you are so angry with me."

"Why don't you ask Cassie. Maybe she could understand why I might not trust you."

"You're jealous of Cassie? Why? I have never been with her."

"She's on a pretty short list then." I stood in front of him wrapped in a towel. His scent and righteous anger were killing me. I realized that was as close to an apology as I was likely to get. I dropped the towel. "Take off your clothes. I accept your apology."

"I didn't apologize."

"Shut up Tristan!"

Well, you know what followed. Before sunrise, Tristan went to his room. Shutting him up with sex was not my proudest moment. When I made it down to the kitchen in the late morning, Tillie was in a great mood. She thought the Lord and Lady of the manor were back together again. I grabbed a mug of coffee and a Danish then followed the voices of my kids coming from the dining room.

I wanted to get myself and the kids around "normal" people for a while. "Why don't we go to the mall today, get you guys some clothes."

"And new shoes," Jacques added, staring at Des.

I texted Lolly to see if she and Al might help supervise the kids buying clothes. She took it pretty hard when she heard about my dad's death. I hoped it might make her think twice about sampling any more vampire blood. She still did not know I was aware of their relationship with Borgia. I knew she had been waiting to hear from me since we got back to L.A. Fashion advice for the kids was right up her alley. She and Al would meet us at Nordstrom.

Clive and his brother Jasper were to be our bodyguards for the day. Clive was clean-shaven and a little shorter than Jasper who sported a very neat mustache. To their relief, I assured them that Al and Lolly would also be there to help with the kids.

I grabbed the kids and we headed out to the Rolls Royce They would soon turn fourteen and fifteen and were taller than me now. It was roomier than the Bentley. Sometimes you have to sacrifice. When we arrived at the Beverly Center, Jasper hated giving up the keys to the parking valet, but the valet assured him this wasn't his first Rolls. Al and Lolly greeted us with big hugs. Each of the kids had their own unique sense of style. Marie preferred dark colors, Tomas liked an athletic look, Des was retro hippy, and Jacques liked button-down shirts.

Lolly was pleased to be engaged in official aunt duties. "I've been thinking about your colors. Tomas, I see you in blue, Desmon in greens, Marie, definitely shades of red, and Jacques in purple."

"Marie replied, "I want black!"

"Don't limit my colors," Des replied.

"I'm good with blue!" Tomas smiled.

Before Jacques could add to the dispute I said, "Thanks Lolly, but let's just see if we can find some clothes they like. To be on the safe side, everyone team-up. Al with Tomas, Clive with Des, Lolly with Marie, and Jasper with Jacques. Okay?"

"And Batu with the Baroness, just to be on the safe side."

Startled, I turned to see my bodyguard standing behind me. "How did you..."

He smiled. "I saw you as the car pulled away. The Baron would be unhappy if I didn't keep watch on you. I borrowed the Baron's Corvette and followed the Rolls."

"I want to drive home with Batu," Des stated.

"No way, I get to go with Batu!" Tomas insisted.

"Enough! No one is going with him. You'll have to put up with the Rolls." I couldn't believe I said that.

As we set off to find the boys some jeans, I felt the floor tremble. For a second, everything went silent, and then people started screaming. I yelled, "Get the kids to the stairwell!"

The kids and their assigned guardians headed to the stairwell. I was close behind with Batu at my back. There was a loud, deep rumble and the floor shook so hard I lost my balance and fell to the ground several feet from the stairwell door. Batu pushed me against the wall and threw himself on top of me as light fixtures came crashing down. He cradled my head against his chest. His strong body protected me from flying debris. I felt something fall on top of him. He did not move. "It will be over soon," he whispered.

I started to tremble, "My kids!"

"They will be fine." His scent and warmth comforted me.

The rumbling and shaking finally stopped. I looked over his shoulder and saw a blinking EXIT sign. I stared at it for a few seconds. Damn! Back in Rossville I asked for a sign. This was not what I expected. Who was I to deny fate? We lay on the floor for several very long minutes to be sure the earthquake was over. Batu stood and carefully helped me up. I looked in his eyes and saw passion chained by restraint. Batu winced when he turned to walk towards the stairwell. I saw a shard of glass stuck in his shoulder.

"Wait," I grabbed a shirt off a mannequin and wrapped it around my hand. "Let me help you." I pulled on the piece of glass, he did not make a sound, but I almost fainted. Finally, it came out. I stuffed the shirt under his t-shirt, over the wound, to try to stop the bleeding. Then we moved some debris out of the way to get to the stairwell. I noticed other people seemed more shaken up than hurt. The dust gave us a ghostly appearance.

I could see Clive and Jasper looking through the small window in the door. Batu pushed open the door. "Mom!" the kids screamed as it popped open. They pushed their way past the other adults to hug me.

Lolly joined the hug, "Randie, are you okay?"

"Batu saved me, but he's hurt."

Lolly told Al to look at Batu."

Batu tried to say it was nothing, but the blood on his shirt convinced Al to check the wound. "The wound needs to be cleaned and dressed as soon as possible, but I don't think it will cause long-term injury."

Jasper stated, "We should get out of here before more debris falls. There might be aftershocks."

Clive took control, "Down the stairwell! I'll lead, and Jasper will go last."

We quickly made our way down four flights of stairs. Other people covered with bits of debris joined us. The kids were adjusting quickly and showed little signs of fear.

Tomas stated, "This is like one of those catastrophe movies."

"We look like Mall Zombies," Jacques replied.

When we got to the parking garage, the cars were covered by chunks of cement. Jasper shook his head, "I loved that car!"

We headed out to the street. There was a small aftershock that caused us to freeze. I grabbed Batu's hand for a minute. Marie seemed to notice. After it passed, we walked across the street to the Cedars-Sinai Medical Center. The E.R. entrance was packed with ambulances and first responders bringing in the severely injured. Al asked us to wait while he went inside and a few minutes later he emerged with some first aid supplies. We sat at a nearby outdoor café while Al took care of Batu's wound. When he took off his shirt Lolly rolled her eyes.

"Stop it," I whispered. The kids snickered. He was in great shape for a mortal. "If he hadn't laid on top of me, I'd be injured or worse."

Lolly whispered, "I wish he would lay on top of me."

I just shook my head, but I appreciated the levity. We were all okay. It was not the first earthquake I had experienced in L.A., but it was the biggest. It was amazing how quickly an earthquake could pass while leaving so much destruction and disruption.

Clive called Tillie and announced, "All is well at home. No one was hurt, and there is little damage to the buildings. The Baron slept through the quake."

"Thank God his Highness was not disturbed," I added, rolling my eyes. I saw Batu trying to hide a smile.

"Unfortunately, Tillie does not drive, so I suggest we call Uber."

It took a while with all the chaos, but finally, we got a ride. The Lyft driver asked us to walk a block to meet her due to the emergency vehicle traffic around the medical center.

When we got to the corner, there was a minivan, and a Prius.

I hugged my friends and joked, "We'll take the kids shopping, what could go wrong? It'll be fun!"

Al smiled, "Just order from Amazon next time."

We left for Stone Canyon. Jasper was seated in front next to the driver. The kids were in the middle section, arguing about who got the most scared. Clive, Batu and I rode in the back. Batu said nothing and made it a point to not look at me. With the blinking of an exit sign, I had made up my mind. I would never know if Batu's actions saved my life but seeing the exit sign was about to rock my world.

Chapter 32

The Aftershock

When we got home, Tillie was beside herself with worry. She ran down the steps, hugged her husband then checked each of the kids before getting to me. She surveyed the dust and bits of debris in my hair. "Baroness, I'll run a bath."

"Don't worry about that. Please ask Lady Lily to look at Batu. He was hurt."

We all went upstairs, and I told the kids to get cleaned up for dinner. Uncharacteristically they quietly obeyed.

As I went into my bathroom and started filling the tub, Tristan ran in and took me in his arms. "Miranda!"

"I'm okay! Really!" I stepped away and started to undress.

"Clive said the children were unscathed, but look at you."

"It's just dust. The store ceiling came down on Batu and me, but the others were safe in the stairwell."

"I'm sorry I was not with you."

"I don't think you could have stopped the earthquake."

He ignored my response, "What can I do..."

"Well, funny you should ask," I looked at him directly, "I want a divorce."

He was stunned. I turned, threw off the rest of my clothes, and submerged myself in the rose-scented bubbles. I did not want to even look at him. Two strong arms pulled me out of the tub.

"You want a divorce because of an earthquake? Are you sure you are not hurt? Are you in shock? You are making no sense. You must have a concussion. I'll summon Lady Lily."

"Stop! I'm fine. You might want to let the kids know you were worried about them." Please tell Mr. Beaudine I would like to see him. Now, if you don't mind, I want to be alone right now and soak. In fact, even if you do mind."

The mighty and powerful Baron Tristan Mordecai struggled for a response that would put his world right again. He stood for a moment, clearly at a loss for words, possibly for the first time in his life. Then he turned and left, presumably to check on the kids.

I felt lighter than I had in a long time. It was like a heavy weight had been lifted from me. I told him that I wanted a divorce, leaving little room for argument. I would gladly give up the Baroness title. It was a small price to pay to be free. I knew he would always be part of my life for many reasons, starting with the kids. He thought I had lost my mind, but actually, I finally found it. I wanted to live with the kids closer to the mortal world rather than at the heart of the undead society. It was why I had gone to Rossville in the first place. I needed more than just distance, and the relationship had to be severed. I imagined how he must feel un-hinged like I did when he first revealed that he was a vampire. Maybe I did hit my head, or perhaps it was just surviving a disaster. I did not care. I was grateful I had been given a sign, although an actual blinking exit sign wasn't exactly what I was expecting.

Downstairs, Lady Lily was finishing dressing Batu's wound.

"Batu, what happened today?" Tristan angrily demanded as he burst into the room.

Batu rose from his seat, bowed slightly, and grimaced from the pain. "There was an earthquake Baron."

"I'm well aware of that," he bristled, "I meant what happened to the Baroness?"

"She lost her balance and fell and as debris started to fall from the ceiling, I shielded her from injury. The others kept the children safe in the stairwell."

Lily added, "The cut on his back took several stitches. The Baroness was fortunate he protected her."

Tristan's tone softened, "Are you sure she was not hurt?"

"I don't think so, though she may have been bruised when I fell on top of her on the floor."

"You were on the floor on top of my wife?"

"Just for a few minutes," Batu quickly responded, "When I helped the Baroness to her feet, she was understandably shaken up but not injured."

Lily intervened. "He was wounded protecting the Baroness. She could have been the one needing medical attention instead of Batu. Tristan turned to Batu and managed to say, "Thank you," then walked away.

I got out of the tub and got dressed. Now I had to tell the kids what was going to happen. They would know something was up soon enough. I just wanted them to know the truth. I found them in the game room. "Are you guys doing okay? Did you eat something?"

Des was sharing a couch with Tomas, and Marie was on the floor. They were intensely focused on a game. Jacques was sitting at a small table drawing. I looked at his comic book artwork. It was Batu wearing a superhero costume. I hoped their father did not see that drawing.

Des broke his concentration for a minute, "Yeah, Tillie gave us snacks, but she said that's all till dinner."

"You can have ice cream later. Now we need to talk."

Des turned off the TV. They all stared at me. "I made a difficult decision today. Your dad and I have some differences that we can't get past."

"Divorce?" Marie asked.

As usual, they were one step ahead of me.

"Does dad know? He must be..." Des began but stopped mid-sentence.

"Miranda!" Tristan bellowed in the hall.

"We'll continue this later," I walked out of the room, closing the door behind me.

"I want to discuss what the hell happened today!" Tristan said.

"Let's go out on the patio," I replied. Tristan followed me outside. We sat at the same wrought iron table where we had discussed my move back to Illinois.

"Everything was fine last night. We made love and fell asleep in each other's arms. Now you say you want to leave me. What is going on?" he asked.

"Last night felt great, but sexual compatibility is not a measure of the health of a relationship. As I recall, you enjoyed yourself with Antoinella, repeatedly."

He stared at me, fuming.

"Since we met you know I have been considering how I might escape from you and all the midnight madness. I guess I've always known our marriage could not last. I will always love you, but I can't be married to you any longer."

"I recall you wanted to marry me. Was that a lie?" His stare was cold and piercing.

"No, I did at the time. I can't stay in the center of your chaotic world or have the kids in the middle of it anymore. I'll give up my station, my

Haute Caste identity, my title, and whatever else is necessary."

"Miranda, I…"

I held up my hand, "As long as I'm mortal, I want a life for the kids and me away from all this craziness."

"What do you mean as long as you're mortal?" His voice softened, "Will you come back to me if you decide to transform?" He gently placed his hand over mine.

"That's a big if, all I can say is I haven't closed the door on that possibility." I pulled my hand away. You can see the children as much as you want. I don't want to hurt your relationship with them. They adore you; you will always be their father, but we will no longer be a couple."

"You're going to give up everything we have together. Who is it? Your bodyguard? Someone else?

I stood and stated clearly, "It's me. I'm leaving you for me. I will always have strong feelings for you, but this marriage has been strangling me."

He stopped a few feet away. I could see both sadness and anger in his eyes. "Baroness Mordecai will always be your rightful title whether or not you are married to me. I will give you whatever you want, but I will always protect you and the children. That is not negotiable." His voice was calmer, almost cold. His eyes narrowed. Tristan rarely showed his scary side to me.

Still, I decided to take it further, "Divorce means I will be free to get involved with someone else if I choose. I want your word that they won't have a weird accident or disappear."

"I will not interfere if they are a decent mortal."

I was surprised that he had specified mortals. "I don't plan on seeing another vampire, but if I did, I still want you to stay out of it."

"Our divorce will make you a highly sought prize among the Haute Caste. You represent status. I will let it be known that if anyone tries to court you, they will have to deal with me. If they should be unkind or improper in any way, they will answer to me."

He moved closer. His searching gaze touched my heart. I wanted to hold him, but I stopped myself. "The chemistry between us is rare. You won't find it with another." I turned and walked into the house. I wondered how long it would take before I heard from the Magus.

I gathered the kids for dinner. To my surprise, Tristan joined us. There was an uncomfortable silence at the table. He sipped from his silver goblet while we ate lasagna.

"Hockey tonight?" Des asked.

"I'm afraid your mother and I will be meeting with the lawyer this evening. I'm sure you can convince the others to play with you," Tristan said.

The room was quiet again. The kids stared down at their plates while they finished dinner.

"I'll tell Tillie to fix hot fudge sundaes later."

The kids excused themselves and set off to recruit players.

He stood, "I'll be in the library. Mr. Beaudine will arrive shortly."

I grabbed a cup of coffee and went in search of my freedom. Mr. Beaudine was sitting on the couch, talking with my husband, seated behind his desk. The well-dressed lawyer rose when I entered the room. He was tan with graying blond hair. He nodded to me and said, "Nice to see you again."

I nodded in reply and sat in one of the chairs in front of the desk.

"I understand your desire to start the divorce proceedings. If you and the Baron are in agreement, I can start the process tomorrow."

"That would be fine. I want joint custody of the kids."

"Of course. He is giving you the property in Illinois, and very generous support. Shall I stipulate monthly visits?"

I turned to Tristan, "He can visit the kids whenever and for as long as he would like as long as he lets me know ahead of time."

Tristan nodded his agreement and turned to me. "I think that is all. Is there anything else you want?" I just shook my head.

Mr. Beaudine looked at both of us and said he had all the information he required and would have the papers with all the details ready for us the next morning.

I looked over at Tristan and sipped my coffee. "I didn't think it would be this easy," I said softly.

There was a cold fire in his gaze. "Did you think I would force you to stay with me? You are the love of my existence. I hate the thought of you rejecting me, but you have always been free. I brought you to my home years ago for protection, not to imprison you. I guess I never really understood you. Goodnight Miranda," he stood and walked out.

I stayed and sat alone, crying quietly. I was not sure if the tears were due to the end of my marriage, his outpouring of love, relief that it was over, or pent-up grief due to Dad's death. Then sense of newfound serenity filled me. I had divorced his ass!

Chapter 33

The Emperor and the Queens

The Magus was in his office and spread out a Tarot deck on a small table between two leather chairs. He selected the Queen of Cups, the Queen of Wands, and the Queen of Plows. He placed the Emperor card in the center and placed the queens around it. The Empress card he placed alone on the side. He took a picture with his phone and sent it to Lady Kananga, Lady Lily, and Lady Sarah, with the caption, Tomorrow night. Within minutes all three responded that they were agreeable.

A few minutes later, the butler announced, "The Baron is here to see you."

"Please show him in."

Tristan entered looking ill at ease. "Miranda is divorcing me. I can't believe she truly desires this!"

"I will try to give you some insight into your wife's decision. You tend to view women in simplistic transactional terms."

"I've given her everything she could want and more." Tristan stood and paced in the room like his panther.

"Exactly my point. I have found that though women appreciate gifts, it is our attitude towards them that can enhance or diminish their affection. How did you respond to her demand?"

"I warned her others of the Haute Caste would pursue her as a prize."

The Magus shook his head, "That is exactly how you view her, as a precious commodity."

Tristan was exasperated, "What can I do? There must be a way to win her back."

The Magus raised his hand, "Continue to cooperate fully with Miranda. The divorce changes your relationship but does not end it." He pushed a button on a remote control and a screen lit up, showing the Baron's hockey rink. Miranda was watching the game with an expression of delight. "See how closely she minds your children; she is a great mother. Your shared devotion to the children binds you."

"I don't understand how she could do this to me?"

The Magus was growing impatient, "She has strong feelings for you. She did not make her choice lightly. Don't you see, she is doing this for herself and your offspring. She is not doing this to punish you. In time I believe she will decide to take her rightful place among us. She has been evolving, yet you have changed little. Use this time to examine your relationships with her, and women in general. Try to gain some insight into the female psyche. It will improve your interactions with her."

"I have always enjoyed my relationships with women. Why should I change the way I interact with them?"

The Magus sighed, shaking his head in frustration. "Because Miranda has stopped enjoying your company," the Magus stated bluntly. "

The Magus was irritated, uncharacteristically he raised his voice, "For a brilliant vampire, you are clueless about the fairer sex. Tomorrow night Ladies Kananga, Lily, and Sarah will meet with you at your home. You will hear them out and listen to what they tell you."

Tristan had expected sympathy from the ancient vampire who ruled his world. He was confused by the Magus' lack of support.

The next day I gathered the kids together in my room. Despite all they had been through over the past few weeks, our divorce would be a big deal in their lives. I wanted to give them a chance to talk about it.

Des was first, "I knew this would happen. Being, you know, normal, you're getting older, but Dad is not going to change."

Jacques complained, "I don't like it. You should stay with Dad."

Marie was the therapist, "We know it's been hard for both of you. I want you to be happy, but I'm worried about dad."

Tomas sounded like the oldest, "We'll be fine whatever you do."

"I appreciate your honesty and concern for your dad and me. He is not happy about this, but he accepts my decision. We'll go back to Rossville in a couple of weeks."

"Mom? C'mon. Can't we stay here?" Marie asked.

Jacques pleaded, "Please Mom, the house is so big you don't have to hang out with dad."

I looked at Tomas who had yet to respond. "What do you think?"

"I miss grandma, the horses, and Bart."

"Well, regardless, we are all flying back in two weeks."

Jacques was getting tearful. "Does this mean we won't see Dad anymore?"

I put my arm around his shoulders, "Of course not. You'll still have lots of time with your father. He said he'll visit more often. His love for you won't change. He isn't divorcing any of you."

Des inquired, "We'll still be royal, right?"

"Unfortunately, yes."

"Cool!" Jacques blurted out.

The next evening Tristan stopped by the dining room as the kids and I were finishing dinner. He was wearing a dark grey jacket over a silk shirt and navy slacks as though going somewhere.

"What's up?" I inquired.

"Dad, will you play hockey with us?" Jacques asked.

"I have a meeting with some Haute Caste in the library. It should not take too long. Then I'll join you."

"Do you want me there? Is it something I should know about?"

"No," he replied curtly and walked away.

After dinner, Billy and Robert joined us in the small hockey rink. As Billy was lacing up, he said, "We heard you're splitting up. Now don't be running off with Robert."

Robert added, "As nice as that sounds, I'd like to stay attached to my handsome head."

Lady Kananga's hair fell in fine curls about her shoulders. She adjusted her dark purple caftan as she sat on the couch in the library. She considered the best response to the Magus' request to counsel the Baron. Lady Sarah and Lady Lily joined her and sat down in the plush chairs on either side of the large coffee table. Lady Sarah wore a leather vest over a denim shirt and jeans while Lady Lily was a bit more formal in a pale blue silk blouse tucked into linen slacks. They had not spent much time primping or adorning themselves for this meeting. At different times over the years, they had all known the pleasure of having sex with the Baron, but it had been over a hundred years ago for Sarah and even longer for the others. He was as handsome and seductive as ever, but his personality had diminished their desire to share his bed.

Lady Kananga started, "It will take all of our intellect to provide the Baron with even a small insight about women, mortal, or our kind."

"I will try to be gentle," Lady Sarah responded.

"Not too gentle," Lady Lily added with a smile.

"I wish Miranda could be involved, but the Magus was afraid she would lose her temper," Kananga told them.

"The Baron certainly will," Sarah added.

"I hope I don't," Lady Lily responded.

Tristan entered, "Good evening," he greeted them with a bow of his head, closed the door, and sat on the end of the sofa opposite them. "Thank you for meeting with me. I know this is unusual, but the Baroness is seeking a divorce. I'm struggling to understand why she would make that kind of mistake. The Magus thought you could provide me with some insight."

"Baron," Lady Kananga began, "The Magus would like us to help you better understand…shall we say relationships with women. It might be helpful if to start you asked any questions you might have."

He shifted uncomfortably, "I've never had any difficulty with women, mortal or vampiress until I met her. The Magus seems to think she has caused me to become clueless when it comes to females. Isn't it possible that she is the one in need of your counsel?"

"It is difficult to add water to a full cup," Lady Lily remarked.

He sat back and glared at Lady Lily, "Do you think I have acted badly towards my wife?"

Lady Sarah responded, "When I met the Baroness, my impression was that she seemed a bit immature and ungrateful, but as I have gotten to know her better, I find that she is honest, sometimes brutally honest, and merely wants to be respected."

Tristan stated, "I respect her!"

Lady Kananga leaned towards him, "You feel passion for her, you adore her, but you punished her with your indiscretions when she decided to move away. You refused to remain monogamous but demanded it of her. That is not respect."

"I told her what I would do if she went to Illinois. She made her decision. Now she wants a divorce. She is punishing me!"

Lady Lily sighed, "No, she is not. Consider, just for the sake of argument, that perhaps this is not all about you."

Tristan looked confused, "She is divorcing me. Acting as if she would be content with someone else just to hurt me."

Lady Lily looked incredulous. Kananga raised a hand to stop Lily from responding. "There is someone else."

"You see!" Tristan said, "Who is the fool?"

"Someone very bright and brave. She is leaving you to find herself," Lady Kananga stated.

Lady Sarah added, "Sometimes your presence is a bit overwhelming."

Tristan looked more confused than ever. "Can't she find herself with me? I've given her everything, including my undying desire, how could she reject me? If there is anything she desires, all she has to do is ask."

Lady Lily was unable to restrain herself, "Has a woman ever walked away from you before?"

"Of course not."

"I suggest you Google Narcissistic Disorder." Exasperated she stood, bowed slightly to Lady Kananga and Lady Sarah, then turned and left the room ignoring the Baron.

Lady Sarah smiled, "I once advised you to lie to Miranda, but you refused, saying that you prided yourself on your honesty. Now, old friend, you must try and be honest with yourself."

Lady Kananga added, "You're obsessed with her because she is not obsessed with you."

He stood and walked to the French doors that looked out on the garden. He turned to face them, "I do obsess about her. I wake up thinking about her. Even when I'm with another, I think about her, which diminishes my pleasure."

"When you begin to see her as a human being with emotional needs and aspirations that go beyond her relationship with you, then this possessiveness will wane," Lady Kananga told him.

"Since I have been with Miranda, the moon rises and sets with her. You really think I can let go so easily?"

Lady Sarah sighed, "She was never in your grasp. You need to understand that she is not a thing to be possessed. She chose to be with you."

Lady Kananga added, "Miranda is coming to terms with life. None of us know where it will lead. Trying to stand in her way will not help anyone, especially not the children."

"I told her I would not stop her."

Lady Sarah responded, "That's good because you cannot stop her."

He appeared a little shaken. "I'm grateful to you both and Lady Lily. You have given me much to consider. I saw Miranda as an extension of myself, much like the children, not standing alone." Then a slight smile came to his face, "Still, she will never find anyone like me."

Lady Kananga, slowly shaking her head. Responded, "Tristan, that is why she is getting a divorce."

♈

At his mansion, the Magus had watched the counseling session on a monitor in his office. He was appreciative of the insight and patience of the vampiresses. He had always been very discrete about his relationships and never let his affairs become public. His deep respect for women and appreciation of their ability to be shrewd or subtle and when necessary cunning, came from watching his mother care for him and protect him when he was a sickly child. His father thought he was cursed and hoped he would die. His mother kept him away from his father and developed a special diet that allowed him to flourish. Remarkable for the illiterate wife of a Mesopotamian goat herder. After all these centuries, he still found himself learning about how to handle people by observing women around him. When Theodore Roosevelt talked about speaking softly but carrying a big stick, he must have been inspired by the women in his life.

The Magus contemplated how Miranda and the children were affecting the societal norms of the undead. The divorce would certainly cause a stir. It was a blow to the Baron's pride. The Magus would tactfully try to help him recover. Tristan kept his tremendous powers hidden, just like the Magus. Unfortunately, emotional insight was not one of Tristan's gifts. For a thousand years he thought he was prepared for all the moves on the chessboard of this world until now. The age of Miranda and her offspring was bringing upheaval to their society, which had been coasting along unchallenged for centuries. He was oddly thrilled to face new challenges where their ancient abilities, long unused might be needed again.

Chapter 34

Marie has a Vision

Back in Rossville, Mom was struggling with the loss of my dad. Grigoryi was showing her how to hand-make pasta when Jeanne entered the kitchen with Bart. Grigoryi had not spent much time with the vampires, and with his past experiences, Grigoryi had yet to establish a comfort level with the undead.

Jeanne and Bart sat at the counter and watched them roll out the pasta dough and cut the noodles. "Good evening Grigoryi" Bart said.

"We trust that you are a friend. We hope you will consider us friends too." Jeanne tried to reassure him.

She did not look like the other vampiresses he knew. She wore little jewelry or makeup, and her long dark hair was not styled. "Thank you," he nodded.

Bart responded, "We appreciate you wanting to help the Baroness and her family."

"I met with Father Rinaldi in Los Angeles. He mentioned a vampire hunter who had changed his ways, was that you?" Jeanne asked.

Grigoryi swallowed and put down his knife, afraid the blade might slip. "Yes, he was kind to me. He helped me leave my former calling to get a job in a bagel shop. Father Rinaldi explained that our job was not to judge but to serve others."

Jeanne smiled, "There was a time when I would have helped you hunt vampires, but then the Magus saved my life."

Grigoryi's eyes lit up, "The Magus scares me, but in a good way, I guess."

Bart smiled, "He often has that effect on people."

"How did he rescue you?" Grigoryi asked.

Jeanne replied, "I was about to be burned alive."

"Holy Mother of God!" Grigoryi's eyes grew large and he crossed himself, "It is you! I had heard rumors of you appearing in convents.

Saint Joan, I am not worthy!" he bowed his head.

Mom responded, "Greg, get a grip!" My mom had figured out who Jeanne was the first night she arrived. Her grandmother had mentioned the French vampiress to her many years ago.

A few days before we returned to the prairie, I decided to get my hair cut. Batu and Jasper would be my security team. Lolly would meet me at the salon. It was broad daylight, so I felt safe to run an errand with a couple of bodyguards. The kids would be supervised by Clive and Tillie, with Delilah as added feline muscle.

We would meet Lolly at Rigoberto's salon in Beverly Hills. He was an old friend of Lolly's. She used to help pay for my haircuts when she was making big bucks modeling and I was still a struggling writer. I was not surprised that she was running late.

Jasper waited outside, and Batu sat in the reception area. He stared at the young Asian woman who greeted us and walked me back. I told him, "Relax Batu, this will take about an hour."

I settled in a chair to get my hair shampooed. The receptionist walked to the back to let Rigoberto know I was there. As another young woman ran the water, I said, "It's a little cold." Suddenly she covered my face with a towel. I tried to push it away, then everything went dark.

Batu's anxiety level rose when the receptionist did not return after several minutes. He signaled to Jasper to come with him. They searched the salon and were alarmed to find it empty except for Rigoberto, and one of his staff who had been rendered unconscious. They called Clive to be sure the kids were safe. Everyone at the mansion was fine. The Magus' staff were notified, but they all decided to wait until closer to sunset to wake and notify the Baron or the Magus. I could not blame them. They hoped I would show up before heads started rolling. Lolly did not answer her phone.

My head ached as I opened my eyes. It was not a bad dream after all. I was lying on a cot in a room with high, unadorned cement walls. There was a metal door which was certainly locked. There was a toilet and a sink in the corner of the room. I lay staring up at a tiny window near the ceiling. I sat up and felt queasy and disoriented. I looked around and saw a young Asian woman sat in a wooden chair in the corner staring at me. "No English," she said before I even spoke.

I hoped the kids were okay. There was a plastic cup of water on the floor. I sipped it and my head started to clear. My arm was sore, and I pulled up the sleeve of my denim shirt. There was a bandage over the spot where a locator chip had been implanted. The Magus had convinced me to take this precaution for myself and the kids soon after Marie had been kidnapped. I realized it had been had removed

My guard called out in Chinese. The door opened and a young man brought in a small tray with a baguette, some Brie, and coffee. He bowed as he placed it on the bed. They both left quickly. I started considering my options. I knew the big guns would not show up until sunset, which gave me a couple of hours. I looked up at the window. It was too high to reach and, in any case, too small for me to fit through. There was no way I could break through the metal door. The only chair in the room was screwed to the floor. Since it was still daylight, I knew they had not taken me very far. I guessed I was being held in an old warehouse somewhere. I expected a rat to sneak out of a crack in the wall at any time. I hoped they needed me alive for leverage. For the first time since I was a child, I got on my knees and said a prayer. I just wanted my kids to be protected. I knew I would need my strength, so I ate the bread and cheese. I slowly savored the still-warm cup of coffee and hoped Team Miranda would be able to find me.

Clive had the misfortune of delivering the news to the Baron when he woke. "Where is my wife?" the Baron yelled as he smashed a table with his fist, causing a lamp to crash to the floor. Clive explained what they knew, and that the Magus was being notified at the same moment. "No one has tried to contact us about her abduction. We have not been able to contact Lolly either."

"Has she been located with her GPS chip?" The Baron asked.

"We haven't yet been able to pick up her signal." Clive quietly responded

"Alexander!" the Baron bellowed.

There was a crisis management meeting at the Bel Air mansion. The Magus, Omar, Anastasia, Pauline, Kananga, Lily, Ruben, Billy, Robert, and Sarah met with Tristan.

The Magus began, "We have underestimated the shameful and outrageous lengths to which Alexander will resort. He has declared war by abducting the Baroness."

"I told him to leave the royal family alone! I swear if he harms her, I shall behead him personally!" Kananga declared.

"You'll have to stand in line for the honor," Omar stated coldly.

Tristan spoke, "I don't believe he will harm her. For many reasons, she is too valuable to him. The botched abduction of her father was an attempt to get to her."

Lily responded, "But the snake bite?"

The Magus said, "He must have known that he could not kill a mortal who was enhanced by our blood and DNA. I believe he was hoping to try and abduct her from the hospital, but we guarded her too well."

Tristan asked, "You still trust Batu? She was taken on his watch."

"Without question," the Magus replied. He did not mention that he suspected the Mongol was in love with her.

Billy and Robert entered with an iPad. "We finally have located her!" Billy announced.

Robert added, "It's a warehouse building in San Pedro."

There was commotion behind them, Batu entered with Delilah and the kids. Marie suddenly stopped seemingly staring into space. "Wait! I can see Mom!"

Anastasia moved over to her and put her arm around Marie's shoulders as though to protect her from the vision. "What do you see?"

"She's in a big room, with a little window. It's not nice. It's an old building. But she's okay." Marie answered tearfully.

The Baron said, "We must go now!"

Batu suggested, "You might take Delilah. The kids have trained her to track the Baroness."

Tristan looked surprised, "Tomas?"

"We just wanted to be able to know where Mom was, you know, when we were staying up late," he squirmed.

The Magus gave everyone orders, "Anastasia and Omar, please take charge of Marie. Tristan bring Delilah. Dr. Lily and Lady Sarah, we may need your medical skills. Lady Kananga, Lady Pauline, and Batu be prepared to take charge of any prisoners."

Tristan turned to Billy and Robert, "Stay here and keep my sons safe."

The Magus rode in his Humvee with the Baron, and the rest of the rescue party split between two Range Rovers. They made record time on the freeway. They located a row of old gray abandoned warehouse buildings and pulled into an alley out of sight of the building where Miranda was being held.

They exited the vehicles and silently assembled, waiting for directions from Tristan and the Magus. The Baron told the group, "We have to do this quickly and quietly, make sure your phones are on silent." turned to Marie, nodded at the last building, and asked, "Here?"

"I don't know, Dad. I can't see her anymore." She started to cry, and Anastasia put her arm around her shoulders to comfort her. Marie put her hand on the panther's head and said, "Delilah! Find Mom!"

The panther sniffed the air and walked to the end, building and pawed at a door. Omar quietly forced the door open; they slipped inside, split up into groups to search the warehouse, but found no one. Delilah walked down a dark narrow hallway and stopped in front of a metal door in a back corner. The door was ajar, and she pushed past the door into the room. Tristan and the Magus followed Delilah into the room. Other than a bed, a chair, a toilet, and a sink, the room was empty. Delilah walked over to a bloody gauze bandage on the floor. The Magus looked down, picked it up and saw Miranda's tracker wrapped up in the gauze. He patted the panther's head. "Whoever took her are clever bastards."

The Baron's phone vibrated with a text from Robert.

Located Antoinella's phone sending coordinates.

"Antoinella!" the Baron spit out her name in disgust.

The Magus was the last to leave the building. He paused and looked at the bloody gauze in his hand. "Miranda, we are coming," he whispered.

I had been moved and was sitting on a cot in another featureless cell. On the floor was a tray of food, but I had no appetite. Suddenly, I felt something like someone from miles away brushed against me. I could sense the Magus reaching out to me, comforting me. The door to my cell opened, and the connection vanished.

"Take away the food!" Antoinella ordered. Two young Chinese vampires did her bidding. Their scent was mingled with Haute Caste blood. I realized that Common Caste, Antoinella had not transformed them.

"Bitch! You better let me go!" I could have been more royal, but I was pissed. "This will not end well for you."

The young vampire almost dropped the food tray. He looked at Antoinella like he was expecting her head to explode. Through a grim smile, she said, "For what it's worth, we were going to trade your father for you. I regret that his kidnapping was handled so poorly."

"You mean his murder!"

"I guess it was too bad he was not one of us," she said with an arrogant smile, "then he could have survived those wounds. In the end, we have you, so I shall be rewarded after all. I will be given my rightful place…"

I cut her off, "On the streets of Rome, where Sir Borgia found you 'working'?" I looked at two Chinese vampires, "You don't have to follow her. I can intercede with the Magus for you."

A tiny smile came to the face of one of the vampires. Antoinella snapped, "Tell the Red Lotus we are ready."

They left and closed the door behind them. Antoinella stood silently next to the door. I tried to stare her down, but she just glared back.

The door opened, and three vampires entered, followed by a figure in a Kabuki costume with a demonic mask. "It's a little early for Halloween!" I said as the masked figure approached and reached out a hand towards me. "Don't touch me!" I struck out and hit the mask. It fell to the floor and I saw his face! For a second, I wondered if he had come to rescue me, but then the reality of the situation crushed my hopes. "Kyoto! I always trusted you!"

"That is unfortunate for you." He turned to the other vampires, "Bind her feet and hands and gag her!"

"Fuck you! You traitor!" I screamed just before a length of duct tape silenced me. I struggled and knocked two of them to the ground as my adrenaline rush was powering my latent vampire DNA. Antoinella grabbed me from behind so the others could tie me up.

Once they had me bound and gagged, Kyoto said, "Baroness, you are probably wondering what we will do to you and why." He paused and made a dramatic gesture that caused one of them to roll in a gurney and some medical supplies. "I will have the honor of transforming you. You will cooperate because if you refuse, you will bleed to death. I don't believe you'll want the children to be without their mother." He saw my confused expression as they laid me on the gurney. "I can no longer bear the disgrace of seeing one of the Haute Caste choose to live as a mortal. I went along with the Magus out of scientific interest. I believe his grand design will harm our kind, though I know that is not his intent. You must set an example for your children. Show them the honorable choice. I shall bestow you with your rightful existence. You will thank me in the end. Shall we begin?"

"And I shall get some of her blood!" Antoinella's vampire teeth were starting to show. It was not a good look.

"I assure you it will be enough to change your powers," Kyoto replied.

I struggled to free myself as they strapped me to the gurney. If I continued to struggle, I would bleed out when he bit my chest, and there would not be enough blood for the transformation. He unbuttoned my shirt and with his index fingernail, made a small cut above my heart. Then he licked his fingernail and grimaced. Chills ran down my spine. He had delivered three of my babies, and now he wanted to deliver me into his Haute Caste hell. I thought of my children, my mom, and Tristan. He opened his mouth enough to display two very sharp fangs. I had stopped struggling, which he took as a sign I would comply. He started to lower his head. With all my might I head-butted him! Kyoto fell and hit his head hard on the cement floor. The adrenaline rush, combined with my enhanced strength, allowed me to break the straps. Antoinella grabbed me and pushed me down on the bed. I pulled up my legs and kneed her in the stomach. She screamed, "Sedate her!"

"Get off me bitch!" I yelled at the top of my lungs.

A young vampire jabbed a needle in my arm. I squirmed, which caused the needle to come out of his hand before giving me the full dose of the sedative. "The Haute Caste will fucking destroy you!" My vision blurred. The door popped open. Tristan entered with Delilah at his side. I heard the young vampires scream. The snarling panther jumped on Antoinella and pinned her to the ground. Tristan rushed to my side and held me in his arms. Anastasia and Omar broke the necks of two of the young vampires like they were pencils, the other one fell to the ground in surrender shaking. The Magus pulled Kyoto up by his hair, and spit on him. Sarah and Lily began to assess my injuries. Tristan saw Lily put a bandage across the cut on my chest, and they knew they had stopped the transformation in time.

Tristan pulled Delilah off Antoinella. She had cuts on her shoulders and face. "All my years of planning," Antoinella cried, "I was so close!" She glared at Tristan, "I did everything a proper vampiress should do, and it counts for nothing! She disrespects us, and you choose her over me! Curse you all!"

"Silence!" The Magus ordered, "You know nothing of what it means to be Haute Caste."

Tristan turned to Kyoto. "I trusted you! I allowed you the honor of delivering and caring for my children!"

Kyoto straightened his ornate robe, "Yes, well, though fascinated with the half-blood experiment I had predicted it would fail. I assumed she would die in time, and our bloodlines would not be further contaminated. I did not believe she would continue this abomination by having offspring. She and the children must transform to stop the threat they represent."

"I sat up on the gurney, "No one can force us to make that choice!"

Tristan put his arm about my shoulders and eased me back down.

Kyoto looked at me with pity, "Your blood is like kryptonite to us. I knew my theory was true. My lab tests confirmed what I suspected. Your mortal blood and immune system developed antigens to your vampire chemistry in order to not be overwhelmed by it. It weakens us and diminishes our powers."

"But you were going to perform my transformation, wouldn't that have harmed you?"

"Likely, but I was willing to make the sacrifice to stop the threat you pose."

Antoinella screamed, "Bastard! You were going to give me that poison as a reward!"

"Enough!" The Magus cut them off. "Kyoto, you are now less than Common Caste. You shall be shunned by our kind. You will be placed in a cell in Tibet where the sun will stream in the window leaving only a bench to sleep under during the day."

Lily stared at the floor, feeling shame for her former lover and the Head of her House.

Kyoto considered his sentence for a moment then responded, "I appreciate your thoughtful invitation, but I must politely decline," with lightning speed, he drew a sharp knife from under his robe and sliced halfway through his own throat. A fine mist of blood sprayed on the Magus. The scent of HH blood was overwhelming.

"Kyoto!" I uttered.

Tristan said, "I will honor his choice." He grabbed the blade and started to finish the job.

"No!" I screamed. Tristan turned to me, the knife trembling in his hand. "Please spare him!" To this day I don't know why I did that.

The Magus looked over at Lily and Sarah then down at Kyoto and gave a small nod. They rushed over and tried to slow the bleeding. Sarah took out a surgical suture kit. Lily knew that Kyoto had consumed samples of other Haute Caste blood over time that had enhanced his ability to heal. She looked up at me and said, "Thank you."

I don't know if it was the drugs or the bloody gore, everything that had happened hit me at once, I turned on my side and threw up. Delilah started to growl. She cornered Antoinella, who had started to crawl towards the pool of Kyoto's blood on the floor. She looked at the panther and backed away from the blood.

Omar held his hand out to me. "Miranda, we must use the gurney for Kyoto. Come, I will keep you upright." Anastasia wiped my face and gently helped me stand. Omar put his arm around my waist. The others lifted Kyoto on to the gurney. He looked pale and fragile, but I knew he would recover. Delilah was standing over Antoinella as the Magus approached.

"You don't deserve to breathe the same air as the Baroness!" He raised a hand; she clutched her throat and started choking.

"Stop! No more killing!" I felt weak and would have fallen over if not for Omar's support. The Magus lowered his hand and Antoinella gasped. Tristan handed me a bottle of water. Everyone was looking at me, waiting for an explanation. My calls for mercy dumbfounded them. In a groggy voice, I said, "I want her gone as much as any of you, but she knows about Alexander's plans. Kyoto thought half-bloods were wrong, so he tried to make me full blood, not kill me. I'm tired of the violence. We have to be better than this!"

The Magus looked at Antoinella, "I shall spare you, which means you owe your existence to the Baroness." She bowed her head. The Magus gave instructions to Lily and Sarah to make the arrangements to send Kyoto to the Tibetan monastery. Omar, Anastasia, Ruben, and Pauline would see to the incarceration of Antoinella and the young vampires.

As Tristan walked me out with Delilah, I pulled away, turned, and called to the Magus, "I've got a lot of questions for you!"

My husband turned to Sarah, "Is there any of that sedative left?"

Marie had been waiting outside with Jasper, and she started to hug me, as Tristan helped me into the car. On the ride home, I only threw up once. When we got to the house, the other kids poured out of the front doors and down the stone steps.

Tomas stopped suddenly, eyes wide, and said, "Mom. Are you okay?" They all took one look at me put on the brakes. I realized how I looked, I had streaks of vomit in my hair and my shirt, not to mention a little blood.

"I'll be fine, I just…" My sentence was cut short as I started to dry heave a little. Tristan held me up. Tillie ran forward to help me into the house.

Tristan looked at the kids, "She was drugged, and it made her sick. She needs to rest now. She will recover fully. Now go to bed and I will be up to see you after I get your mother settled."

They silently stood and watched as Tillie helped me upstairs. When Tristan entered the bedroom, Tillie had cleaned me up with rose-scented soap and put me in a lace nightgown. Clive had brought up a cup of tea and some saltines to settle my stomach. I was lying against some pillows and trying to keep the crackers down.

I looked up at Tristan. "I'm only going to say this one more time, I warned you about Antoinella. She is nothing but a treacherous slut."

"Yes, you did give me that assessment of her character." He smiled, "Don't ever forget that it was you who interceded with the Magus to spare her. I do agree that now she will likely help us take Alexander down. Rest well." He leaned over and kissed my forehead, then left.

Chapter 35

The Offspring's Lineage Revealed

Tristan wasn't surprised to find the kids in the game room at two in the morning, not even remotely ready for bed. As he entered, they switched off the TV and just stared at him, not sure what had happened or if they were in trouble for not being in bed.

"Is Mom better?" Marie asked quietly.

"She will be fine by tomorrow. It's time I treat you more like adults and explain what is going on in our world." He sat in a chair near Jacques. His concentration was briefly broken when he saw the drawing of Batu as a superhero.

Tomas spoke next, "We get that there's a vampire war."

The Baron was surprised by his remark. "Do you know the reason?"

Marie said, "Some of them hate us."

"I think they're jealous," Jacques piped up.

"There is some truth to what you have said. I must ask you to be very mature about what I'm going to tell you. It will help you understand the resentment from some of the Common Caste and who you can trust. But there is something else you should know. You are not half-vampire."

"You're not our dad?" Tomas asked.

"Yes, I am your father. You are actually three-quarters vampire."

"But that would mean, Grandpa Pete was…." Des began.

"No, he was mortal. Your Grandpa Pete was not your biological grandfather but he never knew that. Your grandparents had difficulty conceiving. Your grandmother, for reasons you'll understand when you're older, spent an evening with a member of the Haute Caste, and nine months later, your mother was born."

Marie blurted out, "The Magus?"

"No, though he was the one who set this grand plan in action. Your grandfather is…"

Jacques asked, "Is it someone we know?" Tristan nodded.

Tomas said, "Wait! It's Omar! It's why your middle name is Omar!"

"Yes, you are all of the House of Swords," Tristan said.

Des looked disgusted, "Grandma and Omar? That's messed up."

"Poor Grandpa Pete," Marie was getting tearful, "I hate this family!"

"This sucks!" Jacques stated, "I used to think my name was cool."

Tristan replied, "If your Grandmother had not spent that night with Sir Omar, none of you would be here."

They were all quiet for a minute. They looked at each other, and Des said, "I guess that's true." Marie shrugged, apparently ready to move on.

"Okay, so they wanted Mom because she is half-vampire?" Tomas asked,

"Yes. You four and your mom are the only mortals in existence who are part vampire. When the Magus granted you Haute Caste status, it upset some of the Common Caste. Sir Omar has longed to tell you that he is your grandfather. You should be proud to share DNA with one of the most ancient and honorable vampires in the world."

Marie spoke up, "Everyone lied to us, and to Grandpa Pete."

Des looked at his father, "Tell us the truth. Did they make mom a vampire?"

"No, she fought them off long enough for us to rescue her. She's a little bruised and sedated, that's all. One cannot be forced to transform. I guess Kyoto believed he could pressure her to go along. She has not made her decision one way or the other yet."

"Mom fought off vampires! Wow!" Des said.

"She's tough!" Marie commented. "Will Omar come spend more time with us now that we know the truth?"

"I am sure he will."

"We're part Arab. Who knew?" Jacques said quietly.

Tomas replied, "So much for learning Spanish."

"There will always be a part of your heart that is Mexican. Your heritage is more than DNA." Tristan added, Pete will always be your grandfather.

The kids looked at each other, and without a word, got up and gathered around their father and hugged him. For a moment, the second most powerful vampire in the world felt tears trickle down his cheeks. It was a very odd sensation for him.

I woke a little sweaty but feeling better. The room was dark and as I reached for a glass of water a familiar voice said, "You aren't about to puke again, are you?"

"Ruben?"

"Good evening, at least what's left of it, I just got here."

"You need to work on your bedside manner." I took a drink and then grabbed some crackers. "What about James?"

"Some loyal Common Caste from Toronto are visiting Montana until we resolve this situation with Alexander the Great Asshole. Kyoto should have known better. I heard you were ferocious."

"I feel like I have a hangover. Will you ask Tillie for something for a headache?"

He walked over to the intercom to the kitchen and placed an order. "The Baron needs to update the technology. We need Alexa."

"He'd probably try and have sex with her."

Ruben tried not to look amused, "The meds have not completely left your system."

"Mom!" The kids burst into the room and crowded around the bed.

Des looked me over then pronounced, "You smell better, and look better too."

"Thanks! I think. Aren't you all supposed to be in bed?"

Tomas took the lead, "Dad explained about our other grandpa. We couldn't sleep," he glanced at Ruben.

"Is it really true?" Marie asked.

I was not quite ready for the genealogical inquisition, but Tristan thought it was a great time to tell them. WTF! "Yes. Sir Omar is your biological grandfather."

"Did your dad explain what happened?" I was hoping he had.

"Yeah, sorta. Am I really named after him?"

"Yes, and your great, great, great grandfather, Jacques de Molay, actually I am not sure how many greats, was a Knight Templar."

Des asked, "Why did Grandma pick a vampire?"

"That is a long story and will have to wait for another day."

"I can't wait!" Ruben added.

I shot him a sharp look. I didn't need him adding to the chaos.

Tillie arrived with something for my headache and a cup of tea. She looked at the kids and shook her head. "Aren't you all supposed to be in bed? Your poor mother needs to rest."

Tristan walked in at that moment, "What did I tell you?" he stated in a voice that would make vampires run and hide.

Marie looked right at him and said, "You told us we're seventy-five percent vampire, then you tell us to go to bed like normal kids! Which is it?"

I could see his temper flaring.

"C'mon dad, let us stay up," Des remarked.

"Now!" Tristan flatly stated.

The kids looked at me for support for their rebellion. I shook my head. "Nope! Don't look at me. You heard your father."

Tillie and Ruben ushered the kids out into the hallway. Ruben turned back to say, "And to think I looked forward to them being able to talk." Then he helped Tillie get the inmates to their rooms.

"Are all children this defiant?" Tristan shook his head.

"No, they get it from you."

He started to respond, but wisely changed his mind. Being kidnapped has its benefits. Instead, he simply said, "You look like you are feeling better. I'll retire soon, but first, I'll fill you in about the aftermath. We still haven't located Lolly and Al. The scent of Haute Caste blood was detected at their home, but no foul play was evident. They are…"

"Lolly! I forgot she never showed up. My friends! Do you think they're with Borgia?"

"Yes, we've tracked them to Las Vegas. There is a good chance someone else sent the message from Lolly saying she would meet you at the salon. The Magus and I have made some security changes. Teri and Grigoryi will be flying back today to help us."

"Grigoryi? I mean, he's trustworthy, but not exactly stealthy."

"We needed some trusted shorts in light of Alexander's use of mortals. A few of Camo's friends will be in Rossville to guard your mother. Lady Lily is caring for Kyoto while he is transferred to a monastery in Mongolia. It belongs to the Princess, and Sir Steve will supervise Kyoto's incarceration. His cell will not be as harsh as the Magus originally described. Your mercy has made him reconsider."

"Ruben won't be happy about Lily being in Mongolia. What about Antoinella?"

"The Magus is allowing her time alone in a bare but somewhat comfortable room to contemplate her transgressions. Sir Jorge continues to monitor Franco's movements. No sign of Alexander yet, but his arrival is expected soon. We must not take any more chances. The children will be sent to Hann's sanctuary tomorrow night. They will be safe there."

To his surprise I agreed without further discussion. He started to leave, but I said, "Wait!"

"I must retire soon. It is late." He stopped and came back to the side of the bed.

"What about my blood? Kyoto said my blood was bad for vampires, and Antoinella was pissed at him about it."

"Lily will look into his medical research. I have no idea what he was talking about." He gently stroked my cheek. His hand rested under my chin, and then he leaned down to kiss me. I allowed his affection. His

220

touch, his scent, his lips were a healing balm at that moment. Almost involuntarily I responded, circling my arms around him. I was used to the coolness of his body, and since I felt feverish, it was soothing. He lay down beside me but only held me. I started to get tearful. He wiped away my tears and kissed me again, then rose from the bed.

"Sometimes, I'm not sure what I want."

He replied, "I have never questioned what I desire," and left.

Vegas was always a happening place, even at five in the morning. Jorge, like most vampires, liked to gamble and had bought a home there years ago. Soon it would be daylight, so he took his winnings and left the casino. Near the parking lot, he handed it to a homeless woman. She looked at the large wad of bills then back at him. "You're an angel from heaven."

"Not exactly!" He replied with a grin.

Once home, Jorge paced in the living room that had an autographed picture of Liberace on top of his grand piano, and of course, a small candelabra. There was also a picture of Siegfried and Roy with their great cats. He remembered the interesting times he and Franco had enjoyed with the Las Vegas elite over the years and sighed. He did not believe Alexander would trust Franco. It was hard for him to imagine his old lover as a spy. In his heart, he felt Franco would return to him, but he worried about Alexander's charisma. He had been able to lead vast armies with his charm and brilliance. Finally, he got a text message from Franco:

He arrives this evening at CP

"Of course!" Jorge said out loud. He was not surprised that Alexander would stay at Cesar's Palace. He knew that meant his headquarters were not quite finished. He sent a brief message to update Tristan, then retired for the day.

Lolly and Al had a luxurious suite at Cesar's Palace courtesy of Sir Borgia. They had been invited to a vampire gathering on the condition they kept it a secret from Miranda. He had given them a taste of his blood. It was enough to leave them craving more. Al was uncomfortable with how flirty Lolly was with Sir Borgia, who had picked up on his jealousy and responded by flattering Al about his intelligence and amazing psychiatric career. He was a very cunning vampire who had learned from his years in the most powerful circles in Rome to play all the sides in a conflict if you wish to prosper. Alexander was very interested in using this pair of F.O.V.

Lolly and Al were used to luxury. Her modeling career and his practice had made them rich. They were interested in more than wealth alone. The scheming vampires had preyed on their vanity to lure the mortal couple into the undead world. Lolly had recognized the improvement in her skin and wrinkle reduction after tasting his blood. Al had felt rejuvenated again and found that his cognitive abilities were sharper. Their sex life had been good, but now it was spectacular.

Lolly got into bed, hoping Al would join her, but he stayed at the window looking out on the Vegas nightlife. Lolly asked, "Do you think they want us to become one of them?"

He sat down beside her and took her hand, "Sir Borgia has been hinting at that."

"I have to be honest that scares the shit out of me, but I know it would feel amazing," Lolly said and sighed.

"Their blood makes you perfect. It erases your flaws. The elixir of life," he paused and looked into her eyes, "With a very dark side."

"I wish I could call Randie and ask her about Alexander."

"We should order room service and eat anything we want, just in case it's our last day of regular food." He grabbed a room service menu.

"I am not very hungry," Lolly wasn't sure if they were doing the right thing.

Chapter 36

The Magus Goes to Vegas

I woke up about two in the afternoon, and my thoughts were a bit foggy. A long, hot shower helped wake me up. WTF! Lolly and Al were in Las Vegas hanging out with Borgia, and probably Alexander. My soon to be ex expressed his undying love, and a biker gang was protecting Mom. I needed coffee! I looked at my phone, hoping there would be some word from Lolly, then went to check on the kids. Their rooms and the game room were empty. I rushed to the kitchen where Tillie had a meal ready for me.

"Where are the kids?"

"Clive, Jasper, and Batu are coaching the children in the hockey rink. Please, Baroness, you need your strength, you have to eat."

I took a breath, "Okay, it looks delicious." I poured myself a cup of salvation.

She placed a large plate with half a Cornish hen and all the trimmings in front of me.

I ate about half of the sumptuous meal and put my plate on the kitchen counter. Tillie pulled a sheet of chocolate chip cookies out of the oven. I was full, but I didn't want to hurt her feelings, right? It's just a cookie. I looked at her, "Bless you!"

I checked my phone again. Still nothing from Lolly. I walked out on the patio with my mug of coffee and a couple of warm cookies. The beautiful California sunlight warmed me as I sat on the edge of a planter. How could the world look so perfect and be such a mess? Kyoto knew something about my blood that the Magus was keeping from all of us. I hoped Lily would find the answers. Alexander had a back-up plan, which unfortunately included Al and Lolly! They apparently had willingly gone with Borgia. Lolly had spent thousands of dollars on spa treatments to keep her complexion youthful, but vampire blood was the ultimate beauty treatment. I had not been able to protect my friends from themselves.

Then there was Antoinella. I just wanted to bitch slap her. I should have been traumatized by the abduction, but it just seemed like another bizarre day in my really weird life that I had somehow survived.

"Good afternoon Baroness," a familiar voice broke into my thoughts.

"Grigoryi! Teri!" I stood and hugged my mortal friends. "Is Mom really okay with all the bikers?"

Grigoryi said, "They are very polite around her."

"That's a relief. I hope the sheriff will like them too."

Teri said, "I heard we might be going to Vegas."

"I just woke up and hadn't heard the plans yet."

Tillie called from the patio door, "Come along. I'll show you to your rooms and get you two something to eat."

I met Batu in the hall with the kids. He looked upset. "Clive needs to talk to you in the kitchen. I'll stay with the kids in the game room."

Marie said, "Nobody tells us anything."

Tomas added, "It was a great game, then Clive got a call and said we had to go in the house."

"Go with Batu. I'll let you know what's going on later."

I found Clive and Jasper in the kitchen. They turned to me with an expression of shock. "It's the Magus," Clive uttered, "he's been taken."

"That's not possible!"

"The household was attacked an hour ago, and now he's missing!"

I sat down and took a deep breath, "Alexander!"

"His chauffeur hid during the attack. He said they had tanks of liquid nitrogen that they used to freeze and immobilize the Magus."

It took a minute for the true brilliance of Alexander's plan to sink in. After the Common Caste uprising in L.A., the Magus had subdued his rival, Lena, and froze her in a subzero freezer. His tactic couldn't stay a secret forever. No one even imagined an attack on the Magus!

"The butler said some time ago, the firm that takes care of the gardens had begun hiring Chinese staff. He had not thought much about it. This morning they showed up with a large truck claiming it was for fall yard clean up. He got suspicious when a group of men wearing protective garments with small tanks on their backs emerged from the truck. The staff tried to lock them out, but they broke through the sliding glass doors."

"The staff are okay?"

"Yes, just shaken up and some minor injuries."

Jasper added, "This was well-planned and organized. The attack only took a few minutes." The chauffeur said he saw a freezer wheeled into the house and then loaded back on the truck."

Jasper asked, "Should we wake the Baron?"

I looked at the clock, the sun was descending, but it would be a couple of hours to sunset. "No, not yet. At seven o'clock begin waking the Baron and the vampire guests and tell them the news. Tell them to assemble in the library." It was one of those weird moments when I truly felt like a Baroness.

I went to the game room with a heavy heart. The kids had been through so much, but I had to let them know what had happened.

"First, I want you to know that everyone else is fine, especially your grandma, but the Magus has been taken prisoner. We think that Alexander is behind this.

"He can't be more powerful than the Magus, or Dad!" Jacques exclaimed.

"No, but he's really smart and sneaky."

Marie asked, "Did he hurt the Magus?"

"I don't think so. Because we don't know what they may try next, your father and I want you to go to stay with Hann and Cassie. You'll be safe there while we deal with Alexander."

Jacques said, "We could help you!"

Batu told them, "The best thing you can do is obey your mother. Let the Haute Caste take care of Alexander. I'll come with you to Hann's."

"Knowing you're safe will help your dad and me focus on rescuing the Magus. I want you to go pack for a few days."

They went off to their rooms, grumbling. "And don't forget your toothbrushes!" I called after them. It's weird the shit a mom thinks of, even in a crisis.

"They are brave," Batu remarked.

"I think you're brave to offer to guard them at the elephant sanctuary. Try to keep them out of the mud ponds. And good luck!" I left before the exchange got uncomfortable.

I could not believe Alexander had pulled this off. I stared at the framed Empress Tarot card on the wall in my bedroom. I am sure in time the Magus would give each of the kids a card. We all needed him to survive and stay in power.

The Magus ruled with intelligence and guile. He demanded loyalty and acknowledgment that he was the original source of immortality. When necessary he would use the fear of his rarely used but unmatched and unique powers. I was not surprised, but still saddened that Borgia had turned out to be a traitor. This showed a lack of judgment on the Magus' part. He would need to be more careful about who he allowed into the nocturnal maniac's club. I sent a text message to Jorge, telling him to call the Baron when he woke. I didn't want to tell him about the Magus in a text or voicemail.

An hour before Tristan would normally rise, I went to his suite. Delilah, sleeping at the foot of the bed, raised her head, then went back to sleep. I crawled in beside him and he reached for me like he had so many times, starting to initiate sex. "Clothes?" he muttered.

"Sorry, but I have disturbing news."

"What has happened?"

"Alexander has taken the Magus."

"That's impossible! You're mistaken!" He got out of bed and began dressing.

"It happened a couple of hours ago. He hired mortals, posing as land-scapers to go in during the day with canisters of liquid nitrogen, they froze him with it and loaded into a freezer like Lena. We believe they're taking him to Las Vegas."

"Of course! It had to have been Alexander. No one else would be such a disloyal, deceitful bastard!"

"Clive and Jasper will tell the Haute Caste when they wake them. I asked that they meet us in the library. Luckily the Heads of most of the Houses are already in town and will be here soon. I sent a message to Jorge to call you so you could tell him about the Magus. The kids are getting ready to go to Hann's place. Teri and Grigoryi have arrived."

"Good!"

"Batu, Jasper, and Clive will guard the kids. I'll ask Tillie to go as well to help care for them." I looked at Tristan, so sad and angry, "I don't want anything bad to happen to the Magus."

"You should feel sorry for what will happen to Alexander," he responded.

Jasper pulled up to the front of the mansion in the Magus' armored Humvee. Batu and the kids got inside. They looked anxious.

My husband tried to reassure them, "We will find the Magus and bring you home soon. Follow Hann's directions, and I do not want to hear you've been disrespectful."

I added, "We love you! Give the baby elephant a hug for me!"

I smiled and waved goodbye.

Tristan changed the meeting venue to the Magus' mansion to investigate the attack.

Scheherazade took the elevator to the 29th floor of Cesar's Palace. There were eleven luxurious apartments, the hotel called Villas, five of which were taken by Alexander. A Saudi Prince was using the other six for his large family and entourage. The suites were as opulent and ornate as a Bollywood movie set. Alexander would arrive soon, and she made sure that everything was ready. The staff, who normally took care of the guests in the Villas, had been replaced by his Chinese vampires and the mortals who wished to be transformed. Scheherazade stood and looked out of the window onto the city lights. "Too bad about Antoinella!" she said aloud with a smile. Her rival for Alexander's approval had really screwed up. When she heard the report that the Baroness was still mortal, and Kyoto had been taken prisoner along with Antoinella, she barely hid her delight. Alexander was displeased when Batu had gotten away in London, but that was nothing compared to letting the Baroness escape. Scheherazade would find a way to get back in his good graces yet.

Alexander stood in front of his new headquarters, several miles from the hotel, inspecting the progress of the construction. The four guard towers were complete. The roof, marble columns, walls, and windows were almost complete. Temporary lights were strung up throughout the structure. A limousine came through the gate and stopped at the front steps, and Franco stepped out and straightened his silk suit.

He looked around and then at Alexander, "Camping out?"

Alexander came down the steps and pulled him into his arms. "I'm not sure why I missed you." His kiss left no doubt that he had forgiven Franco.

Franco was torn between Jorge and Alexander. At the funeral for Pete, he realized what a great vampire his former lover was. He also saw the destruction and chaos that followed Alexander, yet now in his arms, he felt such beautiful passion engulf him. His loyalty, again, started to sway.

"I wish you were not so handsome." He stepped away from Alexander, "Why did you put me on that awful ship with that vampiress from hell?"

He smiled, "I wanted the Magus to think I was still in China."

"Antoinella will give you away, they will find you soon."

"The Magus is my prisoner, frozen stiff! They will come after me. I'll show them all who holds the most power!" He moved to the top of the steps and looked down on a speechless Franco.

"No!" Franco sank to his knees. He always had the utmost respect for the Magus. He understood that the balance of power and egos in the vampire world had been kept in check by him. "What have you done?"

"What only I could do. Conquer and rule the empire of the undead. The Common Caste will follow me! They far outnumber the Haute Caste.

I will allow the Heads of Houses who pledge their loyalty to me to retain their stations, and the others will become powerless like the Magus."

"Promise me you will revive the Magus! He must not be destroyed. All we are, all we have is because of him!"

"Franco, I find your lack of ambition disappointing." He signaled to the limo driver. "We shall go to the hotel and discuss how to negotiate with the Baron and Baroness. You know them well; you can help me convince them to cooperate. The other Haute Caste will follow their lead. Once I have consolidated power, I'll release your precious Magus." He climbed into the limo, followed by Franco.

Franco began to understand why the Magus had so rarely showed his powers. He wanted his enemies to underestimate him. Franco looked out the limo window at the dark desert. He wondered how being frozen might compromise the Magus' rumored abilities. Alexander's self-confidence made Franco concerned about what he was not being told. How could he possibly think the Baron and Baroness, not to mention the other members of the Haute Caste, would pledge their allegiance to him?

They arrived at Cesar's Palace, and Alexander strode through the hotel lobby bestowing charming smiles on the staff like they were favors. Even wealthy guests turned their heads to watch the charismatic, handsome figure.

"I need to do some shopping. I did not pack for Vegas," Franco said to Alexander. The Common Caste walked behind Alexander carrying the luggage. "So much for equality," he thought.

He knew he was being watched by those for and against Alexander. Franco wandered into a Prada boutique and bought a couple of shirts. He stopped outside the boutique by a planter to check his purchases. Then he walked to the elevators. A slight built housekeeper was mopping the floor and passed by the planter with barely a pause. A few minutes later, Billy got rid of the uniform and met Robert, who was cleaning up at a roulette table. "Got it! Let's go see Jorge."

Chapter 37

The (Undead) Detective Squad

There was a large group of angry vampires waiting for us in front of the Magus' mansion. I was surprised to see Angel representing the Common Caste. Omar, Anastasia, Sarah, Ruben, Kananga, and Pauline were examining the area where the attackers had parked their truck. They left the empty tanks that held the liquid nitrogen, respirators, and long insulating gloves on the ground. It felt like we were detectives entering a crime scene, except we already knew who did it.

The staff were bruised and shaken up but otherwise unharmed. They had not cleaned up yet, waiting for the Baron to give them permission. Little looked disturbed inside the house until we got to the Magus' suite. The room was in disarray, showing signs of a struggle.

Tristan said nothing but could barely contain his anger.

Kananga noticed that the heavy blinds and curtain were still in place "I don't believe he was exposed to sunlight."

Anastasia agreed, "I can smell his scent, even frozen it does not change. There is no evidence that he was burned."

Omar found a large syringe on the floor. "They sedated him, just like he did to Lena. I believe he was not harmed other than being frozen and sedated." Then he stopped and pointed to the bedside table, "Look!" The Tarot card, The Chariot, was laying upside down which meant defeat, on top of the Magus' card.

Tristan stated coldly, "This will be Alexander's end." He picked up the cards placed them in his pocket to keep the servants from seeing them.

Ruben came out of the bathroom carrying a half-empty gallon bottle of antifreeze. "I have no idea what they did with this!"

Tristan told everyone to wait in the foyer and went into the Magus' office alone. He exposed a small locked refrigerator built into the wall behind a Gauguin painting. He unlocked it and removed a liter bag of blood. Then he closed it again and replaced the painting. He carefully placed it in the Magus' leather briefcase sitting on the desk, then joined us at the entrance to the mansion.

"Have the Haute Caste meet with me back in my library." He turned to me and the others, "I wish to speak with you and the mortals for a moment."

Angel, Grigoryi, and Teri looked anxious. "I trust you to tell no one what you have seen here. We will need you all in Las Vegas. We will leave tomorrow night. I have a precious gift to bestow upon you." He nodded to the butler who had followed him carrying three shot glasses on a tray. Tristan removed the bag of blood from the briefcase and put a small amount in two of the glasses which he gave to Teri and Grigoryi. "This may make you feel a little ill at first, but then a feeling of wellness will prevail. It's from the Magus." He put twice as much in the third glass and handed it to Angel. He did not think I would drink it and didn't give me a glass. Teri swallowed it and steadied herself against a planter. Angel downed the red elixir and smiled, "Thank you!" He felt a rush from the ancient, potent blood.

Grigoryi hesitated, looking at the glass in his hand.

"It will fortify you," the Baron told him.

"I don't think I can. I'm sorry."

I took the glass away from Grigoryi and drank the bizarre pick me up. My husband looked surprised. I started to feel exhilarated, my sense of what others were feeling increased. I would need all my strength for the battle ahead of us.

We then all headed back to the vehicles. I realized all my senses were enhanced more than usual. Tristan's scent was like an aphrodisiac. It was a good thing we were not alone in the car. I guessed that over thousands of years, the Magus just got used to feeling this way.

The Haute Caste were already in the library waiting. Angel looked around the library with a look of awe. When he noticed the Van Gogh hanging on the wall, he exclaimed, "Vincent!" then he whispered to me, "I heard rumors about this place."

"Mi casa es su casa."

He smiled, "Good to know. I'll invite all my cousins."

I liked Angel. He was a vampire, but he was a very clever endearing fellow without the glaring ego of most of the Haute Caste. I hoped I had found an ally.

When everyone was seated, Tristan, who remained standing, began. "We are at war against one of our kind who does not respect our social order or the creator of our society. For too long we have kept the gifts of our caste hidden. We must now unleash them to rescue the Magus."

The room was silent, but the energy level in the room was building.

Kananga spoke first, "We will do whatever we can to right this wrong. I thought that Alexander would be content with the creation of a new House, but his unbridled ambition threatens to destroy our world."

Omar asked, "Is Sir Borgia the only Haute Caste at his side?"

"Yes, since Kyoto has been sent away. A new Head of the House of Cups will be named after we rescue the Magus."

I noticed the look of surprise on Angel's face. Replacing the Head of a House was a huge deal.

"Sarah was pissed. "Do you have any suspicions regarding the other Houses?"

Her question made everyone uncomfortable. Tristan turned to Angel, "Will you please enlighten us about the Common Caste unrest?"

After his one-on-one with the most ancient of the vampires, Angel's respect and loyalty for the Magus had grown, and Angel wanted to do whatever he could to help rescue him. The boost from Magus' blood fueled his self-confidence. "There are disgruntled Common Caste in every House. Sir Alexander and Sir Borgia have used Antoinella and Scheherazade to stir them up. I am loyal to the Magus and he had asked me the same question. I told him you should offer us representation when the Heads of Houses meet. By giving us a voice, you will take away Sir Alexander's claim to be the champion and savior of the Common Caste."

I noticed Anastasia stiffen, and she was not alone. I interceded, "Angel is right. Alexander is using the Common Caste as his army by offering status and power. If the parliament includes the Common Caste, you will undercut him."

Anastasia stated, "The carrot is more powerful than the stick. This rebellion must not be allowed to topple our society. We must realize that we need the Common Caste. They outnumber us. There are several Common Caste to every Haute Caste."

Tristan continued. "Ruben, I would like you and Angel to communicate to the Common Caste in all the Houses. Begin with the aides. Let it be known that next month there will be a parliament meeting that will include their representatives. They will have to choose someone from each House."

Omar said, "Now, let us decide how to rescue the Magus, and depose Alexander."

The Baron continued, "The Heads of the Houses and I will question Antoinella and plan our attack."

"I will be there too!" My tone left no room for argument. Tristan simply nodded.

I went to the kitchen and grabbed a chunk of cheese, and sourdough bread then started the Keurig. Magus' blood gave me a lift but irritated my gut. I took a bite of bread, and my grumbling tummy felt relief. I checked my phone, there were texts from the kids, including a pic with Marie hugging the baby elephant. Tears started streaming quietly down my cheeks. Then there was a message from Batu that all was well. I wished that was really true.

Kananga and Sarah came in and sat down with me at the table. Kananga patted my hand, "Courage!"

Sarah said, "We will be at your side when Antoinella is questioned. Just give the word, and I'll end her miserable existence."

Omar came in and told us to go to the hockey rink. Antoinella was handcuffed and shackled to a chair on the ice. Her feet were bare. Vampires are more susceptible to the cold but do have the ability to survive being frozen. The Magus had figured out the whole freeze the undead to subdue your enemies thing. Too bad that secret got out. I remembered the night I had seen Borgia transform Antoinella here after she had helped with the demise of Lena. I'm sure the irony was not lost on Antoinella. They had picked the rink for her vampiress coming out party instead of the mansion because she was Common Caste.

The Baron spoke, "Antoinella, tell us about Alexander's plans."

She looked at the Haute Caste assembled before her and smiled, "Where is the Magus?"

Sarah responded, "You do not ask us questions! What is Alexander planning in Nevada?"

"It's obvious, he wishes to have all of you pledge allegiance to him, and he'll keep a few of you like the Magus as his pet advisors if you flatter him." I had to admire her composure, though somewhat excessive.

"How can he think he can defeat us?" Omar asked.

"He did not reveal all his plans to me," she sneered.

Anastasia approached her and held up her hand but said nothing. Antoinella flinched then looked down at her hands. The skin was wrinkling, and age spots appeared; her beauty was fading fast. "No!" Her face began to age. She raised her shackled hands and touched the sagging skin on her face. A clump of hair fell into her lap. "Stop!" she shrieked.

Anastasia lowered her hand. "I can restore your youth if you cooperate."

"I'll tell you what I know, please stop," she begged. He has a fortress in the desert guarded by a small army of mortals and unsanctioned vampires. He plans to lure you there and take you all prisoners. He will use liquid nitrogen as he used on the Magus to immobilize you." She glared at me, "It's because of her! He wants her to be his Queen! He wants her to have his children!"

"When pigs fly!" I exclaimed. Kananga put an arm around my shoulder.

"Where is the Magus being held?" Omar demanded.

She looked down at her wrinkled hands. "I don't know for sure. I know he had a freezer sent to Caesar's."

Ruben asked the question on everyone's mind, "Does he have a guillotine?"

Antoinella responded, looking down at her lap, "Yes."

The Baron looked at her with contempt. "We will unshackle you, but you must continue to cooperate." Then to my surprise, he added, "If you help us rescue the Magus and swear loyalty to him, you may be allowed to help lead the Common Caste. Will you give your word?"

Antoinella looked at me, "Why did you spare Kyoto and me?"

"Something you may never understand. Life is precious, even yours."

Antoinella lowered her head clearly in defeat. "I give my word to the Baroness."

Anastasia put her hands on Antoinella's cheeks, and her youthful look slowly returned. She looked relieved, but not grateful.

The Baron held up his phone and played the recording of the conversation that Franco had with Alexander in the lobby of Caesar's Palace, "Their conversation appears to verify some of what you said. Now we need a detailed description of the fortress."

We walked back to the mansion. I smiled at Anastasia, "Nice trick! What else can you do?"

She smiled, "An ear-piercing scream, but I decided that was not needed tonight."

"Thanks! I just got over my headache from yesterday."

She touched my arm, "She swore allegiance to you. That was a nice trick!"

At Caesar's Palace, Alexander announced he would be in the hot tub. Scheherazade started to join him, but Franco stood in her way before she could enter the bedroom suite. "He won't be interested in you."

"Because he prefers men?"

"His preference is Haute Caste, and Mon Cheri you'll never be that. So sad."

She brusquely stepped back. "He might enjoy one of my tales."

Franco laughed, "The God of War? He would enjoy Kyoto's head on a platter. Perhaps, you can find a bored parking attendant to spend time with."

"I expect Sir Jorge may have already entertained them."

Franco's eyes became cold, "It's amazing. You make me miss Antoinella." He barely moved his hand, and she fell backward on the marble floor.

She got up but moved several feet away, staring at him, realizing for the first time he was more powerful than she had thought.

Franco found Alexander in the hot tub and entered the bubbling water. He gradually felt more relaxed despite the tension of the current situation.

"My victory is at hand," Alexander stated, he pulled Franco close. He kissed Franco gently at first; then he became more demanding. Franco responded to his passion though his heart was torn. Alexander let go, climbed out of the tub and walked to the plush king-size bed, "Come!"

Franco decided he had to sacrifice to help the Magus and joined Alexander. Despite his strength, Alexander was a gentle lover. The sexual tension in their bodies built up quickly. Franco kissed Alexander before moving down his chest. Alexander sensed a bit of hesitation and pushed Franco away. "You still want Jorge!" The mood was broken.

"I thought I could return to you, but I was only fooling myself," Franco said, thinking it was truly an Oscar-worthy performance. He slowly got up from the bed, "I'm sorry."

Alexander picked up his phone and sent a message. Soon five unsanctioned guards appeared. "Lock him in the next suite, make sure he does not escape."

He followed them to a bedroom next door, glad he was still near the center of Alexander's headquarters.

Jorge, Billy, and Robert stared at the online camera feeds and studied plans of Caesar's Palace. Billy chuckled, "It's got to be the togas. That's what Sir Alexander loves about this hotel."

"Yes," Jorge responded, "It has an ambiance he appreciates. Alex has always been nostalgic about his glory days. His ambition has made him blind to what it takes to rule."

"Look at all the mortals and unsanctioned he has guarding his suite," Billy observed.

Jorge added, "Divulging our existence to so many was very careless. It's as if he believes the mortal world exists only to serve his purposes."

Robert responded, "Sir Alexander is a Haute Caste fool. The freezer was delivered to his floor, but we don't know in which suite it is. It will be hard for Franco to get another message out."

"I have an idea." Billy grinned, "Just call me a genius. We better run this by the Baron first."

Chapter 38

Everyone Goes to Vegas

The Baron went into his room alone before dawn and called Hann. "I need your counsel. I don't know if the information from Antoinella was meant to mislead us or is true."

"Cassie had a vision. You were in a chariot, and it was snowing. That's all she saw, but she was scared by it."

"She had no insight concerning the Magus?"

"None. She tried to reach him, but she said there was only cold and darkness. You are right not to trust any information you get from Antoinella. Such audacity and stupidity to go after the Magus! He must feel invincible now. Use his conceit against him!"

"We will finalize plans after confronting him at Caesar's Palace. How are the children?"

"Fine, when we can keep them out of the mud. They do seem to have a way with the elephants. Though headstrong, they are all very intelligent and kind. They're making bets on who will defeat Sir Alexander."

Tristan smiled. "I don't want to know. I hope they never go to Las Vegas.

"Or maybe Vegas better hope they never go there!"

"Thanks, dear friend. My children have so much potential. I'm glad they're spending time with ancient Haute Caste instead of the mortals in Rossville."

I was in bed when the Baron came in to check on me.

"How are you feeling?" he asked.

"Weird, between whatever drugs they gave me and Magus' blood, I'm wired and a bit nauseated. What's that unleash your powers thing about? Anastasia was like an X-men character with Antoinella. Can you do that?"

"It's not easy to explain, but we have control of the electrical impulses and magnetic fields our bodies produce, and we can focus that energy. It expresses itself in different ways in each of us. I can levitate objects."

"What the fuck! Why didn't you tell me?"

"We like to keep our talents hidden until needed, and I did not want to alarm you."

"You made me watch you rip out the throat of a pedophile drug dealer when we were dating, but you're afraid seeing furniture rise up might upset me?"

"Would you like me to make the bed move?" he said with a leer.

"You are such an ass!"

"I would love to continue this delightful conversation, but I must retire shortly. I want to give you an update. I talked to Hannibal; the kids are fine. Kyoto is recovering but still unable to speak. He wrote the word, forgive, on a piece of paper followed by your name."

"I've been thinking about Kyoto a lot. He was going to transform me even though it might have diminished his powers. I should hate him, but for some reason, I don't."

"Yes, Kyoto was acting out of a warped concern for our kind. Perhaps we will let him continue to study your blood. Though I will never trust him again, saving him may have been a wise decision."

"Yeah, at the moment, I'm more concerned that Alexander wants to be my baby daddy."

He sat on the bed and looked at me with longing. "My dear Miranda. that will never happen, even when the divorce is final."

"Damn straight! Alexander, the shithead, will never touch this."

Tristan smiled, leaned forward, and kissed me goodnight.

Angel and Ruben had been busy working the phones from Los Angeles until almost sunrise. Billy and Robert had sent a flood of messages from Las Vegas. The word was getting out that the Magus would allow Common Caste representation in the vampire parliament. They only communicated with the lowest status members of the House of Pentacles. They were sure the others would be loyal to Borgia. Jorge sent a text to the Baron before he retired,

```
Bring Antoinella!
She might help sway some of the rebels.
```

Lady Kananga took her private jet to Vegas and met with her aides in her suite. Samuel was a rare Common Caste Knight she relied on heavily. He was small in stature and quite acrobatic. He also adored Lady Kananga, the Head of his House. Lady Kabedi had flown in with him. She had checked out Caesar's Palace earlier in the evening. She had been studying Alexander's movements and his build-up of unsanctioned vampires for a year.

Lady Kananga paced in her suite at the MGM Hotel. Samuel served her a silver cup of blood. She took a sip then said, "We must dissuade anyone from ever challenging the Magus again."

Kabedi responded, "Word is getting out that the Common Caste will be allowed representation. If we offer mercy to the rebels, we will have a better chance of winning their allegiance."

Samuel added, "Of course witnessing your power would also move some of them to change their loyalty."

She emptied the cup, then looked at Samuel, "I will find a way to change your caste, I swear it Samuel."

"Lady Kananga, perhaps the Magus will be more open to your egalitarian ideas when he recovers from his imprisonment." Lady Kabedi asked, "Would you allow me to give some of my blood to Samuel to prepare him for the battle to come?"

"Hold the cup," she commanded Samuel. Kananga took off her gold lion's head bracelet, pressed on one of the stones, and a small sharp blade popped out. She made a tiny slit in her wrist. Blood trickled into the cup. "Share this! You will both need to be fortified for tomorrow night!"

They looked at each other in amazement. They could not remember another time she had shared her Haute Caste blood except for transformations. Because the Magus had transformed Kananga, her blood was more potent than other vampires. Samuel took a sip and then gave the rest to Kabedi. They felt a rush as they drank the blood.

Samuel asked, "Lady Kananga, do you feel like this all the time?"

She smiled, "Yes, it is an exquisite state of being."

When I woke in the afternoon and checked my phone, there was a text from Lily. She had never communicated with me like this before. I was surprised by the content which revealed more than vampires will usually put in messages.

> Miranda, I must thank you for sparing Kyoto. I believe he meant to help you. He believes your blood is a threat to our kind in some way, yet he was still willing to risk exposure during transformation be-

cause he thought that might be the best way to remedy
the situation. I have not yet been able to determine
what his concern is.

See you tonight

He had been trying to help me. The doctor who had cared for the kids and I, did not wish us harm. He wanted forgiveness. What did he know about my blood and what did this mean for my kids? I would have to put my questions aside until I could speak with him personally. I remembered the time I had offered my blood to Tristan when he had given a lot of blood to save Al's life. Fortunately, he had refused my blood not wanting to cause me any harm. Who knows what it might have done to Tristan? I wallowed in self-pity for a moment. Somewhere, someone was complaining about being bored at work. I envied them. Somewhere, someone was making a pumpkin spice latte for the 200th time, and I wished for a moment I could be them. Normal, predictable life was getting harder to find. I missed my kids, their laughter, and snide comments. They had to be protected from all this insanity.

I wandered down to the kitchen, where Teri was watching Grigoryi cook. I could smell the garlic in the sauce. "Grigoryi, you might want to go light on the garlic." His eyes got wide for a moment. "Just kidding. It won't hurt them, but scent might be kind of annoying with their enhanced sense of smell." Teri started laughing and Grigoryi smiled.

"We've got a lot to learn about vampire etiquette," Teri said.

"I poured a cup of coffee and said, "I'm going out on the patio."

"Wait! Baroness, the alarm system!" Grigoryi called out to me. "The Baron had a new alarm system installed after the Magus was taken. He gave explicit orders not to disarm the system until he gets up."

I looked at my watch; it was an hour before sunset. "Fuck that! I'm not going to be a prisoner in my own house!" Maybe I was working through my grief. Maybe I was being an asshole, but I opened the patio door.

It sounded like an air raid siren, loud enough to wake the almost dead. I saw everyone running around like headless chickens, Tristan came flying down the stairs half-naked. I just couldn't stop laughing. Tristan was trying to ask Grigoryi something over the din. Grigoryi pointed to me standing by the open patio door. Tristan turned off the alarm and without a word, returned upstairs.

The kids did not hear Hann when he entered the museum. To his amazement, they were singing a Todrick Hall's song about "The Wrong

Bitch" while helping each other suit up in armor fashioned from bits of material they had salvaged from around the compound. At first, he was stunned, and then his laughter got their attention.

"We wanted to surprise you," Marie told him.

"You succeeded!"

Tomas responded, "We have a plan, but we need your help."

He stared at the kids and realized the power within them. His father had seen it in him as a boy. They were on a mission. He knew if he did not help them, they would find a way around him. "Your parents might never forgive me."

"Yeah, but we'll owe you," Des said.

"And there's four of us," Marie added.

"You promise to obey my commands in the field?"

They all responded with variations of, "Sure!"

In all honesty, he had been up before sunset worrying about the perils the Haute Caste would face trying to rescue the Magus. The chance to do battle with Alexander was a challenge he hated missing. Whatever happened, the children would have to be kept safe. Cassie had told him of a vision about the children, which was influencing his decision. "You knew I'd agree to help you."

"Yeah, you're a warrior," Des said.

Marie held up a poster board with a drawing of Alexander's fortress. "We got aerial pics from the internet."

"Things might have gone differently if we had those in my day!" he told them.

Des said, "Wait till you hear our strategy."

Jacques added, "Alexander will be sorry he ever messed with the Magus."

"Or the Mordecai offspring," Hann stated. "My first command is to pick a different battle song."

I went up to my room to pack for the trip. Teri knocked and came in with some black garments. "These are made of a material similar to Kevlar, only stronger. It will help protect you," she told me.

"I wore one of these outfits once before, in a battle during the last Common Caste attempted revolt" I sighed.

"It will be okay," Teri replied. "We've got a squad of vampire elite doing the heavy lifting. We'll just pick off some of the mortal mercenaries. I heard you're good with a knife."

"Here!" I handed her the gold lion's head bracelet Kananga had given me. "When you push down here, a sick blade pops out. You deserve it for being willing to help us."

"Thank you!" She hurried off to pack.

Ruben came by, "You're such a brat! I needed that beauty sleep. I'm beginning to like your kids better than you."

"Sorry!" I couldn't help laughing

"Sure, you are. The Baron says to be ready in fifteen minutes."

Not wanting to provoke His Highness further, I was downstairs waiting by the front door in ten. Ruben helped Omar carry out Anastasia's trunk. She emerged wearing stilettos, lace V-neck, skintight jeans, and pearls. Tristan had an overnight case and a suitcase that, by the obvious weight of it, was full of weapons. Sarah and Ruben had studded leather backpacks and looked like rock stars. Angel appeared with Antoinella. She looked like her young self again, cleavage and all. Her long dark curls had been pulled forward to hide the bald spot. Anastasia had left it as a small reminder.

We drove to a private aviation area of LAX. Tristan did not say a word to me. The Magus' jet was waiting for us. I felt sad thinking about him being frozen stiff. The Magus had revealed the vampire's Achille's heel in part to save me. I sat beside Tristan, "Where are we going to stay?"

"Lady Anastasia's home on Winter Palace Drive, it is her primary residence. Jorge's mansion is nearby."

"Are there a lot of vampires in Vegas?"

"We tend to visit rather than reside there."

"Fun times!" I muttered. He ignored me. It was going to be a long quiet flight to Vegas.

Chapter 39

It's Fabio!

"Who is taking care of Delilah?" I asked Tristan as we landed in Vegas. It dawned on me the big cat had been left alone.

"She does not like to fly. Billy and Robert drove out with her to Jorge's."

We arrived at a small palace on a manmade lake. Though it was magnificent, it must have been a shadow of the grand residences where the Romanov Tsarina had grown up. Velvet drapes, fabulous art, and furnishings inlaid with semi-precious gems showed off her wealth. Her staff were very courteous and had Russian accents. They brought a silver coffee set on a malachite tray. The china was so delicate I was afraid of holding the cup too tightly. Teri, Grigoryi and I were served petite sandwiches as we sat in a plush living room while the staff put our luggage away.

"Your home is amazing!" I stated.

She shrugged, "It's comfortable."

Omar sat beside me and took my hands gently, "Dear Miranda, I know you must be exhausted. We will protect you at all times. If you wish to stay back from the confrontation with Alexander, we will understand."

I looked into his ancient brown eyes framed by a youthful countenance, "Not a chance! I'm doing this for the Magus and to keep my family safe. Would it be possible to wear a robe like yours? I want to announce to the vampire world my House of Swords heritage."

"Of course!" he was delighted.

Tristan shook his head, "You never cease to amaze me."

I replied, "Because you lack imagination."

Kananga arrived and greeted everyone with a smile and asked, "Shall we discuss how we will take down Sir Alexander?"

Sarah added, "And Sir Borgia, I want him!"

"As always, he is playing both sides. I would not harm him until you see who he chooses at the last encounter." Antoinella advised.

My husband stood and addressed the assembled, "Tonight we will meet at Caesar's Palace to hear his demands. We will appear as though we want to negotiate with him. Teri, Grigoryi, Robert, and Billy will try to discover where the Magus is being held. He is probably being kept in one of Alexander's suites. His fortress has not been connected to the power grid yet, though he has generators powering it. The Magus could be moved there at any time. We intend to spare the lives of the rebels, Borgia and even Alexander, if possible."

Kananga asked. "What of Franco?"

"Jorge is at Caesar's trying to liberate him prior to the talks as a gesture of goodwill on Alexander's part." Tristan added, "To spare any harm to innocent mortals, we will wait until Alexander goes to his fortress before we make a move against him."

The Baron said, "We will leave in an hour. Normal dress with concealed weapons. We don't want to alarm the shorts."

As we walked to our rooms I asked, "Why even carry weapons with your abilities?"

"There is always concern that using our gifts in public might draw unwanted attention, even in this city of excess."

I replied, "In Vegas if you dressed up as Elvis, no one would even notice."

Sir Jorge was shown to Sir Alexander's suite by the guards. "Before any talks begin, I must see Sir Franco to know that he is unharmed," he said to Sir Alexander. Sir Alexander was attired in a black suit and black shirt reminiscent of a mafia don.

"Why should I bother to extend you any kindness after you took Lady Penelope?"

"Your pug is quite happy with Connie, the widow you created. Consider it a small comfort to her. Franco is not a threat to you; free him!" Sir Jorge was looking around the suite as he spoke.

"The mortal's death was a mistake, but not uncommon in a campaign."

"Perhaps you should have let him know that you had started a war."

"Revolution," he sat down in a gold brocade chair. "I let Kyoto have his way and look at the problems that created. I am personally directing all aspects of my military operation now."

"Let Franco go. He is not part of your war."

"Very well, I have grown tired of his whining." He signaled to a guard to get Sir Franco.

Sir Jorge smiled, "After listening to him for two hundred years, I've missed it."

"Why not join me now, before circumstances force you to. I have captured the Magus! No other vampire has ever defeated him."

Sir Jorge waited until he saw Sir Franco. He was relieved to find him unharmed. Then he turned to Sir Alexander, "Thank you for returning him. I shall ask for mercy for you when this is all over." Sir Alexander looked at them both with contempt. Sir Jorge took Sir Franco's hand and they started to leave.

Sir Franco looked back, "Good fucks do not always make good leaders." Sir Jorge shoved him toward the door, and they left.

There was quite a strange assembly taking place in a large conference room at Caesar's. It was close to midnight when it began. Two long tables had been set up about ten feet apart, arranged so that both sides could face the other. We arrived first. The Baron and I sat in the middle with the other members of the Haute Caste flanking us. Alexander arrived several minutes later with Sir Borgia and Scheherazade plus several unsanctioned Chinese vampires. He did not realize that Antoinella was now on our side, spying on his guards.

None of us rose to greet Alexander. The Baron merely nodded. Alexander's retinue, even Borgia, waited for him to be seated before they sat down.

"Release the Magus now, or suffer the consequences," the Baron demanded.

"I will give the orders!" Alexander responded. He was more ancient, but most considered the Baron more powerful.

Kananga stood, "You had a chance to establish a new House, but because of your greed and thirst for power, you will never have that honor. Free the Magus!" She lifted her hand and the unsanctioned vampires started crying out, clutching at their eyes. They had been blinded! But Borgia, Scheherazade, and Alexander were not harmed. She lowered her hand and the blinded vampires began blinking and rubbing their eyes. Their sight had returned.

"Nice party trick! I'm sure the Common Caste will want to follow you now." He turned his mocking tone on me, "Nice costume."

"I am the Baroness Miranda Ortega Mordecai. You caused the brutal murder of my father. Return the Magus or I swear I will bring you to your knees."

"My dear, your father, Sir Omar, seems well to me. I will enjoy having

243

your undivided attention but with a more pleasurable outcome. I see no reason to meet your demand."

Borgia spoke, "We all desire to see the Magus again, though in a different capacity. He will be allowed to advise His Highness, Alexander. Do not bother to try and use your gifts upon us. We have supped on the Magus' blood."

I pulled a dagger from a sheath in my boot, and just as Borgia finished speaking, I threw it at his head. He reacted so quickly it only sliced his ear.

"Bitch!" he exclaimed.

"Van Gogh!" I replied smiling.

He started to raise his hands, which got everyone on their feet. Alexander slammed his fist on the table and yelled, "Enough!" The table cracked in half. "We are done here. If you wish me to spare the Magus, be at my fortress tomorrow at midnight ready to pledge your allegiance."

Borgia held a napkin against his ear and glared at me as they left. I called after him, "My dad taught me how to throw a knife!"

Alexander paused and glanced at me with a look of respect, "Goodnight Baroness." Alexander and his minions left the room.

There were twenty guards, both Common Caste and mortal inside the suite that held the frozen prisoner. It was tense in the room as the Common Caste were hungry. The mortals had gathered together beside the locked door to the bedroom which held the freezer. They suddenly jumped back. "Did you hear that?"

"Quiet!" the unsanctioned head guard ordered.

"We heard something move in there!" One brave mortal told him.

"It's your imagination," the leader said dismissively "Sir Alexander shouldn't have given you such an important job. You're no help to us. Except as a meal," he stared at the frightened mortals.

Another unsanctioned spoke up, "C'mon Chang. No one will miss one of these miserable fools. We can share him."

Just then, the door burst open, and to the relief of the mortals, all attention shifted to Sir Borgia, who entered with a bandage on his ear and Sir Alexander behind him. He pointed at the bedroom door. "Open the door!"

Chang took a key from his pocket and unlocked the door. Sir Borgia entered, inspected the freezer and sniffed the air for the scent of the Haute Caste, or an intruder. He only detected the faint scent of the Magus. Sir Alexander followed and closed the door behind them. He was the only one with keys to the three heavy padlocks on the freezer. Sir Alexander opened the locks and turned to Sir Borgia, "Raise the lid."

Sir Borgia slowly lifted the freezer lid. They leaned over to look inside. The magnificent Magus was an ice blue color, perfectly preserved and motionless in a fetal position. "You underestimated me," Sir Alexander said to the inert Magus. He patted Sir Borgia on the shoulder, "The Baroness was fantastic tonight. Imagine what she will be like when she transforms. The Magus should have taken the Baroness for himself."

"I have long wondered why he did not. Now we know his plans for her do not matter, your highness."

Sir Alexander closed the freezer and snapped the locks back in place. They exited the room. He commended the guards then added, "We leave for the fortress in an hour." Sir Borgia sent the mortals to eat dinner and saw small cups of blood had been given to each of the unsanctioned guards. It was O positive. Chang was disappointed. He wanted more Haute Caste blood to prepare them for tomorrow night.

Grigoryi had been busy in the kitchen of Caesar's Palace. He made friends with some of the staff who were on a smoke break outside, pretending he was looking for a job. He asked about the food they prepared and if they had a lot of requests for foreign cuisine. Someone mentioned that they had prepared some special dishes for the Villas. There had been requests for Middle Eastern fare from one side of the floor, and the other ordered Chinese. He was able to find two unattended carts with Asian meals that were going up to the 29th floor and sprinkled a powder Lady Anastasia had given him on the food. She had assured him the harm would only be temporary.

Antoinella slipped into the conference room as the Baron and the others were preparing to leave. In a hushed tone, she told them, "Sir Franco said the freezer is heavily guarded in one of Alexander's suites. They are all leaving for his headquarters tonight. I saw them back up a truck and a couple of vans to the rear hotel entrance."

Tristan looked at Sir Omar, "There isn't much time."

Omar took my hand, "Before we leave, I'd like to introduce you to an old friend."

We left the rest of the Haute Caste and walked towards a Saudi royal and his entourage in the lobby. When the bodyguards saw Omar, they stood aside. He turned to me and said just nod and smile. He embraced the older Saudi and then pointed to me. I did what Omar said. I had no idea what they chatted about. Then he motioned to me to follow him to the elevators.

"What was that about? Where are we going?"

"I told him my cousin was pregnant and needed to rest, that the excitement of Vegas was overwhelming. He generously offered one of his Villas on the 29th floor."

"Nice!" I replied.

He handed me a black scarf, "Cover as much of your face as possible." He pulled his headdress about his face as well. When we got to the floor, we turned in the direction of the Saudi's rooms. Alexander's staff, at the end of the hall, ignored us. One of the royal retinue allowed us to enter an empty suite kept for guests.

"Dear Miranda," he whispered, "I want you to reach out to the Magus, so we know that he has not been decapitated. Cassie has not been able to confirm he is whole. Please try. We believe he is next door."

"I'll try." My anxiety level rose as I considered what I might see. I moved away from Omar and faced the direction of Alexander's suites. I closed my eyes and took a deep breath then slowly let it out. I thought about the Magus. I remembered his scent, the gentle way he touched my hands when consoling me. Suddenly I felt the same sensation I experienced when I had been abducted, except that my brain filled with darkness tinged in blue. I felt an overwhelming coldness creep over me, and I began to shiver.

Omar put his arms around me and asked, "What do you sense?"

The sensation vanished. "He still exists."

"Excellent," Omar whispered.

I sat down on a plush couch and sighed. "Now what?"

"We make plans for tomorrow night."

"Why not free him while he is still here?"

"We won't risk hurting mortals. There are children in the hotel."

"The code?"

"I do not believe that even Sir Alexander would put a child in jeopardy." I gave him a cynical look and he continued. "Yes, we have all sworn to protect the young."

I thought about how Alexander had saved Jacques. "So, no one would hurt my kids?"

"I do not believe any vampire would ever harm them, not even the rebels."

"I wish I could be as sure as you are."

The Baron did not wait for our return. He took off in Lady Anastasia's silver Jaguar to talk with Sir Jorge and Sir Franco. He was so angry with Sir Alexander that he did not hear the click coming from the dashboard as he accelerated on a deserted stretch of road. Suddenly the car began to fill with smoke. He tried to brake, but nothing happened! He started coughing and choking, the headlights went out, and he could not see the road. He tried to open the door, but it was locked. With all his strength, he forced the door open and rolled out on the side of the road as the Jaguar veered off the road, rolled a few times, then came to rest, wheels in the air. He pulled off his torn shirt and brushed off the desert sand. He took out his phone, but the screen was badly cracked. "Alexander!" he bellowed into the desert night.

At Caesar's Palace, the leader of the Haute Caste rebellion lost sight of what happened to the Baron when the Jaguar crashed and destroyed the remote camera hidden in the dashboard. Sir Alexander assumed his foe survived, but hopefully would not be at his best tomorrow night. "Now, let us move to my desert fortress and prepare for battle."

Scheherazade smiled at him, "My Lord, you have diminished the two most powerful vampires in existence. Wait until the news reaches the Common Caste, they will have to accept your accession as the head of the vampire world."

"Fine. Now help supervise moving the Magus." There was something about her unending praise that got on his nerves. He did not need to hear the opinion of the Common Caste; of course, they would be impressed. He wanted to hear the Baroness herself praise him and acknowledge his victory.

Standing on the side of the road, the Baron was combing his thick blonde mane back with his hands when a car with two slightly inebriated real estate saleswomen saw him. "Pull over Karen!" Nancy yelled. "I think that's Fabio!"

Karen said, "Oh my God! It's Thor, that actor who plays Thor!"

The driver pulled the minivan just past the Baron, "I don't care who he is! Look at that body." They stared for a moment at his bare torso. She opened her car door, "You need a ride, honey?"

"Yes, thank you!" he replied.

Karen turned to Nancy, "Get in the back!"

She waited until he walked up to the car and got as close to the Baron as possible while sliding out. "She noticed the crashed Jaguar off the road. Was that your car? It's totaled. You look great! I mean, not a scratch."

He tried to ignore her as he sat in the front. Nancy just stared, "I'm sure I've seen you in a movie, or on a book cover."

"No. I'm not from here. Would you mind giving me a ride to a friend's house?"

"Sure, whatever you want, hon," Karen replied.

"Maybe we can take you out for a drink somewhere," Nancy said.

Tristan replied, "I don't think I am attired appropriately."

Karen looked him over and said, slurring a bit, "I like how you're dressed!"

"Maybe another time, my friends are expecting me."

They both sighed disappointedly.

Nancy inquired from the back seat, "Where are you from?

He started to reply, paused then said, "Lithuania." He then told them where he needed to go. A few minutes later they pulled into the circular drive of Sir Jorge's mansion. One of his staff came out to offer assistance to the Baron. Karen and Nancy sat staring at Tristan, hoping to be invited in. When Tristan walked up to the front door, he turned and gave a royal wave. Delilah came out and jumped up on his chest. Tristan went into the house followed by the panther.

Nancy yelled, "Siegfried and Roy! I knew it!"

Karen stared for a moment, sighed, and put the car in drive. As they pulled out on the road Nancy said, "My next vacation, I'm going to Lithuania."

Karen sighed, "Don't you love Vegas."

When Omar and I got back to the conference room, the Haute Caste were having an animated discussion with Antoinella, Grigoryi, and Teri. They stopped talking as we approached, waiting for news.

"He is still frozen but intact. There is hope," Omar stated.

"That's a relief," Ruben said for everyone.

Kananga looked at me, "Miranda, your husband is fine, but Alexander sabotaged the car he was driving. He's at Jorge's. We'll go there now."

"He's okay, you're sure?"

"The car is totaled, but he escaped unharmed," Kananga told us.

Teri added, "We've checked out the Range Rovers, they have not been tampered with."

Anastasia moved to Omar's side, "I shall enjoy facing that coward tomorrow night."

"Jorge is expecting us," Ruben said. "If we don't leave soon, I'll feel compelled to watch the Elvis impersonator at the Bar Mitzvah in the ballroom next door."

Chapter 40

The Confrontation Approaches

Sir Franco laughed and said to the Baron, "They think you're Roy or maybe Siegfried!" Sir Jorge shook his head at Franco's remark and gestured down a hall, "There are clothes that should fit you in the guest room, please join us after you have refreshed yourself. The others will be here soon."

"I don't believe I know who Siegfried or Roy are." The Baron's glare made Sir Franco's grin disappear. Delilah followed him down the hall.

Sir Jorge's home was a modern masterpiece of wood, glass, and stone. The shower was river rock with a rain shower, which fell gently, washing away the desert dust. The soap smelled of evergreen and musk, invigorating him. As the Baron stepped out, I handed him a towel.

He looked surprised for a moment, not knowing I was here, then he swept me up in his arms, and I started crying, "Are you really okay?"

"Yes, my love." He kissed me passionately. I yielded to his arms as he carried me to the bed. I quickly shed my Arabian robes. Every inch of my body tightened as he stroked and kissed me. The scent and strength of his body was overwhelming. His hands gently teased my response. I raised up against him as we joined in rhythmic thrusts. My body had really missed him, every intoxicating vampire inch. We collapsed in a delightful state of exhaustion.

There was a knock on the door. Ruben called out, "Seriously? Everyone is assembled downstairs."

A few minutes later, it felt like everyone's eyes were upon us as we entered the spacious living room. What an assembly, the Heads of all the Houses and their aides, Common Caste and mortals. Lily had arrived, and Ruben was whispering to her. His old flame Kabedi sat across the room beside Kananga and Samuel showing no reaction to Ruben. It was hard to keep up with vampire relationships. Jorge sat in the middle of the room and gestured to a spot on a couch across from him. Franco was in charge of refreshments. He had the staff give everyone, mortals as well as undead, a small crystal shot glass of blood. Grigoryi declined.

Jorge announced, "It is enhanced with the last of the blood the Magus left to us in case of an emergency. Even now he honors us with his presence." He emptied his glass, and the others followed, but I just took a sip. I shivered for a minute and Tristan patted my hand. Jorge continued, "Sir Alexander will try to persuade us to join him. He is very cunning, so be wary at all times."

The Baron stood and surveyed the elite of his world, "Keep in mind he conquered and ruled civilizations. Establishing himself as ruler of our empire is not his end game. He once told the Magus that mortals should bow down to our superior natures. Not only must we rescue the Magus, we must keep Sir Alexander from revealing our truth to the greater world." The room was quiet. The Baron was in agreement with the Baroness, that too many have been lost since the rebel uprisings began. "We will capture them, release the Magus, then together decide the appropriateness of punishment or mercy."

Kananga responded, "Rewards for those who are loyal and assist us will be in order."

"Of course," the Baron looked around the room. "Much has come to light because of this conflict. Sir Alexander wishes to take advantage of the struggle of the Common Caste, but I shall see that they are given their due as members of our enlightened kind." My husband, with help from Jorge, began to lay out the plan of engagement in detail. I finished off the gift of the Magus' blood. I felt only a tingling sensation and mild heat throughout my body this time. I guess I was getting used to it. I was trying to focus on the plan my husband was detailing, but I was too tired to focus my thoughts for long. Grigoryi looked nervous and afraid, and even Teri seemed worried. The Common Caste, like Antoinella, Angel, and Samuel, were ready to fight now. Bless their dark little hearts. Pauline would be in charge of the Common Caste and mortals tomorrow. The room broke up into fighting groups, but I was not included. I saw Tristan briefly confer with Lily. She left before I could talk to her. When this was over, I would make her tell me about Kyoto, but even with the Magus' blood, I badly needed sleep. I checked my phone and saw Batu had texted that the kids had a good day and were so tired from chasing elephants they went to bed without a fuss.

Antoinella approached me, "The guards said Borgia has been hosting Al and Lolly, but they did not know which hotel. He said they were still mortal two nights ago."

"Thanks for letting me know." I wanted to hate her, but I just felt like she was struggling to survive like me.

"I'll look out for your friends tomorrow. I owe you," she stated and left. Tristan touched my arm, "We have to go. It's almost sunrise."

"Lolly and Al, he will try to use them."

"He is not the only one with cards to play."

When we got back to Anastasia's mansion, I stopped Omar in the hall. "You did not say much during the discussion tonight."

His expression was very serious, "It is time to observe, and act. Words will make little difference tomorrow. Rest well daughter," he kissed my forehead.

I was just about to enter our suite when Ruben stopped me. "I just wanted to tell you, pay attention to Lady Kananga tomorrow night. She and Sir Alexander spent two hundred years together, and it did not end well."

"So, I shouldn't worry about death by vampire?"

"Are you kidding? Lady Kananga likes you," he smiled and went to his room.

That was kind of reassuring. Had all the Haute Caste had sex with each other at some point? I had only been with my husband. Somebody should light a candle to me. At least until the divorce. I climbed into bed and was asleep before Tristan joined me. I woke up as he got into bed, but there was no more physical passion. We were both exhausted and up-tight about the coming storm. He fell asleep with an arm across my chest which was comforting. My feelings for him were all over the board, but always strong. I fell asleep wishing he was mortal. He probably fell asleep, wishing that I was a vampiress. Such is paranormal love.

Sir Borgia knocked on the door of Lolly and Al's suite at the Luxor. Al was irritated at being woken before dawn until he realized who it was. "Come in, come in."

"I'm sorry to disturb you at such an early hour. I hope all is well and that you're enjoying yourselves?"

Lolly pulled a silk kimono robe about her and entered the sitting area. "Hi Cesare!"

"Hello. I wanted to let you know that Sir Alexander will meet with you tonight at his home. He is looking forward to meeting mortals who appreciate our kind."

Sir Cesare gave Lolly a charming smile, "Casual attire will be fine. His home is still under construction. It is impressive but still a bit rustic."

252

"How should we address him?" Al asked.

"Sir Alexander will be fine," he walked back to the door, "I must retire. Until tonight."

When the door closed, Lolly waited a minute before expressing her concerns, and even then, she spoke softly, carefully choosing her words. "He's something that Cesare, but my gut tells me to get out of here. I feel like something isn't right. Maybe we should tell Randie what's going on."

"Lolly, she would probably make Tristan miserable, until he pressured Cesare to keep us away from other vampires. Cesare sees our potential, and he has arranged a personal audience with Alexander."

"Yeah, well, I would feel a lot better about all this if I could talk to Randie."

"Call her tomorrow, after our evening at his mansion."

"How do you know we can trust Alexander?"

"He saved Jacques, didn't he? He conquered the world, one man. I want to get a glimpse inside his mind. Get some more sleep. We'll be up late tonight."

"You've sure gotten bossy since you drank some of their blood!"

"And insatiable," he added, following her into the bedroom.

"I'm not complaining about that."

Sir Alexander personally supervised the placement of a king bed in the finished portion of his mansion. He imagined the Baroness joining him there. He had taken three wives when he ruled an empire. His marriages had always enhanced his ability to rule. Bedding the Baroness would consolidate his new position of power and satisfy his sexual desire. He would overlook her mortal status for now. In time he would demand she transform. Vases with red roses were placed on small ornate tables, sweetly scenting the candlelit room.

He walked out to the foyer. The freezer was in a room just past the grand front doors. He entered the room and opened the freezer to gaze on his fallen rival. "You will respect me in your new diminished role." The powerful Magus looked the same, lifeless, and slightly blue. He closed the freezer. He would have to be more careful of those he allowed close to him. Sir Borgia and Kyoto had been his only Haute Caste supporters. He felt no threat from them. Sir Borgia was appreciative of not being under the scrutiny of the Magus, and Kyoto had sealed his own fate. "Damn Kananga!" he thought. If only she had chosen to join him. She refused his offer to be his second in command and laughed at the idea he might defeat the Magus. If only he had been able to win her loyalty. He would not mind sharing his bed with her again as well, but she was not open to his advances anymore. He wondered who she might favor now.

Chapter 41

The Duel in the Desert

The next afternoon I woke up about two o'clock with a headache. I wandered around the mansion until I found the kitchen and muttered, "Coffee?"

The cook was a skinny form of Tillie. She smiled and said, "Of course, Your Highness."

This was new. Baroness was bad enough. To her surprise, I said, "Just Miranda, just call me Miranda."

"Yes, of course your...uh, Miranda, this way." She headed out of the kitchen and I followed her to the elegant dining room with an enormous polished mahogany table that could seat a small town. I sat down, she poured my coffee and gave me a chocolate stuffed croissant. I inhaled the wonderful aroma. Then I took a drink. "Ah...the magic elixir of life!" I sighed. My head began to throb less. I took a bite of the flaky, still warm croissant. It was heavenly. I considered my circumstances and preparing to battle Alexander the Great was not the weirdest part of it. I was sitting in Tsarina Anastasia's mansion in Las Vegas having coffee and eating a croissant! Episodes of the vampire game show, "You Thought They Were Dead?" kept playing in my head. Joan of Arc was hanging out with bikers in Rossville. Hannibal the Barbarian, and Casandra the Oracle were watching my children play with elephants. Back in Vegas, Billy the Kid wanted to take matters into his own hands. Not to mention Cesare Borgia scheming to use my friends against me. I felt like I was in the middle of a huge vampire power play, with plots and counterplots swirling around me.

Grigoryi and Teri entered the dining room carrying a platter with Eggs Benedict and hash browns. Teri made a face, "She said to tell your highness that it is soy meat."

I told them in no uncertain terms, "Tonight, I want you both to stay behind the Haute Caste. I mean it. No heroics."

They were quiet for a little while, then Grigoryi said, "Then you stay behind us."

I almost started to cry, "I'll try, but I'm afraid I'll get so mad at Alexander no one will be able to hold me back."

Grigoryi thoughtfully responded, "His followers are like mercenaries, they don't believe in their hearts they are doing the right thing. We do!"

Teri patted him on the head, "You are now the official chaplain of Team Miranda!"

After breakfast, I sat alone on the patio, looking out over the lake. I hoped Grigoryi was right, that we somehow had conviction and right on our side. I thought, "Doing the right thing better be enough because we're outnumbered."

At Sir Alexander's, the mortals keeping watch from the top of the towers were making a lot of trips to the toilet, suffering from the effect of the food that Grigoryi tainted. It was a long way from the top of the towers to the bathrooms at the bottom. The constant trips up and down left gaps in protection. Chang would have to use some of his unsanctioned vampires to fill in the gaps. Although they were given bowls of rice to calm their irritated bowels, it was not helping much. Patrols around the compound were minimal during the day and somewhat limited due to the impairment of the mortal guards. No one noticed when Batu and Tomas took photos from a small hill, a couple hundred feet away. They made it back to their camp safely.

"The camo worked," Tomas said excitedly.

"Of course, I told you it would," Marie responded. The desert camo had been her idea. They had stopped at a military surplus store on their way to Vegas and would add Kevlar vests and helmets for tonight. Cassie had blessed them with funny smelly burnt herbs before they took off. Des joked, "The guards will just think they smell pot."

Batu sent the pics to Jorge. Unknown to Tristan and me, they had set up a strike force under the direction of Hann. Hannibal had convinced Jorge, Franco, Billy, and Robert that extra help was needed and swore them to secrecy. They decided that asking forgiveness later, rather than permission before, was their best option. They were right. Tristan and I would never have approved of involving the kids.

As the sun set, Jorge awoke and shared the intel with Billy and Robert, who were working on their plan to breach Alexander's defenses. They left Anastasia's early, heading out to do some errands.

When Tristan woke, he asked me about Lolly and Al. I wished I had some news, but there had been no word about them. The hours leading up to leaving for the fortress involved meetings with different groups of players. I asked what my role would be, and he responded, "Stay right behind me; you will be safe there." Not particularly comforting. I went back out on the patio to try and calm my nerves. Omar joined me and we sat together looking out into the desert. He was wearing olive green pants and shirt, looking like a dictator from a small, cranky country.

After a few minutes quietly thinking of what was to come tonight, I turned to him and asked, "Omar, do you know how to defrost a vampire?"

"Lena was the only vampire to be frozen and thawed. She was damaged, but I believe that happened when the Magus exposed her to sunlight. If we thaw the Magus at room temperature, he should be fine."

"It's like we're talking about a Thanksgiving turkey." I just shook my head at the thought.

"A very important turkey," Omar responded.

I stared at him in surprise. "You made a joke! I've never heard you do that before."

He just ignored my comment, stood up, and went inside.

If the world was coming to an end, I needed more coffee. Anastasia was in the kitchen. Not one of her usual haunts. She was directing the staff to prepare dinner for the mortals.

"Ah, Miranda, how are you?"

"Great! What could possibly be wrong?" I filled my coffee cup. "When do we go to war?"

"We'll leave at eleven. Everyone will rendezvous here at ten. Can my staff get you anything?"

"A tank would be nice."

She pulled me aside, so the staff could not hear us. "I have something for you. I noticed you gave Kananga's bracelet to Teri." She handed me a beautiful opal ring circled by rubies.

"I appreciate it, but…"

"Look. The opal flips open to reveal a preserved concentration of Omar's blood. If you find yourself in a bad situation, take it. You'll get a surge of power."

"Better than espresso," I said with a grim smile.

"We both want you to wear this tonight." I saw the concern in her lovely features.

Not the time to be a smart-ass. "Thank you. Your concern means a lot."

She disappeared down the hall. I slipped the ring on my finger, and I had a feeling I would need it tonight.

Around nine o'clock, we all gathered in the living room. My husband spoke, "We believe Alexander will have a cellular jammer at his compound, and our phones will not work. We can communicate with these." He handed Jorge a small box with several small earpieces for two-way communication. Jorge kept one and handed one each to Billy and Robert.

"Lady Pauline will lead a group of Common Caste and mortals. They will guard our vehicles and escape route. Sir Omar, Lady Anastasia, Sir Jorge, and Lady Sarah will each take out one of the towers. Lady Kananga, Lady Lily, Sir Franco, and Sir Ruben will be with the Baroness and me as we get close to Sir Alexander. We must be very careful when we liberate the Magus. Lady Pauline will be in charge to safely move him when I give her the signal."

"Who will deal with Alexander?" I asked.

Lady Kananga responded, "The first one to get close enough."

We all broke up into our assigned groups. I tried to find Lily, but she had disappeared again. I went back to my room and checked my weapons in front of a mirror. The black ninja suit and quiet booties were creepy. I had two throwing knives and a dagger. I practiced pulling them out, ready for attack. I made mean faces in the mirror.

"Stop it! You're killing me!" Ruben was standing in the doorway, laughing.

"When I make Alexander laugh, it will be a signal for you to strike."

He just shook his head, "I hope you won't need these, but the House of Plows is giving you brass knuckles." He handed me the small, brutal objects. "The Baron says to be ready in an hour."

I liked the way the knuckles felt on my hands and placed them in my pockets. I removed my sapphire wedding ring, which had been on my hand since we were married. It dawned on me that I might not wear it again. I put it on the dressing table and replaced it with the ring from Anastasia. Some of the Haute Caste had seen me fight vampires during the Common Caste attempted coup in L.A. Alexander had no idea what a pissed off, half-vampire, female could do.

At ten o'clock, we assembled. Black cases containing an assortment of weapons were loaded into four Range Rovers. A hospital gurney and medical equipment were loaded into a van. Once more, each group went over their assignments. Everyone was silent during the ride to Alexander's compound. En route, various weapons were distributed. I looked over at Tristan and saw that he was holding, what must have been a very old, heavy sword with an intricately designed hilt I had never seen before. "You're going medieval on his ass?" I asked. He did not respond.

When we pulled up to the heavy steel gates to the fortress, a guard told us the vehicles would have to remain outside. As we got out of the vehicles, I noticed Billy and Robert sneak over to us from a clump of desert brush. They had large backpacks and gave Tristan and Jorge a nod. Pauline and her contingent of mortal and Common Caste positioned themselves around the cars.

Angel looked at me and said, "Vaya con Dios!" It made Grigoryi smile.

I just replied, "Yeah, you too!" WTF. I wasn't sure if tonight we were exactly going with God. I wasn't sure if a vampire fight qualified as spiritual. I hoped I would have years to figure that one out.

Tristan led us forward. I walked behind him flanked by Kananga and Lily on one side, Omar and Anastasia, on the other. Sarah, Ruben, Kabedi, Antoinella, and Samuel had our back. They seemed to be wearing overly bulky clothing. It seemed odd, but I had more important issues than vampire fashion at the moment. Alexander's unsanctioned vampires and a few mortals took up positions around our group and led the way.

We approached the front of Alexander's palace. He had a flair for the dramatic, and it looked like an open-air stage. A full moon lit up the long, wide stone steps that led to a deep entryway flanked by marble pillars. Temporary lights were strung from the pillars, and several fire braziers blazed on the stage. When we reached the base of the stairs, we all stopped. It was eerily quiet, and the only sound was the low rumble of what must have been a generator providing the power to the lights, somewhere in the distance. A heavy red cloth was draped over a tall structure toward the back. Alexander appeared out of the darkness at the rear of the makeshift stage and strode toward us, wearing flowing gold robes. His muscular chest was bare. A heavy sword at his side, hung from a studded leather belt around his waist. His hair fell in curls about his face. Scheherazade and Borgia placed themselves behind him, wearing black garments that reminded me of executioners. Suddenly Chang appeared leading three dozen unsanctioned vampires. They circled around our group

Omar looked grim. "Stay close to the Baron," he moved behind me with the others who would try to take the towers.

Alexander raised his hand, heavy with jewel-encrusted gold rings in welcome, "We have much to discuss! First, I require each of you to pledge allegiance to me. In return, you shall be able to keep your Houses and standings though I shall give the House of Cups to the Common Caste Lady Scheherazade for her loyalty."

From behind me, I heard Lily say, "Never!"

The Baron ignored Alexander's demand and said, "Where is the Magus?"

"My special guest has been given a special place tonight." He gestured to Chang, who pulled on the red cloth, which fell to the floor, revealing a guillotine. The slightly blue rigid body of the Magus was lying with his neck under the blade.

"Stop this!" I cried, "Let him go!"

I started to move toward Alexander, but Omar and Anastasia restrained me. The Baron shifted his gaze from the Magus back to Alexander. "The Magus must not be harmed further! If you wish to retain any semblance of dignity or status in our world, you will release him now and tell your staff to stand down."

"Baron, you're so short-sighted!" He took a step closer to us, "Perhaps it has been the influence of the Magus. I long for more than the glory of the vampire world, and I will use our powers to conquer the planet. A hundred years from now a new Alexandria will be built in this desert as the capital of a world dominated by our kind." He looked directly at me. "Baroness, I will make you my Empress, and our offspring will be raised to help rule the four corners of my empire. I will even name a city in Illinois, Constance, after your mother, a descendant of the great Knight Templar, Jacques de Molay."

Ruben shouted, "That's no great honor, didn't you name a city after your horse?" His disrespectful response gave us a chance to focus on the reason we came there. I had felt the sway of Alexander's ability to charm for a moment but shook it off.

From the corner of my eye, I saw three of Alexander's horde step forward. Each had a metal canister on their backs.

Jorge quietly said something into his earpiece. Sarah, Ruben, Kabedi, Antoinella, and Samuel, donned protective masks, moved between the guards and us. The guards started spraying liquid nitrogen. Tristan, suspecting Alexander might try that trick again, had outfitted them with thermal protective clothing. They deflected the liquid nitrogen spray, and the canisters were soon empty. Although that threat was averted, we still were outnumbered as the unsanctioned vampires came at us.

I saw Antoinella run up the steps towards the Magus. Borgia intercepted her and threw her to the floor. She got to her feet and screamed, "Bastardo!"

Scheherazade pulled a snake out of a basket and threw it on her, and it bit Antoinella's neck. I ran up beside Antoinella, pulling a knife from a sheath at my waist. With one slash, I cut the head off the viper. I saw Borgia throw Scheherazade against a pillar. Whose side was he on? I rushed over to help free the Magus. Tristan raised his hands to Alexander causing him to rise into the air. Alexander pointed a finger at Tristan's feet. The stone erupted in a mass of blue sparks knocking him over. No longer levitated, Alexander dropped heavily to the floor but was quickly back on his feet.

Alexander looked at Tristan, who had gotten back up, and asked, "Old school?"

Tristan nodded, and they both pulled out their swords. It was like a scene from a weird vampire pirate movie. I heard the clash of their blades. The other Haute Caste were using their powers to fight off the un-sanctioned, but the sheer numbers were overwhelming. Kananga would blind a few but five more would climb over them. I saw Ruben gesture at two assailants, and their shirts caught on fire, but then several jumped him. I turned back to the Magus. Jorge once again said something into his earpiece. There was a small explosion, and the lights suddenly went out. The generators went silent. A second later, explosions went off on top of each of the towers.

I heard a familiar low trumpeting sound. "No! It can't be!" I cried out. the hard rock group, The Kongos' song about war blasted from somewhere behind us. Pauline had the vehicles' headlights turned on. I could feel the ground trembling under my feet, and I knew it had to be Hannibal's elephants. Armored and magnificent, the elephants made quick work of the no longer electrified fences now that Billy and Robert had disabled the generators. Some of the unsanctioned, decided the odds were tipping in our favor and started running into the desert night. Then the lights came back on. I saw Hannibal coming up the drive riding a massive male elephant with more elephants following. To my horror, I realized the kids were riding on top of the elephants! Each had an adult with them to keep them safe.

I started to run to them, but Jorge grabbed my arm, "Franco and I will help the others protect them. Stay here!"

Chaos ensued with Alexander's forces not sure about how to respond to the bizarre attack. Alexander's forces in the elephants' path, know-ing they would be trampled, disappeared into the night. Pauline, the Common Caste and mortals that had been guarding our rear, drove the vehicles up to the house. The last of Alexander's guards ran off or sur-rendered. I got religious again and whispered a prayer for the kids as I turned back to rescue the Magus, the guillotine was empty! The smell of vampire blood was heavy in the air.

The Haute Caste had fought their way up to where the Tristan and Alexander continued to try and decapitate each other. They were so well matched that neither had a scratch nor had either been able to gain any advantage over the other.

"Enough!" Lily said as she lunged at Alexander with a syringe and managed to stick it in his arm.

He looked at the syringe still in his arm as he dropped slowly to his knees, "What have you done?"

With an evil smile, she said, "A gift from the Baroness!"

A figure appeared from the shadows at the back of the stage, flanked by Omar and Anastasia at each side. The Magus! He still looked a little blue but otherwise intact. A murmur passed through the group, mixed with a few gasps. He raised his arms, and all fell silent. The kids came running up to him but stopped a few feet away. He pointed at Scheherazade, who was trying to slip away unseen. She fell to the floor clutching her neck. "You could have killed one of the offspring with the snake you brought to the children's birthday party! You have broken the code!" He moved his hand and blood started to pour from her throat down her sari. She slowly sank to her knees then fell back to the stone floor.

After all the blood that had flowed this evening, seeing Scheherazade's blood flowing from her neck, put me over the top. Afraid I was going to lose it I looked down and saw a glint of light off the ring on my finger. I raised my hand, flipped open the ring and tasted Omar's remedy. It was a strange salty taste, and I felt a rush of energy flow through me. I saw the expressions of horror on the kids' faces watching the macabre tableau in front of them. Without pausing to think, I ran to Scheherazade and held her almost severed head in place remembering how Kyoto had been saved.

"Enough killing tonight! Sarah! Omar! Please, someone, help me!"

Everyone looked to the Magus, he nodded. Sarah grabbed one of the medical bags. Omar pushed me aside as he held Scheherazade's head in place, while Sarah tended to the deep neck wound. I stood, numb, watching Sarah. "You are worthy of being an Empress," Anastasia stated.

Ruben stood beside me and steadied me with an arm around my waist.

I looked at the Magus for a moment, "Thank you!" He gave a nod in response.

Borgia came forward with Lolly and Al, looking unharmed, but appearing shocked by the scene before them. Lolly turned to me, "Borgia kept us safe. Alexander tried to convince us to join him to pressure you.

Borgia pretended to go along with Alexander to protect us. I'm so sorry I should have called you."

"I wish you had, but it's okay now. I'm just glad you two are alright." I hugged her.

The Magus looked ghostly as he slowly walked towards Alexander, "You thought that while frozen I would be totally unconscious, but I was aware of everything while you kept me captive. You will never understand the full extent of my powers."

Alexander looked up at the Magus, "How can this be?"

"I have been treating my body with anti-freeze since the knowledge of how I disposed of Lena became known. I knew it would only be a matter of time before someone tried to use that knowledge on me. I only pretended to be immobilized. You have underestimated me. Now I will impose my judgment." Kananga came forward with a deck of large tarot cards. The Magus reached out to select one.

"Wait! I did not break the code!"

"You were responsible for the attack that killed my father!" I yelled.

"I saved Jacques's life!"

Jacques broke away from Batu and responded, "I'm not stupid! I wasn't going to jump in. The water was too cold."

The Tristan said, "The chaos, pain, and suffering your desire for power has created makes our debt to you null and void."

"But Jacques is my son!" Alexander stated boldly.

There was complete silence. I was in shock. Everyone looked at me, at Alexander and back at me. "That's not possible!" I gasped.

Alexander continued, "You all have underestimated me. I had Kyoto impregnate you with my sperm during one of your post-pregnancy exams. He never thought it would work, but if you check Jacque's DNA, you will find that he is my child! You were to be my Empress and give me more children!"

Jacques yelled, "He's lying!"

Lily looked at me with a grave expression, "He's telling the truth. Kyoto confessed to me in Mongolia. It was why he asked for your forgiveness."

Anastasia added, "I could tell the difference in Jacque's scent from the other children, but I was not sure what it meant."

I had also noticed the difference but imagined it was just because he was not one of the triplets.

Jacques ran to Tristan and hugged him crying, "You're my father, not him!"

There was a look of shock on every face except Alexander's, who had an arrogant smirk on his face. Even the Magus seemed taken aback and at a loss for words.

Tristan leaned over and put his arms about Jacques, "I will always be your father! You will always be my son!" Then he shot a look of pure hatred at Alexander.

The siblings ran over and turned it into a group hug, Tomas proclaimed, "We got your back Bro! Fuck Alex!"

Hann walked over to Alexander, "You overestimate your own power. I knew I could defeat you in battle. Hell, even children could! They planned the attack."

Marie walked over to Alexander still on his knees, and with a look of contempt, gave him a quick kick to the crotch and without a word, turned and walked back over to me.

Des said, "Way to go Sis!"

Tristan urged Jacques to go with his siblings, "We will sort this out in time. Go with them now."

Jacques gave Alexander a dirty look and joined his siblings. Grigoryi walked over to the fallen leader, and with all the disdain, the little monk could muster, said, "Vai a quel paese!" Then he spat on him.

Anastasia whispered in my ear, "He told him to go to hell."

Enraged, Alexander started to get to his feet. I pulled Grigoryi away.

Lily stepped up to the vanquished warrior and inquired, "Alexander, how do you feel?"

"Weak." He struggled to his feet and tried to look commanding, but his presence had lost potency. "What have you done to me?"

Lily explained, "We injected you with blood from the Baroness. It weakened you. As you well know, that was what Kyoto discovered. You never expected that knowledge to be used against you, did you?"

The Magus pronounced Alexander's punishment. "You now have the strength of the Common Caste. The injections will continue until we deem you to be sufficiently punished, and you accept your proper place in vampire society. My choice of punishment would be much more severe, but because you are Jacques's father, you will be spared. Sir Hannibal, will you take charge of him?"

"I would be delighted."

I walked over to Hann and slapped him with all my might. It felt like I had broken my hand. "How could you! I trusted you to keep them safe!"

Hannibal looked at me, then speaking quietly, said, "I expected that and understand your reaction. You do not yet fully understand your children's stations, powers, or latent abilities. They were meant to be here. It was important that they played a part in this moment in our history. Cassie foresaw all of this, but we knew you would never agree. In time you will understand."

"Don't hold your breath," I was still seething. My husband pulled me away. I looked up at him, "The kids should not have been here. They could have been hurt, or worse. Poor Jacques! This isn't how he should have found out." Tristan wrapped me in his arms and held tightly. I still am not sure if it was to comfort me or to keep me from slapping Hannibal again.

The Magus conferred with members of the Haute Caste and they went about issuing orders to take oaths of loyalty from those that stood with Alexander before freeing them. I saw Borgia cradling the barely conscious Antoinella, "Il Mio Cuore," he whispered. Until that night, he had not realized how much he cared for her. Borgia produced a small dagger and made a cut in one wrist and held it over her mouth. A moment later, her eyes fluttered open and then focused on Borgia. "I have always loved you."

The Italians were killing me. I began crying. I was a mess! "Can you help Antoinella?" I asked Al, then I turned to Pauline, "Get the stretcher!" Al and Lolly knelt beside Antoinella; Al grabbed the medical bag someone handed to him and cleaned the snakebite wound. He gave Antonella medication to counteract the swelling and pain from the venom.

Al said, "It was a cobra bite, I doubt there is any cobra antivenom in Nevada. I'm not sure what I gave her will be enough."

Borgia responded, "We'll take her to Jorge's to recover. My blood will be enough to promote her recovery."

Omar left Scheherazade and came over to us, "You and the children should get back to Anastasia's now!"

Teri whistled loudly, which made all the kids' guardians grab a child and head to the cars. Ruben volunteered to drive. Clive, Jasper, and Mayi stayed to help Hann with the elephants who seemed to be enjoying Alexander's fountain, at least what was left of it.

Chapter 42

The Common Caste Are Rewarded

I stared at each of the kids feeling anger, relief, and gratitude. Batu would not look me in the eye. "What do you all have to say for yourselves?"

Des was first, "What happens in Vegas, stays in Vegas?"

They all chuckled except Jacques, "I can't believe he's my father!"

Tomas responded, "I guess it's like Mom and Omar. I mean, Grandpa Pete is still our Grandfather."

Marie surprised us all, "We can still take Alexander out if you want."

"Stop it, you're not going to assassinate anyone," I couldn't believe I had to say this to my kids.

Ruben said, "Look at it this way. Because of Alexander, you had a chance to ride elephants into battle."

I knew he was trying to lighten the mood for Jacques.

Marie added, "He's right, Jacques, there is that!"

Jacques smiled for the first time that night.

When his siblings saw him smile, I realized they all knew he had been helped. I had not totally failed as a mother. "I appreciate how brave you were, but you could have been badly hurt or worse."

"There's a code Mom," Des said, "They won't hurt kids."

"It only takes one vampire who decides not to follow their rules," Batu told him. "Your mom is right to be upset."

I wanted to be mad at him, even though he was backing me up, but I was too tired.

"When we get back, I want you to all take off those camo uniforms and get cleaned up. I don't want to hear any more talk about your glorious battle. Never, never breathe a word about this to your grandma."

"We don't have any other clothes," Tomas complained.

Batu responded, "Sir Jorge said he left some at Lady Anastasia's home for you."

"Jorge knew about the kids and Hannibal? He was in on it?"

Des smiled, "He was our inside man."

"It's a good thing he isn't here right now." I put my arm around Jacques, "The code doesn't say I couldn't take out a grown vampire."

Marie said, "You were awesome Mom. To the matriarchy!" She high-fived me.

Des looked at Tomas, "To the Patriarchy!" Tomas elbowed him. Jacques looked at them like he was about to cry. I hugged him and kissed his cheek.

Batu intervened, "Having Alexander the Great as your biological father is a shock, but nothing to be ashamed of, not to mention your father is a powerful Baron!" He put up his hand, and Jacques slowly high-fived him. Now I was tearful. I was angry at Alexander and Kyoto on so many levels. I felt violated and deceived by Kyoto who I had trusted blindly.

We got the kids loaded into the vehicles and headed back to Anastasia's house.

As the Magus' temperature was returning to normal, his skin color was improving. Sarah had put one of Alexander's cloaks about his shoulders, and one of Alexander's throne-like chairs had been brought for the Magus. He watched the loyal Common Caste and Haute Caste restore order in this corner of his kingdom with pride. Alexander had been shackled and loaded into the back of a truck with one of the elephants. The once-powerful warrior tried to use his powers to make a spark with his fingers, but it fizzled. Acknowledging defeat, he slumped against the side of the truck. The Magus gave Sir Hannibal a tarot Hanged Man card to give to Alexander. Miranda's blood would now be known as toxic to vampires. Kyoto had warned him of a possible antigen that he had noticed in her and Marie's blood. The Magus now hoped the news would make the undead fearful of the Baroness and her brood, offering them more protection. He had not known about Jacques. Alexander did not want the Baron to be the only vampire with a bloodline. The Magus felt sorry for the poor child as he had detested his own father, an ignorant brute. At least Alexander had been known as conqueror of the world once.

Sir Omar sat beside the Magus, "My grandson will be fine. I shall not let Alexander's actions cause him harm. All the offspring were amazing tonight, riding against the enemy like tested soldiers. Sir Hannibal was almost as proud of them as I am." After a moment's reflection, he added, "They will be adults soon."

"Yes. They have exceeded my expectations. They will be interesting as adults like their mother." He looked over at Sir Omar and gave him a rare smile. "She slapped Hannibal the Barbarian! She is amazing! Perhaps we should have left her alone with Alexander for a while. How is Antoinella faring?"

"Recovering. Al is in charge of her medical care, and Lolly is assisting him. We thought they would be used to leverage the Baroness, but Sir Borgia only used them to seem loyal to Alexander, while protecting them."

"He always knew how to play both sides to his benefit," The Magus replied.

The Magus watched Samuel as he lined up the unsanctioned and took their loyalty oaths. Then he sent them to Lady Kabedi to be lectured and given instructions about safe houses in Los Angeles. In time they would be taught the vampire code and assimilated into the undead society. Angel gathered up the scattered weapons and loaded them into one of the vehicles. His shirt was torn and bloody. Billy and Robert were gathering the demolition equipment they had used to take out the guard towers and the generator.

"I must do something for the Common Caste. They have done so much for so long and have been so heroic today. They must not go unnoticed and unappreciated," the Magus stated.

"Lady Kananga has suggested making some of the other blood types Haute Caste," Omar said. "I think her idea has merit."

The Magus responded, "I no longer believe that being born with HH blood should be the only criteria for becoming Haute Caste. Now that Alexander and Kyoto have lost their status, it makes it easier to give it to those who deserve such a station. He got to his feet and declared, "I will do it!" He strode to the edge of the steps and called out loudly, "Let it be known that as of tonight I proclaim Angel, Samuel, Robert, Billy and Antoinella to be members of the Haute Caste. From this moment, they shall be known as Sir Angel, Sir Samuel, Sir Robert, Sir William, and Lady Antoinella! All privileges that are afforded the nobility are theirs!"

Everyone stared at the Magus with astonishment. They hoped it was not just a temporary after-effect of being frozen.

"I hope he means it," Angel said quietly.

"Hot Damn!" Billy yelled.

Scheherazade was brought before the Magus. Her sari was torn and bloody, but she was too weak to be concerned about her appearance. Her neck was stitched up like a rag doll. She hoarsely whispered, "Magus, I am guilty only of desiring to be more than our society would allow."

The Baron glared at her, "You are guilty of attacking your own kind, and trying to usurp the Magus' power."

"Yes," she smiled faintly, "that too!"

Lady Kananga came up the steps, "Magus, The Baroness's request for mercy should be considered. Though I would prefer a quick clean execution." She looked over at the guillotine.

Lady Pauline and Lady Sarah joined them. They took particular offense that a vampiress had acted so traitorously. Lady Pauline inquired, "What if we gave this deceitful bitch a way to redeem herself?"

Lady Sarah smiled, "Let her work at the Café in Rossville for a year."

Scheherazade looked as though she had been condemned to hell. "No!" she protested in a raspy voice. "Let me work with the unsanctioned vampires. I will help them adjust to our world. I beg you!"

The Magus nodded with a small smile. "Two years in Rossville, under the supervision of Sir Bart and Lady Jeanne, it will be. I do not want to hear any reports of unseemly behavior while you are there. You will be of service to the widow of Pete Ortega."

The Baron called out, "Sir Billy and Sir Robert, will you see to the transportation arrangements for Scheherazade? Perhaps tomorrow night."

Grigoryi came forward, "I would like to return to Rossville, may I go with them?"

Tristan responded, "Of course! You have served us with honor. You may go wherever you please and always be assured of our protection."

The Magus turned to the Haute Caste females surrounding him. "Our society owes you all a great debt. I am grateful for your loyalty. The Houses will have another female leader. Princess Khunbish will be the Head of the House of Cups as Lady Lily wishes to focus on her research. I look forward to this new era of greater recognition of the contributions of all members of our society, Common Caste as well as Haute Caste." He looked toward the eastern sky and said, "Unfortunately, we must retire soon. We still have much to discuss tomorrow night." He kissed each of the Haute Caste females on the cheek before descending the stairs. They just stood quietly watching him get into a Range Rover. His public act of affection was unheard of.

"I'll never wash my cheek again," Lady Pauline said with a smile.

I heard the commotion when Tristan and the Magus arrived. I had gotten the kids off to bed about thirty minutes earlier and hoped they would all be asleep. I got in bed and lay on my side, pretending to be asleep when Tristan entered. I heard him shower, then felt him climb in beside me.

"I know you're still awake. No matter. I'm not in the mood for once. Don't worry about Jacques. He will adjust. I heard from the lawyer, the divorce is final, the papers arrived while we were dealing with Alexander. We'll fill you in on the rest tomorrow. You were brave and foolish. I expected nothing less of you."

"What do you mean, fill me in?"

He just smiled and rolled over on his side. "Tomorrow night."

"Fucker," I mumbled.

"Not tonight."

On the other side of the world, the sun was setting. Princess Khunbish was seated on a brocade chair in a meeting room of the monastery where Kyoto was being held. News of the successful attack in Las Vegas had been conveyed to her by Sir Steve. She was elated that the Magus came through with his promise to name her the head of the House of Cups. She felt like being charitable. Sir Steve, dressed in a Mongol tunic and pants, sat down in a chair beside her. A mortal monk brought Kyoto to them, then bowed and left. The Princess gestured for Kyoto to sit on a stool. An incense burner scented the room, and a few candles added light as there was only one table lamp.

Sir Steve served a cup of blood to her highness and then offered one to Kyoto. He took it and quietly said with downcast eyes, "I do not merit your kindness."

Sir Steve inquired, "Are you being treated well?"

"Yes, better than I expected or deserve. Because of the Baroness' mercy, my confinement has been made quite comfortable. I had never meant to help Alexander try and usurp the Magus. My intentions had been to protect our kind, but then I became enmeshed in his schemes."

The princess spoke, "I wish to offer you a position in the House of Cups."

Kyoto's eyes went wide with surprise, "I would be in your debt, and glad to be of any service." He had feared he would be banned from such an honor forever.

"I wish you to be an advisor to my House, as long as you never act in any way disloyal to the Magus, the Baron's family, or me." Her eyes studied his countenance for any sign of deceit. She saw none, only regret for his actions.

"I will do anything to protect those I have wronged and try to atone for my actions."

Sir Steve smiled, "Old friend, the Magus has requested you continue your hematology research. A lab will be set up here in the monastery. One of the monks has a degree in chemistry and will assist you. Blood samples from all the Baron's family and Alexander will be sent here."

"I do not deserve such good fortune." He bowed his head, then asked, "Is it true; her blood diminished Alexander's powers?"

Sir Steve responded, "Yes. He has only Common Caste abilities for now. Quite a blow to his ego."

The Princess went on, "You are considered Common Caste. The Magus has decided that is enough punishment after speaking with Lady Lily."

Sir Steve added, "You are assigned to the House of Cups, and are no longer a prisoner."

"Thank you! Please pass on my appreciation to Lady Lily for her concern, mercy, and kindness. This place suits me. I am content with a simpler existence now. Being Common Caste will hold no shame for me. May I ask who your Knight will be?"

The Princess smiled, "Knights. Sir Steve and Batu. He is being elevated to the Haute Caste due to his service to the Royal family. When Batu arrives, he will be transformed and will be known as Sir Batu. Will you assist with the transformation ceremony?"

"Of course! He will make a fine Knight. Batu is clever, loyal, and brave. Does the Baroness know? I believe she has grown quite fond of her bodyguard." Kyoto asked.

Sir Steve responded, "Not yet. Batu has requested to announce his promotion to the Royal family tonight. Though the Baron is aware and believes it will be beneficial to Batu and the House of Cups if he remains here."

Kyoto responded, "I think the Baron would prefer if Batu would permanently stay in Mongolia."

Chapter 43

Lugosi Mordecai

When I woke in the late afternoon, Tristan was deep in the sleep of the undead. I listened to his even soft breathing, inhaled his scent, and sat up to stare at him in the dim light. He was still the most handsome man I had ever seen with his thick mane of blonde hair, his muscular arms and shoulders, his strong back, and of course, the rest of him. Even with his deep blue eyes closed, his face was perfect. The angles of his cheekbones and jaw were like a Greek statue. We were now divorced. It was official. I knew I would not lay with him again for years, if ever. I fought back tears. It would be so easy to arouse him and imagine that if I transformed, our love would stay like this, contentious at times but passionate and written in the stars. I got out of bed. Fuck the stars. I would decide my own fate. I had run away from him once, but this time, I would walk away.

I showered and dressed in jeans and a Dracula T-shirt I had been saving for a special occasion. I smelled food and the aroma of glorious coffee. I headed for the kitchen where the cook had made an asparagus and cheese omelet with hash browns. I stuck a fork in a bowl of fresh sweet and refreshing melon slices. She handed me a mug of Sumatran French Roast like she had been waiting to ambush me.

I took a sip, and it felt almost as good as a hit of Haute Caste blood. Okay, not that good, but still wonderful. I asked the cook, "Are the kids up yet?"

"Yes. They already ate and are being supervised in the playroom." She pointed down a hallway.

"Thanks," I saluted her with my mug, grabbed my plate of food, and headed towards the sound of video games. At fourteen and fifteen, they were now young adults, too old to call it a playroom. This was a high-tech gamers' paradise. I found the four of them absorbed in a war against flesh-eating space aliens while the butler watched in horror. The video screen was huge, the sound so loud it was unnerving. Last night opened my eyes in many ways. They did not need me like they used to.

"How are you guys?" Their attention was totally focused on the game.

"Good!" Des replied.

"Last night was awesome. I think it improved my game," Tomas said.

"Nothing can help you!" Marie added.

"Die!" Jacques yelled as Des started cursing.

"Good talk! Well, I'll be out on the patio."

It was still afternoon, but the sun was starting to set on the life I had known to this point. Despite what the undead world might call me I was going to do everything in my power to be simply Miranda Ortega again or at least some form of the writer from the cornfields who found a little too much excitement when she moved to L.A. I lost track of time considering my options and my musings were interrupted by Franco. I looked up and realized the sun had set while I had been daydreaming.

"Miranda, there will be a meeting in the living room with the Magus in an hour. You won't want to miss it." When I stood, he looked at my t-shirt, "Seriously? How can a vegetarian writer be so insensitive!"

I sat back down and considered changing. One of the butlers came out and handed me an envelope, "From the Baron," he said.

I opened the envelope, and there was a cover letter for the divorce papers signed by Mr. Beaudine. Freedom! I felt a huge sense of relief. Maybe I would announce it at the meeting. I considered Tristan's feelings for once and decided that it might not be my best move.

When I went inside, most of the vampires I had fought alongside last night were already present, and there were even some who had fought against us. Chang, with a bandaged forehead, nodded to me respectfully. All the seating was arranged to face one burgundy overstuffed velvet chair. The kids came in, and I had them sit near me. The triplets started joking about my t-shirt. Jacques was not amused, "Dad won't like it!"

Omar and Anastasia sat on one side of us. Kananga, Jorge, and Sarah sat in front of us. Tristan arrived and without looking at me, took a seat beside Jacques. At least he was reassuring to our youngest. Angel, Pauline, Teri, and Batu sat the back, and Ruben and Lily were conspicuously sharing a loveseat. Borgia entered, helping Antoinella to a seat beside Kananga. I had never seen him be so attentive to anyone. She gave me a faint smile. She was recovering quickly from the bite.

At the last minute, Franco came over and handed me a cashmere shawl. "Just cover up! Please!" I think he would have been less offended if I had gone topless.

The Magus entered, and everyone rose, even me, without being prompted. He was attired in a blue linen shirt and pants looking refreshed like he had spent a week at a spa not locked in a freezer. His recuperative abilities were amazing. He pushed back his dark hair and took a moment to make eye contact with everyone in the room before being seated. Everyone took a seat.

"My loyal friends and newly welcomed members of our community. We are at a transformation point of our society that will make the vampire world more powerful and secure than we ever thought possible." He paused and looked at Angel, "Lady Kananga and other Haute Caste have requested that the criteria to be members of the Haute Caste be changed. Last night I announced that some of the Common Caste, due to their long service, heroic deeds and loyalty, would now be considered Haute Caste. Sir Robert, Sir Willian, Sir Angel, Sir Samuel, and Lady Antoinella are now Haute Caste."

I turned to look at Angel and gave him a thumbs-up. This was great news. I hoped that the chance to become Haute Caste might lessen the resentment some of the Common Caste felt towards the kids and me. I noticed Batu walking up to the Magus. He knelt before the ruler of the undead. "No," I gasped, unfortunately, loud enough for those nearby to hear.

The Magus put his hands on Batu's shoulders who felt a surge of energy from the Magus' touch. "For years, you have faithfully protected the Baron's family, and last night kept the offspring out of harm's way while fighting to preserve our society. Princess Khunbish has requested that you be transformed by her and become a Knight of the House of Cups. I grant her request. You may return to Mongolia and serve your House, Sir Batu."

As Batu rose to leave, he glanced at me for a second. I held my tongue to avoid ruining this special moment for him. I was pissed and sad. The Magus had not finished.

"The Mordecai offspring showed amazing character and bravery last night. Sir Hannibal was very impressed by their cleverness and spirit. He wished me to tell you the elephants have returned to the sanctuary in fine shape." He nodded to the kids.

That was it! I was done with this insanity. I stood and dropped the shawl. "You should not have endangered my children! They shouldn't have been involved in a medieval battle, they belong in school, playing sports, or riding their horses, not riding elephants into battle. What is wrong with you? You could have freed yourself at any time! No one had to fight Alexander for your non-frozen ass! I thought you were the Great and Powerful Magus!"

The room was silent, the Magus glared at me, and I felt his eyes trying to silence me. "C'mon kids. We're leaving!" The kids started to follow me, except Jacques. I grabbed his hand. "By the way, I'm divorced now, don't call me Baroness again!" I saw Jorge roll his eyes and shake his head. I marched them out into the hall, "Get your stuff! Now!"

"Mom, I want to stay," Jacques protested.

"We can go to school here," Tomas added.

"Not another word!"

They slowly walked to their rooms heads down and I went to pack.

I entered the bedroom, threw a suitcase on the bed, and went to the closet. Behind me, I heard someone slowly clapping. "Quite a performance. Where are you going Ms. Ortega?" Tristan asked from the doorway.

"The fuck away from this looney bin. Don't you care that the kids were in danger?" I threw my clothes in a suitcase.

"They were given a chance to show the vampire world their potential. They did not disappoint. I am proud of them."

"I'd give you the father of the year award, but you'd have to share it with Alexander."

Then I felt it. I was rising in the air. I started flailing my arms and legs to Tristan's amusement. "Stop it!"

"Will you talk to me without being insulting?"

"Okay, I'll try!"

I felt myself slowly lowered to the floor. "Where will you go now?

"I haven't a clue. I don't think I could live in Rossville after all that has happened." I did not add that it would seem pretty empty now without Batu.

"I thought you might feel that way." He handed me a set of keys and an envelope. "I think you might like this better now. It is the keys and a deed to a house near Seattle. A home on a river with ten acres. Six bedrooms, so not as large as you're accustomed to but comfortable. There's a town nearby, Granite Falls, with good schools."

"Vampires?"

"It's a little too remote to interest us, though you'll have a nocturnal caretaker to watch over you.

"It sounds better and better."

"I had bought it as an anniversary present for you, a secluded place to write. I think the kids will like it there."

"An anniversary present? Thanks, now it's a divorce present. We'll check it out. It sounds like a plan for now anyway." I took a breath, calmed down a little, then went on. "Wherever we end up, you will always be welcome. It's important to the kids."

"I have a place in Seattle, about an hour away. I had what you will need for now sent from Rossville. You can work out with your mother what else you will want. No matter what you tell yourself, we are not finished. You should apologize to the Magus before you go." He turned and walked out of the room heading toward the kid's rooms. Once more, he had arranged my life without asking.

I slammed my suitcase shut, took a deep breath, and headed to the foyer. I knew Tristan was right. I had been rude and disrespectful but not wrong. I probably could have handled it better. Manners and protocol were a big deal to the undead, especially the Haute Caste. I headed back to the living room. I saw the Magus speaking with Omar.

I walked over to them, and in front of everyone, I said, "I'm sorry, Magus. I should not have yelled at you. Please excuse my anger." I did not apologize for what I said, just the delivery.

"I'll pardon you when you transform," he replied loud enough for everyone to hear.

I started to respond, but I could see Ruben out of the corner of my eye, making a zip-it gesture. I restrained myself, held my tongue, and turned away. Omar looked relieved. Tristan came down the hall with the kids. Jacques's eyes were red. I know he wanted to spend more time with Tristan. After last night it was going to be difficult to get them back in a classroom. It would be a long drive to Seattle, really long.

I hugged Omar and Anastasia. "Hey, Dad, can I have the car keys?"

He smiled and had the butler get me a set of keys to one of the Range Rovers, "Drive carefully!" he admonished.

Someone tapped me on the shoulder. I turned around and faced Batu. "I'm leaving now too."

"Come with us. You don't have to be a Knight or a vampire!" I stared into his warm brown eyes, and sweet smile. I did not want to imagine him as a nocturnal killer. "Stay mortal, please!" I was tearing up.

"But I want to be those things, and more, I will have the powers I have dreamed about. Is the Baron watching?"

I could see Tristan entering the foyer. "Yes."

"Good!" he pulled me into his arms. He kissed me gently at first, then exerted full-court pressure. He had been waiting for years for this moment. The strength of his body engulfed me. When I came up for breath, he released me from his embrace, "In a year we will speak again. Goodbye, sweet Miranda." He placed an envelope in my hand, turned and walked away.

I stared at him as he left for the airport.

The Haute Caste were trying not to react, but Antoinella smiled at me. Teri came up beside me with a backpack. "You really know how to make an exit. Let's go before they start fighting over you."

"You're coming with us?"

"No one in this room will let you leave without protection."

The Magus gestured to me. I walked over to him, ready to be scolded. He smiled, "Never boring. What did I do all those centuries without you? Just know that you will always be the Baroness. One of us will be waiting at your new home. He has been eager to meet you and the children. Please accept his protection."

"You knew I was going to take off?"

"Lady Cassandra saw it a month ago."

I started to ask about what else she had seen, but I really did not want to know. I knew I could not refuse their protection. Despite my proclamation of independence, I was concerned that some unhappy rogue vampires could still be out there. "Okay, I hope the vamp will be like Bart, he kind of grew on me. Magus, I've got to know what happened to Scheherazade."

"Jeanne and Bart are supervising her. She will be waiting tables in Rossville for the next two years."

"Oh my god, that is perfect!" I would call Mom tomorrow. I had a lot of explaining to do.

"Magus, I'm glad you are unharmed. I should have known Alexander did not stand a chance against you. Please, keep him away from Jacques until my son is ready."

"Of course," until we meet again." With a small bow of his head, he turned and left the room.

Omar said, "We will visit when you and the children are ready for company."

"You and Anastasia are always welcome. Please look after Tristan. He is pretty upset right now. I can't help him."

Kananga gave me a rare hug and whispered, "Tristan is a better vampire because of you and the children. You have had an amazing effect on him. Find contentment dear Miranda. It is in the cards for you." She handed me a tarot card, which was labeled The World.

Tristan stood back and merely watched us leave without a word. He would always be a part of our lives, mortal or immortal. We had been apart for most of our marriage, but this felt different. I had not put my wedding ring back on.

We got in the Land Rover, and I put the Granite Falls address in the GPS. As we left the lights of Las Vegas behind us, I knew, unlike Cassandra, I was clueless about the future. I put the tarot card on the dashboard with the envelope from Batu. Batu was clever to display his affection for me before leaving for Mongolia. Tristan would not forget that slight, but when they met again, Batu would be a magnificent vampire.

I was done with males, mortal or immortal for now. My thoughts drifted to my friends Lolly and Al, who were still relatively normal, and

I hoped their Vegas experience would be enough to keep them that way. James was getting attention from Sarah, but I believed he could handle her. I knew it was not a coincidence that Teri, our bodyguard, had HH blood. I wondered if the Magus was trying to protect her by sending her away from Haute Caste society until she might be ready to transform. I would do everything possible to persuade her to stay in the world of sunlight. I glanced at the Tarot card. I would have to research its meaning. Kananga would not have given it to me if it was not important. I considered sending my Empress card back to Tristan. I loved him but not enough to lose myself. I was ready to figure out who I really was, who I was destined to be. I wanted to be a good mom and a good example for the kids.

Two hours later we stopped at a gas station in the middle of nowhere. While Teri supervised the kids getting snacks, my curiosity got the best of me and I opened the envelope from Batu. It was a Valentine with two intertwining hearts on the outside, inside it simply said, "Your special friend." I started to tear up just as Des ran up to me carrying a Black Lab Retriever puppy.

"Mom, he needs a home!"

Marie was right behind him, holding a baggy of dog kibble, "The clerk said he was just left here, and he's giving him away."

Jacques said, "I named him Lug. You know, short for Lugosi!"

Teri arrived with Tomas. "It's legit. Free to a good home." They had already named the pup. Once you name a puppy it's yours! Jacques could use a dog to hug.

"Sure, welcome to the tribe!"

Jacques took the puppy from Des, "I get to hold Lugosi!"

I looked down at my t-shirt, if Bram Stoker had only known what he had started. Teri took over driving. I stared out the window into the dark desert. I hoped there would not be many vampires in the Northwest. It was too cold, right?

THE END

...OR IS IT?

GIFT OF BLOOD

Chapter 1

The Undead Highway Patrol

Vampires secretly desire to be loved, and that is their hidden Achilles' heel. It's one of the reasons I was created. I have turned their world upside down. I was lost in thought about the turns my life had taken. After growing up in a small rural Illinois town, I went to seek fame and fortune as a writer in L.A., little did I know my life would become much more complicated.

I wrote my first book and, as they say, was swept off my feet by my publisher, who was charming, seductive and unbelievably handsome. It turned out he was the Baron Tristan Mordecai, the second most powerful vampire in the world. In months, I found myself married and pregnant with triplets, and soon after they were born pregnant again with a son.

After we were married, I learned that I was a descendant of Jacques de Molay, a Knight Templar, who gave the Templar gold to the undead in exchange for protection of his heirs. It was on the eve of Friday, October 13, 1307, before the Templars were tortured and killed by King Philip. To my shock, I also learned that my biological father was not Pete Ortega, who had raised me but Sir Omar Sedaghi, the Head of the vampire House of Swords. My rare HH blood type, being half-vampire, and a descendant of de Molay put the kids and me in the center of all the insanity of the vampire world.

For fifteen years, I had tried to make it work with my Thor look-alike husband, but his arrogance, chauvinism, and infidelity became intolerable. He thought it was enough that he would be faithful when I was around. Since being married into the nocturnal clan, I had survived two vampire caste wars. I decided I had had enough and divorced him. The kids and I were on the way to a new home near Seattle to get away from the undead circus before we got pulled into another really weird, dangerous situation. Even though we were now divorced, I was still considered a Baroness and would never be totally divorced from the nocturnal society. My children and I were still being protected and watched over.

"Miranda?" Teri, our ninja bodyguard, interrupted my thoughts. "We are heading to Seattle from Vegas. Wouldn't it have been much quicker just going straight north instead of west through California?'

"I suppose but I really love the ocean and thought the kids would enjoy going up the coast on Route One."

"Makes sense, just wondered." She nodded to the back of the Range Rover, "are they asleep?"

I looked behind me in the Range Rover I had borrowed from my biological father, Sir Omar. My fourteen-year-old son, Jacques, had made a bed out of backpacks in the back. He was curled up with the black Lab puppy we had rescued at a gas station not long after leaving Vegas. His siblings, the fifteen-year-old going on forty triplets, had their heads resting on each other's shoulders. Blissful quiet.

"Yes."

"Batu will return to you," she said softly.

I sighed and thought about our bodyguard in Rossville, Illinois. I had grown up there and moved back so I could raise the kids away from the vampire insanity. Or so I thought. I had developed deep feelings for him. I whispered, "When he does, he'll be a vampire like the others. He's a hot, intelligent, and charming Mongol warrior now. Can you imagine what he'll be like then? What will stop him from being another arrogant bastard like my ex-husband?"

"You!" she smiled.

It was the first time I had called Tristan, my ex. We had been divorced for 36 hours.

A groggy voice from the backseat mumbled, "Dad's not a bastard."

"His parents weren't married, so yes he is. Go back to sleep Tomas."

"Whatever..."

I waited a few minutes until he seemed to have gone back to sleep, then said, "I've never been with anyone besides Tristan. Batu and I talked a lot during the time he protected us, but that was all."

"Seriously?" Teri responded.

I had to chuckle, "Yeah, I was waiting for the right one. I found out later Tristan had kept anyone who might have been interested away from me."

"You had no idea that vampires were watching over you, your whole life?"

"None. Not until Tristan told me after we were married."

"So, what's it like to have sex with a vampire?"

"I've got nothing to compare it with. I never asked you about this before, but don't you have HH blood?"

She got quiet for a moment, just stared at the highway. "Yeah. How did you know?"

"I can smell blood type."

"And you're not even one of them yet," she sighed. "I met Lady Pauline because we had this rare blood type and we had the same doctor and he introduced us. He told me that if I ever needed a transfusion I would be out of luck unless I knew someone else who was HH because it is so rare."

"How did you just "happen" to have a doctor that sees vamps?"

"I donated blood, and the blood bank called me to talk about my rare blood type and referred me to the doctor as a specialist."

"How much you want to bet the whole thing was arranged by the Magus. He keeps tabs on people with HH. He told me the computer age made it much easier to find people with HH blood," I looked at her, "Have they pressured you to transform?"

"No. Pauline just talks about how great it is. They never age, get stronger every day, and live outside of society's petty rules."

I sighed, "Yeah, they leave out ripping apart some unlucky soul's throat. Though I have to admit, they are pretty good about not getting it on their designer threads."

Teri said softly, "I try not to think about Angel that way."

"Angel? You've got a thing for him?" He was a Common Caste vampire from L.A., who recently got promoted to the Haute Caste.

"Kinda, he makes me laugh and doesn't take himself too seriously. You know, like your ex."

I chuckled, "Baron Tristan Mordecai has actually laughed twice in the last fourteen years. I guess women don't like him for his sense of humor."

"Is he that good?"

"If I ever have sex with anyone else, I'll let you know."

"Mom, stop it! We're trying to sleep!" Des complained from the back seat.

"Now, we're traumatized for life," Tomas added.

Marie called out, "I'm hungry!"

I turned around and saw that they were all awake now. "If you're traumatized, it's not because of my side of the family," I responded. Long ago, I knew I was out of the running for a mother of the year award.

Jacques said, "Tacos! Look up ahead."

We were just north of Salinas and came upon a couple of gas stations, a hotel, and a Mexican restaurant. I saw a "Menudo on Sundays" sign in the window. We were saved.

We checked into the Starlight hotel, which was three stars if you were feeling generous. It was clean, and we could get a room with two King beds and a rollaway. I did not trust the kids in a hotel room alone. Just saying!

The restaurant was a bit like the café in Illinois, my mom Connie, and my dad Pete, had opened and operated for years. He was killed in a botched kidnapping attempt as part of an aborted coup by some members of the Common Caste. Sitting in the café got us all a little nostalgic. The food was good, tamales and barbacoa tacos were our comfort food. Des tried to flirt with the waitress who looked about sixteen, while Tomas hit him in the face with a straw wrapper. Marie just rolled her eyes at her siblings. Jacques put a piece of leftover tamale in a napkin as a treat for his new pup, Lugosi. With full tummies, we went to our room. Teri did a security check around the hotel.

About midnight, the kids finally settled into bed. Marie slept with me, Des and Tomas shared the other bed. Jacques had the roll away with Lug, and Teri insisted on doing her bodyguard thing, sleeping on a bedroll beside the door. We were exhausted. I sent a text message to Tristan to let him know his offspring were fine then fell fast asleep.

About two in the morning, I was jarred awake by Teri. She put a hand over my mouth and pointed to the hotel room window. I could see a shadow through the curtains. I reached out with my ability to read people and felt concern from whoever was outside. Lug began to growl. I crept up to the window, and even though it was closed, I could smell her scent, Haute Caste vampire.

There was a quiet knock on the door, "Miranda, Teri, it's me, Pauline."

She was one of the few that I trusted, and I let her in. The sleepy kids all sat up. "Lady Pauline?" Des muttered, "We don't have any more beds."

"You can have my bed," Jacques offered gallantly.

The blonde former surfer-queen smiled at the kids. "I'm glad you're all safe. Teri, how could you let them stay here? There is an approved five-star hotel less than an hour away."

"There's an approved hotel list for vamps?" I asked, never having heard about that.

"Of course. The Magus didn't tell you?" Pauline responded.

I noticed Teri had started petting Lug to avoid looking at me. "No, but apparently everyone else knew."

"They have heavy drapes that block out sunlight, concierge on duty all night..."

Someone thumped on the wall next door, "Shut up! We're trying to sleep!"

"…and security." Pauline got an evil look.

I whispered, "No. Leave them alone." The kid's eyes got big. "It's my decision where we stay. This place is Miranda approved. Are we going to be watched the whole trip?"

"The network has been alerted to your route. It's just to be sure that no one, not even shorts, bothers you."

"The undead highway patrol, nice! We need to get some more sleep before we hit the road. Thanks, but we're staying put till morning. I don't mean to be rude, but good night Pauline."

She left in a huff. Teri walked outside to have a few words with her. I hated the expression "shorts." It was a reference to the short lives of mortals. I got in bed and turned off all the lights except the bathroom, "Go to sleep all of you, we have a long drive tomorrow." I whispered.

After a few minutes, Teri came back, turned off the light, and laid down beside the door. I hated to admit it, but knowing the undead were keeping track of us actually made me feel safer.

*****

Lady Pauline was irritated and was not looking forward to reporting on the travels of the Royal family to the Magus and the Baron. She climbed into a Range Rover identical to the one Miranda was using, also borrowed from Sir Omar. She decided that she needed some vampire "comfort food," pulled out her phone and checked a file that contained "Worthy Targets" in the area. Those on the list were mortals that the Haute Caste found that humanity would be better without. On the list were child pornographers, rapists, drug dealers and other reprehensible members of society that the justice system had failed to deal with. The name at the top of the list was Philip Emerson, aka The Pill King, who recently had a case against him thrown out when the key witness disappeared. She read his bio and thought, "This will be a nice distraction!"

About thirty minutes later, she parked across the street from a seedy bar that Phil was known to frequent off Soledad St. She saw his red Cadillac parked in front of the bar. Checking the area, she noticed a couple of homeless people looking for a safe place to sleep and a prostitute walking off with a man who could have been her grandfather. She wasn't worried about them knowing they would never talk to the police. Despite Phil's money, he still spent most of his time in this shady neighborhood where he started as a street drug runner.

Inside the bar, Phil was having a slow night. He knew he had to stay away from his regular business contacts for a few months until the cops stopped their active investigations. He was forty and afraid some young punk would take his business. The lack of action was driving him nuts. He downed a shot of tequila and threw the glass against the wall behind the bar, then left a hundred dollars on the counter. "These bitches are too ugly to Rufi," he exclaimed.

The chubby, bald bartender, grabbed the money and said, "Out of here Phil!"

Phil muttered some obscenities as he left. The drug kingpin was a small man who carried a Glock in his waistband under his jacket but knew better than to start a fight without his crew. Phil stumbled as he walked towards his car. "Fucking cops!" he stated. Then he saw her, a beautiful, tall blonde in skintight jeans and heels. She was leaning against his hood. His eyes grew wide.

"Hey Phil," Pauline purred. "I'm thirsty."

"How do you know my name?" He looked around, afraid he was being set up, but the street was deserted. He stood a little straighter and pulled in his paunch. She just smiled seductively. He got excited, "I got a bottle of Jack in the car." He unlocked the doors and climbed in the driver's side. With his ego, he never doubted she would join him. He never opened doors for women.

She got in and moved close to him. Phil tried to put his hand on her thigh. She grabbed his wrist and jerked his hand back so hard a bone cracked, he cried out in pain. Pauline wasted no time, reached up, and snapped his neck like a pencil to silence him. She tore into his throat with her fangs. Unlike some vampires, Pauline never played with her food. She gorged herself on his warm blood, causing a surge of energy and a sensation of heat from head to toe. It felt like the rush of riding a perfect wave. She pushed away his drained body with some blood left. She had learned to leave something for the medical examiners so as not to raise suspicions. Pauline pulled a knife from her boot and slashed his neck to disguise the puncture wounds. She pulled a packet of Clorox wipes out of her pocket and carefully cleaned up any trace of her and said, "Thanks Phil." She checked her watch and with a small smile, thought, "the quickest assassination yet."

The street was still deserted when she got back to the Rover. There were no street cams in this part of town to pick up her car and she drove away thinking of her undead mentor, Sarah's admonition that the Haute Caste should let the Worthy Target know which crimes had led to the decision to execute them. Pauline sighed, she had wanted to be the perfect Haute Caste vampire, but she had no patience. She would never take the time to remind a scumbag of all the damage he had wreaked on others. She took comfort in knowing she had removed the wealthy lowlife criminal from society. A few miles away she pulled into a gas station and checked her black blouse for any stains. There were a few spots. "Damn!" Pauline ducked down and changed into a clean t-shirt. The gas station attendant walked by and pretended he had not seen her. "Whatever," she thought. Then she got out and filled the tank for the trip back to Vegas.

*****

About four in the morning, Manny Takeda's phone woke him from a heavy sleep. Another murder in the sweet little city of Salinas. He was the youngest and most junior detective on the force, so he always got the shit calls. Another drug dealer, taken out in Chinatown. He wondered why no one in Salinas ever got murdered at ten o'clock in the morning. When he heard it was Phil the "Pill King" Emerson, he was not surprised. He grabbed a coffee and a breakfast burrito and was still working on the burrito as he approached the crime scene. The Medical Examiner walked over to him, "Really?" she exclaimed, frowning at the burrito in his hand. She appeared a little rattled by the murder. Eula Brock never looked rattled. She usually had things wrapped up by the time he arrived. He shoved his half-eaten burrito in his pocket.

"What's the deal Eula?"

"I've never seen a body left like this. The throat is slashed open, but there's barely any blood on the body or the seats. Where did it go?"

"Are you sure he was killed in the car?" Manny asked.

Eula stared at him and just said: "Yes, I'm sure!"

"Sorry. Anything else?"

"No! Nothing! No prints! No hair besides the vic's, nothing! It's like he was killed by a ghost." She shook her head.

As they walked over to the Cadillac, Manny said, "I know Emerson had a lot of enemies, but I would have expected a gun, not a knife." The drug dealer was pale, and his eyes reminded Manny of a dead fish. His throat wound was wide with bruising, but not deep. "Any other injuries?"

"All that I could find without an autopsy was a broken wrist, so I think he briefly struggled with the killer. He still has his wallet with eight hundred dollars cash and his gun is still in his waistband. Nothing seems to be missing."

"Maybe this was worth getting up for," Manny thought to himself.

An officer brought the only witness over to talk to Manny. "This is Fred Chaney, he owns the bar and saw Emerson dead in the car when he was taking out the trash."

"That's appropriate," the detective commented. "Did you see anyone on the street Mr. Chaney?"

"No, except a black late-model SUV driving away. I'm pretty sure it was a Range Rover. I didn't see who was driving it or notice the license plates. Not a car I was familiar with. Not one of my regulars, none of them can afford a car like that."

"Did Phil have any problems with anyone tonight?"

"Hell, Phil had a problem with everyone, every night, but he always paid his tab and then some."

"He didn't leave with anyone?"

"No, not his lucky night I guess."

Manny went back to look at the body before it was moved. "Where is the blood?" he asked no one in particular.

A young officer shook her head, "You got me. Professional Cartel hit?"

"Probably not, they would have done it with a clean shot to the head." He did not think Emerson was important enough for the drug cartel to go to all that trouble. Emerson had stayed in his lane selling pharmaceuticals and did not get involved with pot, cocaine, heroin, or meth. His pharmaceuticals provided the cartel with new customers when his clients graduated to cheaper opiates. He went back to the station to see if there were any other murders with a similar M.O. Something was bugging him about this case. He was sure he had read about a couple of unsolved murders with the same lack of blood at the scene.

*****

By eight o'clock in the morning, the kids had eaten a million pancakes, and way too much maple syrup to be stuck in a car for hours, but Teri and I were game. She and Jacques took Lug over to a small patch of grass by the hotel office while the triplets and I loaded the car.

"Ms. Ortega?"

I turned to see a plainclothes policeman flashing a badge. He looked about thirty, sweet-faced, with kind eyes.

"She's Ms. Mordecai," Tomas stated loudly.

"I'm divorced, Ortega is fine. Tomas, Des, Marie go get Teri and Jacques."

"How do you know my name, and who are you?" I asked

"I'm Detective Takeda. I'm sorry to bother you, but your car matches the description of one seen leaving a crime scene. A passing patrol saw your car and called it in. I asked in the office whose car it is. Can you tell me where you were at three this morning?"

"Trying to sleep in this marvelous motel with four children, a puppy, and a good friend. I sent a text message to my ex-husband about midnight then fell asleep till the puppy woke us around six. There are my witnesses." I told him as I pointed across the parking lot.

Teri ran up to us while the kids trailed behind. "What's going on?"

"This is Detective Takeda. He says someone driving a Range Rover like ours broke the law last night while we were sound asleep." I gave the kids a "this is serious," look.

Teri stepped in, "We had a boring night. What happened? I used to do private security," she gave Takeda a charming smile. This was a side of Teri I had not seen before.

"A murder," he watched our reactions closely.

Lug walked up to the detective and started to raise a leg, "Lug!" I exclaimed as Manny jumped out of the way. "I'm sorry." I picked up the pup.

"That's okay," he patted Lug on the head. "Are you going to be staying in the area?"

"No, we just stopped here for the night."

Teri chimed in, "I'll give you my number if you want to ask us anything else."

"C'mon kids." I opened the door and started loading my family.

The young detective wrote down both Teri's and my name and number. "Thank you, Ms. Park, Ms. Ortega," and turned to leave. Then called out to me, "Oh, by the way, have you ever lived in Los Angeles?"

I thought that was a weird question for a cop in Salinas to ask, but I answered, "I was born in Illinois, got a scholarship to go to U.C.L.A., met my ex, had the triplets, and moved back to Illinois. I don't have time to tell you my life history, but it's fascinating. Are we free to go?"

Detective Takeda nodded and watched as we drove away. I glanced at Teri, "Damn Pauline! What did she tell you?"

"Not to put the local news on this morning," Teri said sheepishly.

Somehow, I knew we would be hearing from Detective Takeda again...

LOOK FOR

GIFT OF BLOOD
SUMMER 2020

Thank You Dear Reader!
I want to thank you for taking time to read my book and hope
you enjoyed it. I would love if you would take a moment to leave a
review of the book on Amazon or Goodreads.

Reviews are enormously helpful to independent authors, not only
to find out what readers think, but also for other readers to find
the book. It is the best way for independent authors to get the
word out.

You can go to my website for more about Miranda, the nocturnal
maniacs and me. If you like you can also sign up for my
newsletter.

www.susanold.com
www.amazon.com

About the Author

Susan is from Southern California and was a Peace Corps volunteer in Zaire in the late '70s. She went on to earn her master's in psychology and started in the field of Mental Health/Addictions at a street emergency shelter. She worked several years at County Mental Health, a University Medical Center, and at Cedars-Sinai Medical Center. She and her family moved to the cornfields of Illinois (like Miranda), and she became a therapist at a V.A. Medical Center. Over her career, she heard about the struggles of celebrities, bikers, walking wounded Veterans, nurses, felons, farmers, prostitutes, athletes, professors, and musicians. Being a therapist gave her insight into many diverse lives, from a housewife with insomnia to a strange ranger who walked the streets with a suitcase full of Barbie dolls. Writing became her outlet for the emotional stress of her job. In her writing, she created a hidden world that keeps the true nature of the inhabitants, secret.

She first considered herself a writer when her late mother-in-law, an author of English historical fiction, said she liked her writing. The manuscript of her first book was lost when lightning struck a power line and wiped out everything on her computer. Rather than take it as a sign to should stop writing, she took it as a lesson to back up everything on the Cloud. It took her years to rewrite the book from her notes, but fortunately, she never gave up.

She became a widow at a young age, battled Lupus, and is a two-time breast cancer survivor. Her children, family and friends always encouraged her to pursue her dreams. She believes there is a Miranda in each of us struggling to make sense of an insane world while sipping coffee.

She married a widower who accepts her obsession with shoes and helps with the technical stuff. They live north of Seattle on the banks of the Stillaguamish River with two rescued tabbies, a Black Lab Retriever with criminal instincts, and a Pug who has a very high opinion of herself. She is a volunteer at an animal shelter, a Veteran's museum, and the Unity Museum in Seattle. She loves Barbacoa tacos and consumes an inordinate amount of coffee.

Follow Susan and the continuing adventures of Miranda and her offspring at:
zairesue@susanold.com
Twitter @zairesue
Instagram @zairesuewrites
Facebook https://www.facebook.com/zairesue/

Acknowledgments

Big time gratitude to my Readers! I am still amazed when people tell me that they loved my books!

Countless thanks to my hubby Joel who spent so much time, energy, and computer skills turning my manuscript into a book. Yay!

To all my kids in Seattle, Lake Forest, Toronto and Milwaukee I am forever grateful for your love and support. When I've needed you, you've always been there for me. My kids and grandson light up my life.

To my old friends in Illinois, my new friends at the Unity Museum in Seattle, the Northwest Veterans Museum and the Northwest Organization for Animal Help in Stanwood, Washington I express my deep appreciation for all you do to help the world be a better place.

Special thanks to my friend Annette and my sister Megan for taking on the task of Beta Readers. You rock!

Sincere thanks to all the members of the Writers Cooperative of the Pacific Northwest for your support. Thanks to Matt Buza, marketing guru, Roland Trenary for getting it all formatted, Toni Kief, Sonya Rhen, Susan Brown for sharing their experience and knowledge about publishing. Special thanks to Linda Jordan-Eishner for helping get the myriad of details right in assembling the final book research and advise on cover art. All these people are indie authors with a wide array of genres. Check out their books!

Much appreciation to Laurie Zifkin for doing the final proofread and finding everything that was missed in all the previous editing passes.

To my dear friends from childhood who also shared the Hippie dreams of our teenage years, Art and Deb, thanks for still being such cool people.

Enjoy the read!

Also by **SUSAN OLD**

The Miranda Chronicles: Book I

RARE BLOOD

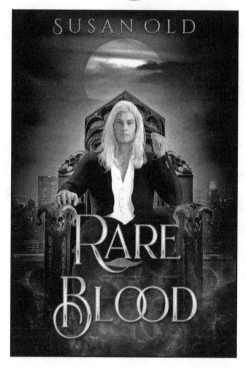

Available at Amazon and Barnes and Noble

AND...

CPSIA information can be obtained
at www.ICGtesting.com
Printed in the USA
FSHW010307150721
83154FS